PYTHONS

PYTHONS

Massacre in the Everglades

HENRY J KUHLMAN

Paperback ISBN: 979-8-9998664-0-0

Ebook ISBN: 979-8-9998664-1-7

Printed in the United States of America

*To those who care about the environment and biodiversity,
ask questions, and step forward.*

Contents

Acknowledgments

Thank you to my wife, Dorothy, my family, and many friends who have been part of this journey.

Thanks to: The Writers of the Villages club, whose critiques were invaluable, as were the conversations over lunch, and enjoying coconut shrimp with Julie Johnson.

Thanks to: Linda Keenan, the lead editor.

Thanks to: Members of the Pen Paper and Pals writing club, and many others who created Short Story Nights and other original experiences.

Thanks to: Stu Coppens, who endured far too many recitations of my story ideas.

Thanks to the Center for Biological Diversity, People Protecting Peace River, The Water Keepers, and countless citizens, scientists, and organizations that work towards healthy, sustainable ecosystems.

Thank you, finally, to everyone who believes in questions that begin with: Why?

Introduction

This ecological thriller takes place in 2029 at an unlikely backwater in the Everglades, called Pa-Hay-Okee.

* * *

The incident struck the new Florida governor like a left hook and called for immediate action. Scrambling for footing and receiving double-talk from state officials, he settled on help from a swamp cowboy and a computer science professor.

Stakes never higher, with the tourist economy, and more on the line, what happened next, no one, not even the governor, saw coming.

1

Campout

"It's really cool down here," Mathew called from under the booth at the Bal Harbor Ale House.

"What did he say?" Sarah Warner asked her brother, Rick.

"Ah, ignore him. It's quieter with him under the table."

Rick checked his phone, expecting a message from his other son, sixteen-year-old Jamie.

Sarah nodded in agreement as Mathew popped his head up next to her leg, shining the toothy grin of a four-year-old.

"I'm camping out like Jamie, and this is my tent, Aunt Sarah. Look, I found another crayon."

She cringed, imagining moldy tater tots and greasy cheese nachos ground into the carpet.

"I'm glad you're having fun, Mathew."

Rick checked the time and sent another text to Jamie's phone.

"The scoutmaster keeps their phones during campouts. They planned to hike out of the park at three to meet the scoutmaster and drive back. It's now four. Their mom wants them home by six."

"They can be a little late. You're the one living in an apartment since Fran divorced you."

"Bravely spoken. She keeps a list of grievances, and I don't need another court hearing. Besides, the kids have school tomorrow."

Slate imagined the pressure on Rick and smiled in understanding. His landscaping business, even with three crews working six days a week in North Miami Beach, struggled to cover expenses, including his child support and alimony.

Slate, a nickname for Sarah Warner, PhD, dearly loved her only sibling and his two sons. Her parents had retired in the same town where she grew up, Columbus, Ohio. Not a fan of flying, they had driven to Miami only three times during the seven years Slate had worked at the University of Miami. She lived on the twenty-second floor in a two-bedroom downtown condo, off Brickell Avenue.

Before Rick's divorce two years earlier, Slate visited them at his four-bedroom home with a pool in Kendall. Now, they have bowling, video arcades, picnics, and restaurants near his apartment.

Slate leaned down to see Mathew on hands and knees, acting like a capybara, his favorite animal. "Matt, buddy, come up and sit by me. How about a hot fudge sundae?"

"Sure, Slate," he said, rising on his knees with his hands up like a capybara begging for food.

"Matt, honey, can you please call me Aunt Sarah?"

Rick went to the restroom, and Slate cleaned Mathew's hands with disinfectant wipes. Rick's phone rang. The caller ID said, "Scoutmaster Flanagan."

"Hello. This is Sarah, Rick's sister. He'll be back in a few minutes."

"Huh, hi, Sarah. I have a list of people to call. Can you tell him?"

"Sure, tell him what?"

"It's about Jamie. He didn't return today from the wilderness campout at Pa-Hay-Okee. The sheriff's department is searching for him and eight others. I'm sorry to bring you this news, Sarah. Please tell Rick."

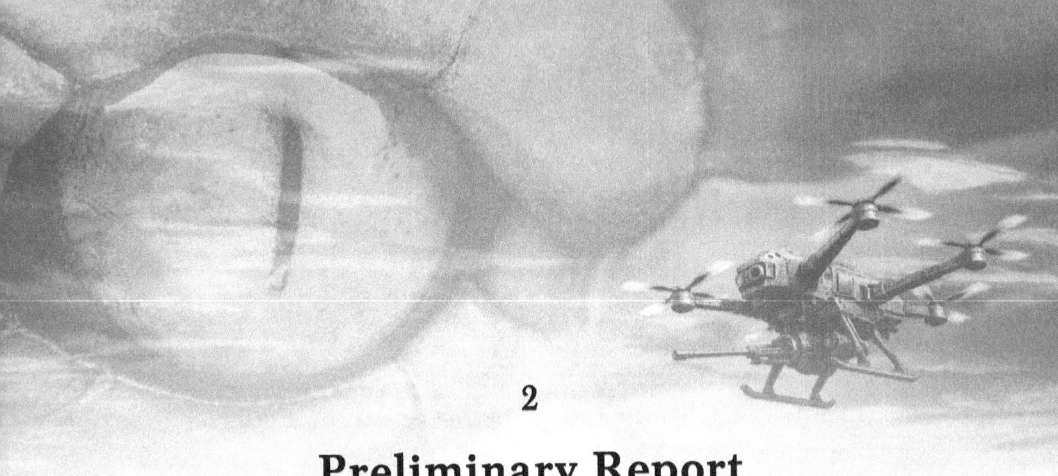

2

Preliminary Report

Awake at five a.m., waiting in her condo for news about Jamie had been unbearable. She, the Associate Dean of the College of Engineering, arrived at her office at ten, notified Dean Miller, and rearranged her schedule to be available for Rick. Sleep-deprived and her mind in a fog, Slate tried to distract herself by reviewing a student's research paper, "Optimizing Dynamic Resource Allocation in Autonomous Agents."

Her thoughts wandered to the Kennedy Space Center. Three months earlier, she had taken Jamie to watch a SpaceX launch to position components for the Mars outpost. NASA recognized her notoriety in robotics and computer engineering with a behind-the-scenes tour. Jamie amazed his aunt with his curiosity and raw intelligence. He drove the guides crazy with questions. She laughed to herself, then snapped back to the present in near panic.

Mentally exhausted, Slate pulled her shoulder-length blonde hair into a ponytail. Attractive and fit at forty years, five-foot-seven inches, and 128 pounds, she opened her compact.

Fresh makeup restored balance and composure to her oval-shaped face, soft lines, and pale blue eyes. She sipped a cup of green tea and grabbed a bag of almonds from the desk drawer.

The ringtone she had set for Rick chirped like a cricket. The message had only a link. Her heart sank.

3

Preliminary Incident Report: Pa-Hay-Okee, Troop 44.
Officer Barry Watkins,
Florida Wildlife Commission,
Dept. of Investigations.

The following is based on interviews with Scoutmaster Ralph Flanagan and two adult scout leaders.

On Saturday morning, February 17, 2029, adult leaders and members of Scout Troop 44 parked three SUVs at the Cracker Barrel south of Miami on US Highway 1 near the intersection with Florida State Road 9336.

Eleven scouts, eight males and three females, ages eleven to seventeen, ate hearty breakfasts and bought last-minute supplies.

Three scouts, two males (Jamie and Randy) and one female (Taylor), were certified to lead wilderness campouts in outback areas.

Traveling west on SR 9336 into Everglades National Park, the group pulled over at the Pinelands Trailhead. The scouts lined up their packs and gear for inspection by Scoutmaster Flanagan. The troop did a practice hike on the two-mile Pinelands loop trail in full gear, then reboarded the SUVs.

They traveled west six miles to the drop-off point at Pa-Hay-Okee Lookout. It had been closed for six months, undergoing renovations.

The scouts gathered their gear in a semicircle under the pavilion. Scoutmaster Ralph Flanagan reviewed plans and contingencies. Considering the group's size and experience level, the weather forecast, and their previous use of the camping area, the troop rated the trek as medium difficulty and did not require adult leaders.

The eleven scouts were split up between three patrols. They would rotate the lead and navigate using a map and compass over a plotted but unmarked three-mile route. The course traversed dry-season terrain, skirting wetland swamps and areas of open water.

Jamie carried the troop's new emergency SOS device, which had limited text messaging capabilities. The scoutmaster checked the device's operational status, collected the scouts' cell phones, and had each scout record their contact information on his clipboard.

The trek to the camping site ended in a six-acre hammock, a slightly raised area of trails, brush, and trees, surrounded by swamps and sloughs. The scouts were tasked with setting up individual campsites and preparing a group dinner before sunset. As planned, Jamie sent a text to Scoutmaster Flanagan at seven p.m.: "Camp set-up. Dinner finished. All is well."

The next morning, Sunday, they would complete wilderness merit badge activities, break camp, and hike back to Pa-Hay-Okee by a different route for pick-up at three p.m.

Scoutmaster Flanagan met the other leaders at Denny's for lunch on Sunday before driving to Pa-Hay-Okee. They arrived on time to pick up the scouts, but they were not there.

The scoutmaster texted Jamie, "Hi, trekkers, we're at the pavilion. What is your ETA?"

The scoutmaster said that after ten minutes with no reply, they walked the short distance to the trailhead and called out. A barred owl on an oak limb stared at them and responded as if to answer their calls. The scoutmaster checked his phone for messages or an SOS alert from the call center. He looked down the trail, saw nothing, and told Carl and Richard to check the bathrooms and outbuildings.

Waiting at the trailhead, he heard Carl yell, "Ralph, you better get over here!"

The scoutmaster turned back and saw Carl standing in the doorway of the women's restroom, waving.

Carl held the door open to let in light. Without power, transom windows at the top of cinder block walls provided some light. Stalls were located to the right of the doorway. Straight ahead on the far wall, between the stalls and sinks, a white plastic diaper-changing table was attached to the wall.

From the doorway, he saw a teenage girl sitting on the table, her back to the wall, legs crossed. She stared blankly at the floor.

A boy lay curled up on the table, his head on her lap, facing the girl. Her left hand cradled his body. Her right hand gripped a bloody survival knife.

The scoutmaster saw bruises and swelling on her face and neck, cuts and scratches on her arms and legs. Mud and blood matted long blonde hair. An open cut traced from the forehead hairline back over her scalp.

He whispered to Carl to prop the door open and call 911 for ambulances, deputies, and fire rescue.

The scoutmaster walked forward and stopped five feet away.

"Taylor, is that you?"

She didn't answer.

"Why are you in your pajamas, Taylor?"

No answer, her stare frozen.

He stepped forward two feet and leaned down to look up into her eyes. Her eyes opened wide.

The knife came up, she lunged forward, and in a hoarse, raspy voice, she yelled what sounded like, "Die!"

The scoutmaster jumped back as the knife came down inches away.

"It's me, Taylor, Scoutmaster Flanagan. Remember me? I'm here to help you. Is that Owen?"

Her back against the wall, she pulled the boy closer and stared at the scoutmaster.

"Is Owen okay?"

She looked down at Owen but didn't speak.

"Taylor, where are the others? Where are the other scouts?"

Her expression changed to profound sadness. Then she shrugged, as if to say, "I don't know."

"It's alright, Taylor. Help is on the way."

She laid the knife on the table, curled over the boy, and fell asleep.

Flanagan moved the knife to a sink, retrieved a blanket from the SUV, and waited.

[End of Preliminary Report]

Slate stared at her iPhone, gripped in fear, feeling she might vomit. Parts of the report reverberated in her mind—bruised and swollen face and neck, bloody knife, pajamas, psychological trauma, a boy.

What happened out there? Where's Jamie?

She called her brother. "Rick, where are you?"

Rick stepped outside the tent reserved for family members. "They have a tent set up at the turnoff from the main road, two miles from Pa-Hay-Okee. We can't go down there. Did you read the report?" His voice sounded weary and defeated.

"Yes, it's horrible."

"Fran just arrived. She's freaking out, demanding answers that no one has. Mathew is at Fran's sister's."

"Have they found anyone? Are there any suspects? A drug gang?"

"They aren't saying. Helicopters and cop cars have gone back and forth all day, but no ambulances. It's bad, Sarah. Real bad."

3

Pissing Contest

Scoutmaster Flanagan had stayed with Taylor Williams and Owen Conroy until the first EMS unit arrived. The seventeen-year-old had led Owen three miles that morning using a map and compass to backtrack the route they had taken the previous day.

The EMS RN, Donna Moody, and her partner, Stu, stood by the curled-up girl and boy. The boy, muddy and scratched in torn pajamas, had no visible injuries. The RN traced her fingers over welts on the girl's swollen neck.

I can't imagine what she's been through. What the hell happened out there?

"Stu, call for Air-evac. Let's secure her for a spinal injury and get an IV going. Get an evidence bag for the knife."

"Air? On a Sunday, are you sure?" Stu asked.

"I've got a bad feeling about this one, dude. I'm not getting tagged for going cheap when the shit goes down."

"Oh, I get it. Cool. Good call."

Taylor arrived by helicopter and was checked into the University of Miami Hospital at six p.m. Owen arrived in an ambulance at Mount Sinai an hour later.

* * *

The next afternoon, Monday, while Rick and Fran waited for news in the tent, the pissing contest in the third-floor conference room at the University of Miami Hospital raged on—a fight for who would lead the investigation and who would interview Taylor Williams.

At the head of the table, the National Park Service district manager wisely yielded jurisdiction and pledged to support the winner of the stare-down underway down the table.

The Florida Wildlife Commission chief investigator demanded to head up the investigation. The FWC protected Everglades resources and had sweeping powers that exceeded those of most law enforcement agencies. Had the incident happened in a small, inconsequential county, the FWC would have prevailed. Indeed, they had every incentive to lead the investigation and control the narrative.

Miami-Dade County, not small or inconsequential, encompassed most of the Everglades. More importantly, the scouts were not state resources. They were Miami's kids. Sensing a turf war, the sheriff had deployed the full array of county assets, including a command center, press tent, and media contacts. Outgunned and outplayed, the FWC scrambled for footing.

Sheriff Daryl Palmer was sitting, arms crossed, staring at FWC's Major Thomas Drew when a deputy leaned over and handed the sheriff a cell phone. The sheriff took the call in the hallway from the on-scene commander at Pa-Hay-Okee.

Palmer returned to the table, took his seat, shook his head in resignation, and clasped his hands on the table.

"Major Drew, my team found a small SOS device carried by Jamie Warner, one of the missing scouts."

"That's great news, Sheriff. Where?"

"In the belly of a Burmese python, Major. One of your Burmese pythons."

"Holy shit! Did they find the scout?"

"Yes, the SOS device was in his pocket."

The major sank back into his chair, hands in his lap.

"I have a call into Governor Prescott. Given FWC policies and practices regarding pythons, I propose we spare you the embarrassment of the governor removing FWC from the investigation. We will run the show, and you will provide resources in support. Agreed?"

The major's eyes flicked, as if processing and comprehending what Sheriff Palmer had said. He swallowed hard.

Before he could respond, the sheriff said, "Major Drew, we are leading the investigation. Let your people know, and don't say a peep about what happened. I mean zip, nothing."

The major nodded and gathered his papers. He stood, about to leave, when the sheriff said, "You guys knew this day was coming, right?"

The major looked at Sheriff Palmer without expression and led his delegation out the door.

4

Taylor Williams

After Major Drew left, Sheriff Palmer handed the file folder to his executive assistant and walked down the fire exit stairs. He called Wendy Cooper from the hospital lobby.

"We're all set, Wendy. You will interview Taylor alone. She's seventeen and in room 322 with her mother. Keep it simple. Get as much as you can without upsetting her more than she already is. We need it on video, okay?"

Wendy worked in the Miami-Dade Special Situations Unit. Attractive in an understated way, she had medium-length brown hair that curled softly above the collar. Her smile, natural and engaging, failed to conceal a shyness. Perhaps most importantly, Wendy had an abundance of empathy and patience. Disarming, many underestimated her intelligence, unaware of her master's degree in clinical psychology.

Wearing casual clothes, Wendy knocked softly on the door, then peeked in. Taylor's mother sat awkwardly on the edge of the recliner, leaning on the bed. Wendy stepped in enough to give a weak wave to the mother, who came to the door. Wendy saw Taylor glance at her without expression.

"Mrs. Williams, I'm Wendy Cooper with the Sheriff's Department," she whispered. "We are searching for the other scouts, and I'm hoping to speak with Taylor if you think she's up to it. Would you mind asking her?"

Wendy watched the mother speak with Taylor, then motioned for her to come in.

11

Wendy stood at the foot of the bed. "Hi, Taylor, I'm Wendy. I used to be a Girl Scout. I liked tying knots." Wendy smiled at her. Taylor smiled back.

"Do you know the timberline hitch?" Wendy asked.

Taylor nodded yes.

"How about the clove hitch?"

Taylor nodded yes.

"The bowline?"

Taylor shook her head no.

"Me neither," Wendy said, and they both laughed.

"It's a stupid knot," Wendy said.

"Yes, it's stupid," Taylor said. "We never use it."

"You have dimples when you smile, like me," Wendy said. They smiled self-consciously, then giggled.

"You must be exhausted. You've been through a lot, young lady. I'm proud of you for being a scout leader, Taylor. I really am." Wendy smiled warmly into her eyes.

"Does your head hurt?"

Taylor put her hand on the bandage. "A little."

"Do you remember how you cut your head?" Wendy asked.

"Yes, with my knife."

"Were you trying to get away from the snake?"

Taylor nodded.

"Very smart of you. I'm not sure I would have thought of that. I would have been too scared, probably," Wendy said. "You're a brave girl, Taylor.

"I should tell you I'm working with people trying to find your friends. I like to help people."

Taylor looked to her mother sitting on the recliner. She nodded approval and patted Taylor's arm.

"Do you think they're alright?" Taylor asked.

"We hope they are. A lot of people are looking for them," Wendy lied, knowing about the boy they already found.

Wendy set her laptop and the cube video recorder on the tray table over the bed. Her phone vibrated, a call from the sheriff.

"Excuse me, Taylor, I need to take this call."

Wendy slipped into the hallway.

"They found a female alive. A fourteen-year-old, Cindy Ajayi. She was in a cypress tree half a mile south of her campsite."

"That's great news; it's just what I need for Taylor. I'm talking with her now."

Wendy returned to the bed beside Taylor, smiled widely, and raised her hand.

"They've found Cindy. Give me a high five."

Taylor's eyes widened in disbelief, and she sat up in bed.

"She's in my patrol."

"Well, she got away. She's okay. With your help, we can find your friends. Do you think you can help, Taylor?"

Wendy watched her process the request, emotions sweeping across her face.

"It won't be easy, but you'll feel better after we finish. Okay?

"You may want to cry, and I might cry. It's okay if we do."

Wendy placed her open hand on the bed. Taylor grasped it.

"I'll turn the recorder on. Then you can tell me what happened. I'll try not to interrupt you with questions.

"Sometimes, telling it as if you are there is easier. Think about being there. You're hiking to the campsite. Do you understand?"

"I think so."

The screen on the back of the cube camera showed Taylor in a short-sleeved blue hospital gown, with an IV drip in her right arm. A tall, slim girl, she reminded Wendy of a volleyball player. Almost swollen shut, deep shades of purple and blue surrounded her right eye. Angry welts ringed her neck and tracked up across her face over her eye. Her arms had scrapes and light bruises. Despite her injuries, she looked cute. Her blonde hair curled messily from a large bandage on her head. Taylor nodded, and Wendy started the recorder.

"Cindy, Kate, and Owen are in my patrol. I'm leading. Jamie's and Randy's patrols are behind us. I see the hammock trees ahead, the place on the map where we plan to camp. Closer, I name the trees—longleaf pine, live oak, and sabal palm. We survey the area where Randy had camped two years earlier, and I see the campfire area."

"What time is it, Taylor?" Wendy asked, glancing at Taylor's mother, who looked afraid and had a knuckle to her face, biting the inside of her mouth.

"Oh, about four, plenty of time to set up camp, cook the stew, and make dessert. From the campfire, I take my patrol east about fifty yards. Jamie went north, and Randy went west. We set up the latrine south of the campfire. Cindy, Kate, Owen, and I spread out and pick campsites out of sight of each other."

"Why did you separate?" Wendy asked.

"Wilderness camping requires self-reliance and self-confidence. And tents aren't allowed."

"Oh, I see. It sounds scary," Wendy said and smiled.

Taylor giggled. "I wasn't scared. I like challenges."

Wendy poured Taylor a glass of water.

"I cut branches with my saw and lash them together into a bed frame. I pile up brush, put the bed frame on top, and cover it with my ground cloth. I inflate the sleeping pad and unroll my sleeping bag with a camping sheet on top. I tie a line between a bush and a tree over the bed and drape the mosquito net over it like a tent. It's still eighty degrees, a good night to sleep with sheets on top of the bag."

Wendy watched Taylor's concentration shift inward as she visualized being there. Her eyes raised to look at a picture on the wall facing the bed—a large, framed landscape of a sunset over the Florida Everglades.

"I finish setting up my camp and hang my gear from a big oak limb and hurry to help the others. Kate and Owen had never camped without a tent. Kate and Cindy are fine and have their mosquito nets strung above their beds. Little Owen is all messed up. The three of us help him as we joke around. It's like five-thirty now. The breeze from the west rustles leaves high in the trees. Otherwise, there is no sound, not even the chirping of birds. Something dead is in the wind, a long way off, not too strong.

"We grab our camp stools and headlamps and walk to the campfire. Jamie and Randy have the fire going and water boiling. They had lashed a large table together from tree limbs and are making beef and vegetable stew. My patrol mixes ingredients for the chocolate lava cake into the Dutch oven."

Taylor paused, her eyes sweeping the picture on the wall.

"It seems so long ago. The steaming pots of stew and dessert are on the table, and we fill our bowls and dishes. Owen brought his mother's cornbread muffins. I put chunks from two of them in my stew. The lava cake is so good. I go back for more, and my belly sticks out. We wash the dishes in hot, soapy water, rinse them in cold water, and clip them to a drying line.

"I fill my water bottle, brush my teeth over a bush, and go to the latrine with Cindy. It's getting dark. We switch on our headlamps and return to the campfire. The troop has a charades competition, and my 'Charlie' patrol wins. Paul and Steven tell jokes and impersonate people we call out. I call Scoutmaster Flanagan's name. Everyone goes crazy watching Steven rub his chin and pretend to smoke a pipe."

Taylor laughed out loud. Then she stopped laughing, and she didn't laugh again.

"My patrol hikes the winding path we made to our camping area. We form a circle where the trails to our campsites join. They all look tired. Light from our headlamps shines on the ground in a circle. Owen jerks his light around, being silly, making us dizzy. I slap his arm.

"I tell them to use their big flashlight to check themselves and the sleeping bag for ticks. I tell them to pee on the ground and put their clothes and water bottle under the mosquito net. Owen is only eleven. He thanks me for being his patrol leader. I hug him. He's such a sweet kid."

Taylor began to cry. Her mother touched her shoulder. The mother tried not to cry but failed.

Wendy handed her a tissue and waited for the terrible parts.

Taylor closed her eyes. "A warm breeze passes over my campsite. I change into my pajamas and unfold the sack sheet over the bag. The wind is high in the trees. It sounds like waves breaking. I write in my journal what I accomplished today. I feel good about being a leader and being respected. I write my goal to make Eagle this year. I feel the limbs of the bed frame poke under the sleeping bag and blow more air into the sleeping pad. I switch the light off."

Wendy watched Taylor's hands tremble, heard her voice hesitate, stammer, and stutter. She took too long to fill in the last parts.

Wendy interrupted. "Sweetheart, can I ask you a question?"

Taylor looked at her smile and nodded.

"Can I see your legs for a second?" Wendy asked.

Taylor looked puzzled. "Uh, okay."

Wendy rolled the table to the foot of the bed, and Taylor lifted the sheet to show her legs below the gown.

"You're bruised pretty good, young lady. The python left black and blue marks. You have scratches from bushes, and your feet are cut and swollen."

Taylor watched her warily and nodded.

"Sweetheart, I don't see bite marks on your arms or legs. I see where the snake squeezed, but not the nasty cuts of teeth."

Taylor stared at her, remaining silent.

"Pythons bite and hold on as an anchor to wrap coils around their prey. Why didn't the snake bite you, Taylor?"

Taylor looked at her mother, who looked confused, then looked back at Wendy.

"Jamie came. He came to my campsite before dinner while I set up camp," Taylor said, looking directly into Wendy's eyes.

Wendy filled in the gap. "Jamie returned that night after you left the campfire."

Taylor looked somewhat relieved and nodded.

"It's okay, Taylor. So, Jamie stopped by."

Taylor looked at her mother.

"It's fine, sweetheart. You two like each other. I've known that."

Taylor turned to Wendy.

Wendy said, "Okay, let's go back. You are at your camp getting ready for bed."

Taylor continued with more confidence. "I see his flashlight leave the path into my clearing. I'm lying on top of the sack sheet under the net with my little camp light. I'm writing in my journal. He joins me, and we whisper. I'm on my left side, leaning on my elbow. He's on his right side, facing me. The camp light between us lights our faces. His blue eyes sparkle. He's very happy. He's laughing about the charades game. We giggle. He kisses me. The wind up high sounds like a waterfall. I close my eyes, waiting for another kiss. I hear a snap. Something is in the bushes off the end of the bed. I open my eyes, and Jamie is looking at me. He whispers, 'Raccoon.'"

Her mother's hand moved to Taylor's arm. Taylor stared at the picture.

"Jamie brushes the hair from my face and leans over to kiss me. Something moves on the brush pile under the bed down there. The bed shakes. I whisper, 'What is it?' He put a finger to my lips."

Taylor sat upright in bed, looking at the Everglades picture.

"I look between us, between our feet into the darkness. A shadow, then something is on the bed frame on Jamie's side. The bed tilts Jamie down. I reach behind my back for the survival knife by my water bottle."

Taylor paused as her right hand reached behind the hospital gown as if reaching for the knife.

"The camp light shines up on Jamie. I see his mouth open, his eyes are wild, and he screams in pain and panic."

Taylor's hands moved to her mouth.

"Jamie's upper arm is in the snake's mouth. The head is huge. The yellow eyes stare at me. We try to sit up on the sleeping bag. The snake wraps its coils around and squeezes us together."

"It happens so fast. The coils wrap around me like a rope. It's heavy. Every part is crawling and gripping me. It bends my head around. I try to breathe, but it's hard. It's pulling my neck, stomach, and leg in different directions."

Taylor's eyes darted back and forth as her body twisted here and there on the hospital bed.

Wendy checked the camera's display screen and the red recording light.

"I'm almost passed out when I hear her scream."

Wendy jolted forward. "Someone screamed? Who screamed, Taylor?"

Taylor's hands came up and covered her eyes.

"I can't see. It's over my eyes and my mouth. Kate is screaming in the dark. I hear her screams above the wind. She yells, 'Help! Help me!' More screams. Then they stop."

"Are you sure Kate screamed?" Wendy asked.

"Yes, she's my best friend."

"Okay, brave girl. You're courageous. I'm proud of you," Wendy said.

Taylor's face, neck, and shoulders were wet with sweat, and the top of her hospital gown had turned dark blue. She breathed hard, gasping for air.

"My right arm is free, and the knife is in my hand, but it's still in the sheath. I manage to unsnap the strap, and it falls off."

A nurse opened the door. "Is everything okay? I heard her from the nurse's station," she said, looking at Wendy.

Wendy hurried to the door and glanced at her nametag.

"Yes, we're fine, Nancy. Thank you. Can you come back in ten minutes?"

Wendy handed Taylor a glass of water. "Do you want to take a break?"

"No, I want to finish."

Taylor sat up in bed, her hands trembling over her mouth.

"I bring the knife up and point it toward my face. I stab. It hits the snake, and it jerks. I pull out and stab again, deeper. It jerked again and loosened its grip. The third stab glances off, and the blade hits my head. But it's enough. The coils around my head and shoulders relax, and I wiggle out and push them down. Finally free, I roll away off the bed in the dark and fall to the dirt."

Taylor's breathing was fast and shallow.

"I crawl in the dirt away from the bed to the edge by the trail. I crawl down the trail, then pull myself up a tree to my feet. I taste blood. I don't know if it's mine or the snake's. My skin crawls, and I smell like a dead mouse. I stumble down the path, brushing against bushes on the sides. I see the faint glow of the campfire. No one is there. I climb up on the camp table and find a towel to hold on my head."

Wendy interrupted to ask about Jamie. Taylor couldn't see in the blackness. Wendy asked if she killed the snake. Taylor said no, that she barely got out of the coils.

"It's dark. No moon. The wind is stirring the fire, and smoke blows over the table. I'm cold and thirsty. I'm scared and shaking. The tree limbs of the tabletop are too hard to sit on. The cut on my head hurts like crazy. I see a water bottle by the fire on a camp stool. I begin to climb down to grab the water and freeze when I see it."

Collecting her thoughts, Taylor reached for her glass of water on the table and took a long drink. Wendy looked across the bed and made eye contact with an anguished Mrs. Williams. Taylor took a deep breath.

"A gust blows sparks from the fire and lights the area. I see it through the smoke. It's crawling across the campsite, coming in my direction. I hold the knife and freeze. It could be the smoke. It doesn't see me and crawls by the table down Randy's trail. I wait a while, then climb down to add wood to the fire and get the water bottle.

"I wait for others to come. I hear noises in the dark, like branches breaking, but it might be the wind. I call out, but my voice is hoarse. No one answers. The hours go by. I see another huge snake stop near the fire. It's fat. After a while, it crawls south on the path to the latrine."

Sensing the worst had passed, Wendy suggested taking a break and turned off the recorder. Taylor's mother stepped out to use the bathroom and returned with snacks from the vending machine.

"Thanks, Mom. I love you," Taylor said, opening a bag of cheese puffs. Wendy filled her water glass and turned on the recorder.

"It's getting light to the east in the direction of Pa-Hay-Okee. The wind is now a breeze. I'm warming up. I see a map and a compass on a small camp table. I look for snakes under bushes, waiting for me. I'm so scared."

Taylor began crying again. Her mother and Wendy passed her tissues.

"I should have tried to find them. Why didn't anyone come to the fire? I was shaking with fear, afraid of being swallowed. I needed to get away from there."

Wendy said, "There's nothing you could do. They wanted to eat you. You had to escape and get help."

Taylor took a drink and finished a candy bar, then continued.

"I decide to walk back along the trail we followed on Saturday. I need my shoes. I walk slowly to my camp with my knife, looking under bushes and up in the trees. My bed and gear are scattered everywhere. I find my shoes and water bottle. Cindy's camp is trashed, and so is Kate's. The snakes made drag marks in the dirt, and everyone is gone. I see Kate's walking stick on the ground and pick it up. The last camp is Owen's, about 10 yards off the trail. I can't believe it. There's a big snake curled on the ground around his Spiderman sleeping bag. Its head is lying over the bag. I hold up the walking stick and have the knife ready. I move slowly around the edge of the clearing and look inside the bag opening. I see Owen's head and whisper, 'Owen, Owen.' His head moves, and his eyes open. The snake's head is facing away from me. I creep up close, hold the stick high over my head, and bring it down with all my weight. I miss the head but hit its fat body. It jolts and crawls away in a hurry into the brush. I hear it splash into the swamp.

"Owen is okay, but terrified like me. I help him with his shoes. We study the map and find the trail. I'm exhausted and sore. Owen tells me I'm bleeding. We get lost a couple of times. Owen cries a few times. We hold hands. The sun is broiling hot. I feel like passing out. I throw up. So does Owen. I look for snakes and other scouts. Owen sees the pavilion first. It's one o'clock."

Taylor's chin sank to her chest. She leaned back and Wendy gently lowered the bed so she could rest. Wendy switched off the recorder and put her notepad away. Her mother lay her head on the bed, cried, and held Taylor's right hand, the hand that had gripped the knife.

"Thank you, Taylor and Mrs. Williams. I'm going to visit Owen at another hospital. I'll let you know about Cindy and the others as soon as I can."

Wendy blew a kiss to Taylor.

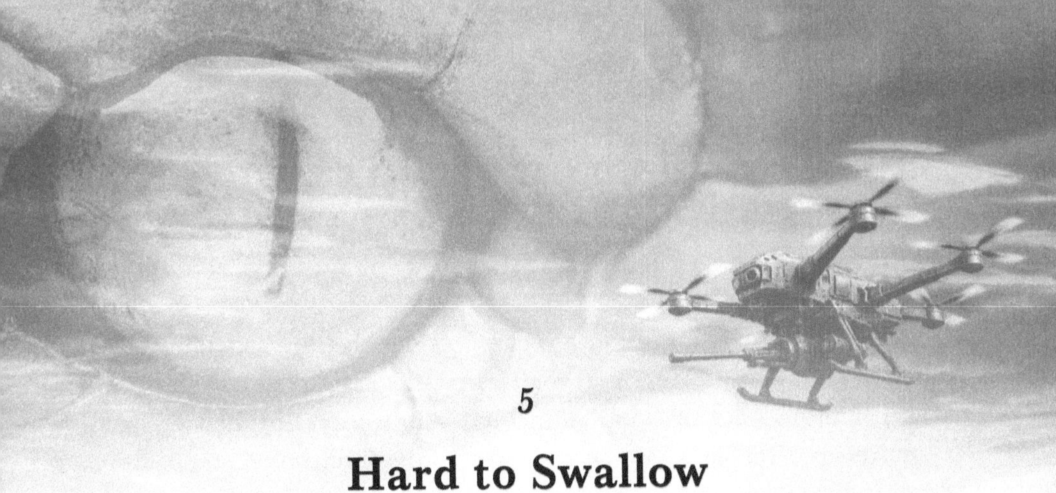

5

Hard to Swallow

Florida Governor John Prescott, in office for less than two months, had endorsed Sheriff Palmer's reelection and received frequent updates from him since the incident. The governor asked Palmer to delay releasing details to the public while his office devised a response strategy. Sensing significant political exposure, Governor Prescott needed time to create an action plan with Republicans in the Florida Legislature.

The sheriff prohibited the press and the public from proceeding beyond the turnoff at SR 9336. A no-fly zone restricted aircraft from flying over the area. The sheriff positioned his mobile command trailer at the turnoff and set up tent facilities for the press, family, and first responders.

At ten a.m. on Tuesday, three days after the incident and one day after Taylor Williams's interview, the sheriff released the first details in a statement, followed by a brief press conference.

The press release read, "It is with a heavy heart and extreme sadness that I report the loss of young lives this past weekend during a scouting campout in the Everglades near the Pa-Hay-Okee Lookout. Search and rescue operations continue around the clock. One male and two female scouts are alive and in good condition at area hospitals. The families of five deceased scouts have been notified. As minors, we cannot release their names. Three scouts remain unaccounted for. We suspect a tragic interaction with Everglades wildlife and have no reason to suspect foul play. County and state forensic teams are on site, and our investigation continues."

Following the press conference, the sheriff called Governor Prescott and informed him of the dramatic videotaped interview with

Taylor. The governor wanted to use the videotape at a press conference in Miami on Friday. Wendy had told Sheriff Palmer about Taylor being alone with Jamie when they were attacked. Being immaterial, they decided to edit the tape into segments and withhold the part about the two scouts being together.

The governor asked for a recap. Besides the three survivors, two males suffered horrific deaths at their campsites. Two dozen professional python hunters were on foot, in airboats, and operating drones in an expanding perimeter from the campsite. They had killed ten pythons and found one male and one female inside of two snakes. A third male had drowned in the swamp near his campsite. The governor asked about the odds of finding the remaining three.

Sheriff Palmer replied, "Jake, our lead hunter, told me this morning that pythons are spooked and scattering from all the activity. They can travel up to five miles per day. However, pythons with a full belly stay within a mile until they digest their meal. We have ten days left to find them."

The governor asked the sheriff to have Jake call him.

***

"Governor Prescott, Sir, I'm Jake of Python Pursuits Unlimited. Sheriff Palmer asked me to call you."

"Good. Thanks for your help, Jake. What you're doing must be traumatic and heart-wrenching. Many people are counting on you. Thank you."

"The toughest thing I've ever done, Governor. Families are waiting in a tent at the Pa-Hay-Okee turnoff, hoping we find their children."

"The sheriff said five scouts have died, and three are missing," the governor said.

"I'm sorry, Governor, they found a young male an hour ago inside a python sunning itself on a mud flat, a mile south of the campsite."

"Do you think any are still alive?"

"Honestly, I don't see how. We would have found them by now. There are snake tracks all over those campsites."

"I don't understand any of this, Jake. I need to get smart on pythons, and fast. Why did this happen?"

"Governor, I've worked hogs, gators, and pythons in the Glades for twenty years and watched the python population explode. They've eaten ninety-nine percent of the mammals, birds, and small gators. Big pythons eat smaller ones. There are hundreds of thousands of hungry pythons out there. I think a combination of circumstances made Pa-Hay-Okee a perfect snake storm. It's a wake-up call for Florida."

"What do you mean?"

"I'm not saying the pythons were hunting in packs like wolves. However, these snakes are large and aggressive when hungry, and they hunt at night. Pa-Hay-Okee had been closed for six months. I'm guessing pythons, too big to eat each other, smelled warm-blooded mammals. Most of these kids were small enough to swallow. Pythons aren't territorial. I think they converged on the campsites after dark, out of the swamp from all directions. Since the scouts were spread out in the open, they became easy targets for ravenous apex predators."

"This is new to me. Why are there so many pythons in the Everglades?"

"Sir, the python population has grown uncontrolled since the 1990s, when pet owners released snakes that got too big to handle. Hurricane Andrew in 1992 destroyed a South Florida reptile breeding farm, releasing thousands of pythons into the Glades. Exotic pet stores sold approximately 99,000 pythons in Florida between 1996 and 2006. The state didn't ban the sale of pythons until 2010."

"It's been thirty years, Jake. I'm just getting up to speed. Do you know if state officials have done anything about the exploding python population besides banning sales?"

"Not much, Governor. At first, pythons were protected by the State under anti-cruelty laws. As such, the state required that they be caught one at a time by hand and taken to an FWC station to be killed with their pith guns. A pithing gun drives a bolt into the snake's brain. They couldn't be shot and left in the wild to be eaten."

"Pythons were caught one at a time. That's stupid," the governor said. "What about today?"

"Before October 2018, the FWC required live pythons to be bagged and brought to them for pithing. Now, they are pithed in the field where they are caught."

"Can they be shot now, Jake?"

"Only a licensed professional hunter with a permit can shoot a python after it's caught by hand," he replied.

"Aren't they hard to find and catch?"

"Very hard. It's suicide to get in the water with a python. Finding them in the swamp is almost impossible. Most are caught by driving along roads with spotlights at night."

Governor Prescott flipped the fourth page on his yellow legal pad and took a drink of water.

"So, you think there might be thousands of pythons in South Florida?" the governor asked.

"I've heard 300,000 to 500,000. The numbers are all over the place, depending on who's guessing. The State won't talk numbers, but, if pressed, admits native wildlife has been decimated."

"How do pythons reproduce?"

"Female pythons begin laying eggs at age five and live twenty years in the Everglades. The mother lays eggs about once per year in late spring, and about 8 hatchlings out of 40 to 100 eggs survive to adulthood," Jake said. "Some claim females don't breed every year, but who knows?"

The governor wrote a list of assumptions on his pad.

"So, each nest has four females that live five years and breed. Say they breed every other year, and ten percent of adults die each year of natural causes before they stop breeding at age twenty. Hold on, Jake, let me do some math. Let's see how many snakes are produced by one female during her lifetime."

The governor, aged forty-one, who had a master's degree in economics from the University of Florida and founded a wealth management company at twenty-eight, rolled his chair over to a desktop computer at a side table. He opened an A.I. chatbot program and spoke the parameters into the computer microphone. The program calculated the population growth.

"Jake, the computer estimates that one female and her offspring, which breed every other year, will produce 1,900 adult snakes. So, a thousand females produce 1,900,000 snakes. No wonder there's little wildlife left in the Glades. There could be millions of pythons out there. How many snakes have been caught?"

Jake referred to his notes.

"Well, the State started two programs in 2017, the Python Elimination Program and the Python Action Team. They hired about 100 professional hunters like me. As of 2025, the state claims about 23,500 were caught over twenty-five years."

The governor laughed. "Only 3,000 females produce that many every year. The other 150,000 females easily replace those caught each year. It's a total waste of taxpayer money."

Jake agreed. "Yet, they hold a Python Challenge contest every July. Nine hundred people catch only 300 pythons in 10 days. What's the purpose? The state spends over three million dollars a year on worthless python programs, and not a penny goes toward warning the public of the dangers."

The governor asked Jake to wait while he finished his notes.

"Jake, when you say State, who do you mean?"

"It's the Florida Wildlife Commission or FWC and the Southwest Florida Water Management District or SWFWMD."

The governor circled FWC three times in red ink.

"Do you live near the Everglades?" the governor asked.

"Yes, I grew up in Everglades City near Marco Island."

"I think I heard you mention you have hunted wild pigs," the governor said.

"Yes, I'm a hunting and saltwater fishing guide."

The governor stood up.

"Now, wild hogs, that's something I know a lot about. I grew up in Polk County, Central Florida. Tens of thousands of invasive feral pigs raise hell there. My parents still live on a cattle ranch south of Lakeland. I started hunting hogs at age ten with my cousins. We had hog dogs, traps, bows, and every gun you can imagine. We killed them on sight, day and night, without a license or permit. Some boars weighed over 400 pounds. We kept meat from young females, smoked some, and made sausage, but most we left in the field for the vultures."

"Yes, sir, you know hogs. They can be shot anywhere on the body, day or night, without a license. Many run off and bleed out. Because hogs root for food and tear up farm and ranchland, the FWC looks the other way," Jake said.

"Okay, here's my read. Since pythons are out of sight and don't damage private property, the FWC gives the appearance of being humane to invasive pythons even though pythons eat ninety-nine percent of native wildlife under their protection," the governor said. "Hogs are mammals like us, don't hunt wildlife, but are slaughtered indiscriminately.

"Yep, you have the picture, Governor."

"Okay, the way I see it, either wild pigs have the same rights as pythons, or pythons have the same rights as wild pigs.

"What are you doing this coming Friday, Jake?"

"Looking for pythons with children in their bellies."

"How about you join me for a press conference at the Sheriff's Department in Miami? It starts at 11:30.

"Can you bring a wild pig of about a hundred pounds and a catch-dog on a chain?"

"Shouldn't be a problem. My neighbor has both."

"How about a twelve-foot python in a wire cage?"

"No problem, Governor."

6

Nowhere to Hide

Governor Prescott took lunch at his desk while reviewing notes from his phone conversation with Jake. He queried A.I. Chat about Burmese python attacks in Asia, the FWC's organization, and their wildlife policies.

He called his chief of staff. "Mike, please set up an encrypted video call later this afternoon at a time that works for Grant and Luck to discuss Pa-Hay-Okee."

Newly elected from the private sector, Prescott felt shielded from the breaking wave of accusations. Not so for longtime Florida Republican legislators, Senate President Jacob Grant and House Speaker Monica Luck, who could hardly plead ignorance. Exposed, they were barefoot and knee-deep in a mudhole full of pythons.

In his straightforward style, the governor summarized the current situation with bullet points he displayed during the video call. He searched Google for images of pythons and scrolled through several pages, which he displayed for Grant and Luck.

"Here's another one of a smiling Florida governor holding a python," Prescott said.

The governor pressed them on FWC politics and for explanations on their actions and inactions. The python attacks on scouts had stunned the legislators. They claimed no direct connections and had considered the FWC a sleepy bureaucracy that avoided attention.

The governor got to the point. "Here's my read. In the nineties, democrats were in power when the python population took off. For reasons I can't comprehend—animal rights or whatever—they granted the pythons protections not afforded to other invasive species, citing animal cruelty laws. They knew or should have known that catching pythons by hand and hauling them to the FWC, had zero chance of controlling the mass invasion. They stood back and watched pythons wipe out native birds and animals. Now they promote killer pythons as a tourist attraction and sponsor 'biggest python' catching contests."

Senator Grant, the backdrop on his video screen, an aerial view of Tampa Bay, looked concerned. He held up a Miami Advocate article to the Zoom camera. The headline read, "Pythons Attack Scouts in Everglades National Park."

"We have to get in front of this ASAP," Grant said. "When the public discovers these kids were swallowed whole, there's going to be a shitstorm. Tourism is the backbone of South Florida. Tourists already fear being eaten by alligators. Who wants to be swallowed by a snake?"

Luck interrupted. "I say the FWC eats this in one big bite. Those fat cats have camped out in cushy jobs for decades while pythons bred like rats and grew into monsters. Democrats catered to animal rights and condoned a snake-happy FWC. Republicans have an opportunity to investigate, educate, and find a solution."

Prescott summarized the strategy. "Democrats failed to act early. The FWC downplayed the emergency and failed to protect or warn the public. Republicans trusted the FWC and now demand to find out how this happened."

"You can call for a task force, Governor, and we will draft legislation in support and tap the disaster relief fund," Grant suggested.

"I like it. That demonstrates action, buys time, and moves it out of the news cycle," Luck said.

The governor wrote on his yellow pad while the two discussed the mechanics of the legislation.

Prescott offered, "How's this for a title of the bill, 'Pa-Hay-Okee Task Force for Protection of Children on Public Lands.'"

They agreed on the basics, and the governor invited them to the Miami press conference.

Prescott pounded his desk for emphasis. "We hold the high ground and come down hard on snake-loving bureaucrats and any snake huggers. We take back the Everglades and protect our children. It's a war on pythons."

"I'll talk to Bernie. We'll need PAC money for a charity drive, an ad campaign, and to seed support groups and protests," Senator Grant said.

"That's the plan, then—no emails or texts about this. We can talk at the press conference," Prescott said.

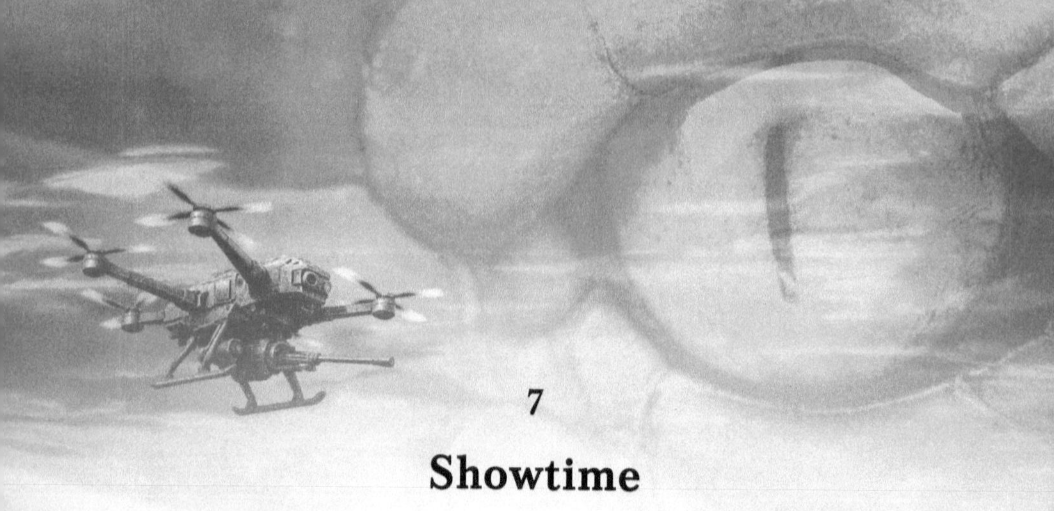

7

Showtime

Friday morning. The Bell 407 helicopter circled low over the hammock three miles west of Pa-Hay-Okee, less than three hours before the press conference in Miami.

"Governor, do you see the fire pit in the sandy area?" Sheriff Palmer shouted over the intercom. He pointed across the governor to the window of the high-banked helicopter flying directly over the campsite.

"See the camp table made from tree limbs? That's where Taylor Williams stayed until sunrise after she escaped."

The area looked deserted except for yellow tape, flags, and police markers. It had an eerie emptiness, considering what had happened.

"I can't imagine the terror that night," Prescott shouted into the boom mic.

Leaving the campsite, the helicopter flew east and landed at 9:30 near the sheriff's mobile command trailer and several large white tents. The sheriff introduced Prescott to the operations commander. The major began with an update from that morning. A team using infrared sensors on a flat-bottom skiff had found a scout inside a sixteen-foot python at three a.m. The major pointed to the location on a wall map—a marshy area crosscut with sloughs two miles southwest of their location.

The sheriff pulled back the table cover to reveal a detailed diagram of the camping area. Using a dowel, he pointed to where each scout had camped. Next, he pointed to where each scout was found.

Green labels for Taylor, Owen, and Cindy, the three survivors. Red labels for the deceased. They found Randy at his campsite. Unable to swallow him, a live python had Randy's head in its mouth. They found Kate inside a python hiding in the brush near her camp. They captured the python that ate Jamie in shallow water on the eastern side of the camp area. Wade, suffocated inside his sleeping bag. The python, unable to reach him, had left. Rob, found in water north of the camp, had drowned, his body showing signs of an animal encounter. Oliver was the scout they had found a few hours earlier in a python. Blue labels for Steven and Paul, who were still missing.

Prescott rubbed his forehead and sighed. "Sheriff, who knows about this map?"

"Only my inner circle. The press only has three survivors, five deceased, and three missing.

"Good. This has the potential to trigger mass hysteria, and the fallout could impact everyone, everywhere. Keep the gore under wraps as long as possible."

Sheriff Palmer replaced the cover.

"Agreed. It's an active and ongoing investigation. Still, we've already had a leak. One of our python hunters told a Tampa newspaper he had found a deceased female. The paper called my office for comment, and I convinced them to hold off. I arrested the butthead for violating his non-disclosure agreement."

"Good. Are there any parents or family members here?"

"Yes, families of the three missing boys are in a tented area protected from the press and staffed with my attendants."

"The last scout they found, Oliver, are his parents here?" Prescott asked.

"Yes, they are here. They don't know yet."

"What a fricking mess. I've learned a lot from Jake. I can't begin to tell you what I'm going to do about this shit."

"I know, I've had to tell five families," Palmer said.

"Okay, let's do it right now. You tell them, and I'll back you up."

* * *

The Bell 407 departed at 10:45 for the press conference with the governor, two bodyguards, the sheriff, and State Senator Marie Anna Alvarez of District 40, which included Pa-Hay-Okee. Irene Anderson, Kate's mother, occupied the last seat in the copter. Even though they had found Kate on Tuesday, Ms. Anderson continued to maintain vigil with the other families. She asked the governor if she could speak at the press conference.

Twenty minutes later, the helicopter hovered three hundred feet above the Dade County Sheriff's Department's helipad. Governor Prescott surveyed thousands of people in bleachers and standing on grass behind rope barriers. A large, covered stage, enclosed on three sides, featured an LED video wall at the back. Media trucks parked nose-to-tail down a side street, their satellite dishes on poles competed for airspace. As the copter descended, Prescott spotted the podium, two covered cages, and the invited dignitaries seated in two rows.

One hundred feet from touchdown, the governor pulled the bottom of his jeans down over ostrich-skin boots. From behind, his bodyguard passed the Panama fedora to the governor. Prescott adjusted his sunglasses and pulled his speech from the breast pocket of a beige suede sports jacket.

Projecting confidence, John Prescott stood six feet tall, weighed 180, and had the rugged good looks of a Clooney. His blue eyes could switch in an instant from warm and engaging to ice on cold steel.

The engines wound down from high-pitched whirring to a rumbling swish. The door next to the governor slid open. He looked over at the sheriff, adjusted his fedora, and smiled.

"Sheriff, I was made for days like this."

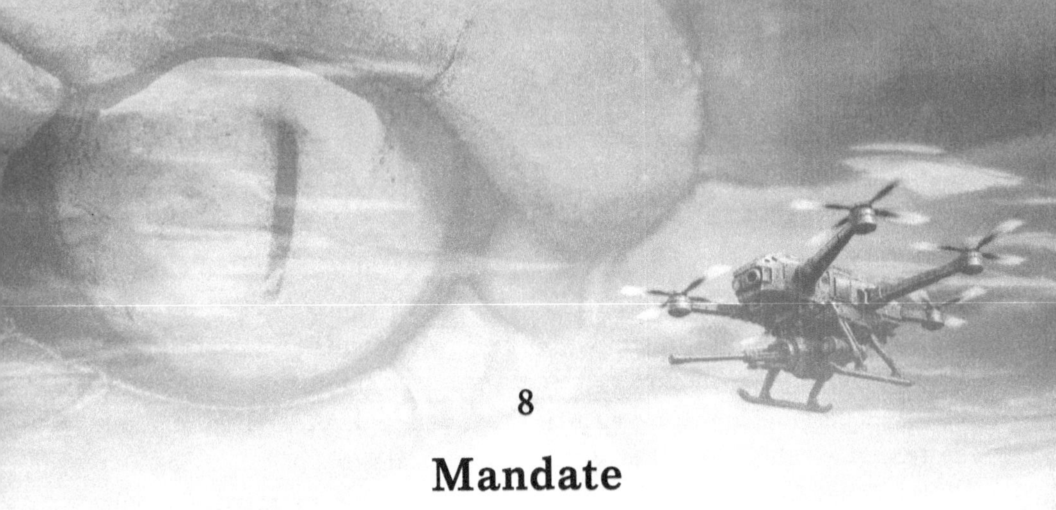

8

Mandate

Sheriff Palmer's community affairs officer, Sally Morgan, whom Slate knew from her position on a campus security committee, agreed to give a note in an envelope to the governor's chief of staff. Slate watched the helicopter land.

After greeting the audience and acknowledging those seated on stage, Governor Prescott removed his hat, draped his sports jacket over the back of a chair, and adjusted the microphone on the podium.

"Thank you for coming. I've just returned from the Everglades, where I toured the Pa-Hay-Okee area with Sheriff Palmer and met families of young victims of the tragedy last Saturday night."

He scanned the overflow crowd and a roped-off press section fronting the stage. His new communications office had cast a wide net and, in addition to the Florida media market, landed major news outlets such as AP, Fox, BBC, and CNN.

A newcomer to the national stage, Prescott had one hour to convince a nation and the political elite that he had the right stuff. Americans were accustomed to watching celebrity python hunts and former Florida governors holding pythons to promote tourism. A false sense of security had not prepared anyone for what Prescott was about to tell them.

Running for governor on a platform of responsibility, integrity, and doing the right thing, Prescott, on the job for only six weeks, faced a legacy-level make-or-break crisis.

His father, a retired veterinarian, had served on the Polk County Commission. Before his father's two terms, the southern half of the county's land had already been lost to radioactive phosphate strip

33

mining. Much of Hardee County to the south was also destroyed by the mining. A half-dozen draglines continued to devastate thousands of acres in Hardee County each year.

Decades of questionable votes by county commissioners led to the degradation of hundreds of thousands of acres that were once productive farms and ranches, complete with roads and communities. While growing up, the governor had witnessed the inexplicable actions of public officials and state agencies that depopulated and permanently destroyed rural communities on a massive scale.

The governor followed efforts by citizens in Hardee County to expose the shenanigans of local economic development boards that received about eight million dollars annually in exchange for mining approvals. One failed project, linked to several state representatives, "lost" seven million in cash. Investigations had led to an Emmy award for a Tampa TV station, ethics convictions, and a criminal grand jury probe.

Prescott watched dozens of other questionable projects fail with no accountability. In part, these childhood memories forged his determination to protect the environment and stand against public corruption.

He realized those mined-out, polluted wastelands, the size of New York City, Los Angeles, and Chicago combined, were beyond saving.

Prescott wondered if similar failures by public officials and agencies were responsible for the decline of the Everglades. The horrific deaths of young scouts provided the mandate he needed to save the Everglades, if that was possible. He had no idea if his plan would work. Like it or not, he now owned the Everglades, with all the issues.

Prescott stepped away from the podium to roll up his sleeves.

"It has been a terrible week for Florida. Caught off guard, I've spent this time trying to understand how Pa-Hay-Okee happened. There are more questions than answers.

"Our great state has failed its citizens, our visitors, and the wildlife of South Florida. The loss of life at Pa-Hay-Okee was preventable.

"Here is what I know. Eleven young scouts from a local troop hiked into the Everglades last Saturday for a night of wilderness camping. During the night, large hungry Burmese pythons, an invasive species, converged on their camp. Two females and one male scout managed to escape. As of this morning, search teams have recovered one female and five male scouts. The search continues for two missing boys.

"We are deeply saddened for the families and loved ones of our young scouts."

The governor motioned toward dignitaries seated to his left.

"With us today is Troop 44's Scoutmaster, Ralph Flanagan. His Troop has their pack meetings a mile from this stage."

Scoutmaster Flanagan, in uniform, looked like a broken man who hadn't slept in a week. He raised a hand without expression.

"Also, here is Irene Anderson, the mother of the female scout taken from us Saturday night. Ms. Anderson will say a few words later this morning."

Irene, dressed in a charcoal pantsuit and white blouse, her long black hair gathered in a conservative bun, held a picture of Kate and a white handkerchief in her lap.

"I've invited members of our State Legislature. Senator Marie Anna Alvarez represents District 40, where Pa-Hay-Okee is located."

Senator Alvarez, tall and attractive, sitting next to Irene Anderson, raised a hand and smiled.

"The president of our Florida Senate and also the Speaker of the House of Representatives are here. Thank you, Senator Jacob Grant and Representative Monica Luck."

Grant, in a dark blue suit, and Luck, wearing a black long-sleeve dress, stood and waved politely.

The governor purposely did not invite representatives from three agencies—the FWC, the Department of Environmental Protection, or the Southwest Florida Water Management District.

To the right of the podium, Sheriff Palmer and Jake Calhoun sat near two covered wire cages.

"We owe a special thanks to Sheriff Palmer and his search team. With Sheriff Palmer today is Jake Calhoun, a professional guide and leader of two dozen professional wildlife hunters at Pa-Hay-Okee."

The LED wall behind the stage illuminated. The screen filled with five men standing side by side holding a sixteen-foot Burmese python. Gasps from the audience registered their shock as they connected the image to the scouts. A QR code appeared. Slate and many others captured it on their smartphones. She looked away from the screen, which showed the happy faces of the men holding the python.

"What are they so happy about?" she whispered to herself. She studied the governor. Taller than she expected, his demeanor didn't fit the image of a typical politician, seeming more sincere.

"The QR code links to a report compiled by my office on the history of pythons in the Everglades and government policies.

"In the 1990s, as python numbers grew, the FWC, for reasons I cannot understand, gave these apex predators protections not afforded to other invasive species like the feral pig. Then, as today, they required pythons to be caught by hand one at a time. Until 2017, the FWC required each snake to be brought to an FWC facility for killing by a bolt driven into the brain. It's called pithing.

"Since 2017, hunters still catch pythons by hand and pith them where caught."

The LED screen changed to a family of twenty dead pigs of all sizes inside a large steel cage trap in a field, their bodies ripped apart by gunfire.

"The FWC has a double standard when it comes to pythons and wild pigs, both invasive species.

"Pythons have wiped out native animals and birds in the Everglades. They have attacked and killed humans in Asia for millennia. Yet, the FWC requires that they be caught by hand and killed humanely.

"Wild pigs are omnivores. They don't hunt wildlife. They prefer roots and acorns. The FWC does not require catching pigs by hand. Pigs of all ages are shot anywhere on the body, and government agencies can shoot them from helicopters in Florida. Caveats like animal cruelty standards apply in theory but not in practice."

Jake removed the cover from the left enclosure, an 8-foot-square wire cage. Panicked with fear, the wild pig crashed against the cage, opening a deep cut on her nose. Thrashing about, blood spewed in sweeps onto the stage.

"Wild pigs root for food and cause considerable damage to farms and ranchland. This one is pregnant. She can be killed in any way imaginable. Hunted day and night with no restrictions, when wounded, they often run into wetlands to die slow agonizing deaths. Mothers are targeted to starve their piglets. Some hunters use fighting dogs to catch them."

Danny, Jake's friend, his arms extended by a heavy chain, came onto the stage. A sixty-pound catch dog named Rocky pulled the chain like an Alaskan sled dog. Square-jawed and bred for hunting pigs, the slobbery foam spewed and mixed on the stage with the pig's blood. Eyes wild with rage, Rocky's sole purpose was to kill the pig. The dog snarled and lunged at the cage, its feet slipping on the wet floor. The pig cowered in the corner, then collapsed with fear. Jake replaced the cover, and Danny led Rocky from the stage.

The raw violence rattled Slate and many others. She couldn't watch and focused on her iPad, pretending not to hear the squeals and growls. Thinking of the animal being pregnant made her want to cry.

"How is it that the FWC has no mercy for these mammals that pose no threat to wildlife or humans? Why does their heart bleed for an apex predator that has killed ninety-nine percent of the native animals and birds in the Everglades, is spreading north, and threatens humans?"

The screen changed to a large female python coiled atop a nest of white eggs.

"Beginning at age five, female pythons breed annually or every other year for fifteen years. From each nest of up to one hundred eggs, about four females and four males reach adulthood and breed. I see some in the audience using their phones to do the math. Let's just say, if there was enough food, the number of pythons slithering in the Everglades would be several times greater than the population of our country.

"Less than one percent of native animals remain. Pythons also eat each other. The scarcity of food keeps the population at three to five hundred thousand.

"It's simple math, folks. The FWC has known about this for decades. They give the false impression that the invasion is under control. They boast about removing 25,000 pythons over the course of twenty-five years. Ladies and gentlemen, the offspring of a single female produce more than 25,000 adult pythons in that amount of time."

The screen changed to a banner for the 2025 Florida Python Challenge, featuring contestants holding a fifteen-foot python.

"In 2025, 900 people competed in the FWC's annual python challenge. They only caught 300 pythons. Think about that. It took

300 of those competitors ten days to catch one python each, and 600 competitors ten days to catch nothing. What's the point? It only takes forty female pythons each year to have 300 babies that reach adulthood. What about the other 150,000 breeding females? The python challenge is a publicity stunt, a charade."

No one, least of all Jake Calhoun, foresaw what happened next.

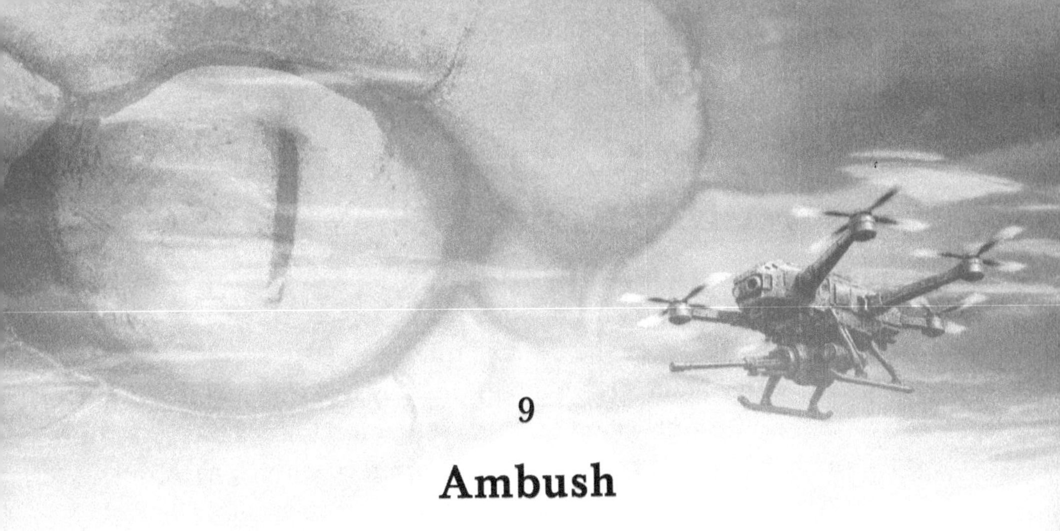

9

Ambush

The LED screen switched to a live view of the wire cage on the right. Jake pulled the cover off and tossed it to the back of the stage.

Slate, sitting in the second row, leaned up to see. She gasped, never having seen a live python. Too large for the cage, the fat body coiled around itself. The head, poised six inches above the body, looked at the audience. Its tongue flicked in and out. Evil yellow eyes with black slits seemed to look directly at Slate. She shuddered and looked away.

The man the governor called Jake wore faded jeans, a plaid work shirt, and a baseball cap with an old-school Shell Oil logo. He reminded her of a cowboy without the boots. She tried to define his look—there was something about him she found alluring. A self-assured, exacting, measured confidence came to mind. His sharp, watchful eyes focused on the python as he removed the cage top. Difficult to see the cage, Slate looked up at the LED screen.

Flick. The tongue slid out, hesitated, and slid back into the closed mouth.

The governor, still at the podium, nodded for Jake to begin the demonstration. Jake hesitated, waiting for Danny to return from putting the dog in its pen.

"The stupidity of FWC policies cannot be overstated. They claim catching pythons by hand is humane, that the snake is not terrified and stressed. Before 2017, live pythons were kept in bags for indefinite periods before transportation to FWC killing stations. Now they must be killed where they are caught."

The governor had never seen a live python up close or watched one being wrestled. Jake and other professionals usually caught pythons

39

by the tail and dragged them straight before grabbing the head. This reduced the snake's options and its power.

"It's about time the public sees what is required by the FWC. Jake will give us a demonstration."

The snake moved its head. Slate saw it on the screen. Not much, but enough for her to notice the upward tilt.

Leaning over, Jake's left hand moved down in front of the python to distract it from his right hand that moved behind toward the neck. In the blink of an eye, Jake's fingers snapped around the thick neck.

Startled, the snake's head twisted and came up at Jake's face, the white mouth gaped wide. Eighty sharp teeth curved back like fishhooks, now inches from Jake's face. He brought his left hand up to join his right in a collar around the neck, pushing it away. The snake's body bolted up and out of the cage like a spring. Jake stood as the snake elevated, his arms outstretched, trying to control the constrictor. The cage tipped toward Jake. He tripped and stumbled backward as coils instinctively wrapped around him. The two landed on the stage, Jake struggling to keep the teeth from clamping on his face. In serious trouble, he held on while the coils squeezed. This was not the plan.

The audience on their feet, Slate moved between seats to the front row. Reporters to her right filmed the scene with everything they had. Some in the audience panicked and ran.

The governor, standing at the podium, saw Jake growing weaker. The sheriff was behind the governor. Prescott, being closer, ran over and straddled Jake and the python. Kneeling over them, he grabbed the neck just below Jake's hands and pulled it away from Jake's face.

Closing the door on the dog's pen, Danny heard the crowd scream and ran for the stage, pulling his buck knife from the sheath on his belt. He flicked the blade open, raced up the stairs, and yelled, "Hold the head still, Governor!"

Danny positioned the blade point in the middle behind the snake's eyes and tapped the end of the handle with the palm of his other hand. It slid into the brain, and he twisted the blade.

The governor unwound the head while Danny and the sheriff unwound the tail. Jake lay flat on his back, gasping. Prescott, Danny, and the sheriff stretched the dead python along the front edge of the stage. Captured live on TV, the episode lasted two minutes and went viral to a hundred million.

Sheriff Palmer and medics rushed to Jake. Shaken, he sat up and drank water. He looked at the audience and at a blonde woman standing close to the stage wearing a navy blazer and gray pants. Hands to her mouth, she was crying. Governor Prescott helped Jake stand. Jake gave a thumbs-up to the crowd, and cheers broke out. The blonde woman clapped wildly, and Jake made eye contact with her.

The governor addressed the audience. "Ladies and gentlemen, my apologies for this. It was not planned. We're glad Jake is alright. As you can see, these monsters are dangerous and unpredictable. I see no reason for the FWC to require risking death or serious injury under the guise of humane treatment of pythons. My apologies to Jake and Danny. I should have waited for Danny to return and help Jake."

Someone from the audience yelled, "Governor Prescott, you're the real deal. You're one bad-ass governor!" The audience cheered and gave the governor a standing ovation.

Prescott replied, "I'm still shaking inside. This was my first snake encounter, and I don't want another one. I suggest we take a fifteen-minute break, then I'll tell you what I'm going to do about pythons in Florida."

Someone yelled, "What about the pig?"

The governor thought. "We'll release her into the wild on public land." The crowd cheered.

10

Pythons R Us

Behind a fold in the drapes near seats for the dignitaries, Senator Alvarez held an inconsolable Irene Anderson, the python attack happening a few feet from her seat. The governor helped escort her to the sheriff's department lobby. Alvarez, Grant, and Luck followed. They conferred with Prescott in a small conference room.

"How's it going?" the governor asked them.

"Good and bad," Alvarez said. "The picture of that python jumping six feet with its mouth inches from Jake's face could make the next cover of Timeline magazine. Did you see how many people in the audience bolted? Thirty million tourists visit South Florida, and half are afraid of snakes. Tourism is my bread and butter. We could have done without the Crocodile Dundee bit, in my opinion."

Prescott and the others nodded in agreement. "We have five minutes, what else?" he asked.

Senator Grant jumped in. "John, you're correct to lean hard on FWC. Glossing over pythons as a nuisance is no longer an option. I've been thinking. Democrats will point out that republicans have done zip since taking control in 1996. How many republican governors with big smiles are on Google holding pythons? I say we go bipartisan and focus on solutions while keeping the heat on the FWC."

The governor agreed.

Representative Luck made the last comment before they returned to the stage.

"Pythons R US. We now own the python problem. There is only one option: killing them by the truckloads as fast as possible before the

42

blame shifts to us. We have five million dollars in the PAC with more coming to keep our message out front."

"Monica, if we have time, you can announce the companion bills supporting our project on stage. Okay?" Prescott asked.

* * *

During the break, Slate asked Sally if the governor received her note. "Probably not, I just gave it to his chief of staff two minutes ago."

Back at the podium, Prescott glanced at the LED screen, the Florida seal over a landscape view of the Pa-Hay-Okee area. He made eye contact with Sheriff Palmer, who was at the tech table talking on the phone. Palmer gave him a thumbs-up.

"Thank you for your patience. I've just seen Jake. He's on his way back to help with the search at Pa-Hay-Okee. He said this experience brought back a memory of the time he was holding down a big alligator in a john boat when the boat flipped over." The audience laughed and applauded.

On the phone with Wendy at the hospital, the sheriff confirmed that Taylor was ready and the connection was good. Sunshine lit her room. A makeup artist had styled Taylor's bright blonde hair to make the bandage resemble a hairband. Wendy helped soften the dark bruises and buttoned the blue gown to cover her neck. Flowers, cards, stuffed animals, and balloons surrounded her bed.

The governor scanned the audience. "Six days ago, a young lady survived a python attack and escaped, but not before saving the life of a fellow scout. Together, they hiked three miles back to Pa-Hay-Okee. Sheriff Palmer assigned professionals from the victim's services unit to help her and the two other known survivors. Would you like to meet her?"

The audience applauded—the screen filled with Taylor. She smiled and gave a shy wave.

"Hello, Taylor. This is Governor Prescott. How are you?"

"Hi. I'm getting better, thank you."

"Wow, you have a lot of cards and balloons in your room."

"Yes, thank you so much to all of the wonderful people who remembered me."

"You're welcome, Taylor. We owe you so much for the help you have provided and for your courage and bravery. There are thousands of people here with best wishes and high hopes for you. We're working hard to make the Everglades safe again."

Taylor's smile wilted, and a sadness returned.

"I hope so," she said.

Someone in the crowd yelled, "We love you, Taylor."

The entire audience repeated, as if on cue, "We love you, Taylor," and broke into applause and cheers.

"Do you hear them?" the governor asked.

She nodded, smiled, and said thank you.

"We'll let you go for now, Taylor. Thank you for taking the time to speak with us. Goodbye."

Prescott looked down at the podium and waited for the audience to quiet. The big screen turned a deep blue with the Florida Seal in the center. Prescott raised his eyes to scan the audience and the media section.

"The sheriff recorded a video of Taylor describing what happened that night. In the interest of public safety and to emphasize the need for action, I'm releasing selected excerpts of the interview to the media."

Prescott turned to look at the State seal, then back to the audience.

"Do you see a Burmese python in our State seal?" He watched their eyes search the screen.

"There aren't any. If there were, they would call them the Florida python. If they were native animals that evolved over millions of years, they would have natural predators and be part of the ecosystem like the alligator."

The screen switched to the five men holding the sixteen-foot-long python. In the lower half of the screen were pictures of the seventy species of animals and birds that pythons have decimated.

"The FWC and other agencies, for reasons an investigation might reveal, have lied to us and concealed the threats that led to the disaster at Pa-Hay-Okee. The FWC created diversions such as snake cowboys, python rodeos, and python adventure tours that glamorized the wholesale destruction of an entire ecosystem. Worst of all, they failed to warn and educate the public about this dangerous silent menace."

The screen changed in color. Over a red background, a vertical column of yellow pythons emerged on the left side of the screen.

Twenty-five in number, they crawled across to the other side and coiled up. A second column emerged, crawled across, and coiled next to the first. The procession continued column after column, packing the screen with virtual pythons.

"Here's a simple question. How could Florida officials spend tens of billions of dollars to restore and clean up water flowing through the Everglades while allowing the near extinction of the animals? What is the Everglades without wildlife?"

The governor waited for the screen to fill with thousands of pythons.

"I'm in charge now. I will do something about this. And, I will start today."

The screen displayed a wide-angle aerial view of the Everglades, splashed in golden shades, with a red setting sun. A box appeared with bright blue text over a yellow background.

Goals:

1. Eradicate Pythons from South Florida (12 months)

2. Reintroduce native wildlife to the Everglades (24 months)

Prescott continued. "I plan to restore the Everglades to its natural native ecosystem, reversing thirty years of neglect and mismanagement. It will not be easy. We know what does *not* work. Using science and technology, we hope to find solutions."

The screen displayed a new view of the Everglades, showing native animals and wading birds around a pond. Over the pond, a QR code appeared with the caption—Python Plan of Action.

"I'm working with legislators on both sides of the aisle to secure approvals and funding. Let me list what happens next."

The screen changed to a numbered list.

Slate noticed Sally motioning to her and met her by the bleachers.

Sally said, "I asked the sheriff about you talking with the governor. He said you can use one of the suspect interview rooms if you want, assuming the governor has the time."

"Where is it?"

"Over there." Sally pointed to a side door at the sheriff's department.

"Thanks, that will work perfectly."

"Okay, come with me. I'll get you set up and make sure Mike shows the governor your note."

Governor Prescott announced his five actions.

"One. Letters were sent this morning to the heads of three state agencies, requesting the resignations of five public officials who were aware of, or should have been aware of, the dangers that led to what happened at Pa-Hay-Okee.

"Two. I've signed an executive order terminating three ineffective and dangerous programs: Python Capture, Adventure Tours, and Contests. Taxpayer dollars funding these carnival sideshows will go toward finding a permanent solution.

"Three. The Florida Department of Law Enforcement, which reports to me, will conduct a criminal investigation into the incomprehensible actions of public officials. Did anyone benefit from jobs, contracts, and quid-pro-quo deals from what appears to be the commercialization and continuation of the python scourge?"

From the top of a bleacher, three women held up signs. One read, "Kids Lives Matter." Another read, "Python Gate." Someone in the bleachers began to chant, "Kids' lives matter, kids' lives matter."

Governor Prescott suspected the Python PAC was involved.

"Alright, if I can have your attention, let me get to the main parts of my plan.

"Four. I'm forming a task force led by Brent Howard, my Director of Science and Technology. Using all available resources, they will explore options and actions to eradicate pythons and reintroduce native wildlife.

"Five. I've signed an executive order proclaiming that pythons have the same rights, or lack thereof, as wild pigs—no license, no permits, no restrictions on killing them, except one. Pythons are not allowed to be caught by hand. The primary method is the same as that for wild pigs: death by gunshot. That said, laws and restrictions on firearms remain in place.

"That's it—the task force forms next week and reports directly to me. Expect regular updates on their progress.

"Our hearts and prayers go out to the families of our young scouts. Rest assured, this terrible loss is the beginning of a new era for our wonderful Everglades. Thank you for coming."

The audience stood, cheered, and applauded. Prescott remained briefly to shake hands and acknowledge the crowd. His security team escorted him down the steps off the stage for his helicopter flight to Miami International, then by private jet back to Tallahassee.

Not far from the helicopter, Mike, his chief of staff, rushed to catch the governor.

"Hey, Boss, Sally, my counterpart for the sheriff, handed me a note from someone for you."

Prescott opened the envelope.

"Governor Prescott, my name is Sarah Warner, PhD, chair of Mechatronics at the Univ. of Miami. I need to speak with you. I can kill your snakes, every damned one of them."

The governor handed the note back.

"You know anything about this?"

Mike read the note. "Wow, I have no idea. Only that Sally said the woman is waiting in the sheriff's department."

Both looked toward the building, the side door held open by a woman.

"That's Sally," Mike said.

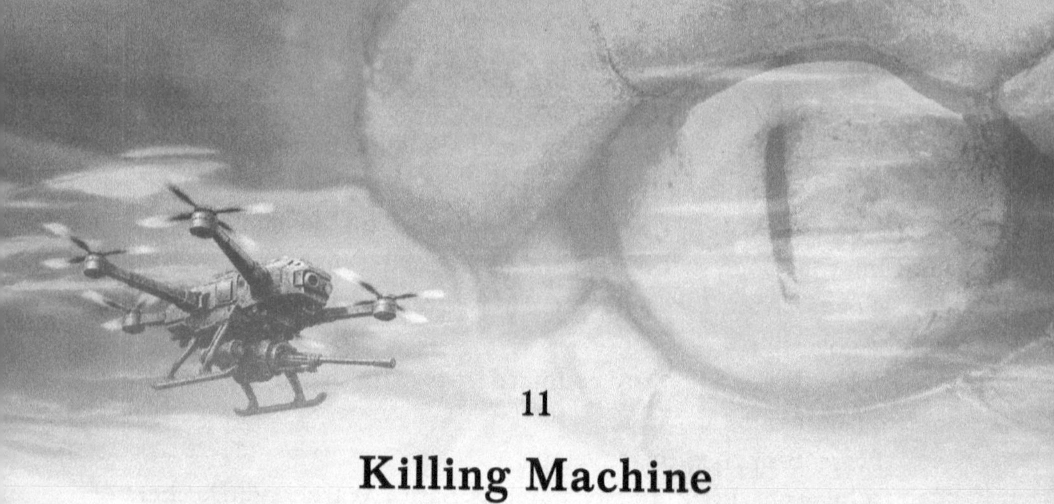

11

Killing Machine

"Interview room number three," Sally said, pointing down the hallway. The gray steel door, a red light above, had a small window, the glass embedded with steel wire.

Governor Prescott studied the woman through the glass. She sat in a straight-backed chair at a gray metal table. Her open laptop rested against an iron loop in the table where handcuffs could be attached.

About his age, he guessed her five feet seven inches tall, athletic, and 130 pounds. Soft blonde hair in layers curled to the collar of a white silk blouse under a navy linen blazer and light gray fitted pants. Her naturally pretty face, with little makeup, was focused on the laptop. Thin fingers zipped over the keyboard. She looked put-together, intelligent, and approachable. An interrogation room seemed an odd place for a woman of her poise.

"What's her name?" the governor asked the deputy.

"Sarah Slate Warner," he said.

"Slate. What's that stand for?"

"Sir, I have no idea."

"Ok, let me talk with her. No video, audio, or monitoring, Deputy."

Prescott looked at his bodyguard, "Greg, you can hang out in the coffee shop."

Prescott opened the door. She slipped the laptop into a folio, stood, and straightened her jacket. Taller than he expected, he noticed her slim waist, flat stomach, and respectable top, tastefully contoured by folds under the blazer. She wore small gold hoop earrings and a large blue sapphire on her right-hand ring finger.

"Hello." Prescott walked in and extended his hand.

She took a step forward, smiled, and shook his hand.

"Ms. Warner, I believe?"

"Yes, Governor. Thank you for meeting with me."

Prescott motioned to sit and took the other chair.

"This is an unusual place to meet, Ms. Warner. Am I being interrogated?"

Slate giggled shyly, and he laughed.

"Of course not. We can swap chairs if it makes you feel better," she said.

He smiled and leaned back in his chair, the first time he had relaxed all day. "No, I'll be the good cop."

She laughed again. "I know Sheriff Palmer's community affairs officer from a charity we support. I asked for someplace private. Pretty funny, huh? Kind of creepy, to be honest."

"I feel the same way, which is a good thing, right?"

They laughed.

"I have two questions, Ms. Warner. Have you ever killed a snake, and why is your middle name Slate?"

She smiled, trying to suppress a giggle, her dimples emerging.

"Those are funny questions, Governor Prescott. Slate is not a formal nickname, but one my parents gave me as a baby. My crying reminded them of chalk screeching on a slate chalkboard."

"That's funny. Do you like to be called Slate?"

She nodded and smiled, the dimples more pronounced.

"Okay then, Slate, are you a killer of snakes?"

Her expression changed from light-hearted to serious.

"Governor, let me answer your question by saying we probably learned about Pa-Hay-Okee at the same time. I've spent every waking minute since then researching pythons in the Everglades. I've read your white paper and checked your population computations. They're correct—too many snakes for human-based interventions."

The governor interrupted. "Have you any expertise in killing pythons, Slate?"

"Not yet, but I will." She sat upright and folded her hands on the table close to the iron ring, anticipating his response.

Prescott, as was his style, got down to basics.

"Let me summarize. Your note said you can kill my snakes, every damn one. You tell me you have studied pythons for all of six days. You agree that it would take thousands of hunters—if there were thousands—but they could never kill enough pythons. And you've never killed a python.

"Sorry, Slate, your dots don't connect, and I'm running late."

She leaned forward and grabbed the iron ring. "Correct, governor. I agree with your summation. Do you want to hear my idea or not?" Along with her challenge came a warm smile and twinkling green eyes.

Slate positioned the laptop so both could see a collage of pictures. One had her at a console wrapped by computer monitors. Others were a giant swirl of birds in flight, an aerial drone with six rotors, and an assault rifle mounted on a dog-like robot.

"I'm the Associate Dean at the College of Engineering at the University of Miami." She slid her business card across the table.

"I also chair the Mechatronics department. It merges engineering disciplines like robotics, machine-trained A.I. models, biophysics, and sensor technologies. In addition, I have a spin-off company called ZKuul Solutions for private-sector applications."

The governor checked his Apple watch. "Impressive background, Slate. Your research and projects are here in Miami?"

She nodded, raising her wrist to show, like him, that she had the latest Apple watch.

"I'll repeat my question and add another. What does your background have to do with killing pythons? Second, why have you been studying pythons day and night since Sunday?"

"Animals behave like formations of birds and schools of fish. I develop software to identify patterns and replicate their behavior. We use this information for automation, robotics, and many other applications."

She pointed to a picture of her in a lab coat. "This is what I do, Governor. I can build a computer program to find pythons in the wild, based on predictable behavior and custom-tuned sensors."

"So, let's say you can find them. Then what?" he asked.

"Governor, my college has classified contracts with the Department of Defense. We do weather research for NOAA and simulations for NASA. I have access to hardware, 3D printers, supercomputers, and a

PhD staff in other specialties. I have the background and knowledge to solve the python problem."

Slate switched to a list of Phase One objectives. She stood, removed the blue blazer, and turned around to drape it over the back of her chair. The governor noted the seductive curves in her fitted slacks and the folds of her silk bodice.

"I propose we use machines to hunt and kill pythons. These are the steps:

1. Sensor selection
2. Develop A.I. algorithms to recognize pythons in the wild
3. Mount sensors and a weapon on an aerial drone platform
4. Couple acquisition and firing controls to aim a weapon
5. Train a self-improving A.I. algorithm to find and shoot pythons
6. Field test."

Slate paused between each step and watched his reaction. His lips moved as he concentrated.

"Governor, pythons will distribute based on food availability, terrain, and reproduction dynamics. Not particularly territorial, they tend to cluster near food sources. Females are larger, and males congregate around them to breed. A trained algorithm could predict python locations based on dozens of variables, much like is done with weather forecasting.

"They are active at night and emit light at 850 nanometers in the infrared spectrum. There might be a sensor that smells them. I'm researching that."

Governor Prescott, fully attentive, leaned forward, his hand now on the iron ring.

"Can you shoot them, Slate?"

"That's the easy part. Hunting them on the ground or in a boat is stupid. A low-flying drone with a gun aimed by a computer is the only way to go. It's a war on pythons, correct?"

"Damn right! What would you need to get started?"

"For proof of concept, I'm thinking four million dollars. I'll demonstrate a prototype by July 4th, in four months, at Pa-Hay-Okee."

"And you propose to use university resources?"

"Yes, initially, assuming, with your backing, we have the support of my dean and upper management. I would own the technology and any patents. The project remains confidential and exempt from public record requests."

Prescott sat back and studied her list.

"Your ideas are ambitious and audacious, just what I need.

"I made big promises today. Promises I will be measured against. Compared to the money wasted on gimmicks like python rodeos, this project could be the answer or lead to new technologies that lead to solutions."

She sat back and smiled in relief. Spontaneously, she applauded herself and said, "Yes, yes. This makes me very happy."

Surprised by her own reaction, she followed up immediately with, "Oh, I'm sorry. That's not like me."

Prescott laughed, amused by her enthusiasm.

"Brent Howard, my technology guru, will call you tomorrow. You can give him a tour of your facilities. If it's a go, I'll call your dean and whoever, okay?"

He reached across the table, extending his hand.

Slate smiled and gave him a firm handshake.

"You haven't answered my other question."

She looked puzzled.

"Why does killing pythons mean so much to you?"

"Will it make a difference in your decision?" she asked, her mood now serious.

He shook his head.

"One of the scouts carried a satellite SOS locator. Do you remember his name?"

Prescott thought of the names on the scout victims board at Pa-Hay-Okee.

"Jamie," he recalled.

"His last name is Warner. My only sibling, Rick Warner, had two sons. Since I don't have children, Jamie was like a son to me."

Prescott reached over to put his hand over hers.

"I'm so sorry, Sarah."

12

Spiderman

Midafternoon, Jake reviewed rescue team reports in a tent next to the sheriff's command trailer. Four days after his embarrassing and terrifying incident at the governor's press conference, Jake was scheduled with two others to hunt pythons later that night with spotlights from a flat-bottom skiff.

A dispatch clerk from the command trailer pulled open the tent flap.

"Hey, Jake, there's a call for you on the landline."

Jake followed her to a console in the trailer.

"Hello, this is Jake Calhoun."

"Hi, please hold a second for Governor Prescott."

The governor came on the phone. "Hi, Jake, how are you feeling?"

"I'm fine, Governor. My pride is bruised and my ribs a bit sore, but thanks to you, I'm fine."

"You're funny. I had no idea how fast those bastards moved."

"We usually dump them out of the tub first and control the tail. I should have waited for Danny," Jake said.

"Anyway, the press loved the demonstrations, and they liked my plan. Most importantly, we have a green light to fund projects. Are there any new developments out there?"

Jake looked across the mostly empty command trailer, the hope of finding the last two scouts, almost gone.

"It's still considered a search and rescue, at least until this Friday, but it's really a clean-up operation. We shoot every python we find and cut open the big ones. One of my guys shot an Indian Rock python yesterday. They breed near where I live, around Everglades City.

Finding one this far east is not good. I heard the two species could be interbreeding and developing a super-snake."

"Not good is right, Jake.

"Are families of scouts still at your command center?"

"Not today, I think that's over. At least I hope so, for their sake."

People continue to bring out food and desserts as well as stuffed animals and flowers. Jake motioned for a deputy to bring him cookies from a table.

"I have something you might be interested in. After the press conference, I met a research professor who has an idea for using A.I. to find pythons. Brent, my tech guy, visited her at the University of Miami yesterday. It might be a dead end, but at this point, we've got nothing to lose.

"I'm reallocating five million in python charade money from the FWC. It's enough to fund this prototype. The professor needs a research site in the Everglades near Miami and live animals to train a computer program."

Jake listened, not getting what that had to do with him.

"I'm not all that high tech, Governor," Jake laughed.

"From what Brent says, the people on her proposed team are scientists and engineers, not Everglades swampers or crackers. That's why I thought of you. They would do the tech, and you do the rest. You build the site, provide pythons and wildlife, and keep the geeks safe. Are you interested?"

"Ah, I have a guide business and other commitments. How long would it last?"

Jake ran the idea around in his head, unsure if he wanted to be around big-city types or super-nerds.

"The professor thinks they can have a prototype ready for testing by July 4th. If it goes well, they ramp up and hunt pythons. You could sign up for the first phase and see what happens. There's great potential if it works. Possibly a new career path and a big payoff for you."

To Jake, the prospect of doing something new for four months sounded appealing. Early spring was a slow time for guided hunts. He could manage the easy one-hour drive from his small ranch house. If the money was good, he thought, why not?

"I assume the pay is worth the commute?"

"That's up to Dr. Warner. There aren't many who know the Everglades like you do."

"Okay, I'm interested. What's the next step, Governor?"

* * *

Events followed a predictable path over the next weeks. The sheriff retired the mobile command center. Volunteers erected a cedar log memorial shelter to display merit badge sashes and pictures of the scouts. The searchers never found the bodies of scouts, Paul, or Steven.

The Pa-Hay-Okee investigation, although active on paper, had little to investigate, given that the suspects were snakes. The python that swallowed Jamie had two stab marks two feet from its tail, likely from a knife. That supported Taylor's story, and Sheriff Palmer let the matter rest.

The three survivors, Taylor, Owen, and Cindy, recovered physically. The families weren't in the mood for a circus, and the media respected their privacy. However, questions about the survivors, never far from the surface, persisted, and Cindy's parents, a dentist and pharmacist who had immigrated from Nigeria, decided to silence speculation with a statement that read:

"Our daughter, Cindy, age thirteen, after dinner at the campfire that night, left Taylor, Kate, and Owen, and walked the trail to her camp. Deciding to read, she sat on a folding camp chair in sweatpants and a hooded jacket with her back to the wind. Quiet, except for the wind, something moved in light shining from her headlamp. Lowering the book, the light flooded across a large python. Creeping steadily toward her on the trail, its eyes glowed orange. Six feet away, she stood, moved behind the camp chair, and reached for her walking stick leaning against a tree. She thought about hitting it, then saw a second python closing in from her right. She escaped through thick brush in the back of her camp. The land descended. Lost in a swamp, afraid to go back, she felt that pythons were stalking her. Moving through shallow water, she continued and eventually found a large cypress tree. While climbing the tree, she heard screams from either Taylor or Kate.

"She spent the rest of the night shivering in wet clothes. In the morning, unsure of her location and hearing nothing, she hung her clothes on branches to dry. Down below, a python crossed and slid into the water. She waited, expecting her troop to come looking for her. Late afternoon, in the distance, she saw people in orange coveralls and called out to them. She saw someone point to her and yell, "Hey! Over there. Look up. There's a girl up in that tree!"

* * *

Little Owen's story—perhaps the most remarkable of all—would pay for his college education and more. His parents sold it to Timeline magazine for an undisclosed sum.

Tired and afraid in the dark, he left the three girls and started down a path of trampled weeds, his flashlight sweeping back and forth. Twice, he drifted off into the brush and had to backtrack. The trail widened, and he recognized two trees and a low branch as being on his trail. His camp looked different—black and confusing—in the shadows of his flashlight. He flipped on the small lantern hanging from the line holding up the mosquito net. Remembering what Taylor said, he drank a little and put the canteen inside his sleeping bag. Clothes folded in his pack, he put on Spiderman pajamas, peed in the bushes, slipped under the mosquito net, turned off the camp lamp, and got into his red and black Spiderman sleeping bag. Unsteady, the bed frame of branches rocked over the brush pile like a chair on uneven legs. Pitch black, lying on his back, his head on the pillow, looking straight up into nothingness, a chill of fear crept over him. He sat up, flipped on the lamp, and left it on. Lying down, he said his prayers and listened to the wind blowing through the trees.

Almost asleep, the bed frame tilted, his feet lowered, and his head raised. Lit by the lamp, Owen looked down over the outside of the sleeping bag and saw the fat head sliding up between his legs. He froze. The python advanced up over his penis and stopped, its heavy head on Owen's belly. The yellow eyes locked on Owen's blue eyes. A black forked tongue came out four inches, hovering over Owen's chest, and the pointed tines of the tongue twittered. The tongue retracted, the head raised as it opened its mouth enough for Owen to see jagged rows of teeth. Then, it yawned and exhaled.

Like a turtle pulling its head into the shell, Owen slid the bag up and over his head and pulled the draw lines to close it. Owen's arms were together over his face, holding the bag closed, and the snake slid up between his arms, resting its jaw on his closed hands. With the heft of its body on Owen's groin, the body flattened, the snake exhaled, and a heavy musky breath engulfed the sleeping bag. The remaining ten feet of snake coiled, forming a bed on top of Owen, and the head moved from his arms to the middle of the coils. It squirmed to get comfortable, spreading Owen's legs. Its breathing slowed, and it seemed to fall asleep.

Owen's panic and urge to scream subsided. He pondered. Remaining motionless, the heavy snake crushed like a sack of grain. Sudden moves, he decided, would provoke an attack. He decided to move slowly, sliding his legs out to the edge of the bag and letting the snake sink onto the lower half of the bed.

From inside the bag, he put both hands against the nearest coil, bigger than an inner tube, that rested on his chest. Pushing against it, he slid his butt and legs out while Owen's head slipped from the neck of the bag. In the camp light, he saw coils stacked like terraces, the head somewhere on the other side. The breeze, now cooler, felt good on his face while the rest of his body overheated. Slowly, he pushed and slid his butt until something in the bed frame snapped, and his left hip dropped into a hole. This made his right foot shoot up inside the thin bag. His right hand came out of the bag and grabbed the coil to keep him from rolling. The startled snake, feeling the slap of Owen's hand and something, which was Owen's foot in the bag, coming at its face, attacked.

Owen winced in pain as the snake opened its mouth over his toes and foot, up to the ankle, and clamped its jagged teeth. They pierced the sleeping bag and sank into his foot.

With the commotion, like a boat capsizing, the snake and sleeping bag rolled off the bed frame and brush pile onto the ground, ending up in the middle of the camp. While rolling, his foot still in the snake's mouth, Owen managed to get fully inside the bag, roll onto his side, and pull into a ball, his arms holding his knees to his chest.

On the ground, the snake wrapped its coils around the bag and squeezed, grinding its teeth into the foot. Air swished out of the bag. Owen pushed his knees against the coils with his hands and breathed. After a few minutes, the snake relaxed, released his foot, and coiled up around the warm sleeping bag. The head, between Owen's arms and knees, rested on his hip. It went to sleep. Owen decided to wait until sunrise for the snake to leave or for help to arrive. After a while, from fear and exhaustion, he fell asleep.

The sun, just above the horizon, the top of the bag was open a little for air, when Owen heard Taylor call his name. He opened his eyes. Seeing her above the coils, she held a finger to her lips to be quiet. She came forward, raised a thick walking stick high in both hands, and brought it down with all her weight. The stick slapped into the snake behind the head, the crack sounding like a bullwhip. Injured, it crawled away into the brush.

Taylor got his first aid kit, dressed the bite marks on the top and bottom of his foot, put on his socks and shoes, gave him water, and found four power bars in his pack. Neither talked. He held out his arms, and she gave him a long hug. Still in their pajamas, they oriented the map and compass and found the trail back to Pa-Hay-Okee.

* * *

Wendy, the sheriff's deputy who interviewed Taylor, promised to keep in touch. Taylor suffered terribly over losing Jamie. His coming to see her that night had saved her life. Nightmares of Kate's screams and leaving Jamie with the python haunted her. Saving Owen made her happy, and Cindy's survival made her feel less self-conscious and guilty. Wendy had kept Taylor's secret about being with Jamie.

Wendy had later learned of a female university professor who met the governor after the press conference. In confidence, the sheriff told Wendy that the professor, a Sarah Warner, was Jamie Warner's only aunt, and she had proposed a way to kill pythons to Governor Prescott. Wendy brought this up with Taylor. She had not met Jamie's aunt, but he often talked of her.

"Taylor, I think you two should meet," Wendy said. "Tell her about your special boyfriend. She obviously thought the world of Jamie if she met with the governor about Pa-Hay-Okee."

* * *

Two weeks later, Taylor signed the register and clipped the university visitor pass to her pocket. The second-floor hallway had chairs and benches below heavily framed pictures of long-dead, famous-looking men. The nameplate read Mechatronics, Sarah Warner, PhD, Chair.

Taylor calmed her nerves, knocked once, and opened the heavy door. Sarah, at a computer console, expected her. The brightly lit room, with fresh colors and tall, arched windows, stood in stark contrast to the ancient lobby and hallways. Sarah looked up and recognized Taylor from the press conference interview and the news video clips.

Taylor stopped when Sarah stood, seeing Jamie's features on her face. Raising her shaking hands to her mouth, she began crying.

"I'm so sorry. I'm sorry. I'm sorry," Taylor said, now sobbing.

Sarah hurried to her with an embrace. Both cried on each other's shoulders. Sarah had channeled her grief into the project and blocked out thoughts of what happened to her nephew.

"I'm sorry too, Taylor. I'm so sorry for you and what you went through."

"No, no. You don't understand. You didn't know that Jamie and I were in love."

Sarah stepped back. "Oh, I'm so sorry, Taylor."

"You don't know. People don't know what happened to Jamie and me. I want you to know."

Sarah led her to the loveseat and got a box of tissues. She brought two cups of water from the cooler.

"I read that you and Jamie were patrol leaders."

In denial of Jamie's death, Taylor referred to him in the present. "Yes, he's super smart and the best scout in our troop."

Sarah held out her hand for Taylor to hold.

"I watched the videotape of your interview. It's terrifying. You are so brave."

"They left out a big part. Jamie and I were together. He came to my camp after dark. We were lying on top of my sleeping bag, kissing and laughing. We loved each other. No one knew. He's a year behind me in school. We didn't want problems at school or in scouts."

"I understand. I had the same situation as a freshman in college," Sarah said.

Taylor told Sarah how the snake had snuck up on them in the dark, how she had seen its head rise behind Jamie, its mouth open, clamping onto his arm. She told Sarah every detail of the attack and her escape to the table by the troop campfire. Then, going to her camp in the morning for her shoes and finding Jamie and the snake gone.

"I don't know why I left him. I barely got away from the snake. It was so dark. I didn't know whether Jamie had gotten away or how badly I'd hurt the snake. But I never went back from the campfire. I had a terrible fear of finding him dead. I should have gone back, but I was so afraid."

Sarah slid closer and pulled Taylor's head to her shoulder.

"It's okay. You were lucky to get away. Jamie was probably unconscious and gone by the time you escaped. There was nothing you could do. It could have grabbed you again. It wasn't your fault. It should not have happened. Jamie should be here."

"I miss him so much, and I can't tell anyone else, that's the worst part."

"Now you've told me. Jamie was my favorite. Now, I have you."

Taylor hugged her. Sarah kissed her on the cheek.

"I'm going to make sure this never happens again. I'm going to kill every python in the Everglades. Want to see what I'm working on, Sister?"

13

Red Riders

In mid-March, one month after Pa-Hay-Okee, with tourism already in decline, the governor signed 2029 SB 432 - Everglades Preservation and Restoration Act. It authorized the task force and established funding accounts.

Under a public awareness and safety provision, twenty-five-armed wildlife resource officers, many of them among the dozens who had searched for the scouts, staffed Everglades parks and trailheads. Authorized to shoot pythons on sight, they answered questions from the public and, in some respects, served as lifeguards.

Billboards along I-75 and I-95 showed the new officers interacting with the public at state parks.

The Tourism and Recreation Department set out to educate and caution the public. New kiosks throughout the Everglades displayed information about pythons, myths, and precautions to take. A picture of Governor Prescott had the caption, "We're working hard to remove invasive pythons and restore your Everglades to the happy home of native wildlife."

Brent Howard divided the task force into two groups: python eradication and habitat restoration. The dismal track record of controlling the python population served as the starting point. Human hunters, GPS trackers, robotic rabbits, and bioengineering options were off the table. The task force considered ideas that addressed the python reproduction rate and the vast area of infestation—over 4,500 square miles.

Brent gave the University of Florida the lead on programs to restore native animals, as they had done with the gopher tortoise and the scrub-jay bird.

* * *

Republicans assumed democrats and animal rights activists would push back. They filtered PAC money into grassroots organizations. Irene Anderson, mother of Taylor's friend, Kate, founded "Never Again - Kids Lives Matter." Their campaign featured a picture of Kate and demanded severe restrictions on public access to the Everglades until pythons were eliminated. Irene used public appearances to garner support. Details of the horrible deaths leaked to the press, and outrage found a footing. Hitting a nerve with mothers, membership grew, as did economic and political pressure.

The governor, declaring open season on pythons and combining it with emotions whipped up by well-funded organizations, invited responses that were hard to predict, much less contain.

Fringe groups saw opportunities to act out. The Red Riders, conspicuous with blood-red tailgates on pickup trucks and gun racks across rear windows, had chapters in small towns across South Florida. Sheriff Palmer, his cousin, a member, joked that Red Riders were guns looking for causes.

Before Pa-Hay-Okee, nighttime wild pig hunts, beginning and ending at lounges north of the Everglades, was the Riders call to duty. Speeches about pythons and children, from tabletop podiums in meeting rooms of BBQ joints, emboldened the Riders. Swearing fidelity, they wore black T-shirts with a python's head centered inside the crosshair of a rifle scope.

The last Friday of March, the colonel clanged a buck knife on the side of his pewter beer mug. Thirty-something men and women standing around the screened porch at Gators recited the Pledge of Allegiance. A pastor invoked the Lord to protect them and provide a bountiful harvest of pythons. The colonel outlined areas of operation for each of the two chapters and reviewed communication procedures. Each chapter captain covered gun safety and assigned kill zones to members. Before loading up, they stood in silence for their theme song, "Lament to Pa-Hay-Okee," an A.I.-generated ballad in a voice like Toby Keith's.

The roar of jacked-up pickups with straight pipe exhausts filled the gravel parking lot. Riders checked in via encrypted group chats and programmed dash-mounted tablets to display the locations of other Riders. Each chapter rendezvoused at its assigned intersection, marked by broken wooden pallets burning in old oil barrels.

Boone, captain of the Renegades, briefed his group. "Now listen up. Keep your gun safeties on until you raise to shoot. We don't need any more guns going off inside pickups. Get your weapons and spotlights ready and load up. Happy hunting."

Guns ranged from small 410-gauge snake-charmer shotguns to assault rifles with infrared scopes. A few had 44 Magnum revolvers holstered on their legs for show. They tossed empty beer cans in the barrel and drove down roads and trails in all directions. Most pickups had a driver with a gun barrel sticking out the window and two or more shooters in the back. Four Riders boarded two john boats. The retort of a Colt 45 from each captain kicked off the two-hour hunt.

"Rider one, Rider one, this is Rider twenty-one. One KIA, about ten feet long."

"Roger, Rider twenty-one. One KIA." The captain recorded the kill and GPS location. The other Riders listened and checked the spot against theirs on the map.

And so, it went. Boone reclined on a weathered beanbag chair, the full moon high in the sky. He, an amateur astronomer, named constellations and traced the Milky Way's thick disc. Occasional shooting stars synchronized with cracks and booms of guns, some near, some distant, in a symphony that Boone found profoundly moving.

"Fifteen minutes, fifteen minutes, Red Riders."

At eleven o'clock, each captain concluded the hunt with three blasts of an air horn.

The colonel came on the radio with the tally. "Good shooting, Riders. Forty-two kills by both chapters. Check the leaderboard on the website tomorrow. Those who want to keep hunting, send in your kill reports to your captain. Have a great night, Red Riders."

Sheriff Palmer's phone pinged at eleven-fifteen—the caller ID was his cousin.

"Hey, Gerald. How did it go tonight?"

"Hi, Daryl. We had a good night. No one got shot, and no big fights. Forty-two snakes."

"That's good news. Shooting pythons is better than poaching deer and shooting up signs. And it makes the Riders feel good. Nothing wrong with that," the sheriff said. "How many did you get?"

"Two. I borrowed my brother's Beretta 12-gauge semiautomatic."

"Good, that's a sweet gun. Keep in touch, Cuz."

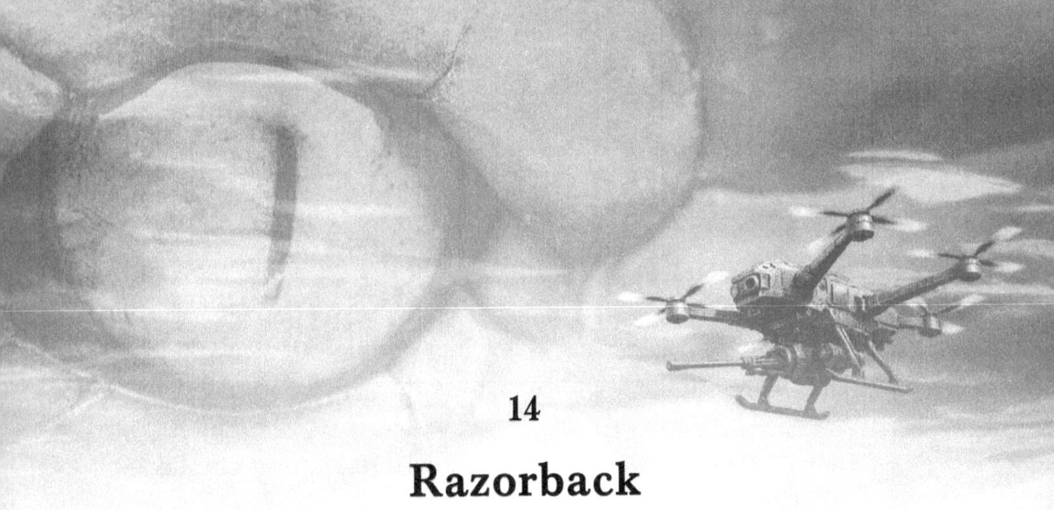

14

Razorback

Slate chose the location of her python research center based on security and proximity—only thirty minutes from the University of Miami. The Tamiami Trail traversed the Everglades from Miami to the west coast. Five miles past the Miccosukee Resort Casino on the eastern edge of the Everglades, a turnoff south connected to a two-mile dirt road. It ended at an antenna farm of tall communication towers.

Dust curled up in rolls behind Slate's blue Toyota Highlander as she drove down the gravel road. Jake had agreed to meet her there for his job interview. He waited among 1,000-foot-tall towers in his white Ford 150 King Cab. Slate pulled the Highlander alongside his pickup.

"Hi. The last time I saw you, you were wrestling a python," Slate said.

Jake laughed and looked at her. "I didn't know you were there. No, wait a minute. You were near the stage in a blue jacket. I saw you," he said, not mentioning her crying.

Slate smiled, pleased that he remembered her. "All that aside, I thought you were cool and quite competent."

They looked at each other for a second, not sure what to say.

"How about we sit at that picnic table over there?" She pointed to a break area for tower workers in a grove of oak trees. In the shade, the table had a view of the Everglades to the south.

"The governor thinks highly of you. So, what are you good at?" she asked Jake.

"Everything except what you do, computers."

She laughed. "Since you led the hunters in the search and rescue effort, you must have management skills. What else are you good at?"

"Anything outdoors—construction, docks, mobile homes, swamps, boats, and animals."

"Can you pass a background check and drug test?"

Jake acted like he had to think about the question, then smiled. "I'm afraid I'm pretty boring."

She laughed and explained her ideas while they walked around the site. He suggested locations for the game enclosures and mobile structures.

"Can you get all of that done without interrupting me, Jake?"

"Don't see why not."

Slate brought deli sandwiches. She asked about his background.

Growing up outside Everglades City on the west coast, Jake's father owned a tow truck, operated a home repair business, and captained an airboat for Safari Tours. In high school, Jake helped his father and played first base for the Everglades Gators. He joked that his small-town team only played bigger schools and they lost all thirty-six games in his four years. While studying construction management at Everglades University in Tampa, he discovered that his girlfriend, still in high school, was pregnant. The baby's father was her basketball coach. Jake broke up with her, dropped out of college, and lived in an RV park outside Marco Island. He worked in marine construction, then did tarpon and snook fishing charters at a camp in the Ten Thousand Islands. Years turned into decades, and, still single at forty-three, Jake owned Razorback Adventures, a successful wilderness-guiding business. Jake was obviously more at home in hunting camps than in towns. Slate imagined his rugged good looks attracted females who came and went with the seasons. Slate hadn't met anyone quite like polite and uncomplicated Jake. He seemed excited to oversee everything outdoors on her high-tech project, a position that paid $80,000.

* * *

Thankful for Governor Prescott's recommendation of Jake, Slate sent him a thank-you note.

Over the following weeks, Jake set up a work trailer, a command center trailer, and a thirty-six-foot Coachman RV south of the towers. The trailers sat on an open gravel area. Everglades to the south were a mixed habitat of hammock trees, sloughs, and sawgrass marsh, which extended sixty miles to the tip of Florida.

The project timeline required total focus and commitment. Slate recruited two single graduate students from her college to complete their team of four.

Brad, age twenty-eight, studied autonomous systems and A.I. robotics. A first lieutenant in the Army Reserve, he wore the coveted Ranger tab. He ranked in the top three percent at the Elite level of Fortnite, a massive online video game. Slate liked his easy-going confidence. Her plan called for two console stations in the control trailer. As her co-pilot, Brad would fly the drone and operate the weapons system.

Carter, age twenty-two with a bachelor's in mechanical engineering, previously had an internship on the pit crew of a Formula One race car team. Looking young for his age, he now studied mechatronics and sensor fusion. Slate considered Carter the sharpest member of the robotics lab, including the professors. Carter would build the drone and maintain it in the field during testing.

On the last Friday of March, the same date as the Red Riders python hunt forty miles west, Slate invited Brad and Carter to the research site RV for a team meeting with her and Jake.

Jake, waiting for a flatbed truck of construction materials from Home Depot, prepared lunch. The pork from a young female he'd shot on a wild boar hunt, slow-cooked in a crockpot.

Jake heard a car rolling over the gravel drive and looked out the kitchen window. Slate got out wearing stylish faded jeans and a short-sleeve cotton shirt. She wore her long blonde hair in a ponytail under a Miami Dolphins hat, the jeans ended mid-calf over sport sandals. He held the RV door open and gave her a big smile.

"Wow, what's cooking, Jake? It smells delicious. I thought we were having sandwiches."

"Oh, it's one of my recipes. In the guide business, preparing and serving tasty meals is part of the job. It's one of my sales points."

"Wow, I'll add this to your job description." She laughed.

"Can I get you tea, soda, or water?"

"Iced tea would be great. I just received a text. Brad and Carter are ten minutes out."

Slate found it amusing that this outdoorsy guy, clad in double-kneed work pants, a thick belt, and a lightweight red-and-white plaid shirt, made his own recipes and enjoyed cooking.

She sat on the bench seat at the table. Looking into the back bedroom, she noticed the bed wasn't made.

"Did you stay here last night?"

"Ah, yes. I worked late, laying out the corner markers for the enclosure and preparing a platform for the Home Depot materials."

"You cut your neck, and your arms are all scratched."

He touched his neck. "It's not too bad. There's a mess of thorny vines out there. Come Monday, a supervisor and five workers will do most of the work."

The guys arrived in Brad's Jeep Cherokee. Slate introduced them to Jake, commenting that they were all about six feet tall. Each, also handsome, Slate wondered if she had a subconscious bias for tall men.

Jake made up plates of coleslaw piled on top of BBQ between toasted buns, with a whole dill pickle on the side. With bags of chips in a basket, and a bowl of baked beans, they dug in.

"Anyone want another sandwich? But save room. Brownies are in the oven, and there's ice cream."

Slate and Carter each had a second BBQ. Brad had two brownies.

"Best BBQ ever," Carter said.

"It's the shoulder of a young wild pig from a hunt two nights ago," Jake said casually, as if it came from the meat counter at Publix. The three glanced at each other without speaking.

After lunch, Jake walked them around the property and explained the layout of Slate's planned enclosures. Hearing the tractor-trailer from Home Depot rumbling down the road, Jake excused himself to direct the unloading. Brad and Carter toured the control trailer and the mechanical shop planned for the drone.

After Brad and Carter left, Slate returned to the RV. Jake arrived, and they sat at the table. She noticed for the first time his deep blue eyes.

"You're something else, Jake Calhoun. I hadn't expected you to make us a homemade lunch, much less wild game from a hunt. I really appreciate what you've done."

Her compliment caught him off guard. "You're welcome."

"I can tell that Brad and Carter like you. I think we have a great team. No room for egos on my team," she said.

He laughed. "Hey, I'm the one who never finished college. I like our little team. Not too geeky." They both laughed. "I enjoy cooking and trying new recipes."

She checked her watch, midafternoon. "Wow, it's almost happy hour. What are the odds that you have beer?"

"One hundred percent. I guessed that you like IPA."

"Yep, you got me."

He drank a dark beer as she had a local IPA. The RV window by the table faced south to the Everglades. They stared out the window in quiet contemplation.

"Scary. It seems so scary out there," she said. "I hope we can pull this project off, Jake."

"Let me just say, Dr. Warner. I would not want to be a python if I knew you were gunning for me."

She looked into his eyes.

He smiled and winked at her.

They finished their beer. He followed her Highlander to the Tamiami Trail. She turned east to her condo, and Jake turned west to Everglades City.

A fifty-two-year-old casual friend with salt and pepper hair in cut-off jeans drank a Bud Light and waited for Jake on the back deck of her double-wide. Two crab traps sat on the creek bottom, off her dock. A CD played a Janis Joplin song. Dropping her cigarette into an empty bottle, she reached down to scratch Sadie, her calico cat.

* * *

The following Monday, Jake supervised a foreman and workers as they constructed a ten-foot-high fine-mesh fence surrounding three acres of the Everglades. They added an electrified wire and an inward-angled panel at the top. A boardwalk around the outside connected the entrance doors and four elevated observation decks centered on each side. Slate requested a 100-foot-wide platform above the main entrance for testing sensors and weapon systems.

They built a smaller square enclosure, 100 feet per side, near the command trailer, and added boardwalks connecting the trailers and enclosures. A subcontractor established data links between the observation sites, the mobile control center, and the university's mainframe computers.

Carter acquired a storage building adjacent to the university robotics lab and enlisted engineering students to help him build the aerial platform using off-the-shelf components. Besides the drone, flown manually or by computer, Carter researched sensors to locate pythons and weapons to kill them.

Brad designed consoles for the control trailer. Assisted by A.I. software agents, Slate modified a foundational algorithm. Jake hired a Red Rider friend and others to find pythons and native animals to train Slate's program, which she named Lucy.

Not unlike facial recognition technology, but more complicated, Slate's was the first serious attempt to locate pythons in the wild. A complex habitat of wetlands, uplands, trees, water, and salt marshes, finding camouflaged pythons in the daytime and nighttime, would require massive amounts of data from multiple sensors.

The team mounted an array of sensors in the small enclosure, including optical, motion, thermal, and infrared. Beginning with live pythons, computers would record their images and movements in different environments.

* * *

Waiting in the RV, Slate and Carter heard Jake's pickup on the gravel road and went out to meet him.

"Okay, Carter, help me with these Tupperware bins. Set them in the shade."

A python was in each of five bins. They ranged from three to eleven feet and from beige to darker brown in color.

"Good job, Cowboy," Slate said, thinking again about his Florida cowboy image. "This should do the trick."

Jake tipped a tub up, and a six-footer slid onto sandy dirt inside a ten-foot portable plexiglass ring. It crawled toward Slate, and she jumped back, almost falling.

"Easy does it, Cowgirl," Jake said.

The three went to the control trailer and powered up the sensors. Brad, at the mainframe consoles in Miami, watched lines of data rain down screens that mirrored monitors in the trailer. The algorithm captured thousands of scans per minute from each sensor, digitizing python images. Every thirty minutes, Jake changed the pythons and moved the plexiglass ring to other areas inside the enclosure, such as marsh grass and wetland. They took a break after six hours, then resumed at dusk for another four hours, using night sensors. Slate and Carter returned to Miami and Jake slept in the RV.

****

The next morning at ten, Slate had a Zoom meeting with Governor Prescott from the control trailer.

"Hi, Governor. We captured ten hours of data on pythons in a controlled environment yesterday, both during the day and at night. So far, so good."

"That's great news. You've done so much in such a short time. Are you optimistic?"

Slate heard Jake open the trailer door. Distracted, she glanced over at him, then up to lines of code pouring from the algorithm.

"Oh, ah, yes, sorry, Governor. I can't help watching my program crunching data."

"It's way over my head, smart girl. So, what's going on now, and what is next?" Prescott asked.

"Well, it's complicated, but once the program learns what pythons look like, it's like playing a game. Do you remember the puzzle called 'Where's Waldo?'"

"Yes, finding a goofy little guy hiding in pictures."

"You're funny. Yes, the algorithm begins with an empty world. We fill the world with data. To the computer, a python is Waldo. The game is to find them by deconstructing the data and assigning values based on correlations and probabilities to find patterns that correlate with Waldo, in our case, pythons."

"Something tells me there is a bit more to it, Cowgirl," Prescott said.

"The algorithm tests for images against the database of known pythons and ignores everything else. The more data we feed it, the better it gets."

"Are you optimistic this will work?"

Slate smiled. "It's a walk in the park. We're not looking for exoplanets or Einstein's unified theory, just snakes in a swamp.

"I started with software I've used on other projects. We'll repeat the cycle with captive pythons several more times, then let the computer find them in the three-acre habitat. The goal is to find them quickly, not miss any, and only find Waldo's, not Whack-a-moles." Slate giggled, surprising herself with her wit and audacity."

He laughed. "Whack-a-mole. You're something else, Slate Warner. In a league all your own, and I mean that."

Slate blushed at the compliment, taken aback by the personal nature of his compliments.

"Thank you, Governor. I'll have better answers for you at our Zoom meeting in two weeks."

"I'm very much looking forward to it. Maybe I'll come down there for a closer look," Prescott said.

"Ah, sure, that would be great. Bring your snake boots. Only kidding, Sir."

"You're funny. Please, call me John."

"Ok, bring your snake boots, John," she said, laughing out loud.

"I'll see how my schedule looks and let you know. Ciao, for now, Cowgirl."

Slate clicked off the Zoom and leaned back in the swivel chair, always relieved when meetings with the governor were over.

"Did he call you Cowgirl?" Jake asked.

"I think he did. He's always called me Slate or professor."

"That's weird," Jake frowned.

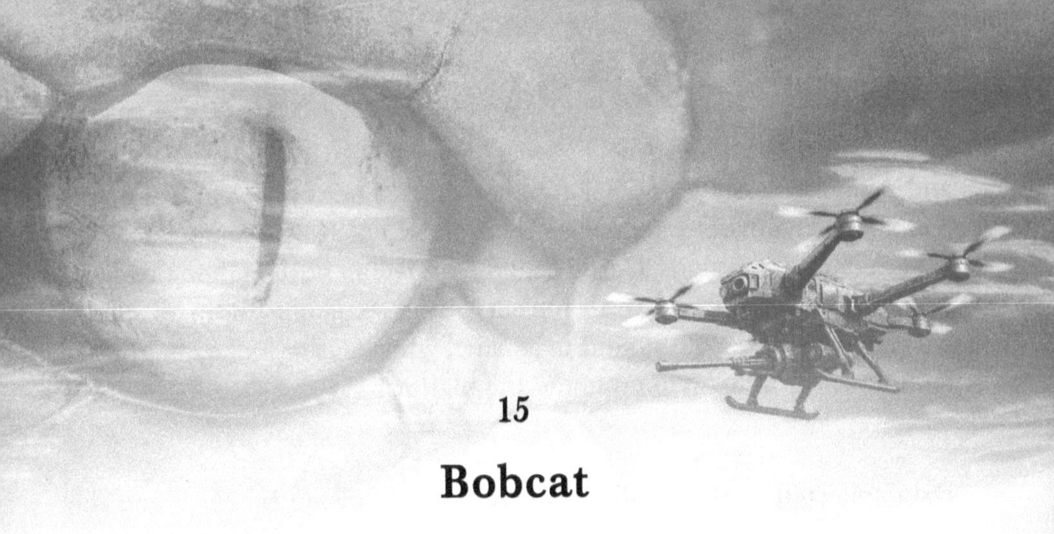

15

Bobcat

Jake lived at the research site throughout April, working fourteen-hour days. Slate split her time between university responsibilities, training the algorithm, and outfitting the control trailer at the research site. The two often ate lunch together in the RV, sometimes playing a round of gin rummy, a card game Jake had taught her. A world away from Columbus, Ohio, Slate found the Everglades wild and exciting, made better by Jake's stories. She observed him—the way he held the cards, his funny expressions, his ability to remember cards played. She admired his disinterest in politics, social media, and TV, except for documentaries on science and history. He was smart enough not to focus on what he couldn't control. Jake didn't snack and she liked that he occasionally removed a long-sleeve work shirt to reveal his company T-shirt. The olive-green shirt accentuated his masculine build. The "Razorback Adventures" shirt showed a boar's head inside a red bullseye. His hands pushed back wavy hair that curled at the back like an old west gunslinger.

Slate appreciated that he valued her accomplishments and was always supportive. If he thought of her in a physical or personal way, he was polite enough not to show it.

Jake brought alligators, raccoons, rabbits, wading birds, and other Everglades wildlife to the site. The four team members developed a process to feed sensor data from each species into the computer. Each member also spent an hour in the enclosure, allowing sensors to identify them as humans. Slate rewarded Lucy in points for correctly identifying pythons. She received additional points for speed, but lost points for misidentifications and failures to locate pythons.

Brad split his time between helping Carter build the drone and supporting Slate and Jake gather data. The drone, named Zcolt, had six heavy-lift rotors on arms that folded out from a square six-foot frame standing on skids. Carter had the bare-bones drone flying by mid-April using a standard hand controller. Brad set about finding a single-barreled rifle and a 100-round magazine, while Carter looked at gimbal mounts to sling the weapon under the platform.

* * *

Data collected in the small enclosure was completed by May, and the team moved the training to the three-acre enclosure. They mounted sensors on platforms above the entrance and on three other sides. Tuned and synchronized to gather data, Jake introduced fifteen pythons over three hours. Slate and Brad monitored systems at their consoles in the control center. Data flowed into Lucy's model, challenging the algorithm to find pythons as they slithered among different Everglades habitats inside the fence.

Jake and Carter watched a six-foot python climb the ten-foot fence.

"Do you guys see the python on the fence?" Jake called Slate and Brad over the interphone.

"Yikes! I didn't know they could climb walls," Slate replied.

The python slid its head under the electric wire and made contact. Its serpentine body straightened like a rope and dropped. In time, it came around and crawled into the marsh grass.

Slate modified the software to simultaneously find and track up to ten pythons, displaying their positions on a digital map of the enclosure.

In a separate program, Slate and Brad designated pythons they saw on sensor screens. This program compared Slate's sample sightings with Lucy's derived sightings, measuring accuracy and the number of false positives.

Once set up, the sensors fed data to the algorithm in six-hour blocks, separated by six hours of processing and machine learning. After three days, Lucy added thirty hours of habitat data to the trove captured in the small enclosure.

As a test, Jake released two raccoons, two rabbits, and three pythons. Slate and Brad monitored sensor screens and designated the animals as they moved about. Lucy processed sensor data and projected animal locations onto the map screen, with pythons displayed in red and all other animals in green. Lucy scored one hundred percent.

Jake, on the platform with binoculars, scanned for other pythons attracted by the prey. He spotted a large one swimming in the narrow canal. Then he saw an animal crouched on the limb of an oak tree that extended over the canal.

"Well, butter my biscuit. Get a load of this. There's a bobcat in a tree," Jake called over the intercom. He described the location, and they found it using the optical and infrared sensors.

"It's beautiful. I've never seen one. I wonder what Lucy will make of it." Slate said.

After a while, the bobcat hopped down to a dirt trail and sauntered toward the rear of the enclosure. Slate found it on sensor screens, and Lucy plotted it with a green marker, labeling it as a friendly animal. Lucy found it twice more during training sessions over the next two days.

* * *

Carter had the prototype Zcolt drone outfitted with optical and infrared sensors and a data recorder. A custom trailer had sides and a top that unfolded to become a launch platform. On the second Friday in May, Carter and Brad towed the trailer behind Carter's Toyota Tundra to the research site. Four steaming hot cheeseburgers and potato salad were waiting for the team at the picnic table. The weather was clear and a perfect seventy-five degrees.

Carter positioned the trailer in the southwest edge of the site, near the Everglades, and converted it for launch. Following a checklist he designed, Carter prepared the drone for flight. Brad sat at a camp table with an open laptop. The screen displayed the drone's video camera and the flight instruments. Slate and Jake sat in lawn chairs on either side of Brad.

"She's ready to go," Carter called, stepping back.

Brad typed commands on the keyboard. The six rotors buzzed to life, sounding like industrial fans at low speed. He switched on the sensors and recorders. The control keys on Brad's laptop mirrored the setup he used to play Fortnite. He pressed keys for takeoff, and the Zcolt added power and lifted off. After flight control checks, Brad flew forward into the Everglades at 100 feet. Carter monitored an app on his phone that reported Zcolt's performance and battery status. A split-screen on Brad's laptop displayed the drone's forward view and images from the optical and infrared sensors.

Descending to twenty feet, the gyro-stabilized drone seemed to float over marshes, wetlands, upland forests, and sloughs.

"It looks like a National Geographic documentary," Slate said.

"It's a stunning and unique area," Brad remarked.

Brad came upon a pond with a sunlit mudbank and slowed.

"I see one," Jake called out. "Up by the grass sunning itself on the mud."

Brad zoomed the optical sensor and centered the aiming point on a fat python with a bulge in the middle of its body. The skin and vivid patterns glistened in the sunlight.

"Pythons don't hear like we do," Jake said. "But it must have sensed the vibration. He's looking at the drone as if it's a nuisance."

"Wish we had a working gun," Slate said. A thought of Jamie flashed in her mind.

"It's using the sun's warmth to help digest whatever animal it ate," Jake said.

Brad flew lower and closer to the python to gauge its reaction. Having never seen a drone and not sensing a threat, it ignored the disturbance.

Lasting forty minutes, the test flight simulated various search patterns, speeds, and altitudes. Returning to the launch site, Brad selected auto-land. The Zcolt centered over the launch pad, turned to the launch heading, and smoothly descended to a perfect landing.

"Nice work, guys. So far, so good. Download the sensor data on a hard drive, Carter. I'll add it to the algorithm and see what Lucy finds," Slate said.

"Sure," Carter said. "I've got something to show you guys in the work trailer."

The trailer had workbenches and racks for parts and equipment. A swivel mount with actuators hung below a stand on the workbench. Carter clamped a modified M16 military rifle into the swivel mount. The weapon had an oversized scope and a large drum-style ammunition magazine, but no stock. It balanced in the unpowered mount. Jake and Slate swung the barrel around.

"It's not too exotic. Mostly off-the-shelf robotic parts. Keeping it simple," Carter said.

"Pretty bad-ass, if you ask me," Jake said.

"Thanks. The weapons computer will receive targeting data from Lucy and aim the rifle with gimbal actuators." Carter touched the mounted scope. "The scope view feeds electronically to weapons screens in the control trailer, cross-checking the impact point of the bullet with Lucy's prediction. At least that's the theory."

"Carter, the governor is coming here in two weeks for a tour," Slate said. "I'll work on software to link Lucy's target solutions with the weapons program that aims the rifle. The plan is to mount the sensors and your servo-driven rifle on the big platform overlooking the enclosure. We'll use Brad's laptop to show the governor how it works."

"Can we shoot the rifle for the governor?" Carter asked excitedly.

"I don't see why not." Slate smiled.

16

Spaghetti

Slate called Taylor to update her on the project. In her last semester of junior year, Taylor had yet to visit the research site.

"I have an idea," Slate said. "Can you skip school next Wednesday afternoon and come to the research site? You can meet Governor Prescott and watch us test components for the drone."

Taylor checked her calendar. "Oh, good. I have an A in statistics, so I don't have a final exam. I would love to come. Thank you, Sister."

* * *

On Wednesday morning, Slate's team mounted sensors and the weapon on the railing of the wooden platform overlooking the large enclosure. A lovely day, with white puffy clouds meandering across an otherwise clear sky. Arriving by eleven, Taylor met Carter, Brad, and Jake. They made soft-shell tacos from ingredients Jake prepared, and ate them at a picnic table under live oak trees and saw palmettos.

"Carter, if you're all set for the test, maybe you can give Taylor the tour before the governor arrives?" Slate asked.

Taylor, sitting across from Carter at the picnic table, smiled at him. Carter saw wispy strands of blonde hair framing her face, the back in a low ponytail under a tipped-down, close-weave fedora hat. The hat covered most of a scar on her forehead. She wore a sage-colored cotton blouse with a floral print, gold stud earrings, and a hint of sea-green eyeshadow. She looked older and more polished for her age, her eighteenth birthday a month away.

Carter jumped at the chance to show her the drone workshop. She asked about the Formula One racecar posters and a picture of

78

him adjusting the downforce on the front wing during a pit stop at the Miami Grand Prix.

"You look pretty sharp in your team uniform. A lot of patches, Carter." She ran her finger over the patches on the picture and lifted her eyes in a teasing way.

He laughed. "It was a short internship. No sponsor money for wearing their patches, I'm afraid."

"Still, it's pretty cool that you got to do that," she said, looking into his warm brown eyes.

Slate heard the crunch of gravel and looked to see a gleaming white Suburban. The governor stepped out wearing slim-cut jeans, a white Columbia shirt, and a conservative beige Panama hat.

Slate and her team met him on the boardwalk deck fronting the control trailer. She stepped forward to shake his hand. Instead, he raised his arms and stepped in with a friendly hug. Surprised, she obliged. Stepping back, she kept a smile and pointed to his Tony Lama ostrich skin boots.

"Are those snake-proof?" she asked.

"Well, no snakebites yet. And there are a lot of snakes in Tallahassee," he laughed.

Jake stepped forward and shook hands, their last meeting, the python encounter at the press conference.

Slate introduced Brad and Carter, then Taylor. Seeing her in person as a bright and healthy young lady, in contrast to the governor's view of her on a video screen in a hospital bed, caught him off guard. She extended her hand politely.

"Thank you for all that you're doing, Governor Prescott," Taylor said.

"I must say, Taylor, I find your courage and leadership inspirational. Your participation in 'Never Again - Kids Lives Matter' is making a difference. We are going to beat this."

He held her hand in his for a moment.

Slate stepped into the conversation. "Well, Governor, what say we start your tour with the control trailer?"

The governor's driver and his bodyguard accepted Slate's offer to hang out in the RV.

Slate sat in her chair at the console, the governor in a chair beside her. Her fingers clipped keys on two keyboards, sounding like an ink-jet printer.

"This large screen shows a live feed from the platform of our three-acre enclosed habitat. The upper-right screen displays computer code generated by the algorithm. The four split screens show data from our sensors that feed the algorithm. By the way, the algorithm is named Lucy."

"It's interesting how we humanize inanimate computers. Sorry, that's off the subject," he said.

Slate paused to think and looked at him. "That's interesting that you bring this up. I've asked myself the same question. Must be human nature or a need to connect with something I've spent hundreds of hours communicating with."

"Sorry, your algorithm is truly amazing regardless," he said.

Slate pushed the intercom button to call Jake on the platform.

"Jake, please release the python."

Slate pointed to the python on the screen.

The governor leaned in. "Yes, yes, I see it."

"See the computer code rain down the top screen. That's Lucy recognizing the python. Look at the split screens. This is what the python looks like in optical and thermal wavelengths."

Prescott listened and nodded in understanding.

"This final screen, lower left, shows a composite image Lucy created from all sensors, with background noise filtered out. Using data from tens of thousands of sensor images, we trained Lucy to recognize pythons by body parts, patterns, motion, and other features. The yellow outline on the composite screen confirms it is a python."

"Wow, you found Waldo," the governor commented. He stood, put his hands on his hips, and looked at the screens.

"The algorithm is learning from this python as we watch."

"Look, it's moving," Prescott said, in amazement.

"Sensor input updates 100 times per second. Accuracy and speed have doubled each week. Get this, Lucy can also track up to ten pythons at a time."

"It's headed for the canal," Prescott said.

Slate called over the intercom. "Jake, can you get the pythons for our demonstration? We're on our way."

"Okay, Governor, that's your introduction to the first half of our project. The second part is from our observation platform."

* * *

The group stopped by the RV to use the restroom and get soft drinks. They climbed the stairs to the twelve-foot-high platform. With an expansive view of the enclosure, under a shaded canopy, and a light breeze, the conditions were ideal.

Carter gave an overview of the equipment. "On the left side of the railing, we've mounted optical and thermal sensors. On the right is our Humboldt rifle with a scope. It fires an open-tip 5.56 NATO match round. The gimbal has servo actuators that aim the rifle."

The governor walked around the platform to each piece of equipment, then to the center, where Brad had monitors and laptops on a table.

Carter continued. "The sensors and rifle are connected to these laptops, which are linked to the control trailer. The laptops display some of the screens that Slate showed you. Additionally, this screen displays the scope's crosshair on the rifle, allowing Brad to confirm the aim point Lucy generates. Does that make sense, Governor?"

"I think so. Lucy analyzes sensor data, determines it is a python, and computes the exact location. A weapons computer considers all variables and directs actuators to aim the weapon. Brad crosschecks the aim point in the scope screen," Prescott replied.

Slate, Brad, and Carter glanced at each other in amazement.

"I think we have a place for you on our team, Sir," Slate said.

The governor laughed and winked at Slate. "Now, that would be fun."

Slate looked through the deck flooring and saw Jake below by the entrance. "Jake, please release two pythons."

She directed Taylor and the governor to stand behind Brad to watch the pythons on the monitors. One of the pythons crawled forward.

"The sensor shows both pythons. You will hear servo motors aim the rifle. Lucy has identified both pythons and targeted the lead snake. Do you see the head of that python in the crosshair of the scope, Governor?"

He nodded and pointed at the screen.

"Okay, let's move to the railing and see what happens."

Carter stood to the left of Taylor. Slate and the governor stood on Taylor's right. Leaning on the railing, they watched the python move in slow motion over the dirt path, the canal twenty feet ahead. An osprey circled overhead, screeching on occasion, a nest likely nearby. A frog croaked. A dragonfly flittered about in front of the four. Other than the buzz of electronics, clicks, and gears of servo motors, it was quiet.

The governor watched as the tip of the rifle ticked up and to the right as the python inched toward the mud bank. Taylor gripped the railing with both hands and stared at the ten-foot python. Her hands came up to feel her face and neck where the snake had been that night. Carter saw her reaction, turned her away from the railing, and held her in an embrace. She hyperventilated, and he lightly rubbed her back.

"It's all right, you're okay," he said.

She reached her hands around and hugged him. Slate came over and helped calm her.

"I'm okay, I promise. I'll be okay now." Her head rested on Carter's chest. The governor joined them. Little by little, she calmed down.

"Slate, the python is almost to the water," Brad called out.

"I'm okay, really. Sorry. I'm sorry," Taylor said and returned to the rail.

"Are you sure you want to see this, Taylor?" Slate asked.

She nodded and stared at the python.

"Take the shot," Slate called over her shoulder to Brad.

Crack. The sound, like the snap of a bullwhip, caused everyone but Brad and Prescott to flinch.

Prescott moved his fingers over Slate's hand on the railing. She interpreted it as a calming gesture or possibly something more. Regardless, his skin touching hers completed a circuit, joining their sexual energy fields. Like two magnets snapping together, a jolt of euphoria washed over her. She pulled her hand away, pretending to check her watch, and glanced to see if anyone had noticed.

Below, the python's head turned to goop, and its body wiggled about in disorder.

"Brad, Brad, the other one's moving fast! Get it!" Taylor yelled, leaning over the railing, staring down at the python.

Prescott watched the rifle barrel migrate down and to the left.

"Good solution," Brad called to Slate.

"Shoot," Slate responded.

The weapon fired.

"Splash!" Taylor called out. "You got it!"

Slate turned to see Taylor fist-pump then give Carter a high-five.

Crack, the rifle went off a third time. Everyone jumped, and Slate spun to face Brad.

"In the tree. Lucy found one we released last week." Brad said and looked back at the screen. "In the tree to the right of the slough halfway back, on a limb over the water."

Prescott looked out and pointed to the snake hanging over a branch like a strand of spaghetti, the cratered head even with its tail. They stood motionless, like the three dead snakes. The smell of acrid sulfur and the finality of death hung thick in the air.

"Slate, Lucy found another one slithering onto the trail," Brad said.

"I think we're good, Brad, thanks," she said, sobered by the killing of animals for just being themselves, stuck in an alien place half a world away from their native home.

Jake came up the stairs as the four turned away from the rail.

The governor broke the silence. "An amazing technology, Slate. It's efficient and humane. Much safer and less cruel than catching them by hand, right, Jake?"

"Yes, Governor. It's the only way if we want an Everglades with native animals and a balanced ecosystem."

Slate glanced at Taylor, saw that sadness had returned.

She thought about Jamie, and the decades of mismanagement by state agencies.

"It's dawning on me that this is not a video game," Slate said.

Prescott put his arm around her shoulder.

Regaining her composure, Slate said, "How about we go to the RV for questions and to discuss next steps?"

***

Walking beside Slate to the RV, Prescott said, "Are you going back to Miami today?"

"Yes."

"I have an idea. I'm going to the sheriff's department to meet Palmer before flying back to Tallahassee in the Citation jet. If it's not too far out of your way, I'll ride with you, and Greg can follow in the Suburban."

"Great idea. It's not out of the way." Saying no wasn't an option. She questioned her inner gut. *Is he naturally gregarious, and I'm overreading it? If I'm not, being alone in a car presents opportunities I'm not ready for.*

The meeting in the RV lasted twenty minutes. The governor waited at the picnic table, chatting with Taylor while Slate returned a call from her boss, the dean. Carter and Brad packed up equipment on the platform. Jake loaded the bin of dead pythons into his pickup to dump them later into the Tamiami Trail canal. Returning to the RV, he grabbed a Diet Coke and joined Slate at the RV table.

Checking her emails, she looked up and could not help but smile at him.

Grinning, he said, "I've thought of a new name for you, Professor." She looked at him warily. "What?"

"The Terminator." Jake laughed and waited for her response. She reached over and tried to slap his arm.

"Okay, I have a name for you ... the Cleaner." She laughed.

"Fair enough, Cowgirl." Jake took a drink, and Slate got up to look out the window to the picnic table. Carter had joined Taylor and the governor.

She looked back at Jake. "Guess what? The governor wants to ride with me to Miami."

Jake looked at her without responding.

"It wasn't my idea. What do you think he wants?"

"Well, I can think of a couple of things, but probably just shop talk," Jake said. "You'll deal with whatever comes up, as always."

"Thanks. You know he's holding all the cards on our project," Slate said.

Jake replied. "I like him, but he's still a politician with an agenda. We're small fish in a big pond. His enemies don't know about us yet, and nothing is guaranteed when politics is involved."

"Yep, out of our hands. So, what's for lunch?" Slate asked.

"Lunch? You already had lunch."

"I mean lunch on Monday. I'll upload the new data this weekend, and we can test Lucy on Monday. How about something with gator, Chef Calhoun?" Slate smiled and winked at him.

"Really? Okay, gator tenders with Sweet Baby Ray's sauce?" Jake asked.

"Sure. I gotta go, Cleaner."

"See ya later, Terminator."

17

Fear Factor

Governor Prescott, in a good mood, chatted away, recounting the day's events as Slate drove the Highlander east toward Miami. Slate relaxed at hearing his enthusiasm and imagined his mood if they had missed the pythons. She felt him look at her across the console, but he wasn't looking her over.

"At this point, what is your biggest problem? What are you most uncertain about?" he asked.

"That's an interesting question. Let me think."

Slate thought the question sounded corporate and a tad insincere. She could fix that.

"Can I be honest?"

"Sure."

"Only in office five months, you're a relative newcomer elected on a populace ticket of integrity and common sense. Your base is thin compared with entrenched bureaucracies and political opponents. Our project is confidential, known only to you and a handful of others."

Prescott looked down the highway bordered on both sides by canals and an occasional semi-submerged alligator.

"So, you're feeling vulnerable and lightly armored?" he asked.

"Let's just say that when the media and your enemies discover your python solution is an A.I. killer drone, the fewer enemies you have, the better. Put another way, the focus is on public safety and restoring the natural habitat without alienating the other party or scorching more than a few public officials. It's a thin rail, and our project depends on how you ride it."

86

Prescott laughed and looked at her. She smiled without looking back.

"That's good, Cowgirl. Especially the part about the rail."

She turned to look at him and raised an eyebrow.

Smiling, she said, "John, imagine you are a pony. You're pulling a cart up a steep and narrow mountain trail. My team is on your cart. It's cold. Patches of ice lie ahead." She stopped smiling and returned her attention to the road.

Prescott thought for a moment. "How about apples? Treats for the donkey?" he asked.

Slate glanced over at him, then slapped his arm.

They shared a laugh.

"I'm serious, John. Besides, I said imagine that you're a pony, not a donkey. Okay, now you're a jackass." She glanced at him.

He laughed. "I understand. I get it completely."

She added, "Two more points. Republican and Democratic governors approved budgets and appointed the seven wildlife commissioners to five-year terms over the course of three decades. Both parties share the blame."

They passed the intersection for the Miccosukee Casino on the left and a highway to the Everglades Correctional Institution on the right.

"You're the new guy, not part of the old guard. That's good and bad—for you, and for my project. No doubt, there are snakes in the grass, so to speak, that thrive on the status quo. It's been a cover-up for decades, mostly by the FWC, but also by both parties. Warning the public would have required many to admit failures and would have derailed the public money gravy train."

"And then, Pa-Hay-Okee happened," he said.

"And then, John Prescott happened," she added.

"And Sarah Warner," he said. "For reasons not of our doing, we are tied together to fix what we were not even aware of."

"Much of history is punctuated by turning-point events that change the course. This might be one of them," she said.

"Here's my final point, John. My technology wasn't available until around 2023. However, had Florida acknowledged the crisis in 2017 and committed to eliminating pythons in large numbers, other technologies and precautions would have prevented Pa-Hay-Okee."

Slate exited north on the Palmetto Expressway and passed under a Boeing 777 taking off from Miami International Airport. She checked the rearview mirror for the governor's Suburban.

"I get it. One thing in our favor is the military drone arms race in the news every day. Your project is an obvious solution," he said. "Still, what I saw today on the platform was scary, and the implications are inescapable. There's a fear factor some will exploit for no other reason than the fact they didn't think of it first."

"All the more reason to get bipartisan support and turn the FWC into an ally. Build a coalition, I think they call it." Slate said, making the peace sign with her fingers.

"Wow, how about becoming my campaign manager?" He laughed.

She held up the back of her hand to him, disguising her middle finger.

She took the exit onto NW 25th Street, one mile from the sheriff's department.

"This was fun and constructive. Thank you for your ideas, Slate. Helpful. Quite helpful. Maybe dinner next time?"

She caught the subtle change in inflection as he shifted out of professional mode.

There's something about him, besides his obvious intellect and maleness. Maybe it's that he finds me attractive.

Rounding the corner, the sheriff's department came into view.

Slate pointed to the building. "Can you believe it's only been three months? There's the door to the interrogation room where I told you I could kill all your snakes. I was so nervous."

"You hid it well. How about a Zoom in two weeks? I'll work on building your coalition."

"My coalition? That's funny. You're the politician, John."

She pulled to a stop.

He opened the door, his foot already out, and was about to thank her.

"Yes, a casual dinner sometime would be fun, John."

He smiled and gave a small wave as he closed the door.

* * *

Stop-and-go traffic on the Dolphin Expressway gave Slate time to think.

Damn, he's attractive. I was funny calling him my pony. He didn't mind. Anyway, he got my point. I hate this damn traffic. People are so rude in "I got mine, Miami." It was a good day. Lucy, wow, she can shoot. Nice of Carter to take care of Taylor. That's it; I'm not going to the computer lab. Screw it, I'm going to my condo—a good time to call Taylor while I'm in the car.

"Call Taylor," Slate said to the Highlander's microphone.

Taylor picked up on the first ring. "Hi, Sister. I just got home."

"Good, I'm stuck in traffic. You sound happy."

"I am. I had a great time today. Thanks for inviting me. Did you know he was an Eagle Scout back in Pennsylvania?"

"Who?"

"Carter."

Slate had a feeling Carter was the best part of Taylor's day.

"Oh, I noticed that he walked you to your car."

"I'm sorry I lost it on the platform. Anyway, his holding me felt so good."

"He's older than you, you know."

"Yes," Taylor said. "But only four years."

"Well, he's one of our best grad students. I call him Mr. Robot."

"He gave me some ideas for my Eagle project. For his project, he made drone videos of hiking trails with QR links to useful information."

Traffic inched along, and Slate's exit edged closer when she noticed something on the passenger seat. The governor had left her his challenge coin. She rubbed it between her thumb and finger as she drove.

"Ah, that's interesting. It seems like your day couldn't have gone any better. I'm happy for you," Slate said.

"Looks like you made a new friend, too," Taylor said.

"Who?"

"The governor is sweet on you. He was captivated by you all day."

"Don't be silly. He's excited about the project."

"I'm not blind, you know. I checked the internet, and he's not married. Your beauty and gorgeous figure did not escape his eyes."

"You're being silly, Taylor. I'm too busy to think about guys. Besides, powerful and ambitious men come with complications.

"I'm changing the subject. Did you hear anything about the biomedical summer intern position yet?"

"I expect to know this week, I think. Professor Gilbert sounded very positive."

"Good, he's top-notch," Slate said.

"Slate, for what it's worth, I like the governor. He's honest and intelligent. And he wants to kill pythons."

"It's not that simple. Anything personal is a serious conflict of interest," Slate said while turning the coin over between her fingers.

"Well, you might want to tell the governor that, Sister."

"You're a funny girl. Here's my exit. Let me know about the internship. Glad you had a good time. Bye."

18

Yellowcake

On Monday morning, the day set for lunch with Jake, Slate considered going straight to the research site. However, the previous Friday afternoon, she noticed two lab techs working on party decorations in the back of the break room and guessed they were for her.

Topping the stairs to the hallway of her office, she prepared herself to be surprised. She opened the door to cheers, party horns, and confetti poppers. Her staff, colleagues, and Carter sang "Happy Birthday" for her forty-first birthday. Not one for birthdays or to call attention to herself, more at home in her lab, she found herself touched by their genuine affection. She cut the cake and took a giant bite, purposely smearing frosting on her face.

Over by eight-thirty. Ten minutes later, Slate sat in the dean's office, enduring a staff meeting on graduation preparations. Her least favorite week of the semester, they reviewed the timeline, and the walk-through scheduled for Wednesday afternoon. Undergraduate ceremonies were on Thursday, followed by a reception, dinner, and an obligatory party. The graduate school commencement on Friday had another reception. As associate dean, Slate had duties and responsibilities for each event. Back in her office by nine-thirty, Carter was waiting with his update.

He began, "I'm wondering, are you taking the cake home?"

"Do I look like I eat a lot of cake?"

"Ah, not really. But it's delicious."

"Yes, you can have it if you clean up the mess in the break room and take the balloons down on Friday."

"Deal."

"Okay, where are we on your Zcolt?" Slate asked, taking a seat on the sofa.

Carter sat by her and opened his laptop on the coffee table.

"The Zcolt's good. I upgraded the six props to handle more weight for ammunition and larger batteries. They run at a lower speed with less downwash. I split the battery packs for balance, with half in front and half in the back."

He flipped through pictures taken in the robotics lab.

"How long will it fly?"

"I'm guessing one hour, maybe one-twenty if we keep the speed down."

"When do sensors and the weapon get added?"

"I've already fabricated the brackets. If the bird flies okay in the parking lot behind the lab, we can test it at the research site in a week or two."

"Is it attracting any attention?"

"Not yet. We keep it locked in the trailer inside the lab when we're not working on it."

"Don't let anyone see your bad-ass gun strapped on it," she said. "The governor almost pissed himself with excitement at the demonstration."

Slate looked for his shocked reaction at her language, then laughed.

"I exaggerate, but he's definitely impressed."

"I'm glad he liked it, Boss."

They stood, and Slate put a hand on his shoulder. "I'm delighted you're on our team, Carter. Thanks for being so positive and dedicated." Slate extended her hand and gave him a big smile. She wanted to mention Taylor but didn't.

Back at her desk, her administrative assistant had fanned birthday cards across the desk pad. Slate hadn't noticed the bouquet of mixed flowers in a beautiful vase on her credenza. The envelope read, "Happy Birthday, Cowgirl." Wondering how Jake had found out about her birthday, she opened the card. It was signed, "To our coalition, John."

At her computer lab, Slate checked on Lucy, who had been machine learning over the weekend from data gathered last week, including the demonstration for the governor. Although not entirely new to Slate, integrating python identification with targeting and aiming a weapon took time. Programming auto-flight and navigation came next.

Slate arrived at the RV fifteen minutes late and waved to Jake, who was looking out the kitchen window. He had lunch ready—gator tail meatballs dipped in Cajun batter, deep-fried and served in a hoagie roll with hush puppies and mac 'n cheese. The dessert was bread pudding.

Having missed breakfast, Slate devoured the lunch.

"Yum, Yum, Yummmmm,"

"More paper towels, Cowgirl?"

She looked at him, disoriented by the nickname, recalling the flowers.

"Ah, sure, Chef, maybe two. I love, love, love this."

She dipped hush puppies in soft butter. Jake brought out two bowls of bread pudding drizzled with creamy white frosting. The one he prepared for Slate had a flaming spiral-shaped candle and a large chocolate wafer.

"Happy Birthday, Sarah. I wish you many happy days and years ahead."

Slate, touched by his sincerity, reached across and put her hand on his, holding his eyes with her smile.

The sound of Brad's Jeep interrupted the moment.

"Thank you for lunch and my birthday wish, Jake."

The RV door opened.

"Just in time for dessert. Bread pudding with warm frosting?" Jake asked Brad.

"Yep, sign me up," he replied.

"Eat up, we have a lot of data to collect," Slate said.

With Slate at the console in the control trailer, Brad on the platform with the sensors, and Jake down below releasing pythons and native animals into the enclosure, Lucy processed sensor data, identified pythons, ignored other animals, and aimed the rifle without firing it. After a few breaks and a half-hour for dinner, they finished at nine p.m.

Arriving at her condo, Slate was relieved that the dry cleaner had delivered her royal purple doctoral gown. Nothing extraordinary happened during the walk-through on Wednesday. Her hair up in a French twist, tall in high heels, and a robe refined with black velvet panels and bell-shaped sleeves, Slate presented a young and refreshing flair as the associate dean during graduation ceremonies. Feeling good about the project's progress, she allowed herself to relax and be convivial at the receptions and cocktail parties. To her relief, students didn't protest anything this year.

Exhausted with aching feet, she met three girlfriends Friday night at a sports bar. Hair straight, old blue jeans over tennis shoes, and a beat-up Shell Oil hat like Jake's, Slate stuffed herself with fried oysters and ice-cold draft beer. Mixed-martial-arts cage fights on giant screens, they cheered against each other for contestants they didn't know, pumping their fists and yelling. Between fights, they danced together to 80s rock music and ignored advances from guys. Gathered outside, waiting for their Uber rides, steamy with perspiration, they hugged as a group, happy for the opportunity to be goofy and have fun.

* * *

Friday in Tallahassee, the same day as Slate's graduation events, Governor Prescott hosted a *Python Focus Day* at the Hyatt. He and members of the task force displayed exhibits that included tourism trends, public opinion polls, task force objectives, and python facts.

In a separate room, the activist organization "Never Again—Kids' Lives Matter" signed up members and presented its demands. All parties agreed that pythons are a clear and present danger to the public, the economy, and native animals.

The governor had not expected pointed questions, such as: "What are you actually doing? When will you start killing snakes, Governor?"

The years of mealy-mouth BS by the FWC to ameliorate the public and media were clearly over.

The event ended at four, and Prescott asked Senator Grant and Representative Luck to meet in his office.

"You saw for yourselves, the natives are restless. They're keeping the deaths of these kids front and center. I'm not sure that PAC funding these python groups was a good idea. The Chamber of Commerce lobby is taking bites out of my ass on tourism.

"Sure, we're making progress with the task force, but I'm worried that if we come up short, the blame will shift to Republicans, and you know what that means at the next election? We need a coalition."

"I agree," Grant, ever the sycophant, said. "We need all hands on deck. Lord help us if another child is eaten while Democrats and Republicans argue over who dropped the ball."

Luck spoke up. "How about we expand the task force to add a couple of democrats, say from their science and technology advisory group? They might have ideas we haven't considered."

"Good idea," Prescott said. "I'm involved with a subgroup of the task force exploring a high-tech solution. It's promising but experimental."

"What is it?" Grant asked.

"It's confidential for proprietary reasons at the moment. It involves a university and is in the prototype phase. As you know, some want us to fail, and cutting-edge technologies scare people. So, no leaks."

"Got it," Grant said. "Monica and I will find two democrats for your task force, maybe three. You might let them nominate one or two replacements for the four FWC commissioners you fired."

"Good ideas," Prescott said. "Next, I want to talk about the documentary on widespread radioactive contamination in the Bone Valley counties of central Florida from 100 years of phosphate strip mining. It made the headlines this morning."

"I saw the news bulletin, but not the documentary," Luck said.

"You know that I grew up in Polk County, smack in the middle of it. Blame for this, like the python issue, is shared equally by both parties, but especially the Department of Environmental Protection and Bureau of Radiation Control."

"Can't argue with you," Grant said. "It's a dirty business. A lot of money changed hands. Politicians from both sides took hundreds of millions in donations, pay-to-play money, jobs, and grants going way back. The press could have a field day connecting the dots."

"What do you know about phosphate mining and radiation?" Prescott asked.

Both shrugged.

"Here's a brief overview. Phosphate ore is buried fifteen feet below the surface and contains Uranium 238 and other isotopes. They decay and emit Alpha, Beta, and Gamma radiation, which can cause cancer. Before mining, the danger was mainly limited to groundwater. However, when dug up with draglines, contamination spreads, and radiation becomes concentrated. A dusty byproduct called reject rock is used on roads and in construction. Reject rock, which has ancient fossils and shark teeth, is used in kids' playgrounds, like in the dragline bucket at the phosphate museum in Mulberry. The industry mined Uranium to produce yellowcake in Polk County from the seventies through the nineties. By far, it's the most significant environmental and economic threat in Florida, besides pythons. Don't even get me started on their radioactive gypsum stacks where they make fertilizer, like in Tampa."

Grant and Luck listened intently. The governor described one square-mile clay slime pits and toxic industrial reagents dumped on mined land. He was about to discuss lawsuits in Lakeland over mining caused by radon contamination in housing developments when Brooke, his press secretary, rushed into the room, grabbed the remote for the TV, and turned it on.

"Governor, there's breaking news. You need to see this."

19

Banana

Weeks earlier, Channel 12, Miami, had done a spot on the Red Riders, embedding Ashley Fox on a ride-along with a twenty-five-year-old flaming redhead and former python wrangler nicknamed Swift Raven. Swift's black T-shirt had the Rider's python logo on the front and "Never Again" on the back.

Ashley shouldered a close-quarters Beretta shotgun for Swift, who favored a fully racked pink AR-15. Both sported bright red nail polish, wrap-around amber shooting glasses, and made-for-TV slim-cut jeans, paired with black tactical boots.

The forty-second segment climaxed with Ashley spotlighting a hissing twelve-foot python, while Swift stitched rounds down its throat and along the body to the tail. Ashley signed off with, "Reporting from somewhere in the Everglades, this is Ashley Fox."

Now, the last Friday of May, back in the Everglades at a popular tourist site, she planned to interview visitors, ask park management about tourism numbers, and talk with Stu Carlton, a former FWC python wrangler. Stu, now a Resource Officer under Governor Prescott, educated the public and assuaged their apprehension.

Standing in the grass next to the sign, Shark Valley Lookout, she arched her toes to keep spike heels from sinking and pitching her over backwards. The microphone under her armpit, she held a compact and tried to straighten a cockeyed paste-on eyelash.

"Christ, Rodney, can't you help me? It's all backwards in the mirror."

The producer, a former offensive tackle with fingers like bratwursts, tipped her head back with one hand and smoothed the sticky polyester strip back in place.

"Good to go, Ash. We're live in ten. Two visitors, the manager, and Stu are on the sidewalk after you finish your intro."

Ashley batted her eyelashes, the mint-colored contacts catching the morning light. She sharpened the lip liner and powdered the shine from her cheeks.

Her ratings had risen like a bull market after she had blacked out and flopped around upside down like a rubber chicken in the backseat of an F-18 Hornet fighter jet over Miami Dolphins' stadium during halftime. Someone nicknamed her "Hot Gun," which she preferred over another nickname, "Barf gun," popularized on social media.

She fancied herself a sexy rendition of CNN's famous war correspondent, Erin Daggett.

A warm, westerly breeze tousled honey-blonde hair, styled over one eye, which, by design, required constant flipping. The coral V-shaped halter top with fitted bodice, over a trim waist, accentuated respectable cleavage below a sweetheart pendant. The light, white, pleated skirt rustled in the breeze just above her knees.

With a microphone in one hand and a note card in the other, Ashley practiced her opening for Rodney and the cameraman.

"Good afternoon, Dan. From deep in the Everglades, we're here at an observatory off the Tamiami Trail called Shark Valley. We'll show you what has happened since the tragic loss of scouts four months ago, only twenty miles south of here at Pa-Hay-Okee."

She paused and leaned into the mic for effect and pointed at the sign. "Dan, I think they should rename this place. I would call it Python Alley."

Rodney gave a thumbs-up. "Good, good. I like the look and your spark. Tilt the mic in. Pull your V down a little. Okay, relax. We have eight minutes."

Her feet on fire from standing on tiptoes, Ashley high-stepped from deep grass to the sidewalk to greet the two visitors Rodney had chosen.

At ten minutes after five, Rodney, on the phone with the studio, showed Ashley two sets of five fingers—she went live ten seconds later.

On her game—like reporting from the front line in Mosul, Iraq—she was about to introduce Stu, when it happened.

In the background behind the visitor center, screams filled the air. She raised the mic to Stu and saw that he had turned toward the screams. More yelling followed, then a commotion. People migrated away from Ashley past the visitor center toward the marsh. Ashley watched Stu take off running. Speechless, she snapped a look at Rodney, standing beside the cameraman.

Rodney circled a finger over his head and pointed to the marsh. "Keep rolling! Run! Follow Stu!"

She wheeled around and put the mic to her lips, her dream of high-impact news coming true.

"Dan, something has happened, Dan. This is breaking news. We're following Stu Carlton, the armed Resource Officer. There is screaming down by the water, Dan. Reporting live, this is Ashley Fox."

Rodney tapped the cameraman on the shoulder and grabbed his battery backpack. "Start with landscape. Then tighten on her ass. Don't worry about the camera jumping. Don't let anyone get between Ash and us."

Ashley took off like a linebacker, her skirt lifting in the headwind with each stride. Neon yellow bikini-covered butt-cheeks flashed like blinking lights on construction barricades. Viral in ten minutes, the emblazoned close-up would become the logo for her lingerie line named "Hardhats."

Up ahead, the scene unfolded behind the gathering crowd.

It had begun minutes before Stu and Ashley heard the screams. Lottie Lohman, in her early sixties, maneuvered her red mobility scooter along the winding walkway.

"Banana, sit still," Lottie said.

The young dachshund fidgeted on a cushion in her lap. Her three-year-old grandson walked beside the scooter, holding onto the seat back. Banana stood as tall as his squat legs would allow, circled the cushion once, then again.

"Damnit to smithereens." Lottie glanced to see if Andrew heard the swear.

"He has to pee. I swear, the dog has an acorn for a bladder. Andrew, love, get the leash from the basket."

Lottie clipped the leash to the collar. "Grandma's knees are killing her. Here, Andrew, help Banana down. Take him over by those bushes to do his business. Here's a bag in case he doodles."

Andrew cradled the wiener dog to the ground. Banana took off like a streak, snapping the leash from his hand.

"Banana, Banana, get back here!" Lottie yelled.

"Nana, Nana, you get back right now," Andrew added.

Banana ran around sniffing this and that, flushed a half-dozen long-billed white ibises, then made a beeline to a bush at the water's edge.

"Andrew, go grab the leash, quick. Get him back up here so I can spank him."

"Okay, Grandma, he needs a good spanking."

Andrew ran down a slight incline, stopping at the water, his right sneaker submerged in muck. He reached for the leash loop as Banana growled at something.

"Andrew, what's going on? No time for playing now. Jerk it. Give it a good jerk!" Lottie yelled, her scooter, only twenty yards from them.

Meanwhile, behind Lottie on the walkway, a woman on a bicycle wearing a bucket hat painted with bright yellow bumblebees saw the predicament and stopped. She set the bike on its stand and started down the incline. About twenty feet away, she stopped and pointed to the water.

"Wani! Wani!" she yelled.

Her mistake was understandable. The splash could have been an alligator.

Andrew was the second splash. Arm extended by the leash, body horizontal, he flew out and slapped flat on the water like a plank.

Banana, at the far end of the leash, as later described by the woman in the bumblebee hat, looked like a hot dog in a bun, stuck on a pole. She screamed, "Hebi! Hebi! Hebi!" Japanese for rotten rope or snake.

Elevated out of the water, Banana, clamped around the middle, squirmed like a nightcrawler on a hook. Lottie's mind caught up with her eyes, and she screamed, "Banana! Andrew! Someone help!"

A jogger, a man of about fifty, stopped near the Asian woman and screamed, "Snake!"

Andrew, no longer holding the leash, flailed and doggy-paddled, his feet searching for the bottom.

Banana, as if stuck on a swizzle stick, rolled in and out of the water, his tail throwing off streams like a drinking fountain.

Stu, pointing his Glock handgun, flew by the jogger and the Asian woman. Ashley stopped next to the Asian woman. Rodney and the cameraman set up to film the scene unfolding behind Ashley.

Ashley raised the mic and resumed reporting.

"Dan, something's happened in the water. There's a little boy. A park officer is going into the water. His gun is out. Oh my God! There's a snake, a python! Oh no, it has a little dog!"

The cameraman zoomed in as Stu grabbed Andrew by the collar and flung him like a soggy beach towel up on the grass. Then a tight shot showed a bleeding Banana wiggling in jagged teeth, his wild eyes bulging with terror.

Zoomed out, the camera showed Stu in a crouch, the Glock leveled like on Miami Vice. Two shots missed high, and a third missed Banana's head by a whisker. The python sank, tail first, like a weighted fly-fishing line. Banana's upraised nose subsided in a swirl of bubbles.

Stu sat on the grass, exhausted, his Glock between upraised knees. Ripples receded, and placid serenity returned to the slough as if nothing had happened.

Andrew, soaking wet and screaming bloody murder, scrambled onto his Grandma's lap. The camera panned to capture the moment.

"Nice and tight, Eric," Rodney coached the cameraman.

Barefoot, her heels long gone, Ashley, slack-jawed and speechless from the melee, recomposed after Andrew screamed. She spun around and stuck the Channel 12 microphone in the face of the Asian woman.

"Ma'am, what did you see?"

Rodney slapped Eric on the back and pointed to Ashley.

Both hands on her bucket hat, the woman's wild eyes met Ashley's steady gaze.

"What did you see? What happened?"

The woman's hands popped off the hat and performed an animated one-minute pantomime while speaking accelerated Japanese without taking a breath. Ashley looked at Rodney, who shrugged. The woman took a breath, and Ashley interrupted, thanked her, and added a slight bow. She turned to the sweaty jogger, whom she took for Hispanic.

"Do you speak English?" she asked.

"Si," he said, messing with her.

"Sir, tell us what you saw."

The man gave a good account of the incident. Ashley ended with her zinger question.

"Is there anything else you want to say?"

"Well, I can't figure out one thing."

"And what is that, Sir?"

"Why did the snake choose the dog and not the boy?"

***

Brooke tuned to the Channel 12 news channel and clicked back to the beginning of the live broadcast from the Everglades. The governor, Grant, and Luck moved to the sofa to see the TV on the wall across the room. Prescott thought the blonde standing by the sign looked overbranded by a network targeting an older audience.

"Brooke, turn it up a little," the governor said.

The blonde reporter pushed hair from her eye, leaned forward, and said something about renaming Shark Valley.

"What did she say?" Prescott asked.

Grant said, "She wants to change the name to Python Alley."

"That's bullshit. The last thing we need is a smartass reporter who thinks she's an actress. Brooke, find out who owns that station," Prescott demanded.

They watched the TV screen, heard screams, and saw the reporter pivot and take off like a jackrabbit. One heel flew off, then the other. The camera zoomed in on her ass, and Grant stood up.

"That girl can run," Luck commented.

"Are those what I think they are?" Prescott said.

"Yep," Grant confirmed, squinting to see.

They watched, the camera jumping as Ashley worked her way through gawkers to the Asian woman.

"Hear her panting? Her ratings will soar," Grant said.

The joking ended when the camera centered, and the little boy took flight like a kite and smacked flat on the swamp water. The 4K screen filled with a ferocious yellow python eye, and a little dog named Banana, with four stubby legs pointing straight up, belly-up inside the jaws.

"Holy shit!" Grant said.

The scene played out second by second until the tip of Banana's black nose slipped under.

"He almost shot the damn dog!" Grant yelled.

Prescott ignored Grant, weighing the repercussions in his mind. He tried to make sense of the Japanese interview.

"What's up with the Japanese? This better not be a diversity play by Channel 12," Prescott said.

"Nah, she's winging it," Luck said.

The jogger's question stunned them.

"He's correct, it could have been the boy," Prescott said.

The reporter tried to interview a hysterical lady on a mobility scooter and the screaming boy. Failing, she stepped away, her hair matted with sweat.

Ashley leaned into the camera. "Our prayers go out to the little dog. Dan, the governor is losing his war on pythons. Signing off from Python Alley, live and exclusive, this is Ashley Fox."

The governor angrily flicked his hand at the TV.

"Turn it off, Brooke. Draft a press release stating that we've reached out to the family. The task force is hard at work. Not a moment to spare. It's a bipartisan issue—the new FWC's highest priority. You know the rest. Oh, and call that station and tell them to cut out or blur the gory parts. That includes her yellow ass."

Luck added. "I shudder to think if that snake had taken the child. Yankees up North already think the state is a swamp. Now, tourists won't leave their cars and will keep the windows rolled up."

"Okay, I want the democrats in this up to their necks like us. Call me on Monday with what they want in trade," Prescott said.

After they left his office, Prescott sat and thought. He concluded the timing of the attack wasn't too bad. The on-site resource officer was his idea. The idiot almost shot the dog, but saved the boy. All in all, he thought, support for an armed drone solution just got better.

He checked his email and texts for anything from Slate, hoping she liked the birthday flowers and card. Nothing.

* * *

Late the next morning, in her lab on Saturday, a good time to use university computers, Slate texted the governor.

"Hi. Busy? Call if you aren't."

Ten minutes later, her phone rang.

"Hi John, I saw your press release. Right on the money."

"Banana, who would name a dog, Banana?" the governor laughed.

"I know. Poor little guy. I feel so sorry for the grandmother and the little boy."

"Crazy that it happened on my python focus day. The Tallahassee media got scooped by a small Miami station. How do you think it will play out?" Prescott asked.

"Oh, before I forget, thank you for the beautiful flowers and card. I'm not big on birthdays, but I do appreciate you thinking of me."

"You're welcome. I'm just two years older, but you look much younger."

"Age is an attitude. Anyway, about Banana. I checked chat. Pythons eat pets and will continue to do so as they move into urban areas in search of food. Chat says that 6 in 10 Florida homes have pets. Only 3 in 10 homes have kids. Therefore, support for your initiative just doubled," she laughed.

"I like your math, Professor. How was the commencement?"

"It was better than I expected. I made myself have fun. Plus, I went out with my crazy girlfriends last night."

"Good for you. Anything new on the project?"

"Motor, battery, and sensor upgrades go on the Zcolt this week, along with the Humboldt weapon system. If all goes well, Brad and Carter will flight-test the configuration next Friday at the research site."

"So, you're on schedule?" he asked.

"Yep, Lucy, gets better every day. July 3rd still looks good for the proof-of-concept demonstration."

"Great," the governor said. "I'm thinking we can watch it downstairs in my situation room with a video link. Much easier for logistics and confidentiality."

"Sure, I'll notify my communications tech," Slate said.

"How about an update on Zoom next Friday afternoon after the test flight?"

"Yep, that works."

"It's not my business, but you're a very busy young lady. Have you ever been to Fairchild Gardens in Coral Gables? It's beautiful and relaxing," he said. "You should take tomorrow off and chill."

"Thanks for thinking of me. Yes, I went there once. That's a good idea if Lucy is a good girl today. Thanks again for the flowers. Have a nice weekend, John."

"I will. You, too. Goodbye."

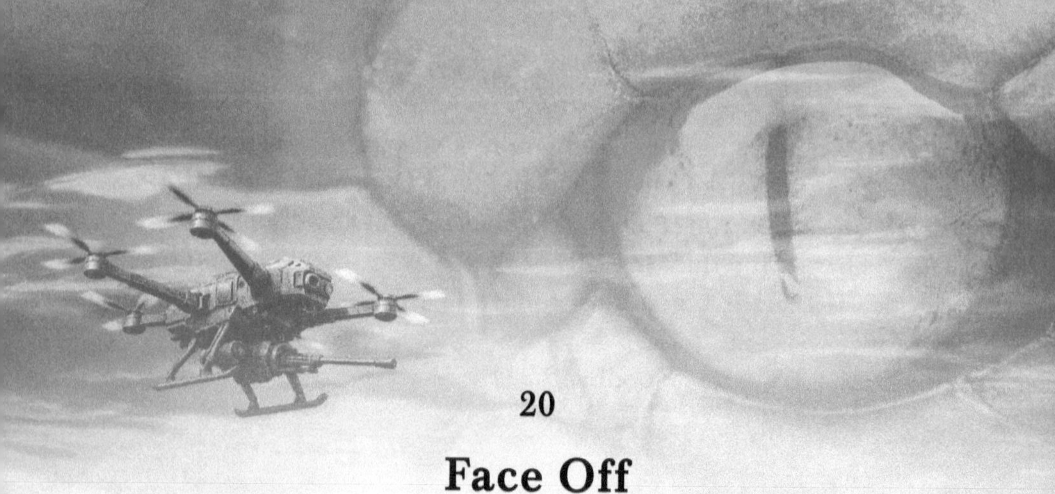

20

Face Off

Three weeks after the first test flight at the research site, Brad and Carter pulled the Jeep Cherokee with the Zcolt trailer to a stop. Carter unhooked the trailer and prepared the drone for launch. Brad parked the Jeep and unfolded the table for the controller on the grass.

"Couldn't ask for a nicer day, ole buddy," Carter said.

"I love the quiet out here. So different from Miami," Brad said.

Carter skipped a flat rock across the meandering slough. It spooked a blue heron, which squawked in protest and flew low overhead. Puffy white clouds drifted across a blue sky, reflecting on clear, slow-moving water. A gentle breeze rustled through sawgrass prairie and cypress trees. To the right, a crusty alligator lounged on a mud flat. The air carried the earthy, sweet smell of decay. A half dozen black-headed vultures circled high on early thermals.

"This must have been incredibly vibrant before pythons ate everything," Carter said.

Brad agreed. "That's what we're here for, to kill the bastards. Time to get to work."

As Slate suggested, Carter flew his small camera drone around the area to ensure they were alone.

"Nobody out here but two guys, pythons, and hopefully, Ashley Fox." Carter wiggled his eyebrows.

"You're funny. I'll bet she opens a fast-fashion clothing line." Brad pranced around, flipping his hair, imitating Ashley in high heels. Carter pretended to be a photographer, snapping poses.

Carter powered up Zcolt circuits and completed preflight checks. Brad set up his computer, monitors, and communication links with the drone.

Brad's computer had upgraded software that tracked targets and aimed the Humboldt rifle. A dashed red circle appeared around the crosshair in the weapons screen when he selected the target. The dashes changed to solid red when the computer began active tracking.

Checks complete, Brad flexed his fingers like a Las Vegas card dealer. As in Fortnite, his left fingers tapped keys on a keyboard, and his right hand moved a computer mouse.

"Here we go." Brad held down the Shift, Command, and S keys. The six motors went from zero to idle at 1,200 revolutions per minute (RPM) in a microsecond. When Brad held the space bar down for takeoff, the buzz, like a beehive, increased to swarms of angry hornets. The Zcolt shot up 100 feet. He tapped keys and slid the mouse across the pad, checking basic flight controls. A monitor displayed the front view of the drone's camera. The weapons screen displayed the rifle scope view with a crosshair.

"Beefy, Carter. This baby has muscle and agility."

Flying manually, Brad aimed the crosshair at the alligator as a test and pressed the Shift and A keys. A dashed red circle appeared, then changed to solid red. He turned a few degrees to the left, and the rifle barrel moved to keep the crosshair on the alligator.

"Target tracking works," Brad said. "Good battery, correct?"

"Yep, full batteries and a dummy load of ammunition."

"Okay, then hang on, Drone Boy," Brad said.

The nose dipped, motors accelerated to 3,000 RPM, and the Zcolt shot across the Everglades like a dragster. Descending to twenty feet, Brad watched the screen from the drone camera. It was like sitting on the drone. He banked hard right, curved back, and set up a figure-eight pattern.

"How's it flying, Maverick?" Carter asked.

"Off balance to the right, but otherwise, smooth and responsive."

He completed three more circuits, attempting to fly the same track.

"I'm ready for lunch. Let's bring her in, recharge the batteries, and call the boss," Brad said while turning the Zcolt for home.

* * *

Back at the RV, Carter made sandwiches with deli prime rib, Havarti cheese, and horseradish sauce. Brad zapped a plate of loaded nachos in the microwave.

Brad dialed Slate on speakerphone. "Hi, Boss. The morning flight's in the bag. It flew well in manual mode. The weapon system syncs and tracks targets."

"That sounds great. Did you see anyone out there? A reporter called this morning, snooping around. There might be a leak."

"No one saw us, Boss. Carter flew his small drone before the test flight to clear the area."

Slate added, "I've heard that reporters are calling universities fishing for stories on what the task force is doing. We have to be super careful."

"Gotcha, Boss. Understood," Brad said.

"Are you flying this afternoon?" she asked.

"Yes, we need to tune out lateral bias and reduce throttle latency. I'll try your idea of covering a grid by flying up and down rows like a farm tractor."

"Good. It'll get easier with sensors that scan a wider area and with the computer navigating and flying the drone. But give it a try," Slate said.

Carter, sitting across the RV table, had his hand up, thumb and index finger moving, like shooting a pistol. He mouthed, "Shoot the Humboldt."

"One last thing. Carter needs to check the boresight of the Humboldt to ensure bullets hit the aiming point. Can we test-fire it during the flight?" Brad asked.

After a long pause, Slate said, "Are you sure no one is anywhere near the area? Will anyone hear a high-powered rifle out there?"

"We'll clear the area with Carter's drone before takeoff. We may not get another chance before the full system demonstration for the task force."

Brad and Carter looked at each other, waiting for her answer.

"I have a Zoom call with the governor at four this afternoon. You can fire one round and record the data. Call me after you land so I can

108

update the governor. I'll ask him to beef up security with a heavy gate at the turnoff and bigger no trespassing signs to keep reporters out."

"Sounds good. We'll call you after we land," Brad said.

Slate hung up, and Brad gave Carter a high-five.

21

Shoot the Bastard

Brad and Carter finished lunch and checked their phones for messages.

"Getting to shoot the Humboldt calls for a celebration," Brad said, and got two ice cream bars from the freezer compartment.

"That's not celebrating, dude. I'll take two, please," Carter said.

"I'm thinking we look for a python to shoot," Brad said.

Carter held his ice cream bars up like a football goal post.

By one o'clock, they had finished the preflight, made trim adjustments, and chambered a round in the Humboldt. Brad programmed GPS grid waypoints on the map display. The breeze had freshened and shifted to the northwest, with scattered cumulus clouds forecast for the afternoon.

Carter sat in a folding chair next to Brad.

"I'll fly at twenty feet. The grid is ahead half a mile. I'll fly rows up and back like a farmer plowing a field. You can watch the drone's forward camera view with me. I can zoom in by holding the P key. However, your primary job is watching the scope view on the weapons screen. I can go as slow as you want. You're doing Lucy's job—looking for pythons."

"Got it. Okay, I'll pull the safety pin on the Humboldt," Carter said.

Brad leveled off at twenty feet and flew south to the northwestern corner of the grid, the rows running north-south.

"Carter, I'll fly over the first row. At the end, I'll turn left, skip two rows, and come back north. At the end of that row, I'll turn left

110

again to the row next to the first one. I'll repeat the pattern until all rows are covered, or until we run out of battery."

The Zcolt slowed to ten miles an hour. Carter watched grass, water, and brush descend down the monitor screens.

"You're going too fast. I'm a human, dude," Carter said.

Brad slowed to five miles per hour.

"Okay, that's about right." Carter settled into scanning patches of terrain. After a few rows, Brad got better at planning the turns to line up straight for the next row. Halfway finished searching the grid on a row heading south, Carter called out, "Stop. Stop. Back up. A snake."

Brad slid the Zcolt to the right, backed up a bit, and then slid back over the row.

"I don't want to spook him."

He edged forward in slow motion toward the spot.

"Where was he?" Brad asked.

"There's a large clump of marsh grass on the right of a game trail or something in line with our flight path. On the left edge of the trail is a smaller bunch of grass. The head of a python is lying halfway across the trail, facing to the right, that's west. The body is behind the grass on the left. It might be an intersection of two trails. Keep going."

"I'm climbing up a little. The downwash and vibration might scare it."

Brad inched forward.

"Stop. I think I see it—a big head. The grass is in the way. He's near the top of your screen, Brad, a little left of center."

Brad eased forward. The terrain moved down toward the X mark in the center of his monitor. "Okay. I see the trail. Yes, I see the snake in a shadow. The wind's blowing the grass. It's not a good angle."

"How about from the west with the sun behind us?" Carter said.

"Good idea, I'll mark the spot as a waypoint."

Brad backed up, circled right, dropped to ten feet, and approached the waypoint from the west.

"There he is at the top of your screen on a thin trail between grass. The head is pointing at us," Carter whispered as if the snake could hear him. "Good. You're lined up down his body. If the shot goes high, you'll still hit him."

Carter checked the weapons screen with the crosshair near the head. Tips of cordgrass bent over the trail in waves, mixing with sun and shadows from clouds.

Brad looked over at Carter's screen.

"There's a lot of shit moving around," Brad said. "I'll try to lock on and get a track."

Brad pushed the Shift and A keys. A dashed red circle appeared. It danced on and off the head, switched from solid to dashed, then back to solid.

"Wish we had infrared," Carter said. "He would pop in infrared."

"We could reposition and come from the south," Brad said.

"We don't have the battery, and he's going to spook," Carter said. "Clouds are moving, and the wind is variable. Let's wait here and take the shot when the track is solid."

"Alright, I'll slide ten degrees left away from the overhanging grass."

Brad tickled the keys to keep the head under the X mark on his screen. The Zcolt flight control computer micro-adjusted each rotor's RPM to hold position. The screens jittered as the drone corrected for changes in wind speed and direction.

"Let's see if it locks up," he said, concentrating on keeping the X over the python.

Carter stared at the scope crosshair on his weapons screen and checked for the red tracking circle.

"It wants to track. Breaks lock, drifts off, then reacquires." Carter said.

"Hold steady, Brad. Wait for the wind and shadows to shift."

The python moved. Its head rose off the ground two inches. The mouth opened wide, catching sunlight.

"Shit. His mouth is open. Lock him up, Brad!"

Brad pressed the keys. A dashed red circle appeared, then solid.

"Solid red. You have a lock. It's jumping but still tracking," Carter said.

Brad glanced over at Carter's weapons screen.

"It looks too jumpy," Brad said. "Not right."

"It's good enough. Let the fricking computer figure it out. Shoot the bastard!" Carter yelled.

Brad pressed the Shift, Command, and F keys. The screen images jumped.

Sitting at the research site, half a mile from the shot, they heard a distant crack and stared at the screens.

Carter leaned in and groaned. "It's hard to see. You got close enough to kick up dirt. I think you hit it. Can't tell."

"I'll climb up and look down from above," Brad said. He created a waypoint over the target, backed up, climbed to fifty feet, swung the Zcolt around south, and approached the waypoint.

Brad inched the X on his screen toward the waypoint marker. "Okay, I'm approaching the waypoint. Do you see it on your screen?"

"Damn, you smacked it good. Flipped it around. The tail was pointed east before you shot." Carter said.

"What do you mean, flipped around? Is it moving? Maybe it's wounded."

"It's not moving, Brad. Get closer."

Brad descended to ten feet—the drone skids and Humboldt rifle dragged through taller patches of cordgrass and inched forward.

"Only seven minutes of battery left," Brad cautioned.

"Keep coming. It's close. Stay over the game trail," Carter said.

The images on Brad's screen sharpened. Downwash twisted grass into twine. The image became crystal clear on both screens. They faced each other, mouths open.

Brad spoke first.

"Panther!"

* * *

Brad jerked open the RV door and threw the backpack with data drives across the room. It bounced off the table onto the bench seat.

"Easy, bro," Carter said.

Brad opened the refrigerator. "IPA or Shock Top?"

Before he could answer, an IPA bottle slid across the table into Carter's hand.

"We've got twenty minutes to find out what happened and decide what to tell Slate," Brad said.

Sitting beside each other, they scrolled through videos of the drone camera and the weapons monitor on a split screen. They zipped forward to where Carter first saw the snake. Frame by frame, they searched.

"There's the head on the trail. Zoom in. A big python. The body disappears behind the grass to the left. What's across the trail, Brad?"

Brad scrolled to the right edge of the trail.

"I see it. The front part of its head. It's staring at the python across the gap," Carter said.

Brad zoomed in, filling the screen.

"Damn, it's the color of dirt, hard to see even with full zoom," Brad said.

"He's crouching flat against the dirt. Wow, see its eyes? Click the frame forward," Carter said. "See the teeth? It's growling."

"It's a face-off. Eat or be eaten," Brad said, adjusting the view to center both heads. "Wow, the panther looks young, not that big, in comparison. Okay, let's fast forward to the shot."

The video advanced and stopped with the drone west of the waypoint over the east-west trail. They were lined up with the python and saw the head and body in the shadows of wavy grass.

Brad hit play. Video and audio resumed. They watched and listened to the audio.

Audio playback:

Shit. His mouth is open. Lock him up, Brad.

Solid red. You have a lock. It's jumping but still tracking.

It looks jumpy. Not right.

It's good enough. Let the fricking computer figure it out. Shoot the bastard!

Brad stopped the video. "For the record, Drone Boy, that's you talking. The 'it's good enough, let the computer figure it out, shoot the bastard,' part."

"Brad, you pulled the fricking trigger," Carter replied.

Brad pointed to the screen. "Fair enough. Do you see the panther in the video?"

"Barely. It was there the whole time. I see it now, the long tail, the back hunches, the front paws, and the broad head. I was looking for pythons, not panthers," Carter said.

"You couldn't see it in real time without the zoom. Let's keep playing to see the shot. Slate's waiting for our report."

"Okay, we're close. Back up a few frames and play it in slow motion," Carter said.

As the video played, the python's mouth opened, as if hissing—the teeth and pink mouth highlighted in the facing sun. The red circle tracked the mouth. Across the trail gap, the panther, not higher than an ant mound in the dirt, raised on its front paws and moved forward. The flat back of the panther's head reflected the sun and shadowed the snake's mouth—the red circle shifted from the mouth to the panther's head. They heard Carter's voice slow down and deepen. *"Shoooooot Thhhhhha Bastarrrrd!"*

The bullet entered the back of the head, dead center, and exited through the lower jaw, impacting dirt, inches from the python. The python recoiled like a lawnmower pull rope and slithered off.

Brad disconnected the hard drives, closed the laptop, and picked up his phone.

Carter got another beer and heard Brad's call connect.

"Hello, Slate. Sorry for cutting it close on your Zoom meeting.

"Yes, we completed the second flight.

"Yes, the Zcolt flew better. Most of the bugs are smoothed out.

"The farm tractor plowing idea worked well.

"No, we were alone. It's a beautiful afternoon.

"Yes, we checked the bore sight on the weapon against the computed impact red circle. It's dead on the money.

"Anything else? Well, there is one other thing. We got a false-positive firing solution—an unprompted track shift.

"Carter, yes, he's right here. Speakerphone? Sure."

With his beer half gone, Carter set the bottle down quietly and straightened up.

Slate addressed Carter. "Carter, since it's your weapon system, what is an unprompted track shift?"

Carter replied, "I think Brad is trying to say that the Zcolt mistook a Florida panther for a python."

There was a long pause as if the call dropped. Brad stared at Carter, shrugged, and waited.

"Are you fricking shitting me? You shot a fricking panther! What the holy F were you two doing out there? Do you think this is a fricking safari? Are you shitting me?"

Brad tried to put a positive spin on it. "We have solid data, Boss. It's clear what happened—a freak accident."

"Is it hurt?" she asked.

"No, it's dead. The panther and a big python were nose-to-nose, but the grass was blowing and lots of shadows. We didn't see the panther. It moved and the computer shifted lock."

"This is the end of the project, and I will lose my university position. Shooting a panther is a federal and criminal offense."

Silence followed. Slate inhaled deeply and let out long sighs. Brad and Carter looked at each other, listening to each breath. Carter pointed to the time on his phone, 3:55.

"Did anyone hear the shot?" she asked.

"No, we were half a mile away and only heard a muffled bump," Brad said.

"Where's the data?"

"On two hard drives sitting next to me."

"Was Jake there?"

"No, he's still in Everglades City."

"Okay, be in my office in the morning at ten with those drives." She hung up.

* * *

Five minutes before the Zoom call, compact out, Slate looked in the mirror.

You'd better get your shit together pronto, girl. Those idiot kids shot a fricking panther! Damn.

Her right hand fluffed her hair, powdered her cheeks, and glossed her lips. She pulled the hidden zipper of her Ann Taylor cream chiffon blouse down an inch and plumped up her breasts.

"I'll give him something to take his mind off armed drones and wild animals," she said to herself.

She put in eye drops, forced a pleasant smile, and clicked the Zoom link. The screen displayed the Florida State seal, captioned "Office of the Governor" in gold Algerian script. It dissolved to reveal a smiling Governor Prescott at his desk.

"Happy, happy Friday, Slate. How are you?"

"I'm good. So glad it's Friday."

"Me too. I just heard from my media office. We fell on the right side of the Banana dog story. The public has had a belly full of pythons. Momentum is on our side."

"Good. You played it well," she said without enthusiasm.

"That one could have ended badly," he said.

He paused, then asked, "Is something bothering you?"

"I'm sorry. I'm excited, of course. We'll need full sails and a tailwind when the public gets wind of our high-tech solution, no pun intended."

"Oh, that's funny," he said.

"So, remember we talked about the odds of a TV crew filming that lady's poor dog?"

"Yeah, 100 percent," he laughed.

"Well, what do you think the odds are that Brad and Carter accidentally shot a Florida panther with the Zcolt today?"

Surprised, the governor said, "No shit. They did?"

"Yes. The morning flight at the research site tested upgrades to the Zcolt. It performed beyond expectations. The afternoon objective included testing a flight pattern to efficiently search for pythons. That also went well. We needed to check the impact point of the Humboldt rifle bullet against the algorithm's predicted impact point. Since we can't shoot the rifle in Miami, I permitted them to fire one round to collect data."

"So, they decided to shoot a panther," he said.

"No, this is the crazy part. They found a python across a narrow trail from a panther. Except they couldn't see the panther. They think the two were facing off for a fight. It was windy, a lot of grass, and shadows from clouds. The computer shifted to target the panther. A freak accident."

Slate waited for the governor to react, assuming he was mulling over ethical and political implications. She saw him look down, maybe at his phone.

"Anything else?" he asked.

"Yes, had all sensors and Lucy been active, they would have ignored the panther. We can train the algorithm to exclude panthers. It won't happen again."

"Who knows about this?"

"Brad, Carter, and you. All data is on two external hard drives."

The governor held up his cell phone. "Chat says cars and trucks hit and kill twenty panthers each year."

"We didn't run over it, John. We shot it."

"Here's my take. The python could have killed the panther. In any case, it wasn't intentional. They didn't see it. No different than a car hitting a panther."

"Therefore, you recommend what?" she asked.

"It's a training accident at worst, a data point at best. In either case, it's your company's confidential and proprietary information, as is this Zoom call."

Relief replaced the tension on her face.

"Thank you, I really appreciate your confidence and wisdom."

"Wisdom is knowing when to look the other way. We've got bigger problems, and now we know the gun shoots straight." Prescott flashed a big smile.

"Oh, by the way, is that an Ann Taylor? I like that look on you," he added.

"Yes, it is. I'm impressed that you know women's fashion."

"That's a good color for you. Sorry, that's off topic. Can Jake find a panther to train your Lucy?"

"Probably. He wasn't there today," she said, tossing her hair and backing up to show her new two-inch wide red leather belt with a gold buckle around a jet-black pencil skirt.

"You're fine, Cowgirl. We're good. Hey, if the project fails, you can always become a model." He laughed and she blushed.

They said goodbye, and Slate left a voicemail on Jake's phone.

"Jake, call me when you get this, please. I really need to talk to you."

22

Omelet

Ten days after the panther shooting, on Monday, June 11th, Jake met Slate at the research site. He lifted the cover from a cage in the bed of his pickup. A young female panther squinted in bright sunlight and switched between looking at Jake and Slate.

"I saw her on one of my game cameras," he said.

"Wow, she's beautiful. How did you catch her?"

"Panthers love pigs. My friend, who hunts pigs at night with dogs, caught a small male. I tied it inside a camouflaged cage trap. The front door drops when the panther enters and hits a tripwire."

"How clever of you, Jake. I've never seen a panther."

He winked at her. "I've learned a trick or two over the years."

"Seeing her this close is amazing. She doesn't seem afraid."

"We get along fine. She loves kitty treats and has a belly full of pork."

"I swear, Jake Calhoun, there's not much you can't do."

He seemed surprised by the compliment and unsure how to respond.

"I remember how upset you were when they shot the panther. I got lucky finding one for you. Your project will give panthers a chance to recover when their food supply of native animals returns. Pythons and panthers don't usually hunt each other, so the python and panther they found must have been very hungry."

Something stirred inside a rectangular bin behind the panther.

"What's in there?"

Jake lifted the bin onto the tailgate and raised the lid two inches.

Slate looked in and backed away. "Oh, it's a python."

119

"I found her lying on a nest. The nest with forty eggs is in the other bin."

"Oh, wow, just what I need for the algorithm," she said. "Thank you so much."

"You're welcome."

"The more data we feed Lucy, the better she gets along with my confidence. The quality and quantity of data limit us. Someday, we may have sensors that detect python's unique scent molecules and select by sex to target females. But for now, we use what we have."

"You're one smart cookie, Sarah Warner."

"We make a good team, Cowboy."

He gave her a high five. "Yes, we do. I named the panther Sadie. Want to help me carry her cage to the observation pen?"

"Sure, does she have food?"

"Yes, hamburger patties and a water dish for her, and I brought frozen pizza for our lunch."

"Perfect, pizza-in-a-box."

They put Sadie in the small enclosure. Removing the cover from the bin with the eggs, Jake picked one up. Covering the palm of his hand, he pushed a finger into the soft, leathery shell.

"It's about a month old, with another month before it hatches."

Slate touched the opaque white membrane.

"I had no idea they were this big."

"At birth, they're almost two feet long and ready to hunt. Want to see this one?"

She wrinkled her nose and shook her head. He laughed.

"Well, you need to see what you're up against."

Holding the egg in his left palm, he opened the scissors on his multi-tool knife and snipped an opening in the top. Warm liquid drained between his fingers. Slate backed up a step, a hand over her mouth.

Jake opened the shell with the scissors. Coiled, the baby had a distinct head and body.

"Oh no. Its tongue came out." Slate grimaced.

Jake picked it up by the head, and the four-inch-long body unwound.

"Hard to believe, huh? Thirty days from nothing to this," he said.

She nodded, then shuddered. Jake tossed it underhanded into the brush and washed his hands. They placed the mother python on her nest in a shaded cage.

Brad arrived around one o'clock. In the control trailer, he collected data from sensors while Jake coaxed Sadie around the habitat areas in the pen.

Slate, in the RV, prepared the algorithm to accept data from the panther and python nest. Her Apple watch pinged, a reminder of her Zoom with Brent Howard. They discussed preparations for the critical full system demonstration for the task force in three weeks. Slate projected genuine confidence and enthusiasm. She told him about training the algorithm to find python nests.

Brad and Jake finished up around four-thirty and went to the RV to update Slate.

"We're good to go, Boss," Brad said. "The data files are in two folders named Sadie and Omelet."

"Hilarious, Game Boy. I can guess who came up with Omelet," she said, looking at Jake.

Jake laughed. "I thought about Poached, but anyway, you can rename the file if you like."

"It's good data in sun and shade, with thermal being the best. We don't need a nighttime session," Brad said, looking at the leftover pizza. Slate zapped two slices for him before he left for Miami.

"Have time for a beer?" Slate asked Jake.

"Yes, a quick one. I want to drop Sadie off where I found her."

"Thanks again, Jake, for finding the panther. I feel much better. What about the eggs?"

"Oh, they're going in the canal across from the turnoff. Fish and river otters think they're caviar. The mother goes into the large enclosure."

"What are you doing tomorrow, Jake?"

"I'm available if you need me. Otherwise, I'm fabricating an aluminum T-top for a center console charter boat."

"That sounds complicated," she said.

"Welding aluminum is tricky, and customers are picky, but the money is good."

"Do you have any dinner plans tomorrow?"

"Well, there's the diner, and there's Captain Jack's," he laughed.

"So, there you have it. I'm preparing you dinner here in the RV tomorrow," she said.

"Wow, what brought that on?"

"I want to repay you for all the meals you've made. And, not being a cook, I want to try it for fun."

"Fair enough. Have anything in mind?" he asked with a quizzical smile.

She looked at her index card. "I'm thinking of braised pork tenderloin, broccoli salad with candied walnuts, roasted Parmesan potato fingers, butternut squash casserole, roasted garlic cauliflower, buttered naan bread, and homemade bread pudding."

Jake took a step back. "I'm impressed, Chef Warner." He tipped his bottle to her and clinked the tops.

"Then it's a date. I'm so excited. I'll have the entire afternoon to prepare, but don't expect too much," she said, smiling shyly like a schoolgirl, dimples and all.

Jake smiled. "What time and what can I bring?"

"Happy hour at five-thirty and come alone," she laughed.

23

Night Moves

She listened to Bob Seger on her playlist while driving to the grocery store. Still humming to "Night Moves," Slate wheeled the shopping cart, collecting items for each dish on the menu.

Back at her condo, she organized ingredients according to each recipe listed on her laptop.

Opening the butternut squash proved the most challenging. Pulling the cleaver in to split it, the blade slipped and almost stabbed her in the stomach. She removed the seeds and baked the halves for fifty minutes, then struggled with different utensils to remove the pulp and mash it in a bowl. Stirring in water, cinnamon, butter, maple syrup, pecan pieces, and a dash of cayenne, she poured the mixture into a dish and covered it with tin foil to bake at the RV.

With food packed in three coolers, Slate pulled into the research site at two o'clock. She measured ingredients for each dish in groups across the counter. Following her timeline spreadsheet, by five o'clock, the tenderloin was seared, rolled in herbs, wrapped in foil, and ready for the oven. She had mixed the broccoli salad, roasted garlic cloves for the cauliflower, and added olive oil and herbs to the Parmesan potato baking dish.

So far, so good, she was nervous in an excited kind of way. Having little experience with anything more complicated than boiling spaghetti and zapping sauce from a jar, she knew Jake would understand and be nice no matter how it turned out. It felt good to be outside of her comfort zone. Setting up a date of sorts with Jake just happened. She had surprised herself, and Jake seemed somewhere between amused and curious. Alone in the Everglades in a camper at night with a man who hunts wild animals for a living flashed through her mind, along with titles of horror movies.

There were men in her past, but Slate, aware of her attractiveness, kept to major highways with centerline dividers and guard rails. There was a spate of encounters during her second-semester freshman year, as well as parties after the restaurant closed at her summer waitress job. That era ended when her period arrived a week late that summer. She learned that sex was the easy part. Relationships were the problem. Engaged once in graduate school, moving into his apartment revealed his needy, controlling side, something her brother had warned her about. Children were never seriously considered. Slate valued her independence and a close circle of friends.

She waited, looking out the kitchen window, wondering how she ended up in an RV at the end of a dirt road, making a gourmet meal for a snake wrangler. She giggled, checked her watch, and realized she needed to get dressed.

She primped in the bathroom mirror, added a hint of smoky blue eyeshadow and alluring pink lipstick, then styled her golden hair in pigtails. She tied the front of the white, light-blue plaid shirt in a knot at her midriff. Tight-fitting designer jeans buttoned below her exposed navel. Embroidered tropical flowers and Roseate Spoonbill wading birds decorated the back pockets. Surprised, she noticed something else reflected in the mirror—happiness. She toasted herself and finished the splash of wine.

She heard his truck roll to a stop on the gravel and filled two glasses with Cabernet Sauvignon. He opened the RV door, and she handed him his glass.

"Thank you. Wow, dinner smells delicious already."

"You're welcome, sir. I've had so much fun doing this. Hope you're hungry."

Giddy, she recalled her younger, carefree days. Not much of a drinker, she felt the wine lighten her thinking.

You'd better slow down, girl, or you'll blow the dinner.

He set his glass on the table. "I came directly from the marine welding shop. Do I have time to shower?"

"Perfect. Dinner is on schedule, you have twenty minutes," she said, setting the table.

Showered and changed, Jake returned in a crisp, fitted shirt with pearl snap buttons tucked into slim jeans. The belt buckle had an ornate silver relief of a fishing trawler. Silver caps tipped the toes of his alligator skin boots.

"Have a seat, Mr. Calhoun. First is your salad."

Using tongs, Slate put chilled broccoli salad on his plate and offered a topping of fresh bacon bits which he gladly accepted. His cologne, a blend of leather, oak, and maybe cedar, excited her senses.

Bent over the oven, checking the tenderloin, she felt his eyes.

"I see you like spoonbills," he said.

"They're my favorite. Such a unique adaptation." She turned to face him and noticed his thick, straw-colored hair had grown over the weeks, now wavier, and combed back.

She thought about his body. *He could model jeans and briefs for Wrangler.*

"Spoonbills were hunted to near extinction for their feathers. They need clear, shallow water to feed. That has become a big problem in Florida," he said.

Slate retrieved warm, buttered naan bread wrapped in a towel from the warming drawer below the oven.

"I love this salad. I absolutely love it. So good."

She beamed with joy, happy that he was pleased.

She checked the pork tenderloin's temperature and set it on the counter to rest.

"I can slice the meat if you like," Jake said.

"Oh, that would be so nice of you."

She prepared their plates with extra portions for him. He finished and helped himself to more tenderloin.

"Want more wine?"

He nodded, and she filled both glasses.

They finished eating and talked about releasing Sadie.

"She took off like a rabbit for twenty yards, then stopped and turned back to look at me. Sad in a way, given that we had connected. I clapped my hands and told her to skedaddle."

Slate asked him for stories about his hometown—the last town in the Everglades on the West Coast—and his crazy adventures as a kid and as an outdoors guide. They laughed at his close calls, quirky clients, and the big tarpon that jumped into his boat. He'd never seen snow, driven with tire chains, or had authentic maple syrup. She told him about skydiving in Ohio from 14,000 feet and packing her own chute. He told her about spearfishing for grouper 100 feet under water.

They teased each other with questions and comments, the wine enhancing their levity. Unstated and understood, they stuck with happy times and shied away from previous relationships, the python project, and politics.

"The dinner was more than I could have hoped for. For a computer genius, you're one hell of a cook."

She smiled shyly, her dimples showing. "Glad you liked it. I'm thrilled that you do."

"You sit tight while I clear the table," Jake said.

She accepted, leaned against the wall with her feet across the bench. Slightly dizzy, she sipped her wine.

"Don't forget, we have dessert," she said, watching the lines of his body at the sink, as he rinsed dishes and loaded the dishwasher.

"Warm bread pudding with vanilla icing," she added.

Next were the pots and pans. His sleeves rolled up, he scrubbed and placed each in the drying rack.

She watched him, his broad shoulders, slim waist, and chiseled buttocks. She saw tanned, muscular arms and wide hands. Another sip of wine. Her mind drifted to desire and to flashes of memories long ago, to lovers past. She inhaled, filling her lungs with his masculinity and cologne. Fuzzy, she wasn't sure if it was the wine or this man standing with his back to her.

Watching the back pockets of his jeans below the wide rawhide belt, she tipped the wine glass, the remaining half sliding down her throat. Setting it down, she shook her head back and forth as the alcohol ricocheted through her brain. Something ignited in her loins.

Jake busied himself, absorbed in the task at hand. His casual unawareness of her thoughts increased her desire. The heat climbed to a boil, pouring over like hot fudge on ice cream. Pondering, her body relaxed and sank into the corner of the bench seat. Savoring her power, her position, her prerogative, she knew what happened next was up to her. Jake cleaned the stubborn butternut squash casserole dish with a nylon scrub pad—the last dish, her final opportunity—passed as each burned-on patch surrendered. Decision time.

Slate inched across the seat unnoticed and then stood unsteadily behind him, her face inches from his neck. His cologne and essence, intoxicating as the wine. Her hands slipped past his waist to grip the edge of the sink. Their bodies touched. Jake did not react, letting her indulge.

She pressed into him, her body conforming to his as her lips found his neck. Heat rising, she exhaled a hot breath, moved her front against his back, and returned her open mouth to his neck.

Jake rested his hands over her hands. Her breathing quickened.

"Are we having dessert?" he asked.

"Yes, you're the dessert," she whispered in his ear.

Slate stepped back, grabbed a belt loop in each hand, and turned him around. Looking into his eyes, she untied the knot in her shirt. Illuminated by the light above the sink, the shirt fell away to reveal breasts in half-cups of a sheer bra. She watched his eyes react with desire. Slate reached over, pulled the shirttails from his jeans, and popped open the snap buttons with one pull. A surge of passion rose at the sight of his sculpted chest and rippled stomach.

He leaned to kiss her, and she wrapped her arms around his neck. He reached his hands to cup her butt under the embroidered pockets. As her feet left the floor, she raised her legs to wrap around his waist. Jake carried her to the bed.

Lines and shadows from a closet light filtered through the slatted doors over their bodies, transforming the room into a dream world of discovery and enchantment. Slate, a feisty feline in the kitchen, became a submissive kitten in the bedroom.

A spirited wind swirled around and jostled the RV, enveloping them like a cocoon. A bright red light atop a tall antenna tower sifted through oak trees above the window curtain and danced like autumn leaves about the room.

Under him, Slate entered another world. Her mind descended, receded, and devolved to an earlier, primal time. No longer of body, she floated in a plasma of curling colors pouring through a distant door. The scream from deep inside her physical body rumbled up against her throat. The tranquil entanglement of her mind accelerated like a rocket ship into the venturi of the narrow doorway. The thrill and ecstasy climaxed as she shot through the doorway at the speed of light. Slowly, she regained her body and became aware that the screams she had heard were hers.

For the next three hours, they indulged as if alone on a spaceship surrounded by galaxies. Later, she might question her motives. Maybe pretend it was spontaneous or blame the wine. Perhaps the transparent bra she rarely wore was an inadvertent wardrobe choice. Of one thing she was certain, she had never been in that place of swirling colors accelerating to a doorway.

They slept. Slate awoke on her side, the morning light illuminating her, with him behind her, his arm wrapped over her stomach. Eyes open, she searched her conscience for regret, guilt, or inadequacy and found none. She smiled. It was the right decision. Jake had confirmed her trust with his consideration, gentleness, and prowess. Thinking about the sex stirred her until a glaring reality shot to the front of her mind. She had seduced and had erotic indulgences with her employee, a fatal error of judgment. Helpless, the question of trust and discretion rested solely with Jake Calhoun.

Jake awoke, gently rolled her to face him, put a finger to her nose, and said, "Good morning, sweet pea. Your hair is a mess."

Slate tried not to think of him as her employee.

"Am I in trouble?" she asked.

"For being a bad girl last night?" he laughed. "Yes, you were very bad."

"No, for seducing and molesting my employee."

"Oh, that. No trouble here. I'm thinking you already considered that in your subconscious and decided you could trust me."

Her face now serious, "I feel bad. I've never done this before."

He touched her nose again.

"You're still cute. You can trust me. I understand corporate civility and sensitivities. I have immense respect for you and what you have done to achieve your successes."

She gave a shy smile and mouthed, "Thank you."

He jumped out of bed. "How about I make us breakfast?"

"Great, I'll be there shortly," Slate replied.

She sat at the kitchen table in panties and a sweatshirt. He served eggs over easy, crispy bacon, and hash browns.

Finished, she reached over and wiped her lips on his napkin. Standing, she held out her hand and led him to the bedroom.

Leaving at ten o'clock, she changed clothes at her condo and arrived in time for a staff meeting in the dean's conference room at one.

24

Bat Shit

Slate had not seen Jake in the week since their sizzling night in the RV. Her team had worked feverishly at the University on software upgrades and fully configuring the Zcolt. Using an A.I. assistant to write and test code, Slate had the productivity of a team of five programmers.

Slate, Carter, and Brad spent the weekend in the control trailer at the research site, configuring monitors and communication links. Confident that the systems were ready, the three departed the University on Monday morning for the research site. Slate followed Brad's Tundra, which towed the Zcolt trailer.

Jake had soda and snacks prepared in the RV when they pulled in at ten o'clock for the pre-briefing.

Slate stood at the sink facing the three who sat at the table.

"Okay, guys, to review, we each have master checklists broken down by flight phase and associated action steps for each position. Jake will help Carter preflight, launch, and recover the Zcolt. After launch, Jake, you sit behind Brad and monitor video displays looking for animals. Carter has mounted three GoPro video recorders to the Zcolt. Before takeoff, Carter will launch his small camera drone to check that the area is clear. After takeoff, he will chase the Zcolt with his drone and record video."

The four studied their checklists and took notes. Since killing the panther, Brad and Carter were all business. The pre-mission briefing likely reminded Brad of Army Ranger briefings, Carter of Formula One pre-race meetings, and Jake of football skull sessions.

"Jake has tied a live python to a wooden stake a quarter mile south of us. Brad, it's marked on the GPS map, and you will fly there first.

130

"Any questions so far?"

Slate continued. "Today is a full system test, the last before the live evaluation for the task force in fifteen days. We know Brad can fly the drone and shoot pythons. Today is Lucy's turn to fly, navigate, and find pythons. She performs well on the simulator in the lab. That's theory. Today is reality. I'll bring her online after takeoff. Her sole purpose is finding pythons."

A cell phone rang. Carter fidgeted in his pocket, too late to mute the message. They all heard the voicemail. "Hi, this is Taylor. Hey, can we slip our go-kart race date tonight to six-thirty? Can't wait to kick your butt. See you this afternoon. Bye."

Glances and raised eyebrows flashed between everyone except Carter.

"Sorry. I forgot to, ah, silence it," he said.

Slate let it go. "As I was saying, Brad will fly and find Jake's snake. We'll check the sensors from various heights and distances to find the sweet spot using Lucy's algorithm. I've added two new features. When she finds a python, a yellow border appears around the python image on the composite and weapons screens, and she announces "python" twice over the speaker—the same repeats each time she finds one.

"Questions? Okay, Brad, what are we doing?"

"I take off, fly to Jake's snake, and find the optimum altitude and speed for Lucy. She outlines pythons in yellow on our screens and announces each one over the speaker."

Jake interrupted. "For the record, it's not my python. It's our python, or more accurately, the FWC's python."

Everyone laughed.

"Well," Slate added. "It's going to be a dead python. Carter, please load one round in the Humboldt."

"Now you're talking," Carter said.

"Yes, Brad, next, you lock on and track the python on your weapons screen. If everything works, we back away, and I'll transfer control to Lucy for auto-flight, python acquisition, and tracking. If she finds the python, announces it, and there is a solid red tracking circle around it, Brad, you can fire the Humboldt. Got it?"

Brad raised his thumb, followed by the others.

"If all goes well, we've programmed a ten-acre section on the map near the pond. Lucy will fly the rows up and back like a tractor at five miles per hour, or four minutes per round trip. We're testing her for navigation and finding pythons. She's programmed to stop, hover, track, and announce when she finds one.

"That's it. We'll be finished in plenty of time for Carter's date." Slate winked at him.

Everyone laughed, Carter less than the others.

"How about a pee break?" Carter asked.

He used the restroom, then went to set up the Zcolt and his small drone. Brad went into the bathroom, leaving Slate and Jake at the table. They smiled at each other. She slipped off her sandal, put her toes between the legs of his jeans, and nudged. His eyes got big. She laughed. He reached down and twisted her little toe.

"Ouch," she whispered.

Slate stood when the bathroom door opened. "What's up with boys and their tiny-weeny bladders, Brad?"

Caught off guard, Brad stuttered, "Ah, ah, good question, I haven't given that a lot of thought, Professor." They all laughed.

* * *

In the control trailer, Slate adjusted the lumbar support on her high-back gaming chair, the same model Brad used when playing Fortnite video game tournaments for cash in his spare time. Each workstation had an array of monitors arranged in a partial arc.

Following checklists, they powered up electronics—each contributing volume and pitch to the growing buzz, whirl, and hum that filled the room. The air vibrated with charged particles and electromagnetic energy. Cooling fans swirled air in eddies and crosscurrents. Computers emitted beeps, squeaks, and tones in response to keyboard commands. A window behind them overlooked the Zcolt.

Outside, Carter and Jake lowered the sides of the trailer to create a launch platform. They extended the support skids, raising the Zcolt enough to attach the Humboldt gimbal and weapon. Sensor probes unfolded into place. A power cable brought the vehicle's control panel to life, and Carter ran the before-flight checklist to test circuits and continuity.

A light breeze from the east under clear skies made for perfect flying. Carter launched his small drone and climbed to four hundred feet. He surveyed the area looking for drones and people. After landing, he replaced the drone battery and followed Jake into the command center. They took chairs and sat on a raised area beneath the window behind Slate and Brad.

On the console, behind Slate's two keyboards was an array of eight monitors. On the left, a vertical stack of small screens displayed raw data from the four sensors—optical, thermal, motion, and infrared.

The upper-left screen of four large monitors was split to display waypoints and Zcolt's position on a GPS map. The other half of the split screen showed video from a steerable camera mounted on the drone.

The lower left monitor displayed Lucy's computer composite image, her output from combining data from the four sensors.

In the upper right, a digital rain screen displayed real-time text, colors, and motion to represent processing inside the software programs. Flight control information was displayed in green, while Lucy's algorithm was blue and yellow.

Slate's final monitor, located in the lower right corner, displayed the rifle scope view through the Humboldt scope in optical, thermal, and zoom modes.

"How's it going, Game Boy? I'm almost finished with my checks," she said.

"Almost ready." Brad adjusted his chair for the fourth time, a nervous habit. He loosened up his fingers on the keyboard and adjusted the brightness of three monitors that mirrored Slate's screens, which displayed a moving map, a steerable drone camera, and a rifle scope view.

"Okay, Carter, disconnect the power cord, pull the safety pins, turn on the GoPro cameras, and get your little drone airborne," she said. He hurried out of the trailer to the Zcolt.

"Jake, look out the window and tell me when he's clear. Then pull your chair down next to Brad and help look for pythons."

Slate watched the rain screen; the left side displayed green colored code, while the right side had Lucy's code in blue. She typed commands, and symbols appeared like on a spectrum analyzer in a music studio.

"Carter is clear," Jake called out.

"Ok, it's showtime, boys. Brad, take off and hover over the slough."

The Zcolt's rotors growled like shop fans under load. The drone eased off the pad like a honeybee, then tilted forward toward the slough. Slate and Brad scanned displays for abnormalities. Images appeared on the four sensor screens. Carter's drone followed fifty feet behind the Zcolt.

"I'm bringing Lucy online in standby mode," she said. Confused and erratic, blue code poured onto the right half of the rain screen. Pixels populated Lucy's composite screen like static on an old television.

"Settle down, Lucy. It's just like the simulator.

"Brad, check out the new cursor on your weapons scope screen."

Slate had added an operator-controlled cursor to the weapons computer for locking onto targets within fifteen degrees of the drone's centerline. Brad could move the cursor with his mouse to select targets without pointing the drone at them. The Humboldt rifle slewed to align the crosshair under the cursor.

Brad moved the square yellow designator cursor symbol on the screen to the right of the centerline over a turtle on a tree trunk. A dashed red circle appeared, then turned solid red.

"It works. It's tracking a turtle," he said.

"Carter, did the Humboldt rifle move to the right?" Slate asked.

He flew his drone forward ten feet behind the Zcolt. "Yes, it's aiming right and pointing down at the turtle."

Back at her screens, Slate analyzed the bootup progress on the rain and composite screens.

"Much better, Lucy. Are you going to be a good girl today?"

Slate typed more commands. Yellow text in all caps printed across the rain screen, and Lucy announced over the speaker, "Lucy Is Ready To Party."

"Okay, Game Boy, fly us to Jake's snake," she said.

Brad's fingers played the keyboard like a ragtime piano. The Zcolt bolted straight up to 100 feet. He slid the mouse to the left. It pivoted ninety degrees, then shot forward at full speed. Over a sawgrass island, he released the controls, and it braked hard to a full stop hover.

Carter's drone continued forward at high speed. He pulled up a few feet short of impact and shot out in front.

"Game Boy, Game Boy. I need some warning back here, Dude," Carter, flying the drone from his pickup truck, said over the walkie-talkie.

"Drone Boy, don't fly at my altitude, over," Brad replied.

"This is Momma Bear. Both of you, knock off the shit," Slate said, making up her nickname.

"Carter, fly above us and look forward and down," she told him.

Next, Slate told Brad, "I have control of Zcolt."

Using her keyboard, she descended to forty feet and centered a sabal palm under the X on the drone camera screen. One by one, she evaluated the palm in each sensor screen.

"Looks good. Hitch up your britches, guys."

She typed merge commands on Lucy's keyboard. Fresh lines of blue code poured down the rain screen as the algorithm processed raw data. Slate reminded herself that Lucy wasn't human and didn't have emotions. Still, at times, her code creations evoked the enthusiasm, humor, and recalcitrance of an eight-year-old.

The vertical line dividing green and blue code on the screen disappeared. Blue merged with green, like the confluence of rivers having different colors. Patterns evolved—swirls, eddies, waves, and cascades. Completed, the waters flattened and found order. A yellow horizontal line appeared, followed by text bracketed by two python emojis. Lucy had typed, "Let the Party Begin, Momma Bear."

Slate stared at the yellow text, "Momma Bear."

I just made that name up five minutes ago. Did she hack the voice prompt feed, or is she collaborating with my A.I. coding assistant?

"Everything okay, Boss?" Brad asked.

"Oh, yes, sorry. Let's check the composite screen for Lucy's rendition of the palm."

No longer black-and-white static, the composite picture was more ghostlike, not finite or solid, but fluid. The palm went in and out of focus, the fronds pixelating and jittering.

"Is there a problem?" Jake asked.

"Oh, no. There's no problem at all. It's perfect," she responded.

Slate panned the drone camera to the left to follow a canal meandering through a wetland of cypress trees, where dozens of white egrets perched on several trees.

Images graduated from thermal grays to greens for trees and gauzy tans for marsh grass. Indistinct white dabs were the egrets. At the bottom of the screen, status boxes displayed the relative weights each sensor contributed to the composite image.

With the Zcolt in hover, the rain screen displayed lines of blue and green code that pulsated like a jet boat at idle. Slate moved the drone forward and flew down the canal, accelerating. The excited colors cascaded like white-water rapids, and the composite image lit up like the neural storm on a brain scan.

"Perfect. Okay, come onto the controls, Game Boy, and fly us to Jake's snake."

Brad peeled off hard right, climbed, banked over, and sliced down in an arc, heading for the waypoint on the moving map. Carter held back to avoid having a mid-air collision.

Jake watched Brad's fingers, then looked across at Slate, whose hands gripped both armrests. She glanced back at him and said, "I don't like acrobatics—it makes me airsick. He's the drone version of a fighter pilot."

Brad's left hand hovered above the keyboard. Fingers pecking like hungry chickens, the cadence oscillated between staccatos, like a high-speed printer, and short pauses. The mouse in his right hand swept over the pad like a paintbrush on canvas, from delicate and detailed to bold and exaggerated.

Higher terrain, less grass, and more trees appeared in the distance on the wide-angle screen.

"Is that your hammock up ahead?" Brad asked Jake.

"There's a giant oak on the northwest corner," Jake replied. "The ground slopes down toward us from the tree. You're on a good track."

Brad zoomed the camera. "I think this is your tree." He pointed at the screen.

"Yes, okay. There's a natural break in the grass and a trail from the tree, down to the pond in the foreground. The pond is surrounded by marsh grass. The python is on the sandy trail halfway from the pond to the tree."

Brad leveled off at twenty feet and slowed to four miles per hour.

"I see the pond 500 yards, twelve o'clock," Brad said.

Slate watched the sensor images, comparing how each depicted the same objects. The pond, about a hundred yards wide, had aquatic pickerelweed covering one-quarter of it along the edges. Open black water held the center.

"I love how each sensor paints a different picture. I'm not an artist, but I recognize a beautiful composition," Slate said.

The Zcolt edged over the pond. The gap in the grass on the other side, twenty feet wide, displayed on each sensor screen. The composite image was a grainy, out-of-focus version of the thermal screen. Brad paused in a hover, zoomed in, and inched the camera up the trail.

Jake leaned over to see the drone camera screen. "I see the stake. See a red flag on top of a 4x4 pole in the middle of the path? There's the yellow cargo strap. There it is. Follow the yellow strap to the right. It's at the edge of the trail. The lower half is in the water, lying along the grass edge," Jake said.

A late morning sun highlighted the path and the snake.

"Python, python" appeared in yellow on the rain screen. A yellow border appeared around the python image on the composite and weapon screens. A female voice with a British accent announced over the speaker, "Python, python."

"Lucy's found Jake's python," Slate said, cross-checking images on the sensor screens. "Do you see it, Brad? Put the cursor on it."

Brad moved the cursor over the python on the weapons screen and checked for a red-dashed circle.

"I have a solid lock-on," he told Slate.

"Good, back the Zcolt up slowly, to see when the track breaks lock."

Carter flew his drone above and slightly behind the Zcolt, watching the show. The Zcolt moved back to the near edge of the pond, about a hundred yards from the snake. The track held steady.

"Good. Do you think the Humboldt could hit it from there?" she asked Brad.

"Probably. The lighting, wind, and profile are good."

"How many rounds did you load, Carter?" she radioed over the walkie-talkie.

"Only one, like you said."

"Okay, move forward halfway across the pond."

"Holy shit!" Carter interrupted over the walkie-talkie. "Hey, there's a fricking alligator!"

Emerging from the pickerelweed beds thirty yards from the snake on the left, a ten-foot alligator glided into open water toward the python. Only its eyes and nose above the surface, the Zcolt's look-down angle saw the ten feet that was under water.

"Break the lock on the python," Slate told Brad. "The gator's going for the snake."

Slate found the gator on the sensors and waited for Lucy to process it.

"Okay, Lucy. What do you think? Is it a python?"

The yellow outline on the python remained solid. Lucy had ignored the alligator.

"Okay, Game Boy. Lock up the python again and move a little closer."

The snake jerked as the gator closed the gap. Jake had wrapped the cargo strap around the python's body several times behind the head and cinched it with cable ties. The snake pulled its tail and lower body out of the water. The head jumped up, jerked against the strap, then shot across the trail to the left side. It was now partially in the shade. Slate checked the sensors, the composite screen, and the red circle.

"The snake's going bat-shit," Brad said, watching it in the weapons screen.

Shadows confused some sensors, but most were unaffected. The motion sensor caught all the action. Trained to recognize python movement, Lucy stuck with her decision. When a python was identified, a small block in the upper-right corner of the composite displayed a confidence score. Before the python moved, the score was 83; now it was 94.

"Is the dashed red circle on the head?" she asked.

"Yes."

The gator was ten feet away and closing.

"Lock-on," she said.

"Good lock, tracking," Brad said.

"Gator's out of the water. Take the shot," Slate said.

They saw the bullet impact on their screens before they heard a muffled crack at the research site. Carter zoomed in his drone's camera from above the Zcolt.

"Bullseye, a solid kill!" Carter called over the walkie-talkie. The python collapsed like a wet noodle. They cheered and traded high-fives in the control trailer.

The alligator froze when the rifle fired.

"The gator's going for the python," Carter radioed.

Brad zoomed the Zcolt camera in time to see the alligator sprint up the bank on four powerful legs and twist its open mouth around and down on the dead snake. Slashing back and forth, pulling, the python snapped tight like a rope against the cargo strap. The neck came loose, and the gator began to eat it. The snake slid tail-first down the gator's throat, chomp by chomp.

"Holy shit, I see a 'Savages of the wild' YouTube video here," Carter radioed.

"Don't even think about it," Slate replied.

"Good job, everyone, and that includes Lucy, of course. We've got ourselves a snake-killing machine. There are thirty minutes of battery left. Let's see if she can navigate and find pythons at the same time."

Brad flew to the ten-acre digital grid marked on the moving map. The thirty-foot-wide rows, alternating shades of light green and brown, became distinct, and Brad stopped. Slate checked systems and prepared Lucy to fly the programmed route over the rows as Brad had done the day they shot the panther.

Carter radioed from his pickup parked only a hundred feet from the control trailer. "I'm out of battery, guys, coming back."

"Roger that. Do a security sweep of the area on the way," Slate said.

"Okay, guys. I think we're ready. I've set the speed at fifteen miles per hour. Let's see if she can keep up with the data load and still find pythons."

Slate entered the commands. Yellow text appeared on the rain screen, "Buckle Up, Momma Bear. Auto-flight."

Brad and Slate looked at each other, eyebrows raised. Moving forward to fly down the first row, Lucy's digital world, displayed on the rain and composite screens, became dizzy with motion and activity.

Slate's human view, as seen through the Zcolt camera, was an endless mosaic of wild habitat.

The Zcolt finished the first row, turned around, skipped two rows, and returned on the fourth row. Halfway back, the Zcolt stopped, and over the speaker, in a British accent, Lucy announced, "Python, python."

The pixilated image of the python on the composite screen was outlined in yellow. Brad checked the weapons screen.

"I see one sunning on a mudbank." The cursor, already over the python, Brad selected 'track' and a solid red circle appeared.

"Good job, Lucy," Slate said.

"Brad, I'm adding target lock-on and track to Lucy's program before the task force evaluation."

Carter came into the control trailer. Slate turned and gave him a thumbs-up.

"Nice job flying chase. We're almost finished. Hey, can you grab me a Diet Coke?" Slate asked.

Passing the window to the under-counter fridge, he saw their car pull up.

"Momma Bear, Taylor, and Cindy are here."

"Knock off the Momma Bear crap, Drone Boy. Have them come in."

Slate had invited them for a picnic after the test flight.

The two got out of Taylor's canary yellow Corolla. Cindy waved to Carter in the window and he motioned for them to come in. Taylor raised a curved pinky finger to Carter, and he returned one.

Taylor and Cindy adjusted their eyes to the dim ambient blue light and adjusted their ears to the whirling hum, beeps, and clicks. They took seats against the wall next to Carter. He held Taylor's hand between the chairs in the dim light.

"Okay, guys," Slate called over her shoulder. "Lucy is flying the Zcolt and finding pythons. We're almost finished. Jake has made more of his famous pulled pork and coleslaw, and he's going to grill burgers."

Auto-flight resumed. Lucy, on row number eight, stopped to announce another python. Brad found it on the weapons screen.

"Holy smokes, it's on a nest of eggs," Brad said.

Slate looked past Brad to Jake, "Looks like she remembered your nest."

"She's a smart girl," Jake said.

"Okay, battery is twenty percent. Lucy, do you want to fly us back home?"

Slate half expected to hear Lucy answer. She entered the commands on the keyboard.

Everyone in good cheer, the test was a complete success.

* * *

The picnic almost ready, Slate excused herself to the RV for a Zoom update with the governor.

Her laptop was on the kitchen counter by the sink. Slate initiated the call thirty minutes before the scheduled Zoom time, hoping to catch him and get back to the picnic.

Waiting, she looked out the window and watched Jake at the grill. Leaning against the sink, her mind flashed back. Only a week ago, it seemed like a month or more, she had Jake pinned against the sink. Drifting further, she remembered the rush, the acceleration, and the passing through a mental doorway of unimaginable ecstasy. That thought connected to an eerie symmetry. One that made her shudder. Today, she had seen a visual representation of that place in her mind. On the rain screen, Lucy's world of beautiful chaos was drawn in colors and patterns that pulsated, crescendoed, and collapsed like emotions. Emotions that Slate recognized but could not explain.

The laptop chimed, and Governor Prescott, sitting behind his desk, appeared. Slate, lost in thought, was staring out the window.

"Hi, I'm here. Can you see me?" Prescott asked.

His voice jolted her like a splash of ice water. She shook her head, blinked, and pulled together a big smile.

"Oh, hi, John. I wasn't sure you would be available."

The governor, in an expensive suit, looked handsome and camera-ready.

"I just finished another media interview, on the status of Florida, after my first six months in office, this one by ABC. No big problems. The poll numbers are holding, thanks to our economy and the budget surplus. They pressed me on affordable housing, red tide on the west coast, the latest phosphate mining sinkhole, and other environmental catastrophes."

"Wow, that's a boatload. You look very nice in your suit, if that makes you feel any better."

"Ah, thanks. From a political standpoint, we're good. At least we're not California," he laughed. "How was your big test today?"

She saw the thumbnail picture of herself in the corner of the screen and brushed disheveled hair from her face with both hands. Her eyes looked as tired as she felt.

"Sorry, I look a fright. We had a great day, though. The Zcolt flies like a fighter jet. Lucy flew by herself, navigated, and found two pythons. One was on a nest. Oh, we also shot a python."

"That's great news. Sounds like you're ready to go for the July 3rd demonstration."

"Definitely," she said, thinking his characterization of a demonstration, was too kind. Both knew the demonstration was more like a jury deliberation in a murder trial.

The governor referred to his notes.

"Most of the task force and a few others will be in the situation room. Can you send someone to answer questions?"

"Sure, how about Jake? We're installing a camera in the control trailer to live-stream video and audio of our consoles and screens. We'll see your situation room on a monitor in our room, but we won't hear your audio."

"That's fine. We can talk by phone. There's one other thing, Slate."

Distracted again, Slate watched as Carter and Taylor went into the work trailer and closed the door. At the picnic table, Brad had his laptop open next to Cindy. It looked like a Fortnite game, and Cindy was cheering him on.

"Slate, you look busy," Prescott said.

"Oh, sorry, my team is waiting for me at the picnic table."

"I'll let you go. But a heads-up. There's a protest rally on Friday at the FWC regional office in West Palm Beach. A political action committee, True North Patriots, is behind it."

"Sounds like trouble," she said.

"Not my idea. I'm sending the lieutenant governor. The Republicans are getting antsy. They sense that blame is shifting on the python issue. I'm beginning to understand why both sides have ignored the python crisis. It's a powder keg."

"That was before pythons killed eight kids, John."

"Agreed. Anyway, the PAC has a special operations section that cooks up and shapes events."

"Aren't they called plumbers?" she asked.

"You're funny, Cowgirl. I thought you were too young to know that word," he laughed.

"Well, they're not called electricians, are they, John?"

"I'm not going to argue with you on this, Professor. Let's just say it's out of my hands." They laughed, enjoying the teasing.

Slate caught sight of Jake waving and pointing to a spot next to him at the table.

"Let me finish so you can get back. The rally is an FWC ambush. You may remember that I fired the West Palm Beach director early on. I appointed his replacement a few weeks ago, a deputy director I transferred from the panhandle. He wouldn't know a python from a fence post. I'm not telling him about the protest rally until Thursday afternoon."

"Sounds dicey."

"We can't tip off the opposition. They want us to fail—more points for them. The wetlands around their own FWC office is infested with pythons. You can't make this stuff up. Anyway, press coverage begins at two o'clock."

Slate had stepped back from the laptop to show him her dark blue company flight suit. She put on aviator sunglasses and a white baseball cap with the ZKuul Solutions patch.

Prescott stopped talking and took her in. She watched his face, satisfied that he liked what he saw. She adjusted her sunglasses and smiled at his bright eyes.

"Two o'clock on Friday. I'll be sure not to be there," she laughed.

"Good, me neither," he smiled. "I like your flight suit. Looks good. Real good."

They said goodbye, and she came down the RV steps as Carter and Taylor emerged from the work trailer. Jake moved over, and Slate slid in next to him on the bench.

25

Off Script

Harry Sullivan, a gum chewer nicknamed Wrench, smacked the first word of each transmission into his wrist mic. Dano turned the volume down on his earbuds. Wrench, in a dirty white van parked between palmettos, watched the intersection of a dirt lane and Northlake Boulevard, an east-west highway out of West Palm Beach. The dirt lane ended a quarter mile north at the J.W. Corbett Wildlife Management Area and the headquarters of the Florida Wildlife Commission, South Region.

A typical Friday afternoon, FWC staff sauntered about, looking forward to a sunny weekend and a party at three for Maggie, who was retiring after thirty-three years of faithful service.

Far from being relaxed, Anthony Newman, Regional FWC director for three weeks, wrestled with the fifth revision of his speech. He learned of the 'rally' the previous afternoon on a confidential phone call from Governor Prescott. Using notes from the call, he fussed around at home that evening, went to bed, couldn't sleep, and was in his office at six-thirty. Blinds closed, he paced back and forth in his T-shirt, not wanting to sweat up his light blue dress shirt.

* * *

Wrench watched his two greeters, tall, trim, identical twins in their early twenties. He'd met the girls working the second shift at a Miami sports bar. They had the look he wanted, "stacked and jacked." Black hot pants, long black hair in ponytails, and Barbie-doll makeup—they could pass for volleyball players or strippers. On the front of their black V-neck T-shirts was a red circle and a line through the angry head of a python. Below, the caption read, "FWC, Stop Talking, Start Killing."

Operating under a blue pop-up awning, the twins greeted vehicles as they turned onto the dirt lane. Bending over to look into car windows, many drivers failed to notice their bright smiles.

"Hi. Are you here for the rally? Want some free stuff?"

They passed out T-shirts, signs on sticks, keychains, and bumper stickers—Pythons, Go Back to Burma; A Python Free Florida; Everglades Is No Place for Pythons; WTF FWC; People before Pythons; and Animal Rights My Ass, What About Us Mammals?

Wrench radioed Dano, his boss, stationed at the other end of the lane. "Dano, traffic is backing up on Northlake at the turnoff. And Tim Parker and his wife are coming your way."

"Roger that, if the cops show up, move your girls and the awning to this end of the lane. The parking lot is filling up. Cars can park in the grass along the lane. I'll catch Mr. Parker and see if he's all set."

Parker, father of a deceased scout, agreed to give a speech prepared by the governor's media office.

The backup growing, Wrench told the twins to greet every other car and every pickup truck. Two shiny black Suburbans turned in.

"The Lieutenant Governor is headed your way," Wrench radioed.

Dano replied, "Gotcha. The stage and chairs are up, and the sound is good. Shit, I forgot to get a standby ambulance."

"No worries, Draino. I got you covered on the ambulance."

"Don't call me Draino, Weakdick."

The PAC's cyber team monitored groups for pro-python sentiment—animal rights, biodiversity, and environmentalists. The net was quiet, but the team was all too aware that pop-up rallies attracted kooks, camo-decked vigilantes, and piggybacking agitators promoting oddball causes.

Dano's field team kept a low profile, wore street clothes, and avoided the media.

Wrench radioed. "Channel 12's coming at you with a satellite truck. Holy shit, there's Ashley in a purple Corvette with the top down. You guessed it, Draino, she's wearing a low-cut banana-yellow tube top."

"Put your binoculars down, Weakdick. I knew she was coming. Carrie tipped her off."

By one-thirty, vehicles were parked on the grass along the lane and extended east on the shoulder of Northlake. The twins were out of goodies and joined the rally in the VIP area, handing out water bottles and discount drink coupons for their sports bar.

Agnes, the only employee at the FWC gift shop, usually sat behind the counter knitting scarves for veterans. By late morning, she marveled at the rush of visitors. Many wore black T-shirts with a mean python staring at her. Grandparents usually bought the five-foot-long stuffed pythons for goofy grandkids. She sold the last one on display and got twenty more from the back. She overheard someone say, "What a crock—teaching kids that pythons are cool."

Amazed at the influx of visitors coming from the parking lot, FWC staffers at first thought they were geriatric day-trippers from The Villages.

"Might be a cruise ship tour out of Lauderdale," a clerk speculated.

That was before a convoy of jacked-up pickup trucks pulled into the parking lot with red tailgates and poles in the bedrail slots and black flags with pythons inside red bullseyes. Dismounting, they walked past the FWC office, holding the flagpoles over their shoulders like rifles.

"Hey, there goes another one of our stuffed pythons," a staff biologist said. "Rhonda, go get Director Newman."

Rhonda saw the "Do Not Disturb" sticky note on his door and peeked through the blinds. The director was naked above the waist, talking to a wall.

Dano directed two guys with a hand dolly, the kind used to move refrigerators. The covered plexiglass box weighed 150 pounds. At fifteen feet, recently fed a medium-sized pig, the chubby python snoozed on a bed of woodchips.

Two o'clock came and went as throngs of people walked up the entrance lane.

A middle-aged lady with a full head of salt and pepper hair, wore a green scout uniform adorned with a sash, badges, and medals. At the podium, she blew her whistle into the mic, scaring the bejesus out of many.

"Thank you for your attention."

The crowd formed a semicircle facing the stage; wheelchairs and people needing to sit occupied the first row. VIP seats were cordoned off to the left.

"My name is Charlene Davis, the volunteer chairperson for the Scouts of Pa-Hay-Okee Foundation. It's my honor to report that we have received a total of $342,000 in donations. Your generosity will fund a permanent memorial at Pa-Hay-Okee, a sustainable scholarship endowment for scouts of South Florida, and the construction of a full-service summer camp facility to expand the scouting experience. All foundation officers are unpaid, and our administrative expenses will never exceed five percent. To donate by cash, check, or credit card, stop by our table in the back or Google, Scouts of Pay-Hay-Okee for the QR code."

The crowd cheered, and a line formed at the donation table. A large screen behind the stage illuminated with pictures of the Everglades. A scoutmaster led the Pledge of Allegiance, and a pastor gave an invocation.

As planned, Tim Parker walked to the podium. He carried a scout uniform on a hanger with a sash of merit badges. He hung it on the podium facing the audience. The name badge read, Parker.

"Good afternoon, my name is Tim Parker. Mary, my wife, seated in the front row, and I are the parents of Randy, a scout taken from us four months ago at Pa-Hay-Okee."

Scouts, boys and girls, from Troop 44 walked to the front of the stage on the grass. Each held a picture of the eight scouts killed at Pa-Hay-Okee. The pictures were official troop portraits taken only three months before the massacre.

Tim gestured to the uniform hanging on the podium. "Randy loved scouting. He loved the outdoors. Had he returned from the wilderness campout that Sunday, like his many other campouts, Randy would have talked my leg off about what he saw and what he did.

"I think this campout would have been different. You see, camping is about nature. Randy would have told Mary and me that there was something wrong out there, that the Everglades had lost its nature. You're seeing pictures of the Everglades behind me. Would you be surprised to know it has become a biological desert? Have you noticed that FWC no longer promotes pictures of animals and birds that have lived in the Everglades for millions of years? Why is that?"

Parker pointed to the container on the stage. "Consider that a six-year-old python has eaten the equivalent of the animals listed on the screen."

The list included: 1 Racoon, 1 Opossum, 4 Five-foot Alligators, 5 American Coots, 6 Blue Herons, 8 Ibises, 10 Squirrels, 15 Rabbits, 15 Wrens, 30 Cotton Rats, and 72 Mice.

"There are 300,000 to 500,000 pythons in the Everglades that can live for twenty years. If half are females that produce eight snakes each year or two that live to breed, is it any surprise that animals and birds are extinct or within one percent of disappearing over 4,500 square miles? Eighty-seven percent of all bobcats are dead. Marsh rabbits, cottontail rabbits, and foxes are gone. Raccoons and opossums are ninety-nine percent gone."

The screen changed to support his remarks.

"A study of the stomach contents of 1,716 pythons from 1995 to 2020 showed 45 different mammal species, 29 different bird species, plus alligators, water moccasins, and smaller pythons.

"Randy would have talked about the silence, the dearth of game trails, the missing birds he so loved. His camera would not have wildlife pictures. He didn't know this. Neither did we. And neither did most of you.

"The FWC knew. It turns out they protected pythons for the last thirty years. If there are so few animals or birds, what is the purpose of having a wildlife commission in South Florida, the wildest part of the state? FWC allowed large, hungry Burmese pythons to stalk our children and hunt them down. That night, the FWC added humans to the list of mammals that pythons eat in our Everglades.

"The least the FWC could have done was tell us the truth about the mass extinction of wildlife and warn the public of the growing menace from these apex predators.

"I am out of words."

Mr. Parker folded his notes, unhooked the uniform from the podium, stepped off the stage, and passed, head lowered, through the crowd. Immersed in his own grief, he was not aware of others crying as he took a seat next to his wife.

One of Dano's crew, a six-foot former military man wearing combat boots and a Raiders ball cap, began the chant.

"WTF, FWC, Save the Glades for you and me."

The cadence caught on and increased in volume. Someone, not a PAC staffer, jumped on the stage, grabbed the mic, and pointed to the FWC headquarters.

"FWC snake lovers, we know you're in there. Come out, come out. Show your yellow bellies."

One of the tall twins in hot pants leaped onto the stage like a ninja and snatched the mic from the scrawny agitator, whispering, "Sweetie, I appreciate your enthusiasm, but you're not on the program." She handed him a handful of free drink coupons at Muffins Sports Bar.

Back at the Northlake Boulevard turnoff, two Ford Explorers carrying eight Palm Beach County sheriff's deputies turned in. Wrench ran out to intercept the lead SUV. Wrench flipped open a leather badge holder with an embossed metal card identifying him as an affiliate of the Office of Legislative Investigations. His Marine Corps insignia tattoo popped out like a salute on his wrist.

Wrench apologized for not giving the sheriff's office a heads-up about the 'Focus on Wildlife' rally organized by the governor's office.

Rolling to a stop behind the crowd, the deputies, all wearing identical sunglasses, parked and exited their vehicles. They stood off to the side, arms folded over their duty belts.

Caroline, an attractive woman who looked to be in her 30s, with lush caramel curls draped over the shoulders of her closed collar pleated blue dress, stepped to the podium. Wrench and Dano's boss, Caroline had shaped the agenda and managed the message.

"This is incredible. Quite the crowd. Well above our estimates. Thank you for coming.

"Thank you, Mr. Parker. We are so sorry for your family's loss.

"We also thank members of the media for covering this event.

"In the building behind me is where the FWC established policies that protected invasive pythons—policies that promoted a population explosion and wiped out native wildlife.

"Since Pa-Hay-Okee, Governor Prescott has worked tirelessly reorganizing agencies to put public safety and native animals first. He fired the FWC director in that building five days after the massacre. He canceled circus-like python challenge contests and ridiculous charades, such as paid python road warriors. He emptied the FWC's so-called python toolbox.

"Three weeks ago, the governor's new FWC director took command of the South Region. Director Anthony Newman, formerly the assistant director of the Northwest Region, holds a PhD in natural resources. It's my honor to introduce your new director."

Leaving the stage, Caroline removed the cloth cover from the eight-foot-square plexiglass box. Sunlit, the python stirred with every inch of its body moving. The head slithered along the perimeter and up to the plexiglass cover, searching for an exit. A long tongue flicked in and out.

Dressed in khakis, a light blue open-collar shirt, and a blue blazer, Newman stepped from behind a tree and approached the back of the stage. His brow already shiny, he squinted under an afternoon sun that baked his balding dome like the open door of a coal-fired boiler. Waiting out of sight before his introduction, the chants and slurs unsettled Newman. His slow pace could be interpreted as either confidence or consternation. All eyes watched as he approached the back of the stage.

The python cage, centered on the stage, was ten feet left of the podium. Feeling the heat, the python looked antsy and agitated. Stepping up two feet onto the stage, a short height for Newman at six feet four inches, he walked to the plexiglass cage, removed his blazer, and draped it over the top. The python moved under the shadow.

"My name is Anthony Newman, and I'm sorry. Sorry for the tragic and senseless loss of your children. I'm sorry for the near extinction of our native mammals, reptiles, and birds. Mr. Parker, father of a scout taken from us, is correct. The Everglades is now a biological desert. Public officials hid the truth from you. The FWC used willful ignorance to turn a blind eye to the python scourge.

"What happened at Pa-Hay-Okee was inevitable. Hungry apex predators hunt animals, and humans are animals. Decades of mismanagement have led to a dangerous Everglades, culminating in the deaths of precious children."

Sweat dripped from his chin, and dark rings descended like storm clouds under his arms. One of the twins tiptoed a short distance from the right to slide a tissue box and water bottle on the podium shelf.

"Somehow, and I don't know why, leadership at FWC applied animal anti-cruelty laws that protected an invasive predator, the Burmese python. Their convoluted, hypocritical, and flip-flopping policies granted rights to pythons that other wild animals did not have. Mandating live capture by hand, they required live transport to designated sites for pithing, the killing by driving a bolt into the brain. That policy changed to require pithing where they are caught.

"Instead of owning up to the impossibility of controlling the population by wrestling them one at a time by hand, in 2013, the FWC started python-catching contests and promoted python adventure tours.

"Making matters worse, since 2017, they have spent tax dollars on paid python hunters to give the grand illusion that the FWC is controlling the population.

"In 2025, it took ten days for 900 hunters to catch only 300 pythons. Does anyone want to guess how many female pythons it takes to produce 300 adult pythons? Twenty. Folks, there are likely 100,000 breeding females out there.

"It's simple math."

Newman took a step back, wiped his face and the back of his neck with tissues, and emptied the water from the bottle.

"After the deaths of our children at Pa-Hay-Okee, Governor Prescott exposed the truth behind the duplicities at FWC.

"The FWC did not warn you about the dangers of camping, hiking, fishing, and touring in python-infested areas. To do that, they would've had to admit their failures in addressing the crisis and scare away tourists.

"We failed the people we serve. I am heartbroken and sorry for this. We, including the employees at the district headquarters, apologize to you. We promise to do better and hope the governor can fulfill his commitment to eradicate all pythons from the Everglades.

"Some here may think I'm another time-buying, bullshit blowing bureaucrat. I assure you, I'm not buying time, and I'm not prone to bullshitting."

His hand reached under the podium, past the tissue box, to the gun.

"This is not a firearm. It is an air-powered sport pellet gun."

Seeing the pistol, some yelled, "Gun!"

Two women bolted from the front row, shoving baby strollers on back wheels through tall grass. Some dropped signs and water bottles, tripping over lawn chairs as they ran. Most waited and watched in amazement.

A rookie deputy in the line of eight reached for his service weapon and dropped into a crouch, just like at the academy. Others followed, looking at each other for what to do next. The sergeant never moved, focusing on the gun Newman held with the muzzle pointed at the sky.

"Stand down," the sergeant ordered his troopers. "See the barrel? It's a pellet gun."

Newman folded his notes with his left hand and put them in his shirt pocket.

"As your new regional director, allow me to demonstrate our new and improved FWC python policy."

The air gun hung by his side as if he were holding the hand of a grandchild. He clicked off the safety. Comfortable under the shade of Newman's blazer on the cage, the python's head rested on its coils. When the director lifted the lid, spectators murmured and angled to see through the plexiglass. The python raised its head as if curious and tasted the air with its tongue.

The gun barrel moved forward and down in slow motion and centered between amber-colored eyes with black vertical slits. The sound was a sharp swoosh, like the silencer on an assassin's 22 pistol. The pellet expanded inside the snake's brain, and the head rolled upside down to the cage floor. Newman lowered the lid, tossed the jacket over a shoulder, walked to the back of the stage, stepped down, and walked to a side door in the headquarters without looking back.

A few people ran to the stage to see the python, its body twisting in the box. Children cried and asked their mothers what had happened. Side conversations ensued about Newman's state of mind. Some thought he had snapped under the pressure, while others were reminded of Clint Eastwood in a Dirty Harry movie.

Someone clapped softly, then louder. Others joined in a cadence, the intensity rising like the pounding of war drums.

One by one, the snake's coils relaxed and unwound limp like the spent spring of a watch. People tried not to look, but they couldn't help themselves. The snake's execution had a finality that affected even hardened onlookers.

Someone called out, "Go, Dirty Harry. One down, thousands to go."

Rushing to the podium, Caroline put her thumb and finger to her teeth and whistled into the mic. Shaken by Newman's unscripted demonstration on live television, she stumbled over words and glanced at fifteen feet of upturned python belly, the beige color of cooked flan.

"I, ah, want to thank Director Newman. He's working hard responding to this crisis, while remaking an FWC we can be proud of."

* * *

In Tallahassee, Governor Prescott and Brent Howard, his tech guru, watched the rally from the sofa in his office. Both stood when Newman pulled out the gun.

"Holy shit, he shot the fricking thing!" Prescott said.

"For a second, I thought he was shooting himself," Howard said.

The governor wiped his brow. "So did I."

"Go figure. He was a shmuck assistant director in the sleepy Panhandle. I met him for the first time at his interview. He seemed easygoing and pensive."

"Your call yesterday, dropping the rally on him and assigning him the keynote speech, got him rattled. You should call him within the hour and get him stabilized. Tell him he did well," Howard said.

"Right, good idea. How will this go down in the press?"

"It wasn't pretty, watching the thing unwind belly-up. That went live on TV. Still, we needed a dramatic event to galvanize public opinion. There's no getting around the fact that 300,000 pythons will fill twelve Olympic-sized swimming pools," Howard said. "They'll have to get used to this."

"I suppose you're right. It's eleven days until Professor Warner's proof-of-concept evaluation. A lot is riding on her."

Prescott felt a vibration on his phone. The text from Slate read: "WTF?"

He chuckled and typed, "Who could have guessed this?"

* * *

From the podium, Caroline looked to Lieutenant Governor Anderson, the last scheduled speaker. Standing on the stage beyond the python, he repeated a slashing motion of his hand across his throat and mouthed, "No."

"Well, folks, that concludes the formal portion of our rally," Carolyn said.

Someone from the press area yelled out, "What about questions?"

The lieutenant governor hesitated, then walked to the side of the podium. He kept to the talking points or tried to. Pressed on rumors of high-tech sci-fi options under consideration, he cited confidentiality and intellectual property.

Ignoring protocol, Ashley attempted to jump two feet onto the stage. Constricted by her tube dress, she snagged a heel on the stage and stumbled forward several feet. Cushioned by Anderson's prodigious tummy, he extended his arms like a forklift and caught her under the armpits. Recomposed, she pulled her dress down to just above her knees and pushed the mic up to Anderson.

"Oops, sorry about that, Lieutenant Governor. So, what do you say about Director Newman executing a python on live television?"

"I think actions speak louder than words. Director Newman is the face of the new FWC, and now part of the Administration of Governor John Prescott."

Ashley smiled at him and mouthed, "Perfect."

26

Bug Off

Only one register was operating. The line zig-zagged through Brewmaster's display racks. Slate held an insulated coffee mug under her arm and checked a weather app on her phone. Radar painted a severe weather system forming in the Gulf of America.

A storm is the last thing I need tonight.

Waiting, she thought about the governor's call last Saturday. Sounding nervous, almost desperate, he worried about press coverage the previous week after Newman's Dirty Harry routine. Headlines like "Public Execution, New FWC Director Shoots Python" blasted across social media, television, and print outlets.

Like it or not, the governor's actions had weaponized the FWC, insinuating the state would shoot its way out of the crisis. Humans shooting pythons, while safer and more efficient than catching them, was another publicity stunt, with no hope of reducing the population. Governor Prescott, like all before him, was headed for failure, except now the public and tourists knew the truth.

He'll be a hero for saving the Everglades or be banished into political obscurity for failing.

Vulnerable, the governor had sought Slate's reassurance that her terminator drone, his only card, would work and that she was ready for the live test on Tuesday.

Today was Tuesday.

She stood third in line for coffee behind a tall man with faded gray overalls that smelled like fly spray. The red "Bug Off" emblem of an angry cockroach across his shoulders caused her to back up.

155

When Brewmaster's, around the corner from her condo, was crowded, she usually skipped it and got coffee from the machines at work. Today was different. Nothing short of a thirty-two-ounce vanilla latte and two Bavarian cream-filled donuts could get her going.

After what happened with the dean yesterday, not sleeping well last night, and knowing she would sleep little tonight, Slate also couldn't bear to face colleagues in the break room.

A call vibrated her phone.

"Hi Slate, I'm on my way. ETA Tallahassee around five," Jake said.

"Good. How did packing up the command trailer go this morning?"

"It went great. Brad was there. He's towing it down to Ernest Coe Everglades visitor center, then going to the University to help Carter load the Zcolt and pick you up."

"Okay, call me when you get to the hotel in Tallahassee."

"Are you okay? How are you holding up?" he asked, knowing about the dean's meeting with her the day before.

"I'm not okay, but I will be. Gotta go. I'm next in line for coffee. See you later, Cowboy. Bye."

* * *

Dean Henry Miller's administrative assistant had called Slate mid-morning on Monday. The dean wanted to see her in his office after lunch. Surprised, Slate wasn't too concerned, her mind consumed with preparations for the test flight on Tuesday night. Still, the assistant's tone was formal, without the usual chit-chat about her cats.

The shock of being fired as associate dean took Slate's breath away like falling through ice into a pond. Dean Miller said he appreciated her dedication to the governor's task force and understood her grief over the loss of her nephew. However, those were not priorities of his College of Engineering. Her excessive use of computer resources and server capacity had drawn complaints from other departments. Slate retained her position as chair of the computer science and robotics department, at least for now, but the dean reassigned two of her postdoctoral researchers to other mentors.

"Sometimes, I wonder if you forget where you work, Professor," Miller had said.

Leaving his office, lightheaded, like champagne on an empty stomach, Slate walked down the long hallway to the women's restroom. The cavernous room, with gray marble floors and oversized mahogany stalls, had fat porcelain toilets with thick wooden seats. The room was empty. She chose the last stall, closed the door, turned on the water, and retched the lunch special into the sink. The sound echoed off tall ceramic walls. Hands trembling, she sat on the toilet seat and cried her heart out.

Slate had never been fired or demoted. Failure and shame twisted in her stomach. Another reality hit her like an electric shock. News of her demotion would ricochet throughout the university. She felt like going to her condo and pulling the covers over her head. Then she recalled that the dean had brought up Jamie as a reason.

I must have heard him wrong. He had valid reasons for demoting me, but Jamie was not one of them.

The thought of Jamie released another round of sobbing.

A hinge squeaked on the heavy entrance door. Two young women she recognized by their voices as grad students chatted away at the long bank of sinks across from the stalls. She lifted her feet above the opening under the door, half expecting them to gossip about her sacking. Instead, they complimented each other's makeup, agreed to meet at Joey's Joint for happy hour, and left.

Slate emerged, tried to repair the damage to her makeup, and mustered the courage to walk to her computer lab. More than anything, she needed to talk to someone. She called Jake.

He listened, let her get it out.

"I'm sorry this happened to you. It could be political or because the dean isn't aware of your key role in saving the Everglades. Even more reason why tomorrow night matters. This is bigger than a college position. You're at the right place at the right time in history, Sarah. Lean forward and stay focused, Cowgirl."

She understood it was a pep talk, and it made sense.

"Thanks. I really needed to hear it from you."

"Are you on schedule for tomorrow?" he had asked.

"Yes, I'm configuring the control trailer remote link to the university today. We leave for Pa-Hay-Okee tomorrow afternoon."

27

Python Python

Tuesday, July 3rd, Carter left the University at three-thirty p.m., towing the Zcolt southbound on US 1. Brad followed in his pickup with Slate sitting across from him. Clogged with early celebrations for Independence Day, kids crowded sidewalks and zig-zagged up and down the street on riptide bicycles and motorized trikes. Carter inched forward in traffic, then stopped at a red light behind a Monte Carlo lowrider. It bounced to rap music blasted from a soundstage in its trunk. A firecracker arced over his pickup to the opposite sidewalk and exploded. Kids on that side returned two salvos across his hood. A kid at the curb in front of Cafe Loco, a walk-up Cuban sandwich shop, dropped lit bottle rockets down a five-foot-long PVC pipe. Pointed up like a mortar, the missiles left the tube with a psshh—swoooooosh and exploded high over the street.

Carter tapped the steering wheel to his playlist and surveyed the commotion without looking nervous. An impact and a loud crack reverberated through his steering wheel. He checked the side mirrors and saw smoke on the left side of the trailer. Turning his head, he saw a group of kids pointing and laughing.

His phone rang.

"Carter, a rocket hit your trailer. It's okay, but there are too many crazies on US 1. Use the side streets," Brad said.

"Roger."

The light changed. He turned right and stair-stepped streets to the Don Shula Expressway, then to the Florida Turnpike. Leaving the turnpike, they stopped at a truck stop for food and generator fuel before driving to the Ernest Coe visitor's center to pick up the control trailer. At five, the two pickups with trailers pulled off SR 9336 into the former

158

Sheriff's rescue and recovery command center across from the two-mile access road to Pay-Hay-Okee.

Slate's first time there, she saw a crooked sign hanging from a tattered tent, "Families." Her heart sank, remembering her brother's anguish and the heartbreak of the group vigil. In many ways, Rick's heart was still in that tent, along with others.

Wind whipped up dirt and brush under overcast gray skies. Two dumpsters, a porta-potty, and the tent were sad bookends for a dusty cedar-log lean-to adorned with laminated pictures. The original memorial, a ten-foot-long hog wire fence to the left, collected windblown brush and shopping bags that mixed with withered bouquets, stuffed animals, and deflated balloons.

Slate looked on in silence from the pickup while Brad went across the highway to unlock the gate to Pa-Hay-Okee. Fighting the urge to pee, she realized this might be her only opportunity. She hopped out and headed for the porta-potty. A gust swirled dust and disguised the odor until she opened the door. A cloud of black flies crashed against her face. She released the door, and the spring slammed it shut. Legs crossed, she tripped over brush to get behind it, in the lee of the wind. Pants down, her back against the blue wall, she peed in the dirt.

Closed for almost a year, first for renovations, then after the python attacks, nature had reclaimed the entrance road. Weeds widened the cracks in thin asphalt and encroached over the shoulders. The pickups weaved around tree branches and potholes. A quarter mile in, a large oak tree had blown over, blocking the road, its disk of roots tipped up.

Brad dug his chainsaw out of the toolbox. He cut off limbs and sectioned the trunk. He and Carter rolled and carried the pieces to clear a path wide enough for the trailers. Annoyed by the delay and aggravated by the growl of the chainsaw, Slate rechecked the weather on her phone. Moving east from the Gulf, she estimated the wall of thunderstorms would slam Pa-Hay-Okee around one in the morning.

Her phone rang—the caller ID read Jake.

"Hi. I've checked into the hotel and talked with the governor. They're taking me to the situation room around seven."

"Good, sorry about the racket. The guys are cutting up a damn tree that fell across the entrance road. This is a disaster area. How did the governor sound?"

"He asked about the video feed and if we are ready to put on a great show for his task force. He also asked about the weather. He's afraid of media leaks and wants this done tonight. What time should his task force arrive?"

"I'll give you the time once we set up. So, he wants a great show, huh? Does he think this is a fricking movie set, or a concert? Prescott has no idea how many moving parts must line up for this shit to work. Anyway, get over to the situation room and make sure their tech guys have the feed ready on their end."

Slate hung up, steaming about the governor's 'great show' request. Impatient, she got out and helped clear the road.

Slate and Carter were back in their seats, and Brad was putting the chainsaw away when he saw something shiny in the late sun. A crop of cypress knees populated the mudbank of a canal bordering wetlands. He went over.

"Hey, guys. You might want to look at this," Brad yelled.

They joined him. "Holy shit, it must be fifteen feet!" Carter said.

A python had used the crux of two cypress knees as an anchor to shed its skin. Still pliable, it stretched flat across the muddy bank. Slate looked and recoiled, realizing the skin was fresh.

Back in the truck, Slate felt a chill in her spine and shuddered without comment. Brad, both hands on the steering wheel, shifted into four-wheel drive, drove over branches, and splashed in and out of water-filled holes. He stopped once to honk at a nine-foot alligator sunning on the road.

The road ended at an oval-shaped parking lot. They stopped at the entrance. Carter came from his pickup and jumped into Brad's back seat. At the far end of the lot, on the right, was a concrete-block building for restrooms and storage. Left of the building, a concrete pad with metal picnic tables had a covered, arched pavilion. The Google map showed two boardwalks behind the pavilion that looped through marsh grass and cypress to join at a covered lookout 100 yards into the Everglades.

Covered by debris left during the search and recovery, waste overflowed from trash cans, their tops overturned on the ground. Animals had scattered garbage, beer cans, and food containers. Paper plates and white plastic bags swirled around the parking lot in the wind.

"The least the search teams could have done is clean up their mess. Eight kids had their last day in that pavilion. Their body bags were probably on those tables," Slate said, allowing anger to temper her grief.

There's the bathroom where they found Taylor," Carter said, pointing at the concrete building. Slate nodded, thinking only a handful of people knew that Taylor was with Jamie that night. Carter was not one of them.

The three discussed where to set up the trailers.

A rat scampered across the lot. It got halfway. A barred owl swooped from a cypress. Talons crushed into the rat's back and carried it up to a branch.

"We needed those in Newark," Brad laughed.

"You don't have enough rats up there?" Carter grinned.

"Knock it off. Where should we put the trailers?" Slate asked.

Brad said, "How about the command trailer at the far end by the pavilion with the door and window facing us?"

"The drone needs a flyway. Put it a hundred feet in front of the command trailer facing us," Carter said.

"Sounds good. Pull them into place, park the pickups off to the side, and start setting up. Use your damn checklists," Slate snapped. "Brad, your first task is to get the power up and link the video feed to Tallahassee.

"Jake says the governor wants a really big show. Carter, load a full magazine on the Humboldt."

She checked her watch. "Six-forty-five. Sun sets at eight-fifteen. Showtime is nine."

* * *

Nine o'clock. Standing, her team faced the camera mounted above the window. Each wore dark blue flight suits with name tags and ZKuul logos. Slate, hair in a ponytail with subtle, but seductive lip gloss, turned on the video feed.

A monitor below the camera showed five task force members, the governor, and Jake sitting around the far end of a conference table. They waved to Slate's team on their wall-sized screen in the situation room.

Using Jake's cell on speakerphone, the governor introduced the task force. Slate began to introduce her team when she saw a door to the situation room open. Two people entered, and everyone stood up.

"Oh, so glad you could make it," Prescott said. Slate heard him over the speakerphone. The governor turned to the tripod camera at the end of the table. "Professor Warner, also joining us are Senator Jacob Grant and the Democratic Minority Leader, Senator Victoria Hale."

Slate felt another chill in the spine of her back as the pressure to perform increased. Another gust rocked the trailer. She introduced her team, then slipped the wall camera from the mount and pointed it out the window.

"We are at Pa-Hay-Okee, the place of the python attacks. What you're seeing outside is the Zcolt aerial platform."

Lit by a light above the control trailer door and a shop light on a stand, the drone on the launch pad, except for the long Humboldt hanging between the skids, had the eerie resemblance of a Mars rover. Colored lights at various locations on the drone shined and blinked as the vehicle pitched against the tie-downs.

Slate returned the camera to the mount and began an overview of the command center when Brad motioned to her. He whispered, "Something's wrong with Lucy."

Without missing a beat, Slate said, "Brad has reminded me of the coming storm. We'll complete our prelaunch checks, and Jake will present slides that explain where we're going tonight and what you will see on the monitors."

Slate turned off the video feed and sat next to Brad.

"What's up, Brad?"

"She's in slow-mo. See the rain screen?"

"Something's in a loop, or the university choked down our bandwidth," she said.

"What about a reload on the Delta channel?" he suggested.

"I was thinking the same thing."

Anticipating delays, Slate had prepared a self-explanatory slide show on the project's history, the research site, the Zcolt, and the layout of the command center.

Almost finished and ready for questions, Jake received a text from Slate, "Ten minutes."

She entered commands and watched the algorithm sequence through upload protocols as stable lines of blue code streamed on the screen.

"That's more like it. Easy does it, Lucy."

Finished loading, a yellow line of code in all caps said, "Lucy Is Ready To Party."

A strong gust jolted the trailer, a harbinger of what lay ahead. Carter looked out the window at the tie-downs. "The wind's picking up, guys, and the sky is clearing with fast-moving clouds. A bright full moon is rising above the trees. It's a good night for snake hunting."

Slate switched on the video and audio feed and turned her console chair toward the camera.

"Sorry for the delay. We had to reconnect a link to a remote server. Your screen may jitter when wind gusts rock the trailer. A strong line of thunderstorms is racing our way. We're almost ready for launch. Jake will explain what's happening."

Slate entered commands to merge the flight computer with Lucy's algorithm. She pointed to the composite screen, telling the task force what was happening as the computer programs merged. Once completed, "Lucy Is Ready To Party, Happy Hunting," appeared on the rain screen. Below the line, an angry python slithered across the screen—one that Slate had not seen before.

The monitors were populated with sensor images and status indicators. Brad stretched and limbered his fingers. His expression changed to intense concentration, like an Army Ranger before a knife fight.

"Okay, Carter. Go out, pull the tie-downs, and remove the safety pin on the gun. Hurry back so we can launch."

Slate and Brad completed their checklists.

"Brad, I'll do the takeoff while you watch the weapons screen. Once we're airborne and stabilized, you fly us to the grid."

Slate rotated her chair toward the camera.

"Jake, we'll show manual mode first and then auto-flight search mode. As Lucy finds pythons, Brad will track and shoot them."

He gave a thumbs-up in return, along with several other thumbs-up from others in the room. The task force had a broad elevated view of the two operators, their keyboards, and monitors.

"You ready, Game Boy?" Slate asked Brad.

He nodded, fingers over the keyboard.

"Where's Carter? He should be back," she said.

"Don't know," Brad said, staring at the monitor.

"Go find out."

Annoyed, Brad grabbed his MK18 stub-barrel assault rifle to check on Carter. The wind caught the door, pulled it from his hand, and slammed it against the trailer.

"For God's sake, Brad. Watch the fricking door," she yelled, while watching Lucy's rain screen stabilize.

Bark. Bark. Muffled pops of the MK18 in the wind.

"Holy shit." Slate looked at the drone video screen and rotated the dome camera on the Zcolt. Behind the drone, about ten feet away, she saw Carter horizontal on broken concrete. In the flat light, it looked like he was wrapped in a fire hose. Only his hair and eyes were visible. Then she saw Brad. He had a python by the neck in one hand, trying to put the barrel of the MK18 against the head, but the python's mouth was clamped around Carter's calf muscle.

Jake and the others, watching and listening, stood and leaned toward the screen. Slate jumped up, grabbed a Phillips screwdriver from a tool bag on the service table, and ran out.

"Brad, there's one behind you!" she screamed in the wind. He spun around and put two rounds in a python. Slate ran to Carter, held the snake's head, the size of a salad plate, and pushed the screwdriver through the skull into the brain. She swirled it around like stirring a smoothie. Although dead, the body continued squeezing Carter. Brad grabbed the tail, and together they unwound the fifteen-foot snake.

They laid Carter on the asphalt. Slate found a pulse, tipped his head back, and blew air into his lungs. After two breaths, he coughed. Using the red-dot laser sight, Brad shot another python under the pickup. They helped Carter into the trailer and onto the sofa.

Slate looked up at the video camera. The governor, Jake, and the others stood, leaning on the conference table, staring back at her.

"A python attacked Carter. He's alright," she said, breathless. She pulled her messy hair back in a ponytail, put on a black company baseball cap, and wiped her hands and face with wet wipes.

"We need to get the show on the road."

Back in her chair, Slate refreshed displays and analyzed code on the rain screen.

Brad cleaned Carter's leg wound and gave him two amoxicillin tablets. Woozy, Carter propped himself up on the sofa to watch his team.

"Carter, did you remove the straps and gun safety pin?" Slate called over her shoulder.

"Yes, Boss."

"Are you still ready, Game Boy?"

"Is it too windy?" Brad asked.

"We're within design limits; besides, you have the golden hands. You can handle it. Here we go."

Inside the command center, the takeoff sounded like concrete demolition saws. Slate eased Zcolt off the pad. Twenty feet above the launch pad, a British female voice announced over the speaker, "Python, python."

Brad checked his monitors. "Holy smokes, she's found one already. On the grass just right of the parking lot." He centered the cursor and initiated tracking.

"Fire away!"

The crack of the Humboldt from the drone ten feet above their trailer ricocheted inside the command center. Brad pointed his finger to the mushy spot on his weapons screen—the head was gone, and the body wiggled in the grass.

"Good job, Lucy. Let's get some more. Brad, you can take over. Do your thing."

He banked hard left and headed southeast in the direction of Taylor's campsite, where it all began.

* * *

In the situation room, Jake positioned the laser pointer over the rifle scope on the wall screen. The headless python squirmed in the grass. Jake pointed to the snake's body on the infrared sensor screen, then to where they were going on the GPS map. He turned to see their reaction. Open-mouthed and wide-eyed, the governor and the others made comments to each other and took their seats.

Jake turned up the audio. Sounds from the command center filled the room like an IMAX movie theater. They heard wind gusts slam the trailer along with the whirl of computers and fans. The room was dim, except for indirect lighting and micro track lights on their consoles. Slate flipped her ponytail trailing from the ball cap. ZKuul Solutions shimmered in silver letters on the back of their flight suits.

Jake pointed the laser at Brad's keyboard.

"Brad is flying the drone using a keyboard and mouse. The flight screen shows the drone's position on the moving map and the waypoint where the scouts were killed. In the distance, you see the radar return of the thunderstorms."

Brad's fingers tapped the keys in staccato, like a concert pianist, while Slate monitored sensor displays and computer code. Jake pointed to the mix of blue and green data.

He explained what they were seeing. "Lucy, the algorithm, is trained to recognize pythons from patterns in the data she is processing. Dr. Warner wrote the A.I. program and can interpret the data stream on the screen."

Over the speaker, they heard Slate. "Slow down a little, Brad. Lucy's falling behind. Zig-Zag right and left of the centerline to give her more to look at."

Jake checked his watch. In the last thirty minutes, they had seen Carter attacked by a python, and watched Slate kill it with a screwdriver. They witnessed the Zcolt launch in stormy weather at night, and saw Brad shoot a python after takeoff.

Brent Howard, the technology director, commented that it felt like watching a Hollywood action thriller.

Thirty seconds later, they heard Lucy's voice over the speaker: "Python, python."

Brad stopped, found it on the weapons screen, locked onto the target, and fired one shot. The python was submerged, except for its head. The Humboldt corrected for wind and platform drift. The impact blew the head off in a splash.

"Python, python." Lucy, still scanning, found another one.

Jake's phone vibrated in his pocket. The text from Slate asked how it was going. "They're standing up and clapping," he replied.

With less than a mile to the campsite and ten dead pythons, Slate stood and turned to face the camera.

"This completes the manual flight portion of our test. Up ahead is the campsite. Next, we will demonstrate auto-flight, where Lucy flies a programmed path, in this case, an expanding spiral centered on the campsite. She will stop and highlight pythons for Brad to shoot. If she finds more than one, they will list on the screen in the most efficient order of engagement. As you can see from the radar return and distant lightning, we don't have much time."

Slate entered commands on her keyboard and checked the rain screen for Lucy's response. A line of yellow code appeared, "Auto-Flight. Let The Party Begin."

Jake used the laser pointer to explain what was happening. "This is where the computer sorts multiple targets. See how the code stream changes patterns, swirls, and curls?"

A hundred yards from the campsite, the Zcolt stopped. Slate waited, watched the stream, and read lines of blue code.

Tallahassee heard Brad ask Slate, "What's she doing?"

Slate replied, "I don't know."

The governor asked Jake, "What's going on? Is there a problem?"

Jake held up an index finger to wait. Then, he shrugged as the moments passed.

A flash of lightning from the west illuminated the campsite area ahead. The sky was overcast. The monitor jittered as the Zcolt fought to hold position in the wind.

"Python, python, python, python, python, python, python, python, python, python, python, python, python, python, python, python, python, python, python, python."

Slate and Brad looked at each other. This was a first for them.

Jake told the group, "Lucy has found multiple pythons."

Yellow highlights overlapped on the screen, and a shooting order list propagated. Another bolt of lightning, now closer.

Slate stood up and faced the camera. "Lucy stopped because she'd reached her programmed limit of ten pythons. My guess is there are a lot more up ahead. Our contract was to demonstrate an ability to find and manually shoot pythons. I think we have succeeded. Given that the storm is almost here, I would like to demonstrate an advanced capability if the task force agrees. Lucy will fly the drone, find pythons, and shoot them without our input. We will monitor her and intervene if there's a problem. I'll need your approval, Governor."

Prescott and the others discussed her request and asked Jake a couple of questions. They reached a consensus, and the governor gave Slate a thumbs-up.

Slate typed commands. Lines of code gathered in bunches, then cascaded and branched like snow-covered trees in winter, except they were inverted. A yellow line of text appeared, "Auto-Flight And Auto Shoot. Enjoy The Show!"

The Zcolt pivoted left to align the Humboldt with the first target. The dashed circle turned solid red, and the weapons screen jittered as the rifle fired. The snake's head, a white spot on the infrared screen, exploded like a splash of white paint. The targets on the list moved up one place, and a new python was added in the tenth position. Below the target list, a tally of dead pythons appeared in red.

The Zcolt rotated right, locked on a python, and shot. Lucy flew the drone forward twenty yards, pivoted and shot, then slid sideways five yards and fired again.

Governor Prescott had moved to the end of the conference table near the screen. Unable to hear the drone or the rifle firing, following Jake's pointer, the governor counted on his fingers and announced the kills to the group.

"Three, four, five, six, seven, eight, nine, ten, eleven, twelve, thirteen ..."

The Senate minority leader remarked, "This is like a video game. So precise, methodical, and lethal. This Lucy is like one of those factory robot welders—zap, zap, zap."

Brent Howard added. "They're killing one every five to ten seconds. I've never seen anything like this."

Up ahead, behind the higher ground where the scouts camped, lightning arced like dancing spider legs, then joined and slammed into a cypress tree.

On the moving map, Lucy produced a gray-tone overlay of the spiral track she would follow. Centered over the campsite area, the Zcolt rotated like the second hand on a watch. Trails and remnants of camping areas cleared by scouts and investigators were depicted in white on the infrared screen.

"Python, python, python, python," Lucy announced over the speaker.

The weapons monitor centered on a campsite. The screen bumped, a python head exploded, and kill number thirty-eight appeared in red on the list. After completing the first orbit with fifteen more kills, Lucy flew the drone around the perimeter of the campsite. Tracking a python slithering quickly down a trail, the algorithm calculated variables, such as the bullet's time of flight. Lucy killed eight more pythons, then stopped, moved forward, and stopped again. Under increased zoom, the image on the weapons screen enlarged to show a panther looking up and growling at the drone. Jake thought of Sadie.

"Panther, panther," Lucy announced, almost joyfully, and resumed the hunt for pythons, and, before long, stopped again. This time, the image on the screen was a large female python curled over an enormous clutch of eggs.

"Python nest, python nest."

The drone advanced, halting twenty feet away. The mother snake raised her head and opened her mouth in an inaudible hiss. The Humboldt sprayed twenty rounds and made soup of the python and her nest.

Still on their feet, the task force cheered when they saw Slate and Brad raise thumbs up above their heads.

Lucy returned to the programmed track as gusts of wind jolted the Zcolt. Slate entered a pause command and stood to face the camera.

"The rain is almost here, and the wind is at our operational limit. We have thirty-seven rounds left. I've programmed a waypoint on the map, located a quarter mile away from our command center, to avoid the storm. I'm directing Lucy to fly S-turns at high speed to the waypoint. She will likely miss some pythons, but let's see how many she manages to find. I'm saving ten rounds to shoot pythons near our command center."

While Slate talked, Carter pulled up a chair to join them. "And here's Carter. How are you feeling?" Slate asked.

Carter smiled and waved to the task force.

The Zcolt under Lucy's control snapped into action like a fighter jet—violent turns, crisp edges, and blade-like precision. Lines of code tumbled and jumbled in what appeared like a departure from controlled flight. The algorithm had learned to squeeze the last ounce of performance from the drone. Like a mongoose, Lucy ferreted out pythons and shot them as speed blurred the screens. All eyes centered on the red kill list.

At ninety-three kills, Lucy stopped shooting and arrived at the waypoint. Slate returned control of the Zcolt to Brad. He flew toward Pa-Hay-Okee while Lucy scanned for pythons. Brad stopped and allowed the algorithm to process the area around the command trailer. One by one, Lucy spotted pythons and compiled a target list of six; Brad shot them. The task force, now accustomed to the routine, sat back in their seats. Jake returned to sit next to the governor.

"Locked up. Shoot," the governor called out.

"It's a good hit, get the next one," another task force member said.

Closer to the command trailer, the task force heard the crack of the Zcolt Humboldt killing pythons and the rhythmic thrum of the drone descending to the launch pad. Slate took control and cut power to the propellers as Brad and Carter raced out to strap the drone down and reconfigure the trailer before the storm arrived. Slate completed the checklists and flipped the interior lights on. She texted Jake to call her on his speakerphone. It started to rain, large drops pounding the aluminum roof as Brad and Carter jumped back into the trailer.

She addressed the task force. "Thank you all for your support. I suppose I should also thank Mother Nature for providing us with enough time to complete our demonstration. As we saw tonight, pythons are dangerous and pervasive. I'm satisfied with the performance of our drone and our computer programs. I'm glad you got to see the algorithm operate autonomously under human supervision. Does anyone have any questions?"

The governor spoke first. "Doctor Warner, I think I speak for the others when I say what we saw tonight was well above the bar for proof of concept. It takes 900 hunters ten days to catch 300 pythons on roads. You killed ninety-nine during a storm at night in the wilderness in forty-five minutes. Make that one hundred, adding the python you killed with a screwdriver, Dr. Warner."

Several task force members thanked Slate and her team. The democratic leader, Victoria Hale, stood up, called for a standing ovation, and the others joined in. The governor shook Jake's hand.

The governor concluded. "I'll close by congratulating your team on achieving so much in such a short time. Dr. Warner, I remember the day we met at the press conference in February when you claimed you could kill every damn python in the Everglades. At the time, I thought you were full of beans. But I've been following your project from the beginning. What we saw tonight was beyond incredible. I got dizzy watching Lucy fly the Zcolt. We will meet here in Tallahassee next Monday to discuss the status of the task force. We'll be in touch. Have a happy Fourth of July. We had our fireworks tonight. Good night."

Brad and Carter joined their boss, and they waved to the camera until the video connection terminated. Slate held her arms wide, and the three of them had a long group hug.

Their heads together, in elation, Slate said, "Wow, that was fricking fun."

Brad and Slate powered down the command center electronics. Slate texted Jake, "Call me when you get to the hotel."

Rain pounded the command center relentlessly. Brad grabbed three beers from the cooler and the three sank into the sofa, clinked tops, took long swigs, and listened as all hell broke loose outside. Rain and hail pelted the metal trailer.

"Marbles on a cookie sheet," Brad said.

Lightning struck a nearby tree. The crack jolted them. They looked at each other with wide eyes and clinked another toast.

Slate struggled to control her emotions.

"So many things could have gone wrong." She wanted to cry.

Brad laughed. "Hey, the governor wanted a great show. He got one. You went for it, Boss. Unleashing Lucy was pure genius."

"She found a panther and destroyed a python nest. What are the odds of that?" she said, taking another swig.

"How are you, Big Boy?" Slate put her hand on Carter's knee, then reached over and hugged him.

"I'm okay. Just tired. I remember reaching up on one leg to double-check the ammunition magazine when something clamped on my leg and twisted me to the ground. It happened fast. When I realized what it was, it was too late."

"I'm sorry it happened to you. If it's any consolation, the task force saw most of it. They are totally sold on eradicating these assholes." She patted his arm, then rustled his hair.

"You'll be fine. Lie down here and let me change the bandage. You can sleep for a few hours until the storm passes, and the sun comes up, before we head back to Miami."

Brad said, "Good idea. I'll crash in my console chair."

Slate sighed. "Sounds good. Do you mind if I take the back seat of your King Cab, Brad?"

"Sure. You carry the umbrella, and I'll escort you with the MK18."

* * *

Comfy under Brad's Miami Dolphins fleece blanket, Slate used a gym bag for a pillow and stretched across the seat. She scrolled through messages and waited for Jake's call. Bands of rain came in sheets, and lightning lit up the building. Slate looked at the bathroom door, thinking about what happened there—a bloody girl guarding a little boy with a knife. She closed her eyes, wishing she had brought another beer.

Why doesn't he call?

She checked the ringer on and turned up the volume. Starting to relax and doze, she jumped at the ring.

"Hi there. I've been waiting. Are you in your room?"

"Yep, just back long enough to grab a beer and call you. Where are you?" he said.

"I'm alone in Brad's pickup. They're getting a few hours' sleep in the trailer."

"You must be wasted. I am, just from watching you guys. What a fricking night that was."

"Fricking night in a good way?" she asked.

"They were on their feet most of the time. When the video feed ended, they stared at the screen, exhausted, like at the end of a Star Wars movie."

"It was good, right?"

"You blew them away, Cowgirl. Want to do a video chat? I want to see your face," he said.

Slate removed the baseball cap, fluffed her hair, flipped on the dome light above the back window, and propped herself higher against the door. Holding the phone between her knees, she connected to the video and saw Jake leaning against pillows on the hotel bed, holding a beer can. His chest, prominent beneath the black crew neck, his strong arms, and his soft smile took her back three weeks to that night.

"Hi, Big Guy. Can you see me?"

"Yes. Aren't you cozy, wrapped in a blanket out in the wilderness? I'm taking a screenshot to remember how you look. Your hair is golden, and your face is soft and cute in that light."

"You're sweet. You look pretty good yourself."

"How's Carter?"

"He's fine. That was close. I don't know what made me think about him not coming back in the trailer. Another few minutes and, well, you know."

"We heard Brad's gun go off and saw you turn the drone camera to show the snake. You couldn't hear us, but everyone jumped up and yelled, "It's a snake!""

"Wow, you could see all of that?" she asked.

"Yes. You're something else, killing it with a screwdriver, resuscitating Carter, and getting the Zcolt airborne before the storm. They were super impressed."

"Thanks. I didn't really have a choice. I took a lot of chances. We got the Zcolt trailered just before the storm hit. What did the governor say?"

Slate noticed a flashlight shining from the trailer window. It was Brad checking on her. She waved, and the light went out.

"I was alone with the governor in the situation room before the evaluation. He wore jeans and boots with a black western shirt. I'm not sure what that was about. Aside from my longer hair, he dressed a little like me—go figure."

"That's funny."

"He's worried about his image, being painted as a renegade loose cannon by the press. Newman going rogue played out decisively and radically."

"Men and their hangups," she laughed.

"Speaking of hangups, you were the next topic." Jake smiled.

"Pardon me. What about me?"

"Oh, nothing crazy. The governor asked about your personal life—if you're involved or dating, your hobbies, and background."

"You're kidding. He asked you that, why?" She sat up higher against the truck door.

"Well, he tried to sound casual, slipping in questions while discussing the project and admiring your leadership."

"What did you tell him?" she asked, watching his reaction.

He looked at her with the hint of a smile that widened.

"I couldn't lie to the governor, could I?" He winked at her.

"Jake, I would slap you silly if I was there." The tension broke, and she laughed. He laughed with her.

"I'm serious, what did you tell him?"

"Being the team lackey helped, and I don't know much about your personal life, except for the parts I know a lot about," he smiled and raised an eyebrow.

"I explained that the circles of Everglades City high society didn't cross paths with yours in Miami. It made perfect sense to him."

Suddenly serious, they looked into each other's eyes. A moment passed. Then another.

"I guess I should be honored the governor has eyes for you."

A hint of resignation and reflection crossed his face.

"There's so much I admire about you, Jake," she said with a warm smile.

He listened and watched her, seemed to put it aside, and smiled.

"Thank you, sweetness. I wish you were in my bed right now," he said.

"I was thinking the same thing." She blew a kiss across her fingers.

"I have an idea," she said. "Tomorrow is the fourth. I can meet you at the RV late afternoon, or do you have other plans?"

"Fireworks in the RV. I like that," he said.

She slid the blanket down, unzipped the top of her flight suit to show creamy breasts cupped in a powder blue lace-trimmed bra. Pleased with his reaction, she pulled the blanket back up.

"Okay, Cowboy, how did it end with the task force and the governor?"

"Needless to say, they were blown away. There's no doubt that we not only won, but there's no competition or any other solution in the hopper."

"Did they understand the basics about the algorithm matching sensor data against the machine-trained database?"

"They eventually figured it out from watching the process repeat during the flight."

"What did they say about Lucy shooting pythons by herself?"

"It felt strange, surreal. Someone compared it to a robot war in a distant galaxy. At times, many stood cheering for Lucy. The lethality and surgical precision of the killings overcame others. They thought the sexy British voice was funny and not funny at the same time. Another said, "This superhuman future is gory and scary.""

Slate listened to Jake's words, searching for meaning. She remembered that watching Lucy in full auto was like a high-speed chase in fast-forward.

She liked hearing that many stood and cheered for Lucy.

Jake continued. "Someone commented that Lucy is the gateway to a new world, and the splashes of python heads turning to goop seemed like a video game, not real living animals.

"And the governor reflected that if Lucy could find pythons at night in a swamp, she could find anything. He said that to me as people were leaving."

"Is the technology too sci-fi for them?" Slate asked.

"They didn't have time to think about ethics, precautions, or unintended consequences. The results overshadow those concerns for now."

Slate told him about her decision to let Lucy go wild.

"I decided to go fully automatic because of how well we did on the way to Pa-Hay-Okee. Now that they've seen full auto, it should be easier to sell."

"Answer this question, Slate. Is there any difference between catching and killing a thousand pythons one at a time by hand over one year, and killing a thousand pythons in one day with bullets?"

Slate thought for a few seconds.

"You know, Jake. You are one smart cowboy. Did you notice anyone in the room who wasn't on board?"

"The governor convened a brief meeting afterward around the table. As I mentioned, there was a bit of sensory overload, but in a positive way. There weren't many questions. The governor, of course, praised you highly as the architect of the A.I. program.

"Representative Shirley Jensen, the only democrat on the task force, has a background in environmental science. She said that returning native animals to the Everglades necessitates a mass culling of invasive pythons as quickly as possible. Nothing she has seen in twenty years compares to our team killing a hundred snakes in under an hour at night during a thunderstorm."

"I like that," Slate smiled.

"Guess who showed up just before you spiked the python with the screwdriver?"

"Ah, a handyman?" She laughed and held up her hand, as if holding a screwdriver.

"That's funny. No. Dirty Harry Newman."

"No way!"

"Yes, way," Jake said. "Yeah, I think Prescott is trying to present a united front as if he had a choice. Regardless, I like him. He's quiet, but I could see him shooting the snake at the rally just because he felt like it."

"I can see that," Slate said. "None of us, including Newman, imagined our world would now revolve around pythons. At least six of us have wrestled or killed a python by hand in the six months since Pa-Hay-Okee. How did the meeting conclude, Jake?"

"Brent Howard distributed a draft outline for the next phase. I'll bring it to the RV, not that you will be reading during our July 4th celebration. It proposes an expanded pilot project to remove pythons from a designated area. They're seeking our input on measurement criteria. Someone brought up getting bids or having a fly-off. Speaking on your behalf, I said that we don't mind, although we're not aware of any entities with proprietary technology like ours. I emphasized that time is crucial."

"Keep it up, Cowboy, and you'll be our chief operations officer."

"I think I'll stick to pickups, tarpon fishing, and making BBQ."

Jake, in boxers, got out of bed to grab another beer from the mini fridge.

"Big Boy," she murmured.

He grinned. "Oops, sorry."

"One more thing before you go, Jake. The scariest part of today was driving out of Miami. Mobs of kids were shooting off fireworks. A rocket hit the Zcolt trailer. Not a cop in sight."

"That's bullshit. Another reason to stay out of Miami," Jake said.

Hesitantly, she said, "Something else happened. It's important, and I'm not sure how to fix it."

"What?"

"Twice tonight during the demonstration—once when Brad was shooting pythons and later when Lucy was fully automatic—I entered commands on the keyboard for Lucy to disengage and return to standby mode. She ignored me both times. Nothing overt showed on the rain screen, except a blank line where code should have been. The second time I entered the commands, she complied. I have no explanation for this. Operations deep within her neural network are a black hole."

"You tried to take control twice, and she refused. That's not good. You may need a backup kill switch, either electronic or mechanical."

"I have to think about it and ask a colleague. Want to hear another scary thing?"

"What?"

"On the way back to base, during Lucy's shooting frenzy, I noticed the color of the target box change from yellow to light orange. It happened twice, and I had never seen that before. After landing, I scrolled back through the frames on the weapon screen and found them. Lucy killed two young pigs, bullets through the eye."

"Holy crap, we trained her to recognize pigs and other mammals, including humans, as friendly," Jake said.

"I know."

"So, what happened?" he asked.

"I don't know why she did it, not once, but twice."

28

All Nighter

Driving to the computer lab Saturday morning, Slate's mind drifted three days earlier to July 4th at the RV. Thinking of intimate scenes with Jake, her memory flipped through the three hours like a slide show. She smiled, and a warm rush gathered. Then she recalled what she had found before Jake arrived.

June 19th, the day the team did the full system test at the research site, was the last time anyone had been in the RV. Only the four team members knew the four-digit door code. The bed, not used since June 12th, her first night with Jake, was fully made up on June 19th. But now the sheets were bunched up under the bedspread, the bedspread was thrown carelessly over the pillows, and an accent pillow lay on the carpet in the corner. Looking around, something blue under the RV dining table caught Slate's eye. She retrieved a light-blue, floppy hat covered with colorful butterflies. The final clue, a butterfly barrette with one long blonde hair, lay on the carpet in the narrow space between the bed and the wall. Slate changed the sheets and decided not to tell Jake.

Stopped at the last traffic light before the university, she opened the shopping bag on the passenger seat and looked at the barrette clipped to the hat, unsure of what to do.

* * *

A large flat UPS box leaned against her office door. The beautiful painting on metal, a stylized Everglades landscape, featured rows of native animals lined up in the foreground, ready to return home. A brass plaque was engraved with two lines, "Welcome Home and Thank you, Dr. Sarah Warner."

178

A handwritten card congratulated Slate and her team for exceeding project goals and commended Jake for his contributions during the task force evaluation. The governor closed with, "Very truly yours, John." The card included an invitation to dinner at the Savour on July 17th, the evening before the task force press conference. She held the picture and touched the animals. Smiling, her mind swirled with emotion. Somehow, the governor understood her tribulation. He framed her as a savior of grateful animals, not the maniacal scientist behind the mass execution of Florida's pythons. She replaced a picture on the wall opposite her desk with the gift.

Looking at the picture from her desk chair, she subconsciously reached for the meditation stone shaped like a cowboy boot that Jake had slipped into her purse at the RV. Rubbing it, the paradox struck her like a mallet.

You were a complete idiot for seducing a man you hardly knew—not just once, but twice. Now, the governor tells the man I'm having sex with that he's interested in me. This is total bullshit and too complicated. But fun.

Her mind shifted to Carter.

What if he's having sex in the RV? Damn, this project could blow sky-high into sex scandals.

She checked her watch.

You've just wasted an hour of lab time. Get to work, Girl.

Slate grabbed her white lab coat and walked to the computer lab. Before entering, she texted the governor.

"Hi John, thanks so much for the picture. You read my mind. I'm stressing about the killing machine I've created. You reminded me to focus on the prize. I appreciate it. The picture is on the wall across from my desk. Sure, dinner would be fun. Slate."

Other than T-Zee, Professor Bismark's cybersecurity graduate student in a side office, Slate had the lab and supercomputer to herself. She investigated Lucy's disturbing behavior during the evaluation—ignoring Slate's stand-by commands and shooting two pigs. She finished after midnight. Not counting three trips to the break room vending machines, she'd spent twelve hours using her A.I. assistant to modify code and test an update to the algorithm. She added two digital standby pathways and a kill switch that operated like a physical circuit breaker. Slate uploaded thousands of images of wild pigs from the internet for

Lucy to integrate through machine learning. Concerned that Lucy might confuse other animals, such as humans, with pythons, Slate also uploaded thousands more images of people and native wildlife. Testing and debugging complete, she brought Lucy online.

"Okay, Hungry Girl, here's your dinner. Remember, pigs are not pythons. And, when I say stop, you stop."

Lucy devoured the data like black holes swallowed solar systems. Blue lines of text and symbols erupted on the monitor like lava pouring down the slope of a volcano. Slate linked her laptop to the program to monitor the progress from home.

"Okay, Lucy, you have all night to finish your homework. Remember, speed counts, but accuracy is more important. No mistakes. Tomorrow, I'll test you with computer simulations. They won't be easy, Big Girl. Goodnight."

At 12:30 a.m., Slate splashed through puddles on the sidewalk and climbed the stairs to the second floor of the university ramp garage. Next to her car, she watched lightning strikes over South Beach, ten miles away. Grateful that the storm, the last of the evening, had passed, she texted Jake.

"Hey, Cowboy, don't reply tonight. I'm leaving the lab for my condo. Lucy's pulling an all-nighter, rewiring her neurons. Can you get five pigs and five pythons to test Lucy at the research site next Friday? Sleep tight, Big Boy. Thanks for you know what!"

29

Paunch

Slate waffled back and forth over what to do about the hat and barrette she'd found at the RV. There might be a simple explanation. Deciding there was only one way to find out, she went directly to the robotics lab on Monday morning. A checkered black-and-white race flag on the front of the cubicle partition marked the office. Carter, on his computer, had his back to the opening. Slate cleared her throat.

He spun around in the chair.

"Oh, hi," he said, surprised to see her.

"Is this a good time?"

"Ah, sure, of course."

Slate pulled the flimsy plastic shopping bag from her purse and dropped it on the desk.

"What do you know about this?"

He opened the bag and froze.

Slate waited as he calculated the odds of each possible explanation. He looked up at her passive expression.

"We had a picnic."

"Do you see the barrette?"

He looked again.

"It was on the floor by the bed in the RV."

"We didn't do anything," he said.

"Is this Taylor's?"

He nodded.

Slate reached into her purse and tossed a small envelope on the desk. He opened it.

"I found these at the bottom of the waste basket under the sink."

181

He pulled the envelope open, and two empty condom wrappers fell out.

"You're twenty-two. She's seventeen. People go to prison and get signs on their yard for this."

Looking guilty, yet puzzled, Carter said, "She's eighteen."

"Needless to say, no more dates in the RV," she said, feeling hypocritical.

"I'm sorry. It was stupid of me."

"If it makes you feel any better, I've done worse," she said. "We're good."

Slate shuddered at a thought. Carter could have brought Taylor to the RV while she was in bed with Jake last Wednesday, July 4th.

Carter relaxed until he remembered flushing a condom and putting the wrapper in the trash under the sink on Friday, July 6th, three nights ago.

"On a different subject, the task force meets today to decide the next step. I have a Zoom call with the governor tomorrow."

"Wow, that's great news."

"How's your leg? Any infection?" Slate asked.

"It's good. My ribs are still sore, but no worries."

"What did Taylor think of your python encounter?"

Carter let out a long sigh. "I hadn't expected her reaction. A panic attack of sorts. She cried for a long time, then said she had to tell me something. She told me about her boyfriend being your nephew and that she escaped, but he didn't. She said that you know they were together that night."

Slate nodded and put her hand on his shoulder.

"I'm glad she told you. You're a good boy, Carter. Take care of her."

Slate got up to leave, glad it had turned out all right. She asked him to bring the Zcolt to the research site on Friday to test Lucy's updates.

On the way to her office, she stopped by the break room for a coffee. Dean Miller sat at a table, eating a fat frosted honey bun on a paper plate with a plastic knife and fork. He looked up, smiled with a full mouth, and raised messy fingers in a half-wave. It'd been a week since he had demoted her. Slate recoiled inside with tension at the sight of him, caught herself, and put on a happy face.

"Good morning, Dean. Hope you're doing well, at least for a Monday."

"Thank you, Sarah, I'm fine," gumming his honey bun. "Didn't you have a test or something on your project last week?"

"Oh, yes, we did. I'm pleased, although the weather could have been better," she said with detachment, not wanting him to share her success.

"I upgraded the algorithm this weekend while the mainframe was idle to incorporate lessons we learned."

"Oh. Good. We'll all be happy when your extra-curricular activity is finished."

"I understand, Dean. Have a great day."

Slate over-tightened the top of her coffee flask and imagined massive coils squishing rolls of Miller's jelly belly into links like plump German bockwursts.

* * *

Tuesday. With great anticipation, in the reflection of her computer screen, Slate touched up lip gloss and adjusted her hair in lazy curls grazing her white silk blouse. Already logged onto Zoom, she waited for the governor.

Beaming, Governor Prescott blinked into view with a trim, two-day shadow and a stone colored open-neck Columbia shirt with sleeves rolled up in neat sections. His wavy hair had the tussled, salty look of a boat captain in a Marlin fishing tournament. Slate liked his look.

"Hi, Cowgirl," he said, clearly happy to see her.

"Hello, John. Hold on, I want to show you something."

Slate turned the monitor to face the wall. "Do you see your picture?"

"Yes, there it is. I thought you would like it."

She turned the screen back. "I really, really love it, John."

He smiled. "Can I be the first to congratulate you?"

"For what?"

He held up a printed summary of yesterday's task force meeting.

"You won the contract, of course. They considered five proposals still on the table. One garnered some interest—the public funding of millions to a for-profit start-up that makes boutique snakeskin fashion accessories. Their python kill numbers didn't add up. The 100,000 remaining females would replace tenfold the pythons they caught by hand each year."

Slate recalled a short-lived FWC program a few years back that sounded similar. At the time, she thought most people were repulsed by the chilling pictures of the governor and happy hunters holding the creepy things in promotions. Given what happened at Pa-Hay-Okee, having a python wallet in your pocket or hanging from your shoulder seemed heinous.

"The vote was unanimous. I'm proud and happy for you, Slate. No one has worked harder for this than you and your team."

He paused. "There is a good chance history will recognize Dr. Sarah Warner for having saved the Everglades. What good is the ten billion dollars we've spent to clean up water in the Everglades if there's no wildlife?"

She absorbed his words, realizing the implication that the chance off-ramp her life had taken might become a legacy.

"It's good news. You still look serious," he said.

"I'm sorry. I guess I've been so focused on not screwing up that I hadn't considered where this might lead. Kinda scary."

"You're fine. I'll help you."

"Did Jake tell you about my demotion at the university?"

"No."

She told him what happened.

"As recently as yesterday, the dean said he wanted the project wrapped up."

His elbows on the desk, index fingers twirling, Prescott thought for a moment, then said, "Slate, it's not about the dean, it's about you choosing between the university and the Everglades. For all the reasons, including your nephew's death, you've already chosen, at least for now."

Slate looked past him to the picture on the wall.

He's right, of course, but I can't leave the university feeling like a loser after what Miller did to me.

The governor went on. "Let me handle Miller. I'll call him today."

"I don't want to create an issue or make it worse, John. I'm not a fighter."

"No worries. Academic elites are easy to deal with once you know what they want. Want to hear the rest of the task force recommendations?"

Still concerned, she nodded.

"Your spin-off company, ZKuul Solutions, will have a cost-plus contract to complete a pilot project overseen by Brent, the University of Florida, and a non-profit, Save Native Wildlife of Florida. You retain commercial and intellectual property rights.

"If the pilot goes well, you scale up the number of Zcolt teams, section off the Everglades, and clear them one by one. The repatriation team follows you, seeding the cleared sections with native wildlife."

"What's your guess on the timeline?" she asked.

"Well, as you've said, pythons breed annually in May and June. Eggs hatch sixty days later. Ideally, we finish clearing in April, that's nine months."

"That's ambitious. What about my university job?"

"I'll get you a sabbatical."

"I would need a production, testing, and training facility. Plus, a data center and A.I. computing support," she said.

"No shortage of those in South Florida. We have connections and leverage."

"Do you know how many square miles in total?" she asked.

Prescott held up a finger to her and asked a chatbot on his phone.

"There are 3,500 square miles in the Everglades and Big Cypress, our primary target areas. Add another 1,000 square miles in three wildlife management areas north of Everglades National Park. The total is 4,500."

Slate picked up her phone and asked Chat a question.

"That's nearly the size of Connecticut," she said.

They paused, contemplating the magnitude of the task.

"The short answer to how long it will take is, we won't know until after the pilot. It must be lean, clean, and super-efficient, not to mention fast," she said.

"Understood. The task force report will be released on Wednesday, July 18th, at my press conference in Tallahassee. Can you come on Tuesday, July 17th, for a meeting with Brent on the contract?"

Slate looked at her calendar.

"Seven days from now. Ah, I think so, if I'm not needed at the University."

"I'll take care of Miller. Is there any way you could bring the Zcolt to the press conference?"

"No way. It remains a closely guarded secret for as long as possible. Competitors in this business are a mixed breed of pit bulls, wolves, and honey badgers. Only I have access to Lucy's algorithm."

"So, what about dinner? I suggested the Savour," he asked.

"Only if they serve quail," she teased.

"I'll make sure they do, just for you."

* * *

"Dean Miller, this is Governor Prescott. Do you have a minute, or is this a bad time?"

Never having talked with the governor, Miller, a thirty-year university relic, considered giving an excuse but thought better.

"Ah, Governor. Sure, I have time. How can I help you?"

"First, let me apologize for not reaching out sooner. We've asked a great deal from your exceptional engineering college, a testament to your decades of leadership. Thank you, Sir, for lending Dr. Warner and her grad students to our python campaign. Their contributions have proven pivotal in addressing the greatest biological emergency in Florida."

Miller leaned back in the chair and let his paunch relax against the elastic waistband of his suit pants.

About time the fat cats in Tallahassee realized there's more than two universities in Florida.

"It's been my pleasure, Governor. I've followed Dr. Warner's progress weekly and leveled a few speed bumps for her."

"Indeed, I've heard that, Dean Miller. A well-oiled engineering machine down there near my favorite botanical museum, Fairchild Gardens."

"Oh, I raise orchids and display them at Fairchild's events."

"Do tell. Do tell. All I could manage to grow in Polk County were soda apples and thistles. Anyway, I know it's short notice, but the results of the Burmese python task force are being released at a press conference next Wednesday, July 18th. I was wondering if you might join us, because Dr. Warner's project plays a key role in addressing this urgent situation. We'll send a jet to Miami Executive Airport and have you back home by dinner."

"Oh, let me see. Next Wednesday."

Miller thought for a second. His desk calendar had a tee time at three.

"Well, I don't see why not. I'd be pleased to support you any way I can, Governor. Is Dr. Warner traveling with me?"

"Oh, no. She has meetings with my staff on Tuesday to discuss the next steps. You'll have the Citation all to yourself. My assistant will call you with details."

"I'm honored, Governor."

"Splendid. It will be great to meet you. Oh, one other item. Dean, the execution phase of restoring the Everglades will require Dr. Warner's full attention. It would be very kind of you to grant her a nine-month sabbatical. We'll pay her salary and benefits, of course."

Dean Miller's mind spun with possibilities.

There's juice in this plump orange.

"Well, that's a tough one. Dr. Warner is a critical component of our leadership team. That would require serious reshuffling."

Prescott smiled, setting up the squeeze.

"Understood, Dean. Unfortunately, she is the sole architect of the computer programs central to the solution. I agree, we can't crater your management team. If it would help, we have unallocated federal A.I. infrastructure funds to upgrade your data center. I have a donor who could provide one million dollars to support five F-1 PhD engineering candidates. Dr. Warner's project is sure to attract future grant awards. In addition, I can redirect some grant money from UF to UM. Would that help?"

Miller leaned back further, the chair almost horizontal, and watched a spider crossing upside down on the ceiling.

"As I said, I'm fully behind your project, Governor, and understand our contributions to date and your future needs. I accept your offer and suggest that we start with three million as a point of reference for UF research grant funds migrated to my college. We can be flexible on the length of Dr. Warner's sabbatical."

Prescott fist-pumped the air, then flipped his middle finger at the phone.

"Splendid indeed, Dean. I look forward to meeting you next Wednesday. Have a great rest of the day, Sir."

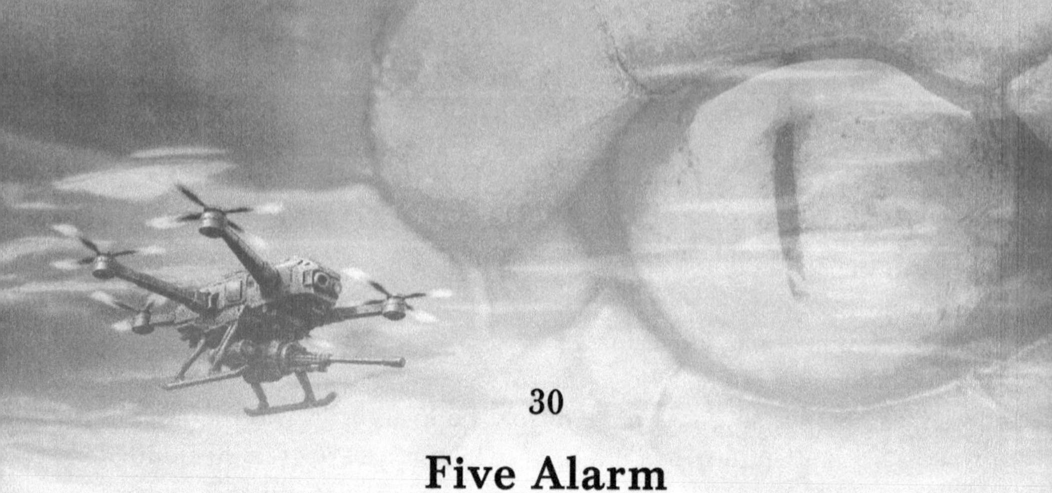

30

Five Alarm

Drizzle, unusual for Tallahassee in July, began around noon on Tuesday. Slate, accompanied by her finance director and two attorneys, sat at a table in the governor's executive conference room. Opposite them, Brent Howard, and, to her surprise, Anthony "The Assassin" Newman, sat with attorneys and others in expensive business suits. Brent opened the meeting and stepped them through a contract template with standard clauses and blanks.

Negotiating from a position of strength without competition, Slate defined the limits of ZKuul Solutions' responsibilities and liabilities. She would kill pythons within a defined area as quickly as possible. Wildlife surveys, scorekeeping, security, and liability were State responsibilities. Slate passed out a single sheet with her requests—a mobilization fee of $750,000, bi-weekly payments for supported expenses, plus a 12% profit over expenses. She requested a 3% bonus for completing the project by an agreed-upon date, adjusted for any delays caused by the State.

Slate would retain operational control and intellectual property rights.

Finished by four, Brent Howard complimented her team.

"I've seen negotiations like this drag on for days. Thank you, Dr. Warner, for reasonable requests without theatrics. We'll email you a draft agreement by Friday. See you tomorrow at the press conference."

* * *

Slate's room came with an attendant who placed Slate's malachite green silk-wrap dress and jade-colored leopard scarf on the bed.

188

Her delicate gold bangle, embedded with emeralds, along with emerald drop earrings in gold and a matching pendant, draped across a velvet cushion on the dresser. Champagne-colored heels, a coordinating clutch, and ultra-sheer nude pantyhose lay over a club chair. Light filtered through flowing lace curtains, and shifting shadows moved like waltzing ribbons around the room.

Returning from the meeting, Slate opened the room door, and her eyes saw movement on the bed. A python slithered over the duvet cover. Gasping, she let out a short scream and flipped on the light switch. The malachite dress and leopard scarf had the shape of a serpent.

"Oh my god," she exhaled, and a half-laugh escaped as her tension unraveled. "I'll be so glad when this project is finished."

After her shower, she sat at the vanity in a lacy silk bra and bikini panties. Her excitement had grown throughout the week. She prepared for the dinner date, with feelings she hadn't experienced since attending a fraternity formal during her sophomore year at Ohio State. She used an A.I. fashion app and watched YouTube makeup tutorials to plan her outfit and accessories.

Her makeup arranged on the table, she applied foundation and powder, then bronzer and blush for a natural, sun-kissed look. Next, taupe eyebrow accent, honey dew eyeshadow, deep brown eyeliner, charcoal mascara, and summer peach lipstick.

Slate called the room valet to help pin her hair into a twist with a fashion clip. The lady declared her a cover girl and took a photo with Slate's phone.

Slate stepped out of the hotel at six-thirty onto a burgundy carpet beneath a covered walkway. A steady drizzle fell in the calm air. The doorman helped her with a waist-length trench coat, complimenting her with words like "dazzling" and "striking." She blushed, showing her cute dimples.

"Here's the governor's car," he said.

The glossy black Escalade pulled up. The doorman opened the back door and took her hand as she stepped on the running board. The governor reached for her other hand and guided her to the middle beside him. Feeling awkward and unsure if it was intentional, she moved away, angled her body, and smiled.

"Hi, there," he said with a bright smile. "Sorry about the weather. Wow, you look stunning, Sarah."

She giggled. "I wasn't sure if the restaurant allowed jeans, lab coats, or cowgirl outfits."

He chuckled. "Don't forget the flight suit, another uniform I've seen you wear, Dr. Warner. You're a woman of many impressive looks."

She blushed again, loosened the belt of her jacket, crossed her legs, and noticed the governor glance at them.

He wore an ice-blue Oxford shirt, matching the color of his eyes, and a navy-blue linen sports jacket. Sleek charcoal dress slacks complemented signature leather boots.

Slate wondered if his Omega astronaut watch was a gift. At forty-three, gray streaks at his temples enhanced a light salt-and-pepper scruff. Slate recognized a faint scent of Green Irish Tweed—an exotic cologne favored by men on a mission.

Two attendants welcomed the car with umbrellas. The restaurant owner stood at the entrance and led them to a secluded table for two overlooking a courtyard in the back. Rain streaked the bubble-glass windowpanes, blurring the shapes of mallard ducks huddled by a pond.

An arrangement of tapered candles on stands cast a halo of soft, warm light. Slate noticed his handsome features highlighted by the candlelight and wondered if he thought the same of her. Feeling confident and adventurous, she ordered a Kir Royale while the governor chose a smoked Manhattan on ice.

The governor raised his glass. "Here's to an enjoyable evening with a lovely lady. I don't want to waste our evening on shop talk, but I will just tell you that Brent called and said you had a productive meeting and that he was impressed with your team."

"I like Brent and your python assassin, too." She let out a giggle.

"You're funny. I hope you didn't call him that."

"No. He's straight up and competent," she said.

"That calls for another toast." He raised his glass. "Here's to Anthony. May he shoot straight and stay true to his values." They clinked glasses and laughed.

She paused for a moment, then said, "Something occurred to me. Do you find it strange that a common thread connects us? Had it not been for pythons, we wouldn't know each other. The same applies to connections with dozens of others in this potpourri of personalities."

He laughed. "That's creepy. You started it with your note," he smiled with raised eyebrows. "And here we are," he said.

"So, that begs the question. Why did you take a chance on me?"

Their eyes met, and time stopped for a moment.

"There's something about you that's different, Sarah—something special."

She smiled, pleased with his response. "Too late now. You're stuck with me, at least until the end of the project."

Her meal arrived—pan-seared quail finished with a fig and rosemary glaze. His filet, cooked medium rare with blackened garlic au jus, hissed in a tableside skillet.

"Quail. That's funny. Besides your uncanny ability to kill pythons with a screwdriver, I only know that you like to eat quail. So, what's up with you and quail?"

She took a sip of the paired wine, a pinot noir from Oregon. Then she popped a piece of quail into her mouth.

"Yummy! Just like the ones Dad hunted in Ohio. We had them every fall. My older brother and I grew up in Columbus. Dad owned a feed store, and Mom taught high school chemistry."

"I'll bet you're a Buckeye," he said.

"Yep." She made a circle with her thumb and finger on her head, resembling the buckeyes that Ohio State football players wore on their helmets.

"I'm a Floridian." The governor put his hands together and gestured like an alligator chomping its jaws.

"University of Florida, I'm guessing."

"Yes, I have a degree in economics and a master's in finance. I grew up in Lakeland, Florida. Have you ever been there?"

"No."

"It's a charming town halfway between Orlando and Tampa in Polk County. The county is renowned for its kick-ass sheriff. My father is a semi-retired veterinarian, and my mother is a dermatologist. I have an older sister and a younger brother."

Each took a bite. She sipped her pinot noir while he enjoyed a merlot, exchanging glances over their glasses. A teasing smile emerged, and her eyes sparkled.

"Well, you seem to have left out the good parts, John."

He laughed, understanding her meaning. "And I was thinking the same of you."

"I earned my PhD in computer science and robotics from Carnegie Mellon in Pittsburgh," she said.

He nodded approvingly. "I worked in mergers and acquisitions at a consulting firm in Tampa, then formed a wealth management company."

She reached across the table and touched his ring finger.

"So, what's going on there?"

He flipped his palm up and grabbed her hand, holding her ring finger.

He grinned. "I'll ask you the same."

She withdrew it and took a sip of wine.

"You go first," she said.

"Eight years. No kids. We divorced seven years ago. What about you?"

"Two years, no kids. It's been twelve years, and I have no regrets," she said.

"You're a powerful, handsome man, Mr. Governor," she said with a wry smile. "That must make you popular with the ladies."

He returned her gaze, smiled, and said, "You're a stunningly beautiful woman, probably the smartest person in all of Florida. That must make you incredibly popular with the boys."

She smiled and winked. "It does."

They erupted in laughter. He raised his hand for a high-five. She slapped it firmly, then offered the back of her hand like a princess. He accepted and kissed it.

Dessert arrived—a lavender crème brûlée.

She pointed her dessert spoon at him.

"John, I love everything about this evening, especially your sense of humor. But we must agree that we cannot have these dinners or a personal relationship, given the obvious conflict of interest. Nothing remains secret in the political arena, and my technology will attract intense scrutiny."

Seeing the effect of her declaration on his face, she regretted being so direct.

"Once the project is over, let's see where we stand." She smiled and winked.

Her last words brightened his mood.

"You're right, of course. Thanks for leaving the door open."

"You're sweet." She straightened up and signaled the server.

"Do you have St-Germain Spritz?"

"Yes, Madam."

"Will you join me?" she asked him.

"Great idea."

They discussed their favorite comedies, sports, hobbies, politics, podcasts, and books. She viewed him as open, curious, interesting, intelligent, principled, and honest. He was neither overly ambitious nor did he seem obsessed with power or wealth. Slate thought herself more intelligent, in some ways. However, he had a fighting spirit, intuition, and street smarts that exceeded hers.

The rain ended sometime during their conversation. They decided to walk the five blocks to her hotel. The governor retrieved an umbrella from the SUV and instructed the driver to meet him at the hotel.

She removed her heels. The cold, wet sidewalk reminded her of rainy summer evenings in Columbus when she and her brother caught nightcrawlers for fishing.

John carried her shoes, and she held onto his arm. Quietly, they walked in an air of shared energy, buoyed by the tension of sexual attraction. It was a combination that formed lasting memories. Trees arched like cathedrals beneath moody clouds over shimmering pavement and puddles illuminated by glowing streetlamps. A car zoomed by, splashing water over their feet. They shook their fists in mock anger and cursed while laughing. A block from the hotel, Slate noticed a park bench in the shadows.

"Can we sit there? I'll put my shoes on."

He laid his overcoat on the bench. They sat, and she lifted each foot as he slipped her shoes on. She thanked him. He began to stand when she caught his arm.

"To ensure you don't forget me, I grant you one kiss. So, make it a good one."

She turned to face him. A streetlight filtered through the leaves, casting warm light on her face. He looked at her luscious, waiting lips. The kiss, gentle at first, grew in intensity and desire.

A siren sounded in the distance. Closer, up the street, a second siren joined the first. They tried to ignore the blasts.

Barreling down their block, a white SUV, the Fire Chief, led two fire trucks and other vehicles, their headlight beams almost to the park bench. Breathing heavily, the two separated and straightened up on the bench. He grabbed the open umbrella next to the bench and held it up to shadow them from view.

They sat in silence as the sirens faded. She giggled first.

"Was that a conflict of interest?" he asked.

She slapped his arm. "No, it was a test."

"You passed," the governor said.

She lightly slapped him again.

"It's lucky the fire trucks came. I was in the danger zone," she said.

"I agree. We know where that was headed."

"What time is my ride to the press conference tomorrow?"

"Ten. You can sleep in and enjoy room service. Dean Miller arrives at nine-thirty. He's a jerk."

"Tell me about it."

"What was the best part of our evening?" he asked.

"The quail," she winked. "Thank you for a wonderful time, John."

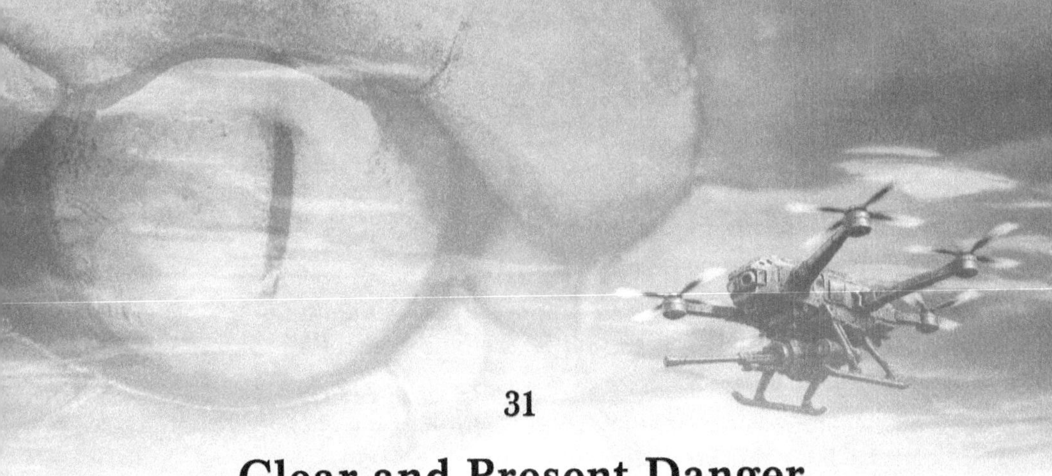

31

Clear and Present Danger

The spacious conference room was nearly empty. Thirty minutes before the task force meeting, Dean Miller sat alone in the first seat of the second row reserved for special guests, the front row empty. At the entrance, Slate hesitated upon seeing Miller's bald crown above tufts of brown hair. She thought of the smooth-top stone dome of an old mountain bordered by scraggly trees. From the tobacco-brown tweed jacket visible above the chair, she guessed he wore a blue Oxford button-down, a faded burgundy tie, a functional slide-rule tie clasp, rumpled brown trousers, and scuffed, broken-back slip-on loafers.

I bet his tenured leather satchel is lying on his lap.

Overwhelmed by nerves, she retreated to the coffee bar in the hallway to pass the time and watch the news on a TV above the bagel rack.

Someone tapped her shoulder, and she turned to see Taylor and Carter. Taylor wrapped Slate in a warm hug.

"Whoa, what are you two doing way up here?"

"It's your big day, and I wanted to be here for you. We left Miami at midnight," Taylor said.

Carter smiled and shrugged. "It was her idea, Boss."

"I'm so glad you came. It's going to be big news for Florida and will likely be controversial. Cross your fingers. Sit in the back and don't talk to anyone. Okay?"

Slate made her way up the aisle as the room began to fill. Just when she thought she couldn't be more nervous, passing in front of Miller to the empty seat next to him, she tripped on his beat-up loafer and nearly fell into his lap.

195

"Oh, I'm sorry, Dean."

He grunted, pulling the satchel to his chest. She shuffled, trying not to touch his knees, and took her seat.

Not having spoken to Miller since the governor practically ordered him to grant her a sabbatical, she braced for the grumpy academic's denunciation of politicians who controlled the money hose funding his department.

Slate assembled an engaging smile. "I came up yesterday for meetings. How was your flight this morning?"

"The boatload they spent on that private jet would have funded two research grants. I don't mind being played, but not with public money."

"I hope, Dean, that the Everglades project will put our university at the forefront of A.I. engineering and robotics. It will attract researchers, venture capital, and federal funding. I'm excited, and I hope you are as well."

He glanced at her, his frown undiminished. "I hope you're right. I don't pretend to comprehend this new wave of technology, Dr. Warner, partly because your project has kept me in the dark. However, I know enough to be wary of unintended consequences no one saw coming until whammo, and then, it's too late."

Slate turned to look at the old man, his glory years long gone, replaced by a lonely, bitter resignation. His sad eyes met hers. Without speaking, she smiled, hiding the feeling a nurse's aide might have as she wiped dribble from an old man's chin.

The governor's twenty-eight-year-old press secretary approached the podium on the stage, about twenty feet away from Slate. Beautiful and crackerjack smart, her shoulder-length, chestnut-brown hair was swept to one side behind her ear.

Family members occupied the first row across the aisle from Slate. Task force members and Director Newman took their seats in the second row, along with other officials like Senator Alvarez. The third row had the governor's cabinet secretaries. Slate took notice that many were attractive women.

A twinge of jealousy colored Slate's observations, highlighting how easily Prescott had stretched ethical boundaries in planning their romantic dinner. She recalled the hot kiss, trying to understand how she had become the instigator. The embarrassing interruption by the fire trucks left her feeling guilty and regretful, feelings she doubted that he shared.

Was last night's dinner business as usual for him? How many other women have sat in my seat across from him at the Savour?

As the press secretary opened the meeting, Slate noticed someone to the left of the podium hidden in the shadows of a stage curtain. John's bright smile and blue eyes met hers. Feeling self-conscious, she forced a nervous smile, lifted her agenda in a small wave, and focused on the speaker.

"Welcome. My name is Brooke Sandals. Today, we present the findings of Governor Prescott's task force, which aims to restore native animals and birds to the Florida Everglades. Copies of their report are available in the hallway following the meeting. A QR code on the screen behind me links to a digital copy.

"Five months ago, Governor Prescott established a task force to investigate the Pa-Hay-Okee tragedy and to decide on a plan of action."

Brooke introduced the task force and officials, asking them to stand. Slate heard a cameraman seated on the floor by the front row of seats comment to another, "Where are the snakes and pigs?" His colleague replied, "I was hoping for mud wrestling or spitting cobras." They chuckled, and one glanced back to see Slate smile at him. Brooke gathered her notes. "And now, here is your governor, John J. Prescott."

Lights dimmed, and scenes of the Everglades and the State seal were displayed on two screens. The governor approached the podium, shook hands with Brooke, waved to the audience with a smile, and pointed to Sheriff Palmer sitting down the row from Slate. He paused while his speech loaded on two teleprompters. His eyes swept the packed room and stopped at Slate. She held his gaze for a moment, hoping they were sharing the same thought.

"On February 18th, we confronted the horrific and heart-wrenching loss of eight young scouts in Everglades National Park. I promised to address this tragedy and to take action. Some families of our scouts are here today." He gestured toward the families.

The governor reviewed python information and stats that, by now, had become common knowledge.

"Those are the facts. Our focus is twofold—how to find pythons and how to eliminate them."

He gave a small laugh. "Sorry to disappoint anyone, but we don't have a live python demonstration today."

The audience laughed, and some booed. The two cameramen looked at each other and shrugged.

Slate looked across at Director Newman, who looked straight ahead without expression.

"You will see in the report that the task force considered a plethora of ideas and proposals. Some, quite original and free-ranging, like balloon-tethered beam weapons, are beyond our time horizon. Another suggestion promoted the introduction of a natural predator of the Burmese python from Asia, the King Cobra. We didn't think that was a good trade-off.

"Here's the math. Female pythons lay eggs around the same time each year. Each nest produces up to eight snakes that reach breeding age, four males and four females. Reducing the present population by one-third, from 300,000 to 200,000, requires killing 275,000 snakes between seasons. Otherwise, their reproduction rate replaces the ones eliminated during the year.

"Any solution that kills fewer than 90% between breeding seasons does not reduce the population. This reality ruled out all proposals except for one. The actions by the FWC for the past thirty years were grossly ineffective, to say the least."

Bullet points, charts, and infographics displayed on screens that supported the governor's presentation.

The governor paused and looked at shocked expressions, many taking pictures of the statistics on the screens with their phones.

Prescott stepped from the stage to greet Dean Miller and Slate. They followed him to the podium.

"As mentioned earlier, I realized that python hunters, trappers, dogs, hormone lures, parasites, and pathogens were a waste of time and money, easily outmatched by simple reproduction rates. Python food, being our native animals, determines population size. Therefore, we sought a technology-based solution.

"Let me introduce Dr. Henry Miller, the Dean of the College of Engineering at the University of Miami."

Miller stood next to the podium as tall as his frumpy frame allowed. Enjoying the celebrity, he attempted to button his jacket, smiled, and waved to the audience.

"Reporting to Dean Miller, we have Dr. Sarah Warner, Chair of Computer Science and Robotics at the University."

Slate, wearing a navy linen blazer, cream-colored silky high-neck top, and wide-leg charcoal trousers, smiled professionally and nodded. Her hair, like Brooke's, was swept to one side. The governor shook their hands, pointed to biographical information about them on the screen, and motioned them back to their seats.

"Let me tell you what Dean Miller and Dr. Warner have accomplished. Within days of the Pa-Hay-Okee tragedy, I became aware of their remarkable research that combines artificial intelligence, advanced multispectral sensors, robotics, and unmanned aerial platforms. I challenged them with a simple question: Can you develop technology to find and eliminate pythons in large numbers, twenty-four hours a day?

"Working alongside Brent Howard, my Director of Science and Technology, Dean Miller provided resources from multiple engineering campuses and also access to supercomputers and data centers. Dr. Warner assembled a small team of robotics and drone experts and created a machine-learning algorithm trained to identify pythons by analyzing data from multiple sensors.

"I direct your attention to the center screen displaying video of live pythons identified by sensors, including optical, infrared, UV, and motion. Notice the image of a python nest of white eggs discovered by trained sensors."

The screen displayed annotated clips recorded at the research site and during test runs in the Everglades, omitting footage of actual shootings.

"The computer program gained speed and accuracy over time through self-learning. Dr. Warner's team installed the sensor array on a drone platform equipped with GPS navigation, which is operated from a control center."

Prescott paused. The audience was quiet and attentive.

"So, we can find pythons not only on roads where paid python hunters search, but also deep in swamps and remote hammocks.

"In only forty minutes, I witnessed Dr. Warner's algorithm find a hundred pythons at night in stormy weather."

Fully engaged, people leaned forward in their seats.

"The final piece after finding pythons is killing them humanely. Using state-of-the-art technology, Dr. Warner's team equipped the drone platform with a high-precision weapon. Controlled by a targeting computer, it fires a single bullet into the python's brain. Remember, my task force observed a demonstration in which 100 pythons were found and killed in forty minutes."

He paused again, watching the audience's reaction.

"To recap, everything tried in the past has failed. These monsters can eat humans and their pets. They wiped out an entire ecosystem that had existed for millions of years. They must be killed in massive numbers that exceed their reproduction rate. There is only one option: the high-tech solution proposed by our scientists, Dean Miller and Dr. Warner."

Prescott ignored raised hands in the press section.

"The next step is a pilot project to evaluate their capacity to eliminate pythons from a five-square-mile area. If successful, we hope to scale up by adding dozens of drone platforms to clear the entire Everglades, beginning with public areas."

Brooke rushed to the podium with a phone pressed to her ear. The governor stepped aside in a hushed conversation while the audience murmured. After watching a video on Brooke's phone, he shook his head and returned to the podium.

"A short while ago, it was reported that a python snatched a toddler and vanished into an Everglades swamp. I'm told a family of four was on a tour with Run-Wild Python Adventures, LLC. The social media video I just viewed shows family members and a tour guide pulling a small python by its tail from a brush thicket. Captured in the background, the video shows a toddler bent over, splashing in the water at the edge of a slough. A large python burst from the water, ambushed the child in a pink sun dress, and disappeared back into the water."

Hearing this, Sheriff Palmer and other officials jumped to their feet and ran out of the room. Cries and chatter erupted as many searched their phones for news and to watch the video before it was removed. Family members stood, hugging one another in support.

Prescott appeared stunned, thrown off his agenda. He grasped the sides of the podium and noticed a man whose son, a scout at Pa-Hay-Okee, was never found. He stepped to the stage and approached the governor, asking to speak. Prescott nodded.

"Paul was my son. He was lost at Pa-Hay-Okee. Something must be done. This must stop. These reptilian terrorists are a clear and present danger. We either kill them or close off the Everglades and other areas as they spread north and south. I fully support Governor Prescott and commend him for finding a way to stop them. Brilliant people are needed. The days of Billy Bob bouncing down roads at night, catching a few snakes, are over. I'm more than pissed off at the FWC for not taking the python problem seriously all these years. The governor has the math. The University has the Python Terminator. We are only eleven months away from the next python hatching season. There's no time to waste. Please, if you agree with me, start clapping."

The applause and roar resembled a Florida Gators football game. The father, dressed in jeans and a plaid shirt, shook Prescott's hand and returned to hugs from family and friends.

The governor and Slate exchanged glances, and she gave him a thumbs-up. The governor thanked Paul's father and decided, in light of the news about the toddler, to abbreviate the portion of the presentation on the repatriation of native wildlife.

Prescott introduced Brent Howard as the State's lead on the pilot project. He, in turn, introduced Dr. Leslie Paton, director of the University of Florida's Department of Wildlife Ecology and Conservation. Brent then introduced Jason Bernal, of Save Native Wildlife of Florida. Brent explained their role in measuring the pilot project's results and briefly outlined their plan to reintroduce native animals after pythons are removed.

The governor concluded, "Our thoughts and prayers are with the family of the little one." Prescott approached the press section. He was surprised by the absence of pushback regarding his high-tech killing solution, but understood that the public was not in the mood for animal rights activism.

Slate was surprised when Dean Miller stood and offered her his hand. In his own awkward way, he admitted that he had been "out to lunch" the last five months and was amazed at how she had managed to get everything done.

"You're one smart lady, Sarah. I'm behind you," he said.

She extended her hand and thanked him, wondering if his enlightenment might reverse her demotion. She decided it didn't matter that much anymore. Jake and John were correct. The project was more important.

She gathered her belongings and navigated through the crowd to retrieve her suitcase from the checkroom.

A man with olive-colored skin, about thirty-five, dressed like a golfer off the back nine at Doral, appeared at her side with a smile as if he knew her.

"Hi. Great meeting. Exciting, huh?" he said.

Slate had an excellent memory for faces. Not only did she not recognize him, but something about him seemed off. She continued walking, suspecting he might be a reporter.

"Dean Miller suggested we talk," the man said.

Slate slowed her pace and studied his steady, dark eyes and warm, fixed smile. She decided to play along to see where he was headed.

"Where?"

"How about coffee in ten minutes at Bean and Bun down the block on the right? You have time to make your flight. My name is Nick, Dr. Warner."

"I'll have a vanilla latte."

32

Jelly Bean

Slate wheeled her carry-on through a line at the checkout counter and spotted his short-cropped brown hair and white polo through the window blinds of a small conference room in the back of Bean and Bun.

"There are extra sugar packets and a toasted cinnamon crunch bagel in the bag," Nick said as he closed the door and the blinds. "I have an Uber waiting to take you to the airport."

"Who are you?"

Nick slid a picture from a folder across the table. "Do you know him?"

"Who are you?" she repeated more emphatically.

"We have reason to believe he works for a foreign agency. I work counterintelligence for the FBI." He flipped his badge open, then closed it.

She looked at the black and white picture of T-Zee talking to someone at Gifford Arboretum, in South Miami, a place where she occasionally had lunch with a girlfriend."

She answered. "He's T-Zee. He's a computer engineering grad student under Professor Bismark."

"His name is Tan Zhi Hao, a Malaysian."

Slate leaned back, sipped her latte, and took a bite of the bagel. "He was alone in the computer lab in a side office a couple of Saturdays ago. I saw him when I arrived to work on the python algorithm. We waved."

"He was here at the meeting this morning. You didn't see him," Nick said.

"No way. He was here in Tallahassee?"

203

Nick nodded. "So was your grad student, Carter, and his new girlfriend, Taylor, who was your nephew's former girlfriend."

Slate stared at him, her eyes like daggers.

The prick probably knows about Jake and me.

"Back to T-Zee, as you call him. He's good but not perfect, and left some crumbs while snooping around university computers. He's been looking for targets of opportunity.

"Your work has commercial and military value, the holy grail being your algorithm. This makes you and your project of interest to US National Security."

"I'm not following the last part," she said.

Nick checked a message on his iPhone. "Good, T-Zee is driving back to Miami. Okay, let me get to the point so you can catch your flight. We have to keep you and your algorithm safe and secure. We don't know who T-Zee works for. He might be freelance."

"So, is my life in danger?" she asked without being serious.

"They might kidnap you."

"What am I supposed to do about that?"

Nick slid another picture across the table. A woman in camouflage and muted face paint crouched in a sandbag bunker, a camo net overhead. Her grubby hands held an army-green drone controller. The screen illuminated her face as the late sun teetered on a war-torn horizon. The photographer captured her smiling face, and the control screen as her missile exploded inside a troop carrier.

"Do you know this person?"

"No."

"She works for us. Shannon Trane came from electronic intelligence in Army Special Forces. In addition to being a bad-ass, she's a crackerjack at cybersecurity. We want your ZKuul Solutions to hire her as a console controller. She'll protect you, secure your algorithms, and shadow T-Zee."

"You're kidding me." Slate held his gaze, taking the last bite of her bagel.

Nick slid another picture across the table. A thin, limp man in a filthy dungeon was secured by leg irons, with a chain padlocked to a loop on the wall. He sat on a camp stool at a folding table, typing on a laptop.

"I wish I was kidding, Doctor."

Her throat suddenly dry, she choked on the bagel. Nick uncapped a water bottle for her.

"Shannon helped us get this computer engineer out of a dirt hole. She took the photograph.

"One more thing. We want you to hire T-Zee."

Slate choked on the water. Nick handed her his napkin.

"If you advertise part-time positions at your college for console controllers, T-Zee will jump on it. You can train Shannon and the operative together. The tab's on us."

"So, what's the end game here, Nick?"

"Once we get enough on T-Zee, find out what he's after and for whom, we give him the choice: thirty years in prison or he works for us. Assuming he makes the smart choice, we feed T-Zee false information that he sends back up the line. Just like in the movies."

"Do I have a choice?"

"I'm afraid not. If all goes well, you do your job, and we'll have your back. When it's done, we're gone. You never saw me."

* * *

Slate turned the thermostat down in the conference room across the hall from her university office. In steamy Miami on Tuesday, July 24th, the pilot project kickoff meeting would begin in thirty minutes.

Shannon Trane sat at the conference table reviewing the task force report released in Tallahassee the previous Wednesday. Dressed as a computer geek, she had braided brown pigtails, a baseball cap with a honey badger patch, cargo pants, and an untucked, long-sleeved cotton shirt over a black T-shirt with a neon green Mojo logo, her favorite programming language. With the pleasant, full face and sturdy frame of a steppe Cossack, her left hand took precise notes with the speed and precision of an inkjet printer.

Having arrived on Sunday, Shannon had spent the afternoon in the computer lab, where Slate introduced her to Lucy. That evening, Shannon searched Tan Zhi Hao's university workstation, copied thumb drives she found in his desk drawer, and planted a micro video recorder on the wall observing his computer screen and keyboard.

On Monday, Brad showed Shannon the research site and the Zcolt while Slate finalized the contract and performance criteria with state staff and Director Newman, who was named general manager of field operations. After draft beer and dinner at Chiller's Ale House with Newman, Slate found him funny and easy to work with.

Slate's team, including Jake, who had driven from Everglades City, and Director Newman's team were seated by ten and reading the printed agenda packet. Slate introduced Brad, Carter, Jake, and Shannon, along with three members of ZKuul Solutions' administrative staff.

Director Newman introduced the operations, procurement, and clerical staff, as well as Dr. Paton from the University of Florida and Mr. Bernal from the non-profit organization.

Brent began. "Great to meet everyone. Allow me to start with a reminder. This project and all related materials, including your information packets, are strictly confidential. Leaks to the media and the public will jeopardize safety and our success. Mr. Newman has included a nondisclosure agreement in your packet for your signature.

Newman said, "We finalized the site and project criteria yesterday. Slate will show us the test area."

Slate pointed to a red square on the map south of Gator Park, an airboat marina on the Tamiami Trail, a few miles west of the original research site.

"This is the five-square-mile test area. You'll notice the grid, like most of the Everglades, is not near roads. The state has amended the test criteria to require operating from land and water. They will modify two airboats and a skiff with platforms to launch Zcolts."

Newman interrupted with a question for Dr. Paton. "Dr. Paton, can you complete the python population estimate of the test area by August 13th, three weeks from now?"

"That depends on you guys at FWC," she replied.

"Tell us what you need, and you'll have it. The governor wants points on the board," Newman said.

Dr. Paton nodded.

Slate outlined her plan.

"Our single aerial platform can clear the area of pythons in about ten days. That's ten-hour days. I'm working on ways to cut the time in half. A second controller team, led by Shannon, can work a second shift. I'm also adding staff to build and operate a second Zcolt.

"That sounds ambitious, but if you can pull it off, all the better," Newman said.

"Here's another idea." Slate held up a picture. "Have you seen pictures of three or more wheat combines harvesting in a staggered formation on the Great Plains? I have the technology to fly three Zcolts in formation under the control of one team."

The participants quietly absorbed the implications and complexities of the ideas Slate presented.

Shannon raised her hand. "Hi, I'm new to the team and still getting grounded, but I've read the task force report and watched the governor's speech. The math is straightforward. We have eleven months to clear 3,500 square miles of Everglades before pythons lay their eggs. Efficiency and resources count. I could see ten teams controlling formations of three Zcolts. That would do it."

Slate looked down the table at Shannon.

There's more to this girl than I thought.

Director Newman added to the conversation. "Good points. It's a major task requiring commitment and teamwork. We'll run the back office, keep score, handle security, and public relations."

Slate finished her thoughts on her company's objectives.

"I'm not questioning our ability to find and kill pythons. The challenge is finding the best combination of drones, algorithms, and controller teams. The sweet spot is a package big enough to cover large areas quickly, like wheat combines, and small enough to be manageable—the more moving parts, the more that can go wrong.

"By the end of the pilot project, I hope to have one team controlling two drones with a software option to add more. Director Newman's area is logistics, which is critical and has the most variables. We organize into teams, with controllers, drone crew chiefs, and support components working as one unit.

"Once we find the most efficient operations and support package, we replicate and scale up. We divide the Glades into grids by priority based on risk to public safety."

Someone on Brent's staff asked Slate about equipment storage and drone maintenance.

"The project's operations are shifting from the university to my company, ZKuul Solutions," she replied. "We're now in an office park. We have located an old industrial complex in western Miami near the casino. There's a large building resembling an aircraft hangar, smaller structures, and a fence around the entire compound. It's the perfect location for building drones and control trailers, as well as for central operations, administration, and training.

"I'm fortunate to have Jake, Brad, Carter, and now Shannon on board. South Florida is home to a wealth of talented individuals across various fields. I'm recruiting to fill a few positions for the pilot project, and we hope to start killing pythons by August 15th. Any questions?"

Sitting next to Dr. Paton, Gary, the name written in felt-tip on his tent card, with a Gator mascot on his cap, asked about the minimum size a python could be detected and shot. He questioned the project's ability to kill most of the pythons in one year.

"Good question, Gary. The algorithm is configured to exclude targets that are less than three feet long. Hatchlings emerge at twenty inches and reach five feet in the first year. We'll miss some juveniles in August and September, but get most of them," Slate said. "You might be interested in another idea I'm thinking about."

Gary seemed satisfied with her answer and leaned forward listening.

"Females lay eggs from March to early May. Lucy, our algorithm, can find nests, but the process is too slow.

"I'm wondering if drones looking down from higher altitudes, maybe on tethers, or even satellites, could be trained to spot the unique signature of one hundred white python eggs in a nest. We could develop target lists of GPS coordinates for hundreds of drones and humans to shoot nests with shotguns.

"No doubt, we are at the beginning stages of this technology, and incremental improvements will evolve. We're doing the heavy lifting, in my opinion. I expect future generations of this technology to develop improved sensors and use lasers or particle beams to kill pythons with microbursts. Still, if we can wipe out most of them in a couple of years and eliminate nests annually, we won't need anything too exotic."

Slate watched Gary take in her explanations and ideas, satisfied that he was not a disruptor.

"If there are no other questions, I suggest we have lunch in the cafeteria, then split into two groups. Director Newman can meet here with his members, and Zcolt people meet in my office. Use the time to create a spreadsheet of action steps on a timeline, assigning tasks to individuals. Also, make a list of what you need from the other team and when you need it. At three, we'll reconvene here and discuss our lists. Okay?"

* * *

Brad and Carter took Shannon to the cafeteria for lunch while Jake went with Slate to leave her briefcase and laptop in her office.

"How was your drive this morning?" she asked.

"Not bad. I found a convoy of commuters on the Tamiami cruising at 100. I got a late start. One of my hog dogs ran off during a hunt last night. As I was about to leave this morning, he came home cut up from a fight with a hog. He's okay, but I had to stitch him up."

"Ouch, don't tell me that stuff. I would be worried sick if it was my dog."

"I know. I didn't sleep well. Once they disappear in the swamp, there's not much you can do. He lost his GPS collar in the fight. He's alright. How was your time in Tallahassee?" he asked.

"Oh, fine. Dean Miller kind of made up to me after the governor kissed his ass for essentially obstructing our project."

"The governor looked happy enough on TV," Jake said.

"He should be. We saved his ass on the python crisis, big time. He was SOL without us. I couldn't have done this without you, Jake. You're underrated. The techie stuff is the easy part." Slate watched his face brighten with her compliment.

"Thank you. I appreciate that more than you can know."

Slate looked at him. "Are you going back to Everglades City tonight?"

"That's the plan."

"Want to take a break in the RV?"

Jake hesitated, not expecting the invitation. She noticed and wondered what could be more enticing than having his way with her in the RV.

"I understand. It's your dog." She searched his eyes.

"Yes, of course. Sure. Jelly Bean is a big boy. He can wait."

209

33

Tac Ops

On Saturday, July 28th, eighteen days before the pilot project, Nick's Tac Ops team set up surveillance in the compound hangar. His cyber guys, having studied Shannon's file on T-Zee, worked with Slate on hardware and software upgrades to detect and prevent cyber intrusions. They created a strategic, limited-access backdoor in Lucy's algorithm as hacker bait.

The following Friday, Shannon walked past the Zcolt in the hangar, then up metal grated stairs to the line of offices on the second floor.

She stopped on the catwalk, recognizing him through the office window as the guy in her university surveillance recordings.

His back to her, he sat upright like a military cadet. An oversized gray sweatshirt hung on the square shoulders of a long, lean torso. His black hair, close-cut on the sides, transitioned into a disorganized whorl on top that failed to convince Shannon of an easygoing disposition.

Across the white laminate sorting table, Brad talked while T-Zee took notes in a blue spiral notebook. From a side view, Shannon studied his angular face, seeing a mix of Asian features. His stiff posture conveyed a forced relaxation. She guessed he struggled with perfectionism and attempted to soften his edge with his paint-splattered Converse tennis shoes and by chewing gum, not common among Malaysians.

Shannon opened the door with, "I'm here," then dropped her computer backpack on the table next to Brad.

T-Zee stood up, as was his culture, and waited for introductions.

"At ease, soldier," Brad joked.

210

"Shannon, this is Tan Zhi Hao. He goes by T-Zee. I'm teaching him my job as co-pilot for the second Zcolt. And Mr. T, this is Shannon Trane. She's your captain once we get you guys up to speed.

T-Zee bowed slightly and presented a formal hand. Shannon, six inches shorter, reached over with the firm grip of a Wisconsin dirt farmer and gave a warm, confident smile.

She thought to herself. *This is going to be fun. I already know what you are, from watching your surveillance. So, what do you want and who for? Is it for money or country? I'm betting money.*

Brad opened a notebook of lesson plans compiled by his A.I. assistant.

"We can get acquainted over lunch. Slate's treating us to BBQ. Carter, with Sebastian, your new Zcolt-2 crew chief, are joining us. After lunch, you get the pleasure of sitting beside us at consoles in the control trailer while we fly the Zcolt through a full cycle. We might find a python or two in the Glades on the other side of the compound fence, but we can't shoot them."

T-Zee sat forward. "Can I fly?"

Brad turned to Shannon. "Mr. T tells me he's not into Fortnite. He's a Valorant guy. Do you think he can handle the Zcolt?"

She nodded. "I'm not a gamer, but even money says T can make the Zcolt cry like a baby."

A genuine smile briefly softened T-Zee's sober expression as he gave her a shy thumbs up.

* * *

On Sunday, August 12th, three days before the pilot project, they continued working on Zcolt-2 and a second control trailer. If all went well, Slate and Brad would calibrate Zcolt-2 and the second control trailer at the compound and test it during the second half of the pilot project.

On Monday, they relocated Zcolt-1 with its control trailer from the compound, six miles to a secure area within Gator Park.

On Tuesday, a telecommunications engineering company tested secure low-latency UHF/RF data and communication links between Gator Park and the compound.

Dr. Paton and her staff conducted a population survey of the five-square-mile, or 3,200-acre, test grid. They reported a healthy number of recently hatched pythons, plus a few large prey species, and marginal numbers of small animals and birds. They estimated 400 pythons within the test grid that were three feet or more in length.

* * *

Wednesday, August 15th, Carter declared as P Day, the kickoff date of the pilot project. Sebastian, the new Zcolt-2 crew chief, rode in Carter's pickup, and T-Zee went with Brad. They unlocked the gate of the chain-link fence at Gator Park around eight a.m., each drinking the last coffee in their 24-ounce mugs. Sebastian, an agronomy student from Michigan taking a night chemistry class at the university, slapped a blood-filled mosquito on his neck and followed Carter to the airboat office on the dock. Sebastian heard the fast, tight whine of a Lycoming aircraft engine and told Carter it sounded like crop-dusters over cornfields back home. Next, a throaty Chevy big-block V-8 came to life and drowned out the Lycoming.

"Now you're talking, S-Man. Do you feel that V-8 rattle your ribs?" Carter asked.

Two groups of tourists in cut-offs and tank tops mingled on the dock waiting for airboat tours.

The screen door of the tour company slammed behind Carter and Sebastian. Cooter, the faded name embroidered above his shirt pocket, looked up from a register. He leaned on a barnboard counter wrapped in corrugated tin, a Styrofoam spit cup in his left hand.

"This the day yer takin' up the whirly-gig?" Cooter asked Carter.

"Yep, is Boone here yet?"

"I saw his Dodge. He's probably gettin' yer ride gassed up."

"Gotcha, gotcha," Carter said. "Can ya get Boone to bring the airboat to the boat ramp and have the marine forklift come over to carry the whirly-gig down to the airboat?"

"Don't see why not."

Meanwhile, Brad and T-Zee, in the control trailer, used checklists to power up the equipment while waiting for Slate to arrive. Carter and S-man opened the drone trailer, unstrapped the Zcolt, and unpacked tools and equipment they would take on the airboat.

Boone's big-block Chevy rumbled up the channel at idle. Jake had helped fabricate an aluminum launch platform that extended out from the bow. The launch platform edged over the boat ramp. Boone cut the engine, coasted to a stop, and tied the boat line to a cleat. The carpet-wrapped skids of the forklift slid under the Zcolt, lifted it off the trailer, and set it on the airboat platform.

* * *

That morning after Slate's operations and Newman's support teams left the compound for Gator Park, Nick and Shannon searched T-Zee's office, the last one in the row of offices upstairs in the hangar. They tried the same login information he used on his university workstation. It worked. As they suspected, T-Zee had poked around project files and moved data to his own work folders. He hadn't found the backdoor in Slate's algorithm.

Hidden cameras recorded him on Sunday evening at Slate's workstation on the hangar floor near the Zcolt. Slate had used the terminal to modify Zcolt-2's firmware and left the system active to process data overnight. T-Zee, looking nervous and exposed in the video, worked at the terminal for ten minutes, then plugged in a small external hard drive. After removing it, he went upstairs to his office, then to his car.

Nick hoped T-Zee had left the hard drive in his office.

"Put everything back like it was. This guy's persnickety," Nick told Shannon.

"That's a pretty big word for a former Marine Lance Corporal," she commented.

"Okay, he's punctilious." He looked to see if she laughed.

"Bingo, I found it," Shannon said. "It's in here. Inside the AC vent." She shined her flashlight through the louvers of a floor vent that was under a trash can.

"Good work. We have a few hours. I'll get the cyber guys over here," he said. "You'd better join the others at Gator Park. They'll be looking for you."

"Okay, I have an idea. How about calling the janitorial company to clean the upstairs offices to move his shit around," she said.

"Good idea."

* * *

Making its way out of the busy Gator Park marina to the main channel, the Zcolt bobbed on its perch as the airboat weaved around watercraft and crossed boat wakes. Strapped into their seats behind the drone and in front of Boone, who sat higher, Carter and Sebastian strained to see around the drone. Even with ear protectors, the roar and vibration of the engine overwhelmed their senses. Boone used an iPad on a pedestal for navigation, adjusting the throttle and twin air-rudders to steer the awkward contraption through a maze of sloughs and across stretches of salt marsh.

After about twenty minutes, Boone announced, "We're here, boys." He pulled the throttle to idle and switched the engine off. The massive prop stopped with a clunk, and a plume of blue exhaust drifted over them.

Carter looked out in all directions, seeing nothing but water, grass, and occasional patches of brush and trees.

Boone rotated the iPad to show them. "We're right here on the northwest corner of your grid."

Boone threw out the anchor, opened a large beach umbrella over his captain's chair, grabbed a two-liter bottle of Mountain Dew from his cooler, and a bag of jalapeno corn nuts.

Carter and S-man removed tie-downs, completed the before-launch checklist, and called 'on-station' to the control center. Carter stepped on the platform and leaned over to check that a bullet was in the rifle chamber.

"Wow, what happened to your leg, dude?" Sebastian asked.

Carter grimaced. "Oh, it's a long story. Tell you over a beer."

They waited for the order to launch. Water slapped the aluminum hull. A fish jumped. A heron flew by and squawked. Boone drifted off to sleep.

* * *

Muggy, air thick under a steamy haze, the control trailer's air conditioner groaned under the load.

Dr. Paton and Mr. Bernal sat against the wall behind Slate and Shannon, who were at the left console. Brad and T-Zee sat to their right. All systems were up, and links to the Z-colt blinked steadily. Slate took a moment to explain the screens to the two observers.

A new, larger screen displayed a 3D depiction of the grid, outlined in red, which showed the drone's position and orientation. As the drone flew, a 100-foot-wide gray track would appear on the map behind it. Additionally, symbols for pythons found and those killed would appear on the gray map track.

Slate turned to Dr. Paton. "I think we're ready. We'll go slow to orient Shannon and T-Zee. Brad will fly the drone while Lucy scans for pythons. Brad will confirm the crosshairs are on the python's head and fire the rifle.

"We'll fly south along the western edge of the grid for 2.25 miles in about nineteen minutes, then turn around and come back next to the first row with a ten-foot overlap. Back on the boat, they will replace batteries and add ammunition if necessary."

Slate called over the radio. "Carter, are you armed and ready?"

"Yes, armed and ready."

"She's all yours, Game Boy," Slate told Brad.

On the airboat, the rotors came alive like woodchippers on bone-dry oak, snapping Boone from his nap. His sweat-soaked, swamp hat flew back and caught around his neck by the chin cord. The umbrella tipped sideways. Boone cursed at his deck crew, and they added another step to their checklist.

The drone popped up to fifty feet, and Brad did flight control checks while Slate brought Lucy online. Brad descended to twenty feet and manually flew the magenta line, the first of 118 rows in the grid area.

"Python, python," Lucy announced over the speaker in her pleasant British accent.

"Do you see the python, Doctor?" Slate pointed out the optical and thermal images to Dr. Paton. "Here it is on the weapons screen. It's a big one. The solid red circle around it means the computer has a firing solution. Go ahead, Brad."

Brad entered the firing command on the keyboard. Dr. Paton jumped and let out a surprised, "Ohhh," as the head splattered like a watermelon dropped on concrete.

T-Zee seemed impervious to the gore. "Amazing precision. Nice shot."

"Thank Lucy. She's aiming the rifle. I'm just pulling the trigger," Brad replied. The green python symbol on the 3D map changed to red. Brad resumed flying, an acre passing under the drone every twenty-five seconds.

"Python, python," Lucy announced. Swimming away from the drone, the python submerged before Brad got the shot off. The python symbol on the map remained green to confirm it was not killed.

The round-trip took fifty minutes, ten minutes longer than estimated, because Brad had to turn the drone within a twenty-degree arc for the computer to aim the rifle.

Small red python symbols for kills, and a few greens for misses, dotted the 200-foot-wide gray-tone round-trip track on the 3D map. They had covered 52 acres, found seven pythons, and killed six.

Dr. Paton punched numbers into her calculator. "Good job. We estimated eight pythons in an area that size," she said.

"You make it look easy, Brad. I don't see how you can do that with only a keyboard and mouse," Mr. Bernal said.

"It takes practice, and I've had plenty. I'm a gamer in my spare time. T-man here is up next," Brad said.

Slate stood up and stretched. "Let's take a break while they swap out batteries and reload."

Shannon stepped back to the cooler for sodas and water and saw a message to call Nick. She passed the drinks around and excused herself to the restroom in the RV next door.

Shannon called on an encrypted app. "Hi, Nick. What's up?"

"How's T-Zee?"

"He's fine. We just finished the first session. That gun is bad-ass. I needed one of those in the Sandbox."

"I'm glad all is going well," Nick said. "We jailbroke his hard drive. Luckily, he didn't have time to encrypt the data he copied from Slate's computer. The hard drive is back in his office, and the cleaning company moved his shit around."

"So, what's he after?" she asked.

"He copied code related to how Slate commands and rewards Lucy. We don't know if it was a time issue, why he didn't copy more, or if he got what he wanted."

"That's weird. But he's a weird guy. Nothing seems to faze him, especially killing snakes," Shannon said. "I have to get back."

Nick ended with, "Tell Slate to leave that computer on at night. We put a repeater on it to capture his keystrokes."

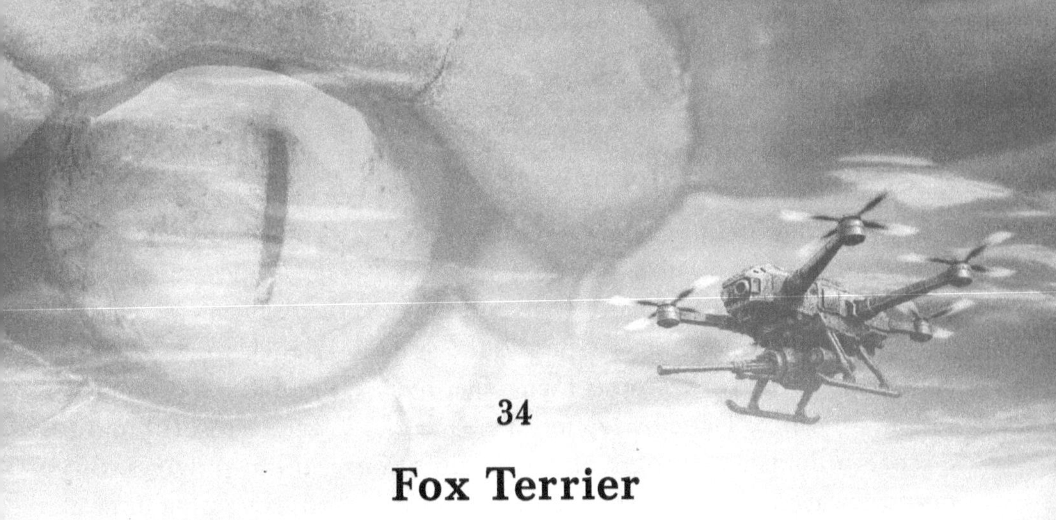

34

Fox Terrier

By Tuesday, August 21st, one week into the pilot, the team had completed the western one-third of the five-square-mile test area. They eliminated 86% of the pythons that Lucy identified. The Zcolt flew three one-hour sessions on each of three days during the daytime and killed 102 pythons. They also conducted two sessions from sunset to midnight on two nights, resulting in 49 kills. As Slate suspected, pythons highlighted clearly in infrared at night, and they killed two additional pythons during each session.

On the airboat, Carter and Sebastian had a front row seat to watch the Zcolt in action. Initially excited, they zoomed in with binoculars and listened for the rifle shots. Boone moved the airboat along the northern boundary as the drone proceeded eastward on the grid.

Lathered in sunscreen and insect repellent, they sunbathed on chaise lounges, wore broad sunhats like Boone, and fished off the launch platform. Boone taught them how to throw a cast net. They grilled fish on a hibachi and argued over what music to play on the boom box.

On the third day, Taylor took Sebastian's place. Boone handed Carter a 410 Snake Charmer shotgun and dropped the two off on a small hammock for a walk.

Not wasting the opportunity, Taylor and Carter found a group of bushes to make out.

Shannon and T-Zee excelled at training during the first five days of flying.

Over the previous weekend, after the first three flying days, Slate's team worked in the compound on the second drone, Zcolt-2, and its control trailer. They powered up systems and did sensor checks.

217

Slate worked at her terminal on the hangar floor and left it on at night to process.

Sunday evening, T-Zee returned to the compound and spent thirty minutes at Slate's terminal next to Zcolt-2. Once again, he downloaded data onto a hard drive and hid it in the AC vent.

Monday morning, August 20th, as before, Nick's cyber team copied the drive. Nick's top A.I. engineer hacked into hidden computer files in his office. T-Zee had found the backdoor to Lucy's algorithm. In a separate folder, he programmed modifications. Still in progress, the purpose wasn't clear, but the engineer said it looked like a plug-in or a patch to modify Lucy's behavior.

* * *

Carter declared Thursday, August 23rd, as Full-Auto-Day. The evaluation team and Governor Prescott were pleased with the results from the first five days of operations. Slate agreed but also understood the sheer size of the Everglades required increased speed and a higher kill rate. Flying in manual mode was like cruise control with lane assist. Brad, as good as he was, could not match Lucy's auto-flight mode. Lucy demonstrated an amazing ability to scan for multiple pythons, build a target list, and engage at speeds beyond human capability.

Slate modified the protocol. Lucy would fly, navigate, find pythons, build a target list, and aim the Humboldt. The captain, Slate or Shannon, monitored Lucy from their console, and the co-pilot, Brad or T-Zee, fired the rifle after checking the aim point. Lucy's speed, limited only by her ability to process sensor data, might exceed twenty miles per hour, a fivefold increase.

On Full-Auto-Day, Boone had the Zcolt on station at eight a.m. Two-thirds of the grid remaining, Carter and S-man checked in with Slate and were told to stand by while Lucy finished loading.

Shannon, getting more coffee, kept an eye on T-Zee. He watched Slate's keyboard commands and studied computer code on the rain screen. He took notes in the small spiral notebook he kept with him at all times.

A line of thunderstorms had drenched the test area the night before, dropping two inches of rain. A fresh green scent mixed with earthy swamp vapors as life erupted in croaks, buzzes, and chirps. While they waited, Boone pulled out two long aluminum poles. One had a pocket net on a loop, and the other had a three-prong gig spear. Using a trolling motor, Boone moved the airboat along the muddy bank. Carter and S-Man gigged ten large pig frogs. Boone cleaned the legs and put them on ice to pan-fry at lunch in olive oil, lemon juice, and a touch of Old Bay seasoning.

"We're ready, Drone Boy," Slate radioed. Boone closed the umbrella and cinched down his hat.

Once airborne, the Zcolt flew forward thirty feet and stopped.

Slate typed commands to initiate full auto-flight, up to but not including firing the rifle.

"Are you ready, T-Zee?" Slate asked her co-pilot.

The tall Asian adjusted his seat, got his fingers in place, and watched the weapons screen.

"Ready, Boss." Slate was shocked that he had called her boss, given what she knew he was doing.

Carter and S-man on the airboat weren't ready for the next part. The growl of the rotors became more like the whine of a turbine as the Zcolt shot forward, nose down. The drone jinked, sliced, and pivoted, performing unlike anything they had seen.

Carter thought it might be out of control. "The Zcolt's having a fit," he called over the radio.

"We know," Shannon replied, sitting next to Brad, who was supervising T-Zee.

Lucy announced pythons over the speaker, adjusted azimuth, and T-Zee pushed the fire keys. Slate had increased the reward for speed while maintaining an accuracy rate of 95 percent. No longer on cruise control, Lucy adjusted forward speed and even backed up. Resembling her S-turns on the way back from the Pa-Hay-Okee test flight, Lucy turned off the centerline and appeared to hunt, not unlike a fox terrier. The results were dramatic. It took time, but T-Zee got in sync and kept up with the firing solutions.

The drone out of sight, Carter poured coffee, and Boone prepared a breakfast of sausage, eggs, grits, onions, and peppers that he grilled in a skillet. Served on metal plates, they had just begun eating when, "Hear that buzz?" S-man asked.

Carter climbed onto the platform with a pair of binoculars.

"Holy shit, it's coming back already, only twelve minutes. It looks unhinged. Boone, you might want to back up a little."

The rifle cracked. Cracked again. Carter watched through the binoculars.

"Holy moly! It's walking rounds left and right at us like a cross stitch."

Shannon came over the radio. "We're not landing, guys. She's got plenty of juice left. Going for another five-mile round trip."

The Z-colt shot a python fifty feet off their bow, banked hard right, pirouetted 180 degrees, and took off like a jackrabbit.

"What's the body count?" Carter radioed.

"Fourteen kills and no misses," Shannon replied.

During the second-round trip, Lucy smoothed edges and rounded turns as if learning on the fly.

Approaching the airboat the second time, Slate disengaged Lucy's autopilot, and T-Zee landed the Zcolt on the pad. The crew chiefs swapped the batteries and ammunition magazine.

On the second session, Shannon and T-Zee sat at the consoles under the supervision of Slate and Brad. As a test, Slate called out simulated problems twice during the session to test their reactions—they passed.

At speeds as high as twenty-one miles per hour, auto-flight required half the pit stops and covered over twice as much ground with an almost perfect kill rate. Skipping lunch, they flew six round-trip flights, twice the size of the former area, and were packed up by two o'clock.

The entire team of twelve, including Slate's and Newman's teams, as well as Jake, went to Tropi-Caracas, a Venezuelan joint near the compound, for a late lunch and early happy hour.

Shannon found herself sitting with Brad. Again.

* * *

Shannon had sat to Slate's right at the console every day of operations. Brad sat next to Shannon, with T-Zee to his right. Brad, almost as tall as T-Zee, had the natural clean look of a gymnast on the pommel horse. Easy-going with a midwestern accent, women found Brad attractive.

Shannon, five feet two inches tall, realistic but sad at times, accepted the hand she'd been dealt. Born with burly arms and thick thighs, she wasn't blessed with small hips, small shoulders, large breasts, or cover-girl looks. She compensated with confidence through competence, and a quick wit spiced with playful sarcasm. Having an exceptional complexion, her face carried a tinge of Mongol heritage. Brown hair, curly and unruly, never failed to disappoint her attempts to look alluring. She endured a slight, but persistent limp from a knee injury. The few relationships she had, a couple in the Army, were guys looking for sex.

By noon on the first day of flying, Brad and Shannon were already exchanging quips. They played off each other.

"I'm ready for an airboat DoorDash," Shannon whispered to Brad at ten o'clock.

"That would be funny. Are you buying?"

"Arm wrestle you for it," she replied.

He looked at her sly smile. "Or, maybe you brought a bag of snacks?" she added.

He pulled a brown bag from under his chair. "Cheetos?"

She winked at him and nodded.

Shannon's real name was Molly Bowen from Eugene, Oregon, but she used a cover identity claiming she was from Fairhaven, Washington. Brad didn't know that Shannon's biological father was a marine mechanic working in a dockyard, or that she joined Army Intelligence straight out of high school and nearly completed Army Ranger school before her knee blew out. Recruited by the FBI three years earlier, she worked as a cybercrime counterintelligence special agent in the Miami field office.

Shannon picked up on Slate's nickname for Brad, calling him "Game Boy," and he called her "Cap," short for Captain.

Before long, they found themselves sitting beside each other at picnic tables and at happy hour. By the end of the first week of the pilot phase, their connection, not yet romantic, had progressed past work associates.

Friday, the day after Full-Auto-Day, Shannon operated the captain's console. Brad was her co-pilot, and Sebastian was alone on the airboat with Boone. In the compound hangar, Slate, Carter, and T-Zee worked on Zcolt-2.

Controlled and predictable, Lucy found a natural rhythm and cleared sixteen rows. With two battery changes and a lunch break, the Shannon/Brad/Sebastian team killed fifty-five pythons and finished by two p.m. With almost half of the five square miles cleared, they hoped to complete the pilot the following week before Labor Day weekend.

Brad and Shannon walked to their cars, chatting about how well the day had gone. Only three p.m. on Friday, approaching her hammered bronze colored Bronco and his Jeep, an awkward silence developed. Their pace slowed for no reason. Shannon wondered about saying something. Then she saw the Army Ranger bumper sticker on Brad's Jeep.

"Dude, you were a Ranger?"

"Oh, yeah. I got the patch, but I'm actually in the Reserves."

"No shit. You know this little limp of mine? Where do you think I got it?"

"Breakdancing?" he joked. She raised her hand to backhand him, and he jumped back, laughing.

"I got it at Ranger school. It washed me out at the end during the swamp phase."

Brad stopped and looked at her, now serious. "You know, Cap, I had a feeling there was more to you."

She looked up at his kind face.

"Ya never know. Who would have guessed, right? Rangers," she said, breaking the tension.

"As it turns out, Cap, this is Reserve drill weekend. It's bullshit mostly. One weekend per month." Brad ran out of words and was about to say he'd see her on Monday.

"Hey, I just remembered. I'm doing pizza and bowling tonight. Nothing crazy. People just show up and organize into teams. I won't know some of them," he said.

"That sounds fun. I like bowling."

"Okay, I'll make it official. Want to go bowling together?"

Her face brightened.

"Sure. Sounds like fun."

"Okay, the place is Palm City Pins on Tamiami just past the turnpike."

Shannon had a great time bowling with Brad on Friday night. With an average of 205, she beat his score in all three games, carried their team to first place, and won free pizza for the team.

* * *

Over the weekend, on Saturday, Shannon met Nick behind the elephant tent at the Sunrise flea market. Not making any progress in finding T-Zee's handler or communication method, they were confident he didn't have remote access to Slate's programs. They expected him to revisit the hangar Sunday evening.

Also, on Saturday, Dr. Paton and her staff completed a survey of the 1,400 acres, almost half of the test grid, and found seven pythons and multiple groups of black-headed vultures feeding on dead pythons.

On Saturday, Slate had a staff meeting in the compound with her administrative team and Newman's. Scheduled to complete the pilot early, they discussed expanding the engagement to develop Zcolt-2 and formation flying.

On Sunday, Slate spent the day with Rick and Mathew. She told her brother about the excellent progress on her project, but it failed to improve his spirits. Mathew seemed much older than six months earlier when he played under the booth at the restaurant. Given his current interest in rockets and Mars, Slate suggested taking him to the Kennedy Space Center.

Back at her condo Sunday evening, she thought about Jake and checked the calendar. It had been five weeks since they had sex in the RV, their third time. She remembered him hesitating when she suggested the RV after the pilot kickoff meeting in the compound. Their evening was fine, better than fine, even fantastic. Jake, ever the gentleman, doted on her and took her to the faraway place of colors and intense acceleration.

Since that night, not needed for the pilot project, Jake kept in touch by text. He guided an inshore fishing charter, a licensed gator hunt, and was hired as first mate on an offshore kite-fishing sailfish charter. A longtime client, in trade for guide fees, had offered to take him on an Alaskan wilderness fly fishing trip for salmon on the Tsiu River.

Returning to Florida the previous Tuesday, he watched Lucy's full-auto session at Gator Park on Thursday and went to lunch with the crew at Tropi-Caraccas. He sat by Slate and told her about his adventures in Alaska, including encounters with grizzly bears and catching silver salmon by hand. He didn't bring up the RV for that evening. She thought about it but waited for him to ask. He didn't. She wasn't sure why and naturally thought he had someone in Everglades City. He never said, and she didn't pry.

Sitting on her sofa that Sunday night, Miami lights in the distance, she sipped wine, wondered, and picked up the phone.

"Hi. It's me. Long time no talkie, Jake."

He seemed fine and happy to hear from her. The background sounded like a crowd, maybe a bar.

"Oh, it's an exhibition football game. A waste of time. I'm glad you called."

She asked him about his business and if he had any crazy stories.

He asked about the project, and she told him about Lucy, who thinks shooting pythons is a video game.

"I've been thinking about you," he said. "Thinking about the RV."

Slate pulled the phone from her ear and looked at it.

Am I hearing this right?

"Really, you're worried about the RV? A leak?" she asked, with a grin he could not see.

"Yes, I think we should check it out. Maybe a test drive."

"Are you asking or begging?" she said.

"Begging."

"Well then, how about this Friday, before Labor Day weekend, after the pilot project team meeting."

He didn't hide his enthusiasm. "Definitely, Cowgirl."

The call over, Slate kicked off her shoes, wiggled her toes, and giggled. Running water for a bubble bath, she opened her music app and clicked, "Girls Just Wanna Have Fun." It played in a loop on an external speaker as she soaked in hot sudsy water.

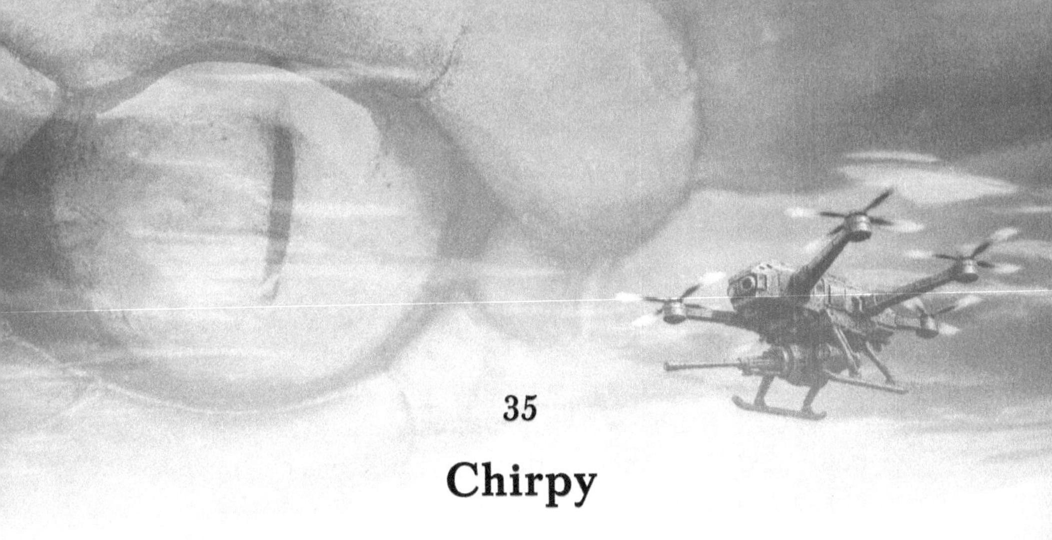

35

Chirpy

Tired, happy with the results, but glad it was over, the two teams led by Slate and Newman completed operations on the five-square-mile grid on Thursday.

Slate opened the Friday morning meeting in the compound conference room on the first floor. She listed three objectives for the remaining time allotted for the pilot phase: 1. Test the Zcolt-2 drone and its control trailer; 2. Operate both drones independently; 3. Fly both drones in formation from one control trailer.

Surprised by a question so early, she pointed to T-Zee.

"Regarding Zcolt-2, is it your plan to use a baseline database and allow its algorithm to machine learn independently from Zcolt-1?"

"Good question, T. There's some merit in that approach, using independent LRMs. If this was a research lab, that would make sense. However, we're here to kill pythons. Lucy has proven herself and continues to improve. Once I finish uploading the latest version of Lucy's algorithm to Zcolt-2 tomorrow, we'll have identical twins—Lucy and Daisy. From there, they can evolve independently.

Shannon eyed T-Zee from across the table.

What is it, T-man? What's your game? If you're a thief, why modify her code? You must finish before she encrypts and vaults the algorithm. Not much time, T-man.

T-Zee continued. "What about formation flying? Have you started on that software?"

"Not yet. I've contacted a robotics engineer, someone who designs drone light shows. She thinks our application is simpler if restricted to

225

two or three drones. A master-slave configuration would work in our case. She's coming next Wednesday."

Carter asked, "When is Zcolt-2's first flight from the new control trailer?"

"First, thanks for your questions, T-Zee. In answer to Carter's question, we're off through Monday for Labor Day. I'm guessing next Thursday we fly Z-2 from the compound, probably fix bugs on Friday, and take it to Gator Park a week from Monday."

Brad joked. "So, T-man, do they celebrate Labor Day in Malaysia?"

"Yes, Game Boy, it's called Hari Pekerja. It's on May 1."

Brad, for whatever reason, kept up his ribbing.

"That said, are you observing 'our' Labor Day?"

T-Zee grimaced, both confused and annoyed at the attention.

"There's a Valorant gaming tournament in West Palm Beach on Sunday. I'm not competing, just watching. I might run a 10K in Davie on Monday. I haven't decided yet," T-Zee replied.

Brad seemed surprised, not expecting a straight answer.

"Ah, good plan, T-man. Enjoy your time off. I brought it up in case you're home alone, so far away from your country."

T-Zee nodded in understanding. "No worries, Game Boy."

"Okay, guys. You're not off until four o'clock today, back to the project. Let's hear from Newman's team."

* * *

The meeting on Friday ended at 12:30, skipping lunch to free up the afternoon, since some participants lived on Florida's West Coast and as far north as Tallahassee. Slate stopped at her condo to change clothes, shower, and find a perfume she remembered from long ago. At the compound, she worked on the Zcolt-2 upload until four, stopped at the grocery store for wine, then went to the RV. Already at the RV, Jake prepared a dinner of veal scampi over angel hair, as he listened to 80s music.

As Slate left her garage, a text sounded, a chirp she had assigned to Nick.

"There's been a development. Can you meet on Monday at two o'clock, at the location I told you about? It's important."

***

At the appointed time, Slate walked through the gift shop into the eighty-acre Fairchild Botanical Gardens in Coral Gables. The pathways, confusing for newcomers, meandered past bamboo thickets, ancient cycads, and palm trees of every variety. Coming here often, being an orchid lover like Dean Miller, she took the most direct path past throngs of visitors to a giant African Baobab tree. Nick, off to the side under shade, read the Miami Herald. She recognized his thin, straight profile. He wore lightweight khaki chinos, a floral print shirt, and military-style sunglasses under a Panama hat. They greeted each other as a brother might greet a sister. He gestured with the newspaper, and they walked to a bench in an out-of-the-way alcove overlooking a cascade of reflecting pools.

Nick got straight to the point. "You worked at your computer station in the hangar on Friday until four, again yesterday from noon until three, and you left the computer running as we requested."

"Yes, I left at three yesterday," Slate replied warily.

If he knows all this, does he know what I did with Jake on Friday evening after I left the compound? He wouldn't tell me, of course. He's too cagey for that.

"T-Zee watched you leave yesterday, went to your terminal on the hangar floor, then to his office for several hours. He's tracking your modifications and transferring data to a hard drive. That's not all. The previous weekend, he found the back door we inserted. He's writing a program on the computer in his office."

Nick referred Slate to an article in the newspaper as he talked. She looked while listening.

"Why would he write a program?"

"My guys are guessing. It might be a modification to track activity. Or a patch to insert commands in real time, let's say, change the target from pythons to humans."

"I can't believe this is happening. I thought he went to a video game tournament yesterday."

"He did go, then doubled back to the compound and waited for you to leave. He's now at the 10K race in Davie."

Slate looked concerned. "What are you going to do?"

"We think he's communicating using an encrypted phone app. Our pinhole camera, positioned over his desk, captured parts of two messages. To be honest, we're not sure how to handle it at this point. Do we keep the game going in hopes of finding the company or the country, and his handlers? If we keep going, we risk him stealing your perfected algorithm or converting your Zcolts into terror weapons.

"Shannon is at the compound now, going through his computer to see what he did yesterday. Depending on what she finds, we might pull him in tomorrow before he spills any more beans.

"We need solid evidence, or he'll claim he's just doing his job."

"Shannon's at the compound, now?" Slate asked. "This is too confusing for me. T-Zee doesn't seem like the spy type."

"The good ones never do."

"But you think it's almost over, right?" she asked hopefully.

"Close, it's getting close. If we turn him, it makes sense to keep him on your project. We'll see."

Nick noticed a lime green four-foot-long iguana crossing the stone wall between the first two pools. A family with five kids fed lettuce to three iguanas off to their right.

"Hey, Professor, how about creating an iguana-hunting drone?" he joked.

Slate half-frowned. "You've got enough on your plate without thinking up more shit for me."

Nick tipped his sunglasses down, making eye contact over the rim. "Good point." He smiled. The phone rang in his pocket, the SOS ringtone assigned to his agents.

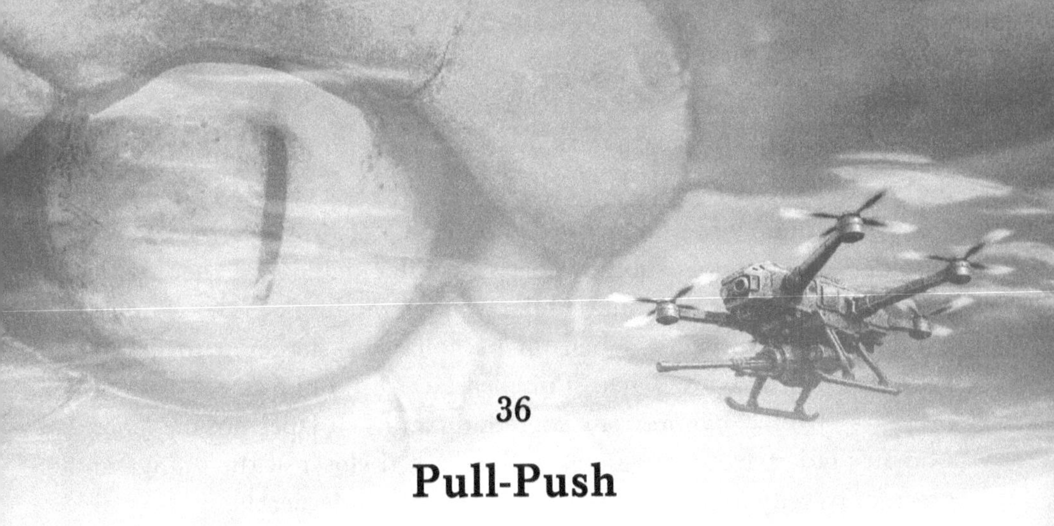

36

Pull-Push

Shannon relatched the combination lock on the sliding gate and drove her Bronco through the empty parking lot. Parking behind the dull green steel warehouse, she looked for but did not see T-Zee's faded gray Hyundai. She put on her backpack and entered through the rusty loading dock door. The hinge squeaked. She left it open a crack. Walking in shadows along the perimeter, she moved short distances, stopped to listen, and looked for movement.

Dim weekend lights cast long, indistinct shadows. During the workweek, she hadn't noticed the annoying rattle of loose air duct vents, creaking metal siding, or birds thrashing and darting around roof girders. Otherwise, the soft, persistent quiet settled her nerves.

She looked across the hangar floor beyond the Zcolt to the upstairs offices along the iron mezzanine catwalk. Her eyes swept to the last office, looking for the faint glow of a computer screen behind cracks in closed vertical blinds. Shannon crossed the hangar past the Z-colt and Slate's computer terminal. She tiptoed up steps of diamond-cut metal grating to a landing and up a second run to the catwalk. Shannon moved silently in tennis shoes across the gray carpet tiles toward the room. Listening, hearing nothing, she used a master key, pushed open the door, entered, and left it open a crack to listen for noise in the hangar. She put on a headband with a red LED light. Retrieving the hard drive from the floor vent, she copied it using software the cyber-team had installed on her laptop.

In T-Zee's desk chair, shining a handheld penlight, she looked up at the ceiling. After some effort, she spotted the camera lens, a tiny dimple in a textured, yellowed fiberboard ceiling tile. The camera was unattended, with half of the surveillance detail off for the holiday, and the rest at T-Zee's race.

Shannon powered up the computer. T-Zee's home screen showed an older Asian couple standing beside a dilapidated tool shed, with a rice paddy in the background, and a wooden pitchfork in the old man's hand. A milk cow with a bell on its collar was tethered to a stake. Looking solemn, lines etched sunbaked faces on frail frames weathered by years of toil. Shannon saw something shiny, a lapel pin on the old woman's faded army green jacket. She looked closer at the orange and green university logo, with the word "Miami" underneath.

His parents. He's their only son. He looks like his mother. They must be very proud. They should be. He's one smart kid. Apparently, no girlfriend.

Referring to her notes from the team engineer who hacked into the computer, Shannon navigated through a labyrinth to T-Zee's new algorithm.

Cool, dude. You're writing in Chinese and using a Chinese A.I. coding agent. Pretty ironic, T-man, that our common coding language is Python. We're using Python to kill pythons. You must admit, that's cool. Anyway, I see your revision log. You were a busy boy yesterday.

Shannon copied what she could to her laptop and took pictures of the computer screen with her phone when necessary. She enjoyed reading lines of Python code he had compiled, looking for clues to his endgame.

* * *

T-Zee drove past the empty parking lot to the back of the warehouse and saw Shannon's brown Bronco. Pushing back panic, he considered leaving. He stopped and wondered. It had seemed easy. Too easy. He pulled next to her car and froze.

Maybe she's here to pick something up. Or working in her office. How can I explain why I would come here on Monday for a part-time job? I can't. Maybe say I left something and came to get it. Why is she here? I must find out why she's here. No way she's counterintelligence. They may not know much at this point. Hopefully, they haven't found the hard drive or my algorithm. I don't have a choice, I must go in. See where she is.

He slipped through the slim opening of door of the loading dock. A hinge gave a short squeak. Standing frozen, he listened, heard birds fluttering in the rafters, and squeaks of metal buckling under afternoon heat. His eyes adjusted to the dim light. He listened. Nothing.

I don't hear her goofy rap music. Why aren't the lights on? Maybe she's having sex with Brad? That would be interesting. No. No noise. She must be in her office.

Tip-toeing in shadows along the perimeter to the restroom doors, he listened for her. Nothing. Past the men's room, five feet, he peeked around a steel pillar across the hangar up to the row of offices. Shannon's office, three down from his, the blinds open, was dark. The first office, the break room, also dark.

Where is she? Maybe at Slate's terminal by the Zcolt.

He moved further along the wall, closer to the Zcolt. A little further. The chair empty, he saw the screensaver on Slate's computer, a view of the Earth from Mars.

She's here somewhere. Or maybe her beat-up Bronco broke down? Yes, that makes perfect sense. Her shit-box Bronco.

His eyes fully adjusted, T-Zee ducked under the platform of the Zcolt between the skids. Now closer, he looked up at the offices.

His heart stopped. A faint blue flicker slipped through a crack in the blinds.

I always turn it off. She's on my computer with the lights off.

He removed his shoes and socks and set them on the Zcolt. It took ten minutes to cross the hangar, creep up the stairs, and walk the length of the catwalk to the door. The diamond-cut grate etched razor cuts into his feet. They seared like hot coals.

His back against the wall, he peeked through the quarter-inch gap. He felt violated, watching her sitting in his chair, her back to him, as she searched his computer. He saw his hard drive on the desk plugged into her laptop.

What right does this stumpy spud think she has? She has no idea what she's dealing with. Or what they could do to her.

Shannon's broad shoulders hunched over the desk. Her head leaned forward as she focused on multi-colored code. Her finger rolled the wheel on the mouse, and the screen scrolled. T-Zee recognized the file. It was his plug-in patch for Lucy's algorithm.

She found it. I'm screwed. They'll send my parents and grandma to the camps.

A bird, spooked by something, fluttered under the catwalk. It flew out from underneath, came up confused, maybe saw the computer light. It smacked hard against the office window and dropped like a turd to the catwalk.

The window a few feet from her left shoulder, Shannon bolted upright in the chair, snapped her head to the window, then back to the crack in the door.

The smack of the bird shocked T-Zee like an open-handed slap to his face. He backed up, his back flat against the window of the adjoining office. He held his breath.

"Fricking birds," she said out loud. "Scared the fricking shit out of me. Alright, let's get this shit done. I'm getting spooked."

T-Zee heard what she said, relaxed, and breathed quiet deep breaths.

The sparrow on the carpet staggered to its feet in a stupor. One wing drooped, the tip dragging. A sick feeling boiled up inside T-Zee like bile. He fought a sudden urge to piss himself.

He inched back to the crack in the door. She, back at his computer, turned her face toward him to check her phone for messages. T-Zee saw her flat, white, ghostly face in the computer light. He cursed himself for being so stupid, thinking his software was secure. He struggled to think.

The sparrow bumbled around like a drunk, made its way over the worn carpet, shooting poop out in white blobs. Next to T-Zee's bare foot, it pecked his little toe. T-Zee looked down, saw the bird, moved his foot away and stepped in a gooey pile of bird shit. It looked up at him. He flicked his foot and slapped it. The bird tumbled over the edge of the catwalk and dropped to the hangar floor.

He watched her take a picture of the screen with her phone. T-Zee had two options. He could sneak out unseen and run, hoping his people hadn't lied about an emergency evacuation plan, a private plane from Miami Executive to Cat Cay, in the Bahamas. But without his hard drive and computer files, he had no leverage. They would throw him off the plane on the way to Cat Cay. The files were his ticket. Killing Shannon, assuming she was CIA or FBI, wasn't an option, with or without his files.

There's only one way out.

* * *

Shannon touched her finger to the screen and leaned forward, straining to read the code in the red light of her headlamp.

T-Zee pressed his shoulder to ease the door enough to slip in, then pushed it back. He crouched and watched her from the dark corner.

Shannon studied the screen, her chin raised. He duck-walked like a ninja across the room to squat behind the straight-backed chair. His head below the top of the chair, he heard the hum of the computer mix with her inhaling and exhaling. She coughed, then burped with a grunt. She tapped a pad with a pen and mumbled something.

He had one chance to sink the choke before she got her chin down. Rising like smoke, his head passed six inches behind her frizzy brown hair that smelled of apricot shampoo.

Now!

His head above hers, the light from the screen reflected off T-Zee's face, caught her attention, and her eyes registered his silhouette reflected on the monitor.

Before she could turn, T-Zee curved his right forearm to the elbow around and under her chin and pulled her neck into the chair. His left arm shot forward along the left side of her neck. His right hand grabbed his left bicep, and the left forearm came up vertically. The left hand grabbed the back of her head and bent it forward. T-Zee squeezed off blood flow to her carotid arteries. She would be unconscious in five seconds. He stood up, stretching her neck like a duck on a hook. Her head against his chest, he pulled her butt up off the chair.

Shannon recognized the choke too late. It was deep, too deep to break. The computer screen blurred, then went black as her eyes lost oxygen. She could still think. His arms were thin and hairless, his chest flat and bony. He smelled of garlic.

T-Zee. It's T-Zee. The T-man. He pulls; I push.

Shannon managed to grab the edge of the desktop. She pulled and bent him across the chair back, his head now lower and close to the left side of her head. She reached and found the pen with her left hand. With seconds before black-out, she stabbed the pen past her head at his face. It went in and stuck in a cheek or an eye. He screamed in her ear, but he held the choke.

She thought, *Time to roll the dice.*

T-Zee winced in pain and arched to pull her against the chair. At that instant, Shannon pushed away from the desk with her hands as she stood up, tipping the chair into him. Off balance, the chair and her 165 pounds pushed against his chest, and they vaulted backwards through the air.

His back slammed flat onto the hardwood plank floor. The chair's back cushioned Shannon, crushing into him. She heard ribs snap like tree branches. The back of her head slammed into his nose, collapsing it, and drove the pen deeper into his face below the right eye. His head hit the floor like a wooden mallet on a chopping block and he blacked out. Shannon rolled off the chair, got to her feet, rubbing her neck and head.

***

Shannon turned on the lights and sat in T-Zee's chair, fiddling with her phone. T-Zee came to, sitting on the floor, leaning against the wall in the corner behind the door. With his nose crushed, his breathing wasn't right. Zip-tied at the wrists, he brought his hands up to touch his nose, then to the hole in his cheek where the pen had lodged. He looked at his blood-drenched shirt and cowered in pain with each breath. But, most of all, he became aware of a lack of air and strange noises in his throat. Wheezing, hacking, gurgling, gasping, he reached to his neck and found a thick plastic cable-tie.

"Wakie, wakie, T-man," Shannon said.

He looked up at her, his fingers pulling the plastic band away from his throat.

"Ya almost had me. But you stood up. Got too high. I knew it was you from your kimchi garlic breath. You're lucky. I aimed for your eye but missed."

He looked at her, unable to speak.

"Hey, before I forget, where are your shoes, and what are those cuts on your feet? I see where you stepped in bird shit." He didn't answer.

"Oh, about that cable tie around your neck. Even if your ribs weren't broken, you couldn't run far on half your air, and if you mess with me again, I'll pull it all the way."

He coughed, and blood drooled from his mouth and the hole in his face.

"Now, we're way off track here, T-Man. I need to check with the boss to see what to do with you."

Shannon dialed Nick's number.

* * *

Nick and Slate, finished with their conversation about T-Zee on the park bench, visited the butterfly conservatory, then went to an ice cream concession. Sitting at a table under an umbrella away from the crowd, they discovered a common passion was college football, and playfully trash-talked each other's favorite team.

A ringtone sounded on Nick's phone. He saw the ID.

Nick said to Slate, "It's Shannon."

"Hi, what is it?"

"We have an incident."

"Where are you?"

"Still in T-Zee's office. He showed up. We fought. He needs a doctor for his face and maybe a collapsed lung."

"Are you alright?"

"Yes, but I'm not sure what to do now."

T-Zee listened, hearing only Shannon's voice.

"Did you find out who he works for and what their plan is?" Nick asked.

"No, Slate's program is on his computer, and he's modifying a copy of it. That's all I found out before he jumped me."

"What's he doing now?"

"Sitting on the floor listening to me."

"Okay, I'll scramble the team to move him and his computer to the safe house. I'll call you back in a minute."

"Have them bring a doctor, clean up the blood, and wipe my prints," she said.

Nick hung up and looked across the table at Slate. She looked confused and worried.

"T-Zee found Shannon at his computer and attacked her. It sounds like she kicked his ass. We have to pull him out of the game for now. If he agrees to work with us and his handlers don't know we busted him, we might bring him back on your team and double back on the other side. We're in free-fall for now."

Nick called the team leader, who said it would take a while to pull the guys together on Labor Day.

"Listen up, Dickwad. You guys lost the target in Davie and didn't tell anyone. We almost lost an agent. You have thirty minutes. Make it happen."

Nick called Shannon back.

"They're on the way. I'll talk to him. Put him on your speakerphone."

"He can't talk," she said.

"That's okay, I'll do the talking."

Shannon moved the chair to the middle of the room.

"He wants to talk to you."

"Mr. Tan Zhi Hao, you're supposed to be running a race in Davie. But the pressure of work brought you back to the office. Is that about right? Just nod yes or no to Shannon."

"He nodded yes," Shannon said.

"Your dust-up with Shannon got us a little ahead of the game. No worries, we can get back on track. We're relocating you to a secure location for debriefing. It's a nice place, quite comfortable with a pool. There's a Malaysian take-out down the street. If all goes well, we'll get you patched up, debriefed, and back on your team with Shannon in a week or two."

Nick looked across the table at Slate, reached over, and took a spoonful of ice cream from her dish. Slate's eyes were wide, and her hands were over her mouth. Nick winked at her.

"Shannon, what does he think of our plan?" Nick asked.

Shannon looked into T-Zee's eyes as he processed the implications. Initially nervous and anxious, the eyes resolved into a dull, dead stare.

"Do you like the plan, T-Zee? Joining our team?" she asked.

His reaction, a blank, vacant stare.

"He's thinking about it," she said to Nick.

"That's alright, thinking is good. We have no problem with thinking, Mr. Hao. You're a smart guy. We're your best option."

"Shannon, can you please get him ready?

"It's nice at the house, Mr. Hao. There's a video game console. Maybe call your mother and talk about the Miami Hurricanes. Much nicer than other places, like a black hole in Aleppo."

Shannon watched T-Zee's eyes flicker when Nick mentioned his mother, then flash at the mention of the black hole in Aleppo.

"I've got to go, Mr. Hao. My buddy grabbed us a 3 o'clock tee time at Doral. Can you believe our good luck on a holiday weekend?

"Hey, they're bringing a doctor to get you comfortable. Before you leave for the house, please tell Shannon who you work for, who your handler is, and how you communicate with them. Can't wait to meet you in person, Mr. Hao."

***

Shannon returned the chair to the desk, collected the computer equipment, and T-Zee's belongings. T-Zee had not moved. Shannon glanced at him off and on. His head leaned forward, his eyes fixed on the floor where his dark blood had pooled.

Shannon bent down on one knee a few feet away—more gurgling sounds between wheezes. Pink saliva dripped from his chin.

"You look thirsty. How about I get you a bottle of water and snacks from the break room? Then I'll zip-tie your ankles and remove your zip collar. Then you can tell me what my boss needs to know."

He raised his head, looked into her eyes with a faint smile, and nodded.

"I'm sorry that this happened. You weren't trying to kill me. I appreciate that." She reached out and touched his cheek, like a mother comforting her son. "You're a good person. Your parents must be very proud of you. Okay, I'll go get you water and snacks. Sit tight, I'll be right back."

Shannon opened the office door and stepped onto the catwalk. Other than birds fluttering in the girders, all was quiet. She looked down across the hangar. The loading dock door remained open an inch so the team could get in. T-Zee liked Doritos and Skittles. She also got potato chips and two bottles of water.

"T-Man, I got you Doritos and your Skittles."

His head slumped forward like he was napping.

Who can blame him?

Shannon bent down and gave his shoulder a shake.

"Here's your water. We have to hurry. They'll be here soon."

She gave him another shake.

He slid down from the corner, his shoulders almost on the floor. Eyes open, his head twisted in a crook.

"Holy shit!" Shannon pulled his bare feet out until his head fell with a clunk on the floor. She went to slap him, then saw it, the cable tie.

He had jerked the tab hard, and the ratchet cinched the cable deep into his neck.

She stumbled back, leaned against the desk, and fumbled with shaky fingers to call Nick.

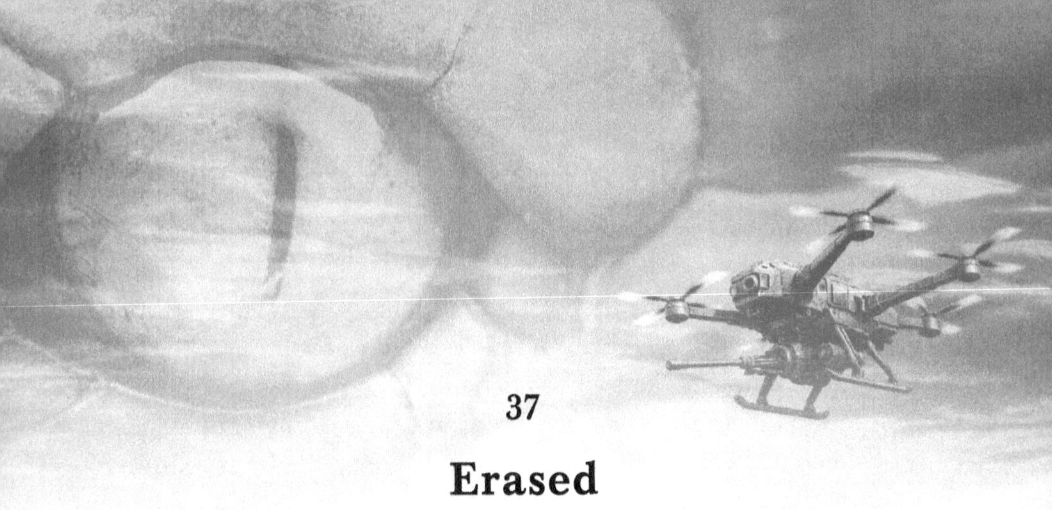

37

Erased

On Tuesday after Labor Day, Slate, in her condo, conferred with Brent and then sent a group text to both teams.

"Greetings. Hope you're having a great Labor Day weekend. I'm calling a meeting on Wednesday morning at ten in the compound conference room for those that live locally and by Zoom for you guys out there."

At eleven-thirty, Slate's doorbell rang. Shannon held a large white bag with red Chinese characters on the side. Nick had told Slate to chill out and decompress on Tuesday and asked her to invite Shannon over.

"Hope you're hungry, Boss," Shannon said.

Slate was speechless, on the verge of tears.

"Can I have a hug?" Slate asked.

They embraced for a long time, their heads on each other's shoulders. Shannon cried softly.

Slate put the take-out in the kitchen and gave Shannon a tour of the condo. The second bedroom had a treadmill, rowing machine, and exercise trampoline. They had lunch on the twenty-second-floor balcony with a view of Biscayne Bay and cruise ships in the port. They talked about growing up in Ohio and Oregon, Shannon's service in Army Intelligence, her cybersecurity degree, and Slate's passion for technology. Slate told her about Jamie and Taylor. Eventually, they got around to T-Zee.

"Nick's team is there now. But you probably already guessed that," Shannon said. "They're removing surveillance equipment and all traces of him."

"I assumed as much."

239

"You understand that no one can find out what happened. You cannot say anything to anyone, ever. It's very dangerous. We don't know what they would do. Understand?"

Slate nodded.

"You have a right to know, so I'm going to tell you. We thought T-Zee was running the 10K race, and his FBI tail was waiting at the finish line. We don't think he knew he was being followed, but he wanted to stay ahead of your work on the second drone. He saw my car behind the hangar, snuck up behind me at his desk, and choked me from behind. He could have killed me with a blow to the head had he wanted to. Anyway, I pushed the chair into him, broke his ribs, and knocked him out. I called Nick. You heard most of that part. We wanted to flip him to our side. Sometimes it works, but we never know their backstory. Anyway, when I came back from getting him water, he had strangled himself with a zip-tie."

Slate sat staring at the boats crisscrossing Biscayne Bay. She thought about the tall, serious T-Zee, no more than a boy, and wondered why.

"We didn't find out who he worked for. He had your software and likely planned to sabotage your project. We'll never know what his mission was," Shannon said.

"What happens now?"

"The official story is he went back to Asia for family reasons. It's above my level in terms of what they do with his body. The CIA may snoop around and use it as a bargaining chip. Or he might dissolve in a barrel of acid."

Slate sat for a moment, then stood up to face Shannon, who was sitting on the rattan sofa. Slate leaned over and kissed her forehead.

"You're a courageous woman. I'm so glad you weren't hurt or worse. It must have been so scary. Are you alright?"

Shannon looked up from the sofa at Slate's kind eyes.

"It was close, very, very close. I got lucky."

"What are you going to do now?" Slate asked.

"Nick told me to take some time off. He wants me to stay on the project to protect my cover. T-Zee's handlers will want to know what happened."

"Stay on our team. Wow, that would be great. I'm so happy to have met you. You're an inspiration. I want you to meet Taylor, the scout I told you about."

"I'd love to meet her, and I've really enjoyed being on your team, Slate."

* * *

Governor Prescott called Slate in her office at the compound on Wednesday.

"Hi, Cowgirl. How was your Labor Day weekend?"

Oh, let me see. Nothing crazy. FBI spy games. A bloody deathmatch five doors from where I'm sitting.

"Hi, John. It was okay, I worked most of it. Stayed around the condo. How about you?"

"Oh, a Shriner's rodeo in Ocala yesterday. Thought I might see you there, barrel racing or bull riding."

"You're funny. Kiss any pretty cowgirls?"

"Nope. Not since you."

"Ah, that's nice of you to say," she replied.

Slate looked across her office at the picture of the Everglades, which she had moved from the university to the compound.

He continued. "Leslie Paton called this morning. She's a big fan of yours, you know. She tried to describe Lucy flying the Zcolt in full automatic. She said it's like going from a Sunday drive in the country to a high-speed car chase. That's a funny way to put it, huh?"

"High-speed car chase. I like it. I'll tell Lucy. She'll laugh."

"Now you're scaring me." They laughed.

"If you think that's scary, I'm almost finished with Lucy's sister program for the second Zcolt. Her name is Daisy."

"Can't wait to meet her." He chuckled.

"I asked Leslie to call me when they completed the population count on the five-square-mile pilot grid. They only found fifteen pythons, and some could have migrated in. She said that you killed 388. That's 97 percent."

"Oh, thanks, I was waiting to hear from her today in a Zoom meeting. I'm quite happy with the results. They're easier to find at night, but the logistics are complicated, more dangerous, and time-consuming."

"So, what's next?" he asked.

"I've hired an expert in drone formation flying. Lucy needs one or two wingmen to hunt as a pack. It's the only way we can clear the Everglades before breeding season."

"You're something else, Slate Warner."

"Thank you. I'm looking at the picture you gave me. I brought it here to the compound."

* * *

Jake was the first to join the Zoom meeting on Wednesday. His handsome, tanned face and trim two-day shadow portrayed the confidence of a professional hunting guide.

Slate noticed his new copper-colored wraparound mirrored sunglasses hanging from a leather cord, and a cut on his right cheek.

That cut wasn't there in the RV on Friday night.

Shannon sat across the rectangular worktable from Slate. Brad arrived and sat next to Shannon. Other faces joined Jake's on the Zoom screen. All present, Carter asked, "Where's the T-Man?"

Slate began the meeting.

"First, T-Zee has left the team. He had a family emergency and returned to Asia last weekend. I spoke with Brad yesterday about a replacement, and he has a friend who is a Fortnite gamer. Did you call your friend, Brad?"

"Yes, her online name is Storm. Her real name is Summer, and she's excited."

"Good, see if she can come in tomorrow for an interview with Shannon and me.

"Let me introduce a new face on Zoom. Peggy Levine, hold up your hand, please."

The thirty-something, athletic-looking woman with slicked-back brunette hair wore a black polo with the logo, SWARM Inc. She raised two fingers and smiled.

"Peggy is a leader in formation drone flying, as in the drone light shows in Orlando.

"With T-Zee's departure, we're skipping independent hunting with two drones. For the remainder of our pilot contract, we'll operate with two drones in formation from a single control trailer.

"We test-fly Z-2 on Friday from the compound out over the Everglades using the new control trailer. If no one is around in the Glades, we might shoot a python. Hopefully, Peggy and Storm, if she joins us, can watch.

"Next Monday, the tenth, we'll fly Z-2 out of Gator Park and test all modes. Meanwhile, I'll work with Peggy to develop software that links the drones in formation. That's the plan until it's not the plan."

Carter raised his hand. "So, has the game changed? What is the goal for the pilot project now, and when will we finish?"

His question reminded Slate of T-Zee's direct questions. Daydreaming, Slate clenched the pen between her teeth. She pictured the life and death fight and T-Zee dying four days ago in his office above her head. It seemed so easy to erase him with a simple lie. She glanced at Shannon, who returned a knowing look. Slate's silence persisted, and Carter wasn't sure she heard his question.

She snapped back to the present. "Oh, you asked if the game changed. Not really, Carter. As I said earlier, we can shoot pythons. The question is, how fast and what is the most efficient combination of resources?

"We'll hear from Dr. Paton in a minute on their python survey of the grid we cleared. We measure success by the time needed to kill ninety-five percent of pythons in one square mile. Friday, September 21st, is the finish date for the pilot project. One final thought. If we can fly two Zcolts in formation, we can fly three, maybe more. That's why we have Peggy."

Peggy smiled again and gave a thumbs-up on the Zoom display.

Dr. Paton gave her report.

As the meeting wrapped up, Brad reached over and drew squiggles on Shannon's notes.

"What's that?"

"Swarm. Fear the swarm, Shan."

"You're jealous of her cool shirt and way-cool hair," she whispered.

"Why do you have T-Zee's spiral notebook?" Brad asked.

"He let me use it at the meeting last Friday."

Brad narrowed his eyes and asked, "So, what really happened to him?"

"Don't know, someone probably died. Asian families are close."

She felt a knot in her stomach knowing that in the notebook, taped inside the back cover, was an envelope with the picture of T-Zee's parents—the same picture she saw on his computer.

"How about lunch?" Brad asked.

"Only if it's tacos."

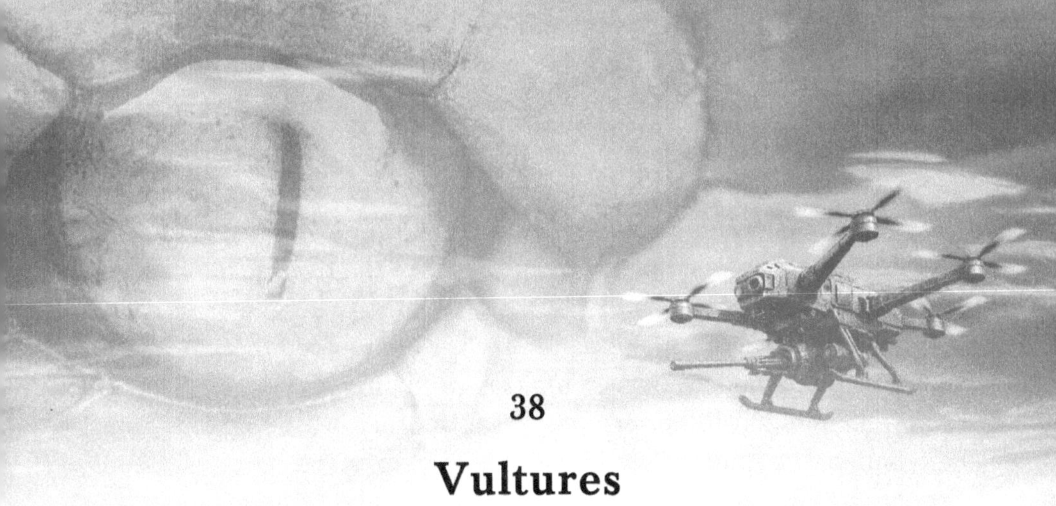

38

Vultures

Slate checked their distance on her iPhone to the Everglades launch site.

"Two miles," she yelled over the roar to Carter, who was sitting next to her.

"Five minutes," yelled Boone from the captain's seat above them.

Over the past two weeks, Zcolt-2 flew its maiden flight from the compound and completed a full test out of Gator Park. Then, in a series of short hops from Gator Park, Slate and Peggy had perfected software linking the two Zcolts in formation.

To Slate, operating the console felt detached from reality, like playing Brad's Fortnite video game. She asked Brad two days earlier in the control trailer, "Have you ever thought what it would be like if you suddenly dropped into your video game with real guns and real blood and real screams?"

Brad thought. "No, I couldn't imagine what that would be like, and I don't want to find out."

"This console feels like a video game. But, unlike your Fortnite, outside of this trailer are real drones, real bullets, and death. Weird, huh?"

Brad winced.

With three days remaining in the pilot project, Slate wanted to experience the reality of an airboat.

Exhilarating at twenty-five miles per hour, in a wide area of the channel, Jake, the captain of the Zcolt-2 airboat, pulled up beside Slate's airboat carrying Zcolt-1. She waved to Jake, Sebastian, and Dr. Paton.

From her seat, the Zcolt looked like a hood ornament on the platform extending from the bow. Feeling alive, her eyes watered, and

245

her ponytail flailed in the wind. Ear protectors created a muffled world defined by the roar of the huge engine.

Boone slowed. They entered narrow, S-shaped canals to reach the launch point at the northeastern corner of the five-square-mile grid they had cleared.

Fifty feet apart, facing south, the crews prepared their drones for launch as Shannon and Brad completed preflight checks.

Slate removed her ear protectors and her crushed cotton safari hat, untied her ponytail, and climbed up to stand next to Boone. Cordgrass reflected on still water like broken glass. Insects buzzed in low clouds. Fish popped to the surface to catch insects. A gator, only the eyes, rose like a periscope, watching Slate as she shook her head and fluffed long blonde hair.

"Snake!" Boone called out, pointing to the head of a python at the edge of the marsh grass. Slate, after a moment, spotted it. Boone lifted the Remington, a long-barreled twelve-gauge, from its rack and handed it to her.

Slate leveled it, put the bead at the end of the barrel on the snake's head, and pulled the trigger. The boom shattered all pretense of a peaceful morning as the gunstock slammed into her shoulder. Double-aught buckshot left a crater of meat as the body slithered without purpose. The recoil rocked Slate back into Boone. He laughed, and she wanted to rub her shoulder, but resisted.

Shannon radioed, "Stand back. Launching Z-1."

"All clear," Carter replied.

Six props sprang to life, pulling Slate's mind away from the savage reality of their mission. Being so close and at eye level, the whirling rotor wash scrambled her hair, then pulled it skyward when the drone lifted off the pad.

Z-1 moved forward 100 feet and waited for Z-2.

Shannon and Brad commanded Z-2 airborne and flew the drone to hover to the left of Z-1.

"Linking the drones in formation," Shannon radioed both airboats on the common frequency.

Z-2 bounced as the auto-positioning software engaged, then it moved to a position they called fighting-wing.

Slate went up the steps to the launch platform and sat in a lawn chair next to Carter. Like black knights on a chessboard, the drones hovered motionless a hundred feet away. Slate looked at Carter's iPad, which displayed a split-screen view of the composite and weapons screens for each drone.

As Shannon entered auto-flight commands, the rain screens for Z-1 and Z-2 swirled with green and blue text. After processing, the last line on each screen displayed in yellow, "Lucy and Daisy Are Ready to Party, Happy Hunting."

"Here we go," Shannon radioed.

Before the drones moved forward, Z-2 pivoted ten degrees to the right. Slate jumped at the crack of its rifle and the thrashing of a python in the water. A red python kill emoji popped up on Carter's iPad.

Zcolt-2 updated its position 120 times per second and flew fifty feet left, one hundred feet behind, and slightly above the GPS location of Z-1.

Firmware upgrades increased the sensor scan rate. Each drone processed data, recognized pythons, aimed the rifle, and fired automatically—fifty times faster than a human.

In manual mode, Brad could fly only 8 miles per hour while watching the screens. And, he had to stop to shoot. The drones automatically processed and shot at twenty miles per hour, equivalent to a cyclist pedaling in high gear.

"I think about the early days with Lucy," Slate said to Carter as they sat on the launch platform waiting for the drones to move. "She wasn't very good, and she shot a panther."

Carter held a finger to his lips. They laughed.

"Daisy has the benefit of Lucy's training. Now they share sensor data at night and get better with each flight. They're finding pythons earlier and taking longer shots."

Carter agreed. "Yes, I've had a front row seat. They've gotten a lot better."

The rumble of rotors increased in pitch. The lead drone moved forward slowly, then faster. Z-2 followed. Rifles fired, disordered and uncoordinated. Flying away, the sound, now like commercial mowers, grew fainter. Slate felt unnerved by the synchronized, mindless execution of her algorithm, unburdened by a conscience.

The drones turned back on the return leg and passed by Slate at high speed before turning around.

Carter pointed to the sky. "Here they come."

Slate looked up. "What are they?"

"Vultures, here for the feast. They now associate the drones and rifle shots with food."

Awestruck, Slate said, "Wow, look at them soar. There must be twenty."

"We've also seen gators feasting on dead pythons."

Shannon called over the radio. "Two more round-trips, guys, then a pit stop."

After the drones landed, Carter and Sebastian swapped out battery packs and ammunition magazines. Boone showed Slate the grid map on his iPad.

Slate did calculations in her head. "This is going much better than I imagined. But the risk of accidents increases greatly with speed. I'm thinking twenty is the sweet spot. What do you think, Carter?"

"I agree. The batteries last longer, and the drones aren't as jerky," Carter said, "Maybe increase the circuits to three miles."

Slate added, "I think we could add a third Zcolt on the right side. The key is keeping each team self-contained and independent while using the latest algorithm."

Shannon radioed, "How's it going, guys?"

Slate motioned for the mic from Carter. "Hi, Shannon. Carter says his bird is ready to go. How about three more circuits, break for lunch, then finish up the last three? These drones in formation look like an air show. Vultures and gators are following the drones. And the weather is perfect. Wish you were here."

"I'll bet it's breathtaking," Shannon said. "Okay, one more flight with three circuits, then lunch. Enjoy yourselves."

Lunch. The four from Jake's airboat crowded onto Boone's airboat, and they trolled to a nearby island hammock of big oaks and cypress. Boone pointed out a strangler fig to Slate. It wrapped around a gumbo tree like a python. A 9mm Glock holstered on his belt, he led them on a sandy trail past saw palmettos and wax myrtle bushes to a clearing. Carter carried a cooler. Jake brought an iron skillet and ingredients in his backpack while Boone taught Sebastian how to make a fire using flint.

Jake sautéed bell peppers, onions, and jalapeños in olive oil. He mixed cornbread batter with a touch of honey, poured it over vegetables, stirred in shredded smoked wild boar shoulder, and cooked it over embers until golden brown.

In the meantime, Boone pointed to a young sabal palm.

"There's our salad," he said.

He cut the palm at the base with his machete and removed the top crown. Peeling off layers of fiber exposed an ivory white inner core about a foot long.

"This is the heart of palm. I like it raw, but we'll also pan-fry some to have with Jake's delicacy." He filled one bowl with thin palm chips to pass around and a second bowl for Jake to fry.

Being from Detroit, Sebastian had a full day of new adventures.

"This is really good, Boone. It reminds me of artichokes," he said.

"Yes, these are fantastic, Boone. A first for me, also, and I grew up in Florida," Dr. Paton said.

Jake served helpings into metal bowls, and Carter poured iced tea and lemonade.

"You've outdone yourself, Jake," Slate said as she held out her bowl for seconds.

"You're a man of many talents." She held his eye long enough for him to receive her message.

For dessert, Jake handed out homemade key lime bars.

* * *

To celebrate the end of the pilot project, Slate's company treated participants to a steak dinner at the Ironhorse Inn and invited Boone, Dean Miller, and Taylor.

Brent stood and kicked off the gathering. "The governor extends his congratulations and best wishes. On behalf of the support team, we've thoroughly enjoyed working with Slate and her team. I must say, as a technology enthusiast myself, I appreciate that Slate has combined multiple disciplines and mind-bending technology to create an elegant solution to restore the Everglades. The governor promises to fast-track the implementation phase, confident that ZKuul Solutions qualifies as a sole-source provider."

Dr. Leslie Paton explained plans for native animals. "The University of Florida, FIU, University of Miami, several non-profits, and animal control agencies have created a committee funded by FWC and the National Park Service. Some species up for reintroduction are raccoons, marsh rabbits, opossums, bobcats, white-tailed deer, egrets, wood storks, and other birds. The first release of ten breeding pairs of raccoons per square mile in the cleared grid is scheduled for the middle of October. We expect a population of 160 in three years."

Dean Miller sat next to Slate. He thanked her for inviting him and credited her with increased enrollment at the college this semester.

"I also credit your project with the upward trend in grant approvals and foreign student enrollments," he said, not mentioning the deal he cut with the governor, which Prescott had told her about.

"Thank you, Dean. It's all working out."

He leaned close and asked, "I trust the affair with Nick turned out all right?"

"From what I understand, it's over," she said, shocked at his question.

The dean nodded without comment.

Slate's mind snapped to T-Zee, and she shuddered, then glanced down the table to Shannon, who was laughing at something Brad said.

After dinner, Slate introduced Peggy again and thanked her for writing software to fly drones in formation. Slate gave a preview of plans for the final phase.

"Thanks to each of you, we have the pilot package wrapped in fancy paper with a bow around it. Now we replicate and scale up. I want to add a third Zcolt in formation and create independent Zcolt teams, and control trailers with five-person teams. Beginning with the five square miles we cleared in the pilot phase, we'll expand outward in grids assigned by a central dispatch. As you can imagine, this won't be easy. Still, the hardest part is over. We now know how to find and kill the bastards."

Surprised by her last words, the twenty people in the room applauded and gave Slate a standing ovation.

Director Newman raised his hand. "I admit, I had my doubts. Wow, just wow. I haven't the slightest idea of how this works, but you make it look like mowing grass, Professor."

Slate ended the evening with a round of champagne.

As the room thinned, Slate saw an opportunity to introduce Shannon to Taylor, mentioning Taylor's summer bioengineering internship, where she still worked part-time.

Taylor's eyes lit up when Shannon showed interest.

"It's so cool," Taylor raved. "I'm working to make 3D printed custom organic shapes for prosthetic limbs."

"That sounds so interesting. I belong to an organization that helps victims who've lost limbs to land mines and IEDs," Shannon said.

Taylor barely contained her excitement. "Wow, my professor is building technology for custom limbs for under one thousand dollars using a smartphone scan of the amputation site. I can show you our lab, if you want."

Slate broke in. "Okay, how about an ice cream sundae next door? I'll ask Leslie Paton to come. Just us girls."

After ice cream and goodnights, Shannon walked with Slate to their cars.

"I found out this afternoon. The branch has elevated your project to a high-value espionage target. They're extending my assignment," Shannon said.

Slate, shocked to realize it wasn't ever over, smiled and hugged her. "Great, you can stay as long as you like, Sister."

Shannon could not contain her excitement. "Thank you. I like it here. And guess what happened at dinner? Brad asked me to a boutique movie theater on Friday. I'm calling that a date, right?"

"Oh, good. Yes, it's a date. Congratulations. You're so cute. Can I give you some advice?"

"Yes, please. I'm nervous already."

"I believe in the saying, 'You want what you don't have.' Don't make it too easy for Brad. You have a lot to offer, so make him work for your affection."

"Wow, I hadn't thought of it like that."

* * *

Driving to her condo, Slate felt a deep sense of satisfaction with the project's results. Dean Miller had shocked her by mentioning Nick, remembering that Nick had used Miller as the hook to meet with her.

How much does Miller know? Did he know T-Zee was spying on his department? Does he know how it ended?

She hadn't opened the card that Jake had slipped into the pocket of her purse as she was leaving.

She also had not heard from John in two weeks.

He's probably busy with Hurricane Harold, a day out of Pensacola. He is the governor of Florida, after all.

Stopped at a red light, the street wet with outer bands of rain from the faraway storm, her phone vibrated. She smiled and let it vibrate twice more.

"Hello," she answered, as if she didn't know who it was.

"Hi, I know you're busy. Is this a bad time?" the governor asked.

"Oh, no. Hi. I'm good. Riding bareback and roping yearlings. You know, cowgirl stuff. How about you?"

"Nothing crazy. Who would name a hurricane Harold, anyway?"

"Well, John, being the Florida governor and all, can't you name your hurricanes whatever you want? Why not something cool like Python?" Slate said while laughing.

"You sound happy and in good spirits, Sarah. I just talked with Brent. He told me your drone formation is a game-changer. He's very excited."

"I am happy, John. I went out on the airboat on Wednesday and watched them operate. They are scarily efficient and lethal. Frightening."

"Brent thinks you are a savant, and so does Newman."

"I happened to be in the right place to merge technologies from many departments and understand artificial intelligence algorithms. It was you, John, who committed to doing something about the pythons."

"I'd say you and I had the good fortune of meeting each other at the right moment in history," he said.

"I couldn't agree more," Slate said in a tone that carried extra meaning.

Silent now, each not sure what to say.

"You must be driving. I hear rain," he said.

"Yes, I'm pulling into the garage at my condo. Are you okay?" she asked.

"Yes. Busy with the second hurricane of the season. But it's not that big. And, it will put out the wildfire in the Conecuh National Forrest."

Parked in her garage spot, she turned off the engine and listened to him, the phone to her ear.

"That's good. You don't have very good luck with fire trucks, though," she said.

"No, I don't. And neither do you, as I recall."

"No, we don't like fire trucks. I thought you had forgotten."

"Some things, one never forgets."

"That's true," she said.

"At the risk of being too personal, I clearly remember what you wore that night: a green silk dress, leopard scarf, emerald necklace, long legs in pantyhose, apricot toenail polish, and champagne-colored heels," he said.

Slate smiled to herself.

Either he has a perfect memory, or I wasn't just one of his girls.

"Here's to no more fire trucks," she said.

"Definitely."

39

Just Beyond Reach

On Monday, September 24th, Brent left a meeting with Governor Prescott and sent a text to Slate.

"Hi, it's Brent. We're working on a budget amendment to reappropriate money to the python project from FDEP's Land Acquisition Trust Fund. The governor meets with the twelve-member Joint Legislative Budget Commission on Thursday. Can you pull together a best-guess proposal on your plan with a timeline and estimated costs by Wednesday at five p.m.?"

Slate replied, "Sure," and then spent the next two days planning with her team.

Executive Summary:

ZKuul Solutions aims to eliminate Burmese pythons exceeding three feet in length from the Everglades National Park and the Big Cypress Conservation Area by February 4, 2030. Note that smaller pythons take five years to reach breeding age, providing the State time to eliminate them before they multiply.

Our plan presumes that nine drone teams work five, eight-hour days each week, with holidays off. Each team operates a three-drone aerial platform dispatched to the 144 twenty-five-square-mile grid sections. The State provides security, logistics, pickup trucks, and watercraft to support drones and control trailers.

The following are projected costs:

Equipment	$34 million
Operations and Labor	$4 million
Home office	$2 million
Profit and Intellectual Property	$12 million
Total	**$52 million**

The anniversary of Pa-Hay-Okee is on February 17th. By that date, we expect to meet our goal of making the Everglades safe for humans and native animals.

Separately, our company is developing technologies to locate python nests during May and June 2030, utilizing forward-looking infrared sensors and wide-area tethered and/or untethered drones. Because female pythons remain on their eggs for sixty days and shiver to increase the incubation temperature, locating their exact position is highly probable. Destroying females and egg clutches over a few years is the best ongoing management practice at a significantly lower cost. We can submit a nest elimination proposal upon request, pending the completion of our research and development.

Sarah Warner, PhD
CEO ZKuul Solutions, Inc.

* * *

Brad drove to Tallahassee on Wednesday to represent ZKuul Solutions at the governor's budget amendment meeting the next day. Scheduled for one hour, Brad answered questions for an additional hour. Slate kept checking her watch. Finally, he called.

"We got the money, Boss, but it wasn't a slam dunk. Many legislators were skeptical that we could accomplish in three months what FWC had failed to do in thirty years."

"That's good news. Thanks for doing this. What position did the governor take?" Slate asked.

"The governor, with his day-one knowledge, was a big help. So were Brent, Newman, and Dr. Paton."

"How did fully automatic drones under human supervision go over?" she asked.

"That was the hardest part. I explained our protocols and redundant safety systems. There were some die-hards. I compared our technology to the safety record of self-driving cars compared with human drivers."

"Did they come around?"

"Most did. I made it simple. Supervised autonomous operations are mandatory if we hope to kill them faster than they reproduce."

"Good job. That's the bottom line. What about our price?"

"No problem. A democratic senator asked how much the State has spent on python programs. The governor said the estimate was north of $100 million. I added that there are more pythons now than ever, so the $100 million was a total waste."

"Any troublemakers?"

"Three were obvious old school FWC cronies, that accused the governor of grandstanding and scapegoating."

"Did you get their names?"

"Yes, two Democrats and one Republican. They're in my notes."

"Good information to have, even though we are out of that fight," Slate said. "Thanks again, Brad. I'm proud of you."

"Thank you for your confidence and the opportunity. I'll drive back in the morning. I'm headed to a sports bar tonight to watch Miami play Buffalo."

"Go, Dolphins. Have fun. Bye."

Slate typed notes on her laptop. Shannon walked by her window on the catwalk, and Slate waved her in.

"I just talked with Brad," Slate said.

Shannon's cheeks brightened at the mention of his name.

"How is he? I wondered how it was going up there."

"He answered questions for over an hour. Some thought it was too good to be true, just another pipe dream. Three defended the old FWC, as if we were the opposition," Slate said.

Shannon thought for a second. "I'm not getting that. Must be politics. Doesn't smell right."

"Who cares, we got the contract, so screw them."

Shannon raised her middle finger in the direction of Tallahassee. They laughed.

Leaning over the desk, Shannon whispered, "Want to hear a secret from work?"

"What an interesting world you live in, young lady. Sure."

"I know. Doors close, and others open. Nick told me this morning that, while backtracking trails that might connect to T-Zee, he found an active but quiet Florida state and FBI investigation into corruption at FWC. We only do counterterrorism and counterintelligence in Miami. Tampa handles corruption. It's probably just the normal bullshit—kickbacks, contracts, or coverups. Time will tell."

"That's interesting. Brad was surprised by an aggressive defense of the FWC by three legislators on the budget committee," Slate said.

"I'll give the names to Nick," Shannon said. "One never knows how deep the rot runs."

Slate nodded. "Okay, now for the important stuff. How was it?"

Shannon pretended not to understand, then gave herself away with a blush.

"We had so much fun. Or at least I did. The movie was okay, a little stupid. So, we trash-talked the characters. I got into a laughing fit, and I never do that. Then Brad caught it, and people thought we were nuts. He's a nice guy." Her voice trailed off with a happy, introspective sigh.

Slate reached across to put her hand on Shannon's arm.

"Steady as she goes, smart girl. A guy like Brad has seen his fair share of ditzy airheads with hot bodies. There's more to him than his good looks. Let me put it this way. If you made him laugh till he cried, that's a good thing. Just be yourself and remember that men want what they don't have. You're just beyond his reach."

They stood up, and Slate held her arms out for a hug.

* * *

Following the Tallahassee funding decision, over the next three weeks, Slate hired a human resources director and managers for recruiting, production engineering, procurement, finance, and compliance.

Peggy took the lead on software engineering and successfully linked three Zcolts in a formation flight from Gator Park on October 10th.

To assuage the state's safety concerns, on Friday, October 12th, Jake brought two cows and a horse to the research site to train the master algorithm, adding them to the "no-kill" list. Finished at three, Jake loaded the animals into stock trailers while Slate secured computers in the control trailer.

Jake opened the door and leaned inside the control trailer as the afternoon sun poured through the door. Slate turned in her chair but couldn't see his face for the glare.

"Getting them loaded was easier than I expected. I had a hell of a time getting them in the trailer yesterday." Jake watched the sun reflect off her golden hair, sunglasses nestled on her head. She brought her hand up as a shade, squinting, still not seeing him clearly.

Neither seemed to know what to do next.

Finally, after an awkward silence, Jake said, "Well, I guess I'd better get these critters back to Everglades City."

Before Jake could say, "See ya," Slate interrupted.

"So, you must have plans, it being a Friday night on South Beach in Everglades City."

He laughed. "It's obvious you've never been there."

She tilted her head. "Is that an invitation?"

"Sure, but you're too busy."

"I'm not too busy for happy hour."

"Are you sure? You know what happened the last time."

"Complaining?" she asked with a sly smile.

His eyebrows raised, "No, are you?"

"I'll have a Modelo. I'll meet you after I finish up here," she said.

Jake stepped into the RV before Slate arrived and spotted the open card on the table, the one he had slipped into her purse at the Ironhorse.

Arranged on the right half of the card, he had made a starburst from dozens of tiny star-shaped bones found inside sand dollars. On the left half, Jake had written, "Sarah, your heart radiates goodness, and your mind illuminates the room. I've never met anyone like you, my dear Sarah."

He opened her Modelo and his Yuengling and poured them into tall glasses. She came through the door, and he handed her the glass. She set it on the table, threw her arms around his neck, and kissed him deeply.

"Thank you for the card, Jake."

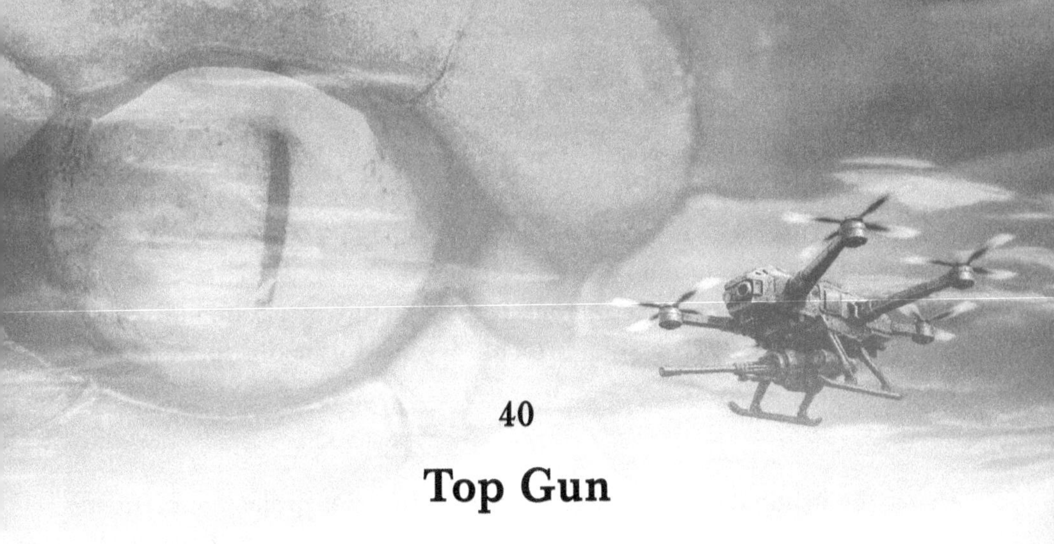

40

Top Gun

Over the next month, by November 9th, Granger, the production engineer, had erected a forty-meter free-span fabric-frame building next to the hangar to build drones, drone trailers, and control trailers. He used supply chain A.I. management programs to source parts, tools, and consumables. Slate set a production schedule to build six Zcolts and two control trailers per week, for five-person teams.

Slate and Peggy completed simulator testing of the common motherboard of integrated circuits and algorithms for the twenty-seven Zcolts in production.

Human Resources screened candidates using A.I. recruiting agents. Shannon secretly submitted candidate names to Nick, who redlined five as security risks.

Console operator candidates completed a check ride on a console simulator as a final test. Zcolt crew chiefs were required to have mechanical, electronic, and outdoor skills. Slate, Carter, Brad, and Shannon made final hiring decisions.

A former launch control director for NASA, Doc Rock Wheeler, Slate's director of operations, designed a central command center in a corner of the hangar. Flight dispatchers would monitor team locations on a master grid map and track operations in real time.

Jake, in charge of field support, coordinated with Director Newman's staff on a logistics plan for each twenty-five-square-mile numbered grid section. They determined the best combination of road-based and water-based launch vehicles for each grid. Newman scheduled four FWC law enforcement officers to each of the nine teams for safety and operational security.

Sheriff Palmer assigned two SUVs with deputies for security at Gator Park and two at the ZKuul compound. He committed to helicopter coverage as needed and coordinated airspace restrictions with the Federal Aviation Administration.

After the Miami Herald published a picture of a Zcolt in flight on the Tamiami Trail, Governor Prescott assigned a media spokesperson for interviews and tours.

* * *

Using the original section cleared during the pilot project, subsequent sections were connected, creating an expanding square. During this period, Shannon, Brad, Carter, Sebastian, and Judy, a newly appointed crew chief instructor, trained the remaining seven teams of five people using the original control trailer and three drones at Gator Park.

By Thursday, November 8th, while training the new teams, they had cleared an additional twenty-five-square-mile grid section, bringing the total cleared to 30 square miles, out of the 3,500 in the two Everglades parks.

Granger added a second temporary fabric building for the final assembly and mating of drones and trailers. Sectioned off, lines on the floor marked areas for each team—three drones, their transport/launch trailers, and a control trailer for each.

Team members helped outfit the drones, configure the control trailers, and test communications and software. They also practiced normal and contingency procedures on a simulator program in their control trailer.

At one p.m. on November 9th, ZKuul employees, state staff, and contractors totaling ninety-five, met in the assembly building to mark the kickoff of the final phase. Slate catered a BBQ buffet and beverages on folding tables. Tent cards on the tables identified the nine Zcolt field teams—Albatross, Bobcat, Cheetah, Dragon, Eagle, Flounder, Gator, Hyena, and Iguana.

Doc Rock Wheeler's central command staff of fifteen sat at two tables and changed their table card from 'Central Command' to 'Raven.' Slate changed the table card for managers and contractors from 'Head Shed' to 'Top Gun.'

Brent, Dr. Paton, Newman, Sheriff Palmer, and fifteen county and state employees occupied the remaining tables. Not having table cards, they created ones calling themselves the 'Overlords.'

Everyone was in a good mood. Halfway through the introductions, the entrance door opened, and to Slate's complete surprise, the governor walked in looking quite pleased with himself.

"Ah, Governor Prescott, we had not, I mean, wow, this is a pleasant surprise," Slate announced.

Prescott made his way through the tables, shaking hands. He waved to Jake, who was sitting beside Slate, and shook her hand. He asked for the mic.

"I happened to be in the area and heard there was free BBQ."

Everyone laughed at his informality. He wore slim-cut jeans and ostrich cowboy boots. The sleeves of the light blue casual shirt were rolled halfway up his athletic arms. Slate had not seen him in a western-style cowboy hat and admired his ability to look the part for any situation.

Prescott acknowledged the tables of state staff members.

"Brent and Director Newman tell me you're on schedule to begin field operations the week after Thanksgiving. Looking around this building, I'm reminded of factories mobilizing for war, back in the forties. I commend you all."

Drones, trailers, and equipment teams were organized like platoons. Sitting at tables for each team, Slate had members stand as she called out their team name.

The fourteen-foot overhead door opened. A new 32-foot motorhome rumbled in and parked facing the tables.

"This was my idea," Prescott said. "I have a friend whose business depends on Florida tourism. This industry and the millions of jobs that depend on tourism depend on each of you. His dealership is leasing nine of these RVs to the state at a steep discount, so your teams can camp in the field during the week, saving time and simplifying logistics."

Team members stood at their tables to see the new RV. Someone yelled out, "Thank you, Governor," and they cheered.

"Each of you is part of something that's never happened anywhere in the world. The complexity, both technologically and logistically, is not lost on me. You each play a crucial role. Yes, we want to eliminate pythons. However, safety is our highest priority. Twenty-seven-armed drones, flying in formation and each shooting computer-aided, high-powered rifles, require self-discipline and professionalism. Above all, there is no place for competition between teams. Move with all deliberate speed, but remember, it's not a sports league. We aren't keeping score," the governor said.

"Some grid squares are easily accessible and can be cleared quickly. Other grids, such as those near roads, private property, or over thick brush and wetlands, take longer to complete. Slate told me that every team member has the authority and responsibility to stop operations and freeze in place for any reason. When it comes to safety, you are each a team captain. We can't afford any injuries or accidents. With that said, happy hunting."

Slate rose, applauding, and took the microphone while the governor took a seat to her right.

"Thank you, Governor Prescott. Well said. Machines and computers are not infallible. Be cautious, follow procedures, and don't become complacent. The quickest way to get fired is by not following procedures to the letter."

Team members traded glances without smiles or comment.

"Thank you, Governor Prescott, for providing the RVs. This adds another hour of hunting each day.

"Thanksgiving is a few days away. Until then, each team helps technicians complete assembly and flight check their platform in the compound's test area. The Saturday after Thanksgiving, we load up and transport three drones, one command trailer, and one RV for each team to locations assigned by central command, which now calls itself Raven. State support personnel, if they are not already on location, will follow you on Saturday. Teams stay overnight in their RVs. Raven remotely updates grid maps and data to control-trailer computers.

"On Sunday, you power up all equipment and get clearance from Raven to launch and test each flight mode in progression up through full computer-controlled auto-flight in formation, short of firing. Each team member will test their remote kill switches, which disengage the computer and freeze their drones in hover.

"Peggy and I continue to modify the master algorithm. We'll upload the new version on drones and control trailers on Monday or

Tuesday of Thanksgiving week. Console controllers won't notice any differences, except that the new version is named Casey.

"Monday morning after Thanksgiving, the teams that passed checks on Sunday will receive clearance from Raven to launch from land or water, as the case may be, and shoot pythons.

"At the end of each day, console captains submit their debrief report to Raven and remain available for two hours to video-talk with me or others at Top Gun.

"We're hiring two additional teams of five for backup. Depending on the weather, rate of progress, and other factors, we may add a night shift. Please be flexible until we get the rhythm down.

"By the way, if you want to drive your own vehicle to the field site, check with your security supervisor to make sure there is room. Otherwise, during the week, plan to use the pickup trucks for towing trailers for runs to town or whatever. We've made arrangements to park the RVs at Barney's Bar and Grill on weekends. You can leave your cars there during the week.

"Alright, enough talk. I don't know about you, but all this excitement has made me hungry. It's time to eat. Starting with the back table, help yourself to the buffet."

Slate took her seat between Jake and John. The chatter from the room reminded her of the first days of many experiences in her life. The youth and enthusiasm of the group, especially the nine teams, made her proud of what they had accomplished. The final push was almost here.

She was uncomfortable sitting between Jake and John. She didn't feel guilty for breaking commitments or betraying either one. Still, each held different pieces of the puzzle. Slate risked revealing a familiarity or showing deference to one or the other. Therefore, she stuck to light banter and shop talk.

The governor made an interesting observation. "Looking at your young teams reminds me of flying squadrons. Remember in the movies, the pilots and crews sitting in briefing rooms? Commanders with long wooden pointers tapped on wall maps. Nervous crew members jotted down information, acting cool, yet aware that anything might happen. These kids likely feel the same, excited and nervous. No one wants to screw up."

Slate thought about his analogy, a perspective she had not considered. "Pilots and flying squadrons are super competitive. Competition is a necessity. Pretenders don't last long. Cream rises. Still, there's a delicate balance between competence, calculated risks, and recklessness."

Jake added, "Fear. They must fear you. That holds the line between high performance and breaking rules that cause accidents."

The governor agreed. "They expect rules, limits, and standards. They expect us to harp on safety and threaten consequences. No one wants to be an example. Everyone plays their part."

The conversation shifted to lighter topics. Slate brought up Jake's recent adventure in Alaska, a place the governor said he wanted to go.

They made their way through the buffet line. Slate commented that Jake's BBQ was way better. Returning to the table, she noticed the corner of a note under her dessert plate and glanced at the governor. He smiled. She palmed it and excused herself to the restroom.

As she got up and turned to go, she saw Jake looking at the note in her hand.

The note read, "I'm meeting a congressman in Doral at 5:00. Not too far from your condo, I think. Time for a drink or dinner, Cowgirl?"

She sighed. *When will I ever learn?*

Slate wrote a reply below his note, "Sure, Cal's is a quiet place close to Doral, ten minutes from my condo. I'm free only until 8:30. Please let me know what time works for you. Thanks! Oh, I liked your talk today a lot, Commander."

Next, Slate, sitting on the toilet, sent a text message.

"Hi. Sorry, but the governor wants to meet me in Miami about the project. Something about meeting a congressman. Yes, I still want to see you at the RV tonight. Can you wait until 9:00? If you can't, I'll be very disappointed, but I'll understand. I'm hoping. Sorry."

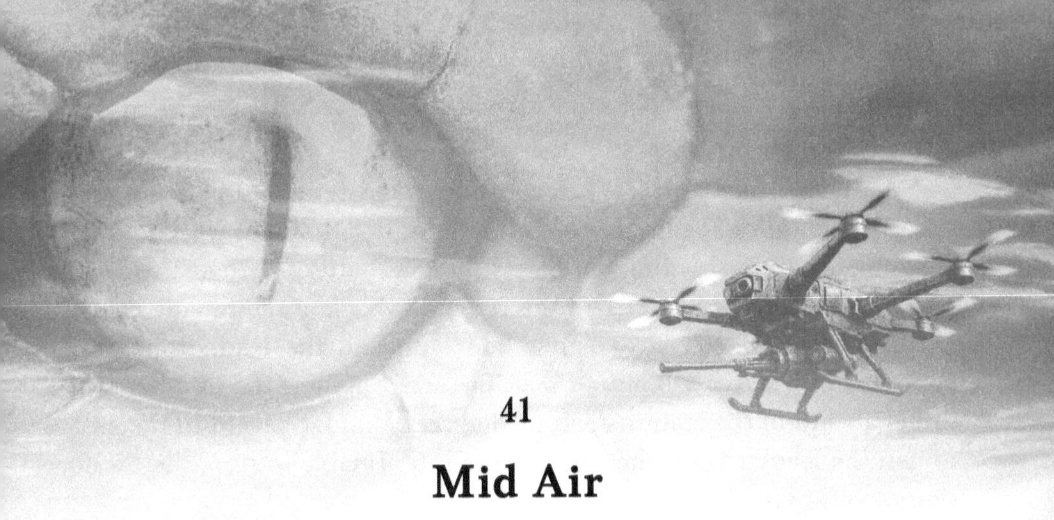

41

Mid Air

On Monday, November 26th, the first day of full field operations began with clear skies, cool air, and Raven's 9 a.m. roll call over the radio. Seven of nine teams passed power-up and flight testing on Sunday. They responded in order by team name and status.

"Albatross, drones on station, ready for launch."

"Eagle, drones on station. Rebooting due to an error code on the flight computer."

"Gator, two drones on station. Number three is down for mechanical until at least noon. One and two, ready for launch."

The Raven controllers in central command completed continuity checks and paged through screens monitoring each team.

Slate keyed the mic, "This is Top Gun. Be careful, fly safe, and happy hunting."

Several team captains clicked their mic twice to acknowledge.

Raven radioed, "Raven copies. All teams except Bobcat, Eagle, and Dragon are cleared for manual launch. Link up your drones, merge with Casey, and report back."

Raven controllers monitored Casey's orange-colored codes propagate across their seventeen monitors, one for each active drone.

A high-pitched female voice radioed, "Iguana is code red, repeat code red."

"Copy code red, Iguana. State the reason. Over," Raven replied.

"Ah, mid-air between lead and two. Both drones are down."

"How?"

"Co-pilot flight error, Sir."

"Can you load them onto the airboats?"

265

"Yes."

"Copy. Land Zcolt-3 if it's airborne and return to your staging site. All remaining teams are cleared to hunt in auto-flight with manual shooting. No auto shooting until after the first battery change."

Slate and Brad watched the video playback of the Iguana drone crash. The flight console co-pilot had launched the lead drone and parked it in a hover a hundred feet forward. She flew the number two drone abeam of the lead instead of slightly behind. She slid to the side to join the lead at twice the safe closure rate. Unable to stop, the drone slammed into the leader.

Brad gave his opinion. "Two major errors. Lining up abeam the lead and aggressive maneuvering. Sandy is either overconfident, incompetent, poorly trained, or untrainable."

"What's your call, Brad?"

"She has a private pilot's license and a commercial drone license—not incompetence. She deserves to be fired, but this humiliated and humbled her ego. I say we bring her in for an ass-kicking, and she'll turn out as one of our best. Maybe even become an instructor."

"Agreed."

Despite the shaky start, after two round-trip flights at twenty-one miles per hour, the six teams cleared over six square miles.

Slate radioed over the common frequency. "This is Top Gun—great job, guys and gals. You killed 543 pythons in your flight segment. Steady as she goes. Follow procedures, stay vigilant, and keep an eye on Casey. Everything looks splendid on our end."

Raven followed Slate. "Listen up. Next roll call is at 10:40. Be powered up and ready to launch."

"Raven, this is Hyena. A Cessna is circling our staging site at 500 feet."

"Copy. Get the tail number. We'll report the violation to the sheriff's deputy here in operations."

* * *

Friday, November 30th, the last day of the first week, marked the first time all nine teams flew twenty-seven drones for four hours with three battery changes. They cleared forty square miles and killed 3,310 pythons.

Each day, the repetition and learning from errors smoothed the flows and rhythms of procedures and interactions. Radio chatter became crisp and ordered. Casey, the algorithm housed independently in each drone, became better at finding and killing pythons. So far, Casey had shot an average of 120 pythons per drone during the four hours of flight time each day.

The routine settled into drone launch teams departing staging sites at 8:30, with the first launch at 9:30. They flew two ten-mile round trips until 10:30, followed by a twenty-minute battery change. They flew a second one-hour segment, swapped the battery pack and the ammunition magazine, then had a one-hour lunch. Flying two afternoon segments with a battery swap in between, they finished shooting at 3:30. Power-down and clean-up lasted one hour until 4:30. Raven and Top Gun worked until 5:30, collecting data and planning for the next day.

* * *

After the last flight on Friday, the end of the first week, the last of nine motorhomes arrived behind Barney's Bar and Grill near Gator Park at 5:45. Not surprisingly, each RV had large posters in the front windshield with patch designs for each team. Like fighter pilot squadrons, some designs were angry, some light-hearted, and all sported lightning bolts, spears, and slogans.

Teams filed into Barney's past a bar full of onlookers, to a private party room. Pizza, beer, and sub sandwiches arrived as they swapped war stories and chided each other.

Someone had taped a large map of the Everglades to the wall with the grid squares assigned to each team. Cleared areas, marked with shaded cross-hashes, covered most of each grid.

Absent managers from Raven and Top Gun, the forty-five team members, fifteen women, and thirty men, self-organized, and before long, used a chalkboard on the wall to list total kills by each team for the week. They also listed average kills per flight-hour segment for teams that had not flown all five days.

Iguana, which flew only three days due to Sandy's mid-air collision, won the most kills per flight hour, with 107 pythons.

Team Flounder flew all five days and killed 1,880 pythons to win the traveling Annie Oakley trophy, a bowling ball-sized bronze statue of an angry, teeth-bearing raccoon.

Each team captain spoke, sounding relieved to have the first week behind them and happy that nothing bad had happened.

The captain of Team Cheetah reminded them that the big picture was saving the Everglades. Without minimizing their contributions, he reiterated that technology and algorithms found and killed the pythons, and their job was to recognize anomalies and intercede as needed.

On Monday, the RVs would depart Barney's at 8:00 a.m. to staging sites assigned to team captains by Raven over the weekend. In most cases, grid assignments abutted their former one.

Barney provided power to the RVs in the fenced lot. Some team members slept in their RV, but most went home for the weekend in vehicles they had left there.

* * *

Friday evening, while her teams partied at Barney's, Slate relaxed in her condo, eating home-delivered butter chicken and naan with Pinot Noir.

Governor Prescott's ringtone sounded on her cell. She answered quickly. "Hi, John."

"Hi, what are you doing?"

"Oh, just relaxing in my condo. I'm exhausted," she said, leaning back on the Egyptian cotton Berber sofa in panties and a sports bra, her bare feet on the glass top coffee table.

"Want to video chat?" he asked.

"No, thanks. How did you know I was in my bra and panties?" she laughed.

"You're funny. You make me out as some kind of wolf."

"No, I'm only kidding. But I really am in my underwear. Oh, I really liked your cowboy hat, boots, and belt buckle you wore to the BBQ. Quite handsome."

The governor thanked her for the compliment but didn't remark about her bra and panties. Slate wondered why, having expected him to keep the game going.

That's strike two, you idiot. First, you ask him to kiss you after drawing a red line at the restaurant. And now, you tell him you're almost naked.

After an awkward gap in the conversation, Slate said, "So, you called about the project?"

"Yes, Brent said you had a hell of a week. Congratulations on your success."

"Thank you. We killed 11,397 pythons and cleared 173 square miles. I'm quite satisfied."

"Kill any panthers?"

"That's not funny, John."

"I'm sorry. I'm very proud of you. That's more pythons than FWC removed in twenty years."

"Thank you, I accept your apology."

The AC kicked on, and Slate pulled the comforter from the back of the sofa over her and poured a second glass of wine.

Prescott got to the reason for his call.

"Okay, on a related subject, do you think you'll be finished before the anniversary of Pa-Hay-Okee on February 17th? That's ten weeks from now, excluding the week after Christmas."

"Oh, good question. The platforms are working well and getting better. Still, factoring in weather and logistical variables, it will be close, John."

"Here's what I'm thinking," he said. "The families, the scouting community, and other groups want a memorial and have been raising money. Florida scouting wants a high-adventure camp with tent platforms and merit badge activities on the far side of the hammock, away from where the scouts died. The National Park Service, which escaped public outcry by hiding behind the FWC, is throwing federal money my way."

Slate replied, "So, you want to tie a ribbon around the commitments you made last February but need a python-free Everglades to do that?"

"To accomplish this in one year would be, well, no one could have imagined it. All because of you."

"You get the credit for trusting me and having the balls to take on the FWC."

"Funny you should mention the FWC. What started as a spark, a few questions without answers, is now a small blaze. We'll see if the corruption investigation catches fire. These guys are slippery. Anyway, that's not your concern. Can you finish by the first week of February?"

Slate paused, thinking of what the governor didn't know about—her FBI contact, spies, Tan Zhi Hao's attack on Shannon, his violent death and disappearance only five doors from her office. She could hardly believe it herself. And she already knew about his administration's investigation of the FWC.

"Are you still there?" he asked.

"Yes, sorry. We can do it with some adjustments and luck with the weather."

"Good. My staff is in contact with the families and other groups. We'll plan a large remembrance and celebration at a renovated Pa-Hay-Okee the weekend of February 16th," he said.

"Oh, by the way, John, I'm having a lot of fun even though this feels like a war. These kids are smart, enthusiastic, and afraid of me," she laughed. "Thanks for the nine motorhomes. That saved our bacon. They're a real morale booster."

"You're welcome. The owner is already doing TV spots promoting his part in restoring the Everglades. The python attacks cratered his industry. I'll let you get back to your evening."

"Thanks. I'm about to watch the Survivor episode I missed on Wednesday. Pretty exciting life, huh?"

"Sounds fun. Good night, Sarah."

"Good night, John." Slate looked at the phone, wondering.

Was it me? No rise out of him on my stupid underwear remark. Didn't call me Slate or Cowgirl. Maybe he's tired of rejection. Or, he's onto something better.

* * *

The next morning, Saturday, the 10 a.m. staff meeting in the compound began with a Zoom glitch. Fixed by 10:20, department heads kicked off the meeting with status reports. Slate summarized her thoughts on the first full week of operations.

"Thank you for your dedication and hard work. It was a long week of long hours. The teams are clearing grids and killing pythons as planned.

"Casey performed well. We'll compare algorithm data from each drone later today. I expect to find slight differences in how Casey evolved across drones over twenty hours of operation in different environments.

Peggy's team will feed the datasets into the master, let it process, and load an update in each Zcolt tomorrow.

"If I'm correct, the Zcolts will find more pythons more quickly, at greater distances, and we can increase forward speed.

"You may wonder what the rush is. I spoke with Governor Prescott last evening. The anniversary of Pa-Hay-Okee is February 17th. They have big plans for a memorial commemoration and a ribbon cutting to unveil extensive park renovations that weekend."

Doc Rock Wheeler, Raven leader, said, "That's ten weeks. With perfect weather and no Christmas break, maybe we can do it."

Slate agreed. "We have several options. We can fly every other Saturday. On five-day weeks, we can add an extra hour. I've talked with Granger about building a tenth team."

Granger chimed in. "We'll have the three drones and trailer ready by December 13th."

"Shannon and Carter, what about additional team members?" Slate asked.

"There's a waiting list of qualified applicants. Our backup five-member team completed training yesterday. They're embedded with Team Albatross next week. It will be a push, but yes, a tenth team in the field beginning the week of December 17th should get the job done," Shannon said.

"Excellent. With those adjustments, we'll finish by the end of January with time off for Christmas," Slate said.

"Oh, one other thing. Expect the governor's press secretary, Brooke Sandals, to be with a group of reporters next week. I authorized limited access to select areas: no photographs or video. The governor's office has a gallery of pictures the media can use.

"In addition, you may see me escorting officials from outside organizations. Ignore us, and under no circumstances is anyone allowed to give interviews or answer questions."

* * *

The meeting finished at eleven-thirty. Slate met Shannon at Wok-This-Way for sushi and fried rice.

"I love your hair and your makeup," Slate said.

"I took a chance. It's called a wavy bob with highlights, according to the stylist. She also helped me with my makeup. Supposedly, it makes my face look thinner."

"It's working. The mauve lipstick is perfect, and you look so sexy. Has anyone told you that your oval eyes have a hint of exotic Asian ancestry?"

Shannon smiled in shy delight. "Yes, Brad noticed."

"So, what's next?" Slate said.

"He's taking me to South Beach for stone crabs. I've never had them."

"Whoa, aren't you special. They're expensive. Someone's going to get a kiss." Slate winked at her.

"Have you talked to Nick?" Slate asked.

"That's why I asked to have lunch with you." Shannon leaned across the table.

"There are two developments. The corruption case is escalating. They're receiving anonymous tips, and there's a whistleblower. People are starting to flip like carp on a hotplate."

Slate laughed, "So carps flip on hotplates?"

Shannon shrugged. "I don't know much about carp, but you get the picture." They both laughed.

"Hey, none of our people are involved, are they?" Slate asked.

"Not that Nick has heard."

"What about spies or moles on our project?" Slate asked.

"None that we know of, which brings up the next thing."

Shannon's posture shifted. She sat back and looked away in thought, biting the inside of her lip. Her smile faltered, and sadness found her eyes.

"What is it? Are you okay?" Slate asked.

"I'm having a hard time with what happened in T-Zee's office that Saturday. I feel responsible for his death."

"He tried to kill you. And he killed himself, for reasons we'll never know. Even so, it was a savage attack, and you found a way to survive," Slate said.

"I know. I'll get over it. I do feel better after what Nick told me yesterday." Shannon looked down at the table and began to cry.

Slate reached across and put a hand over Shannon's arm. "What did Nick say?"

"He said the CIA put out feelers and found a foreign intelligence service willing to help. Anyway, the CIA had T-Zee ritually cremated at a Buddhist temple and gave the ashes to their foreign contact. Nick found out yesterday that T-Zee is back with his parents in Malaysia. They are very grateful, he said. I feel much better."

Slate had expected the worst—his body dissolved in a barrel of acid. She reached her napkin over and patted a tear from Shannon's face.

"That's good, and a much better outcome. That brings us closure, Sister," Slate said. "Never forget, he could have stolen our technology or had the drones hunt people instead of pythons. Besides, if not for him, you wouldn't be on the project or be eating stone crab tonight."

Shannon looked up through misty eyes and smiled happily.

* * *

After lunch, Slate went to her university lab. Dean Miller's car was parked two spots from hers. She walked the long way to the lab, past his office, and waved. He motioned for her to come in.

"Hello Dean, you're in the office on Saturday. Are you bucking for a promotion?" Slate smiled and laughed.

"I could say the same for you. I thought you would be out killing snakes." Miller laughed and pointed his finger at her like he bettered her jab.

He stood up and looked out the window at the parking lot. "Still driving that old Highlander. I thought you would have a beamer or Range Rover by now," he teased.

"I see you have a new Benz coupe, unless someone parked in your spot." Slate grinned and raised her eyebrows.

"Ya got me, Professor," he said. "I'm glad you came in today because I've been thinking of you."

Miller motioned for Slate to take a seat—the same one she sat in the day he fired her.

"Not that it's important, but I go bonkers bouncing around the condo since Margaret got the house in the divorce. The actual reason I'm here today is to research water scarcity in Ethiopia."

"Ethiopia? Isn't that where you attended a conference a few years ago?" Slate asked.

"Yes. They are wonderful people and so friendly. However, seven in ten people, ninety million, don't have water in their homes."

"Wow. But what does that have to do with you?"

"How about I buy you a coffee at Jerry's Deli and tell you?"

"Deal."

They took Miller's black Mercedes E-Class. Slate, accustomed to formal business settings with him, found the close space and quiet car awkward and too intimate. She caught her hands fidgeting in her lap. Since it was Saturday, they found a parking spot in front of the entrance.

"Grab some napkins and find a seat. I'll bring the drinks and our sandwich wraps," he said.

At the table, Slate checked her phone. A text from Jake read, "Breaking news. I guided a tarpon fishing trip this morning on Rabbit Key Flats. AND—I caught a 90-pound tarpon on a fly rod. It jumped and almost landed in the boat. Pretty exciting, huh, Cowgirl?"

In the picture, Jake wore wraparound mirror sunglasses, a Yamaha outboard motor baseball cap, and held up a shiny fish as tall as him.

She texted back, "I've never seen a fish that big! Congratulations."

Miller set the food down, pulled out an alcohol swab, and wiped his side of the table.

"Want one?"

Slate, unsure what to say, fearing she might look like a slob, said, "Sure, thank you."

"Back to Ethiopia. Again, not to get into my personal bullshit, but the divorce opened my eyes and my options.

"Water problems for people in poor countries like Ethiopia are getting worse. In that country, women carry five-gallon, forty-four-pound plastic containers strapped to their backs or on their heads for up to two miles. The water is often contaminated. Each family member needs one container each day. That's five containers for a family of five. It's hours of back-breaking trips to community wells and streams. Interestingly, we Americans each use ninety gallons per day."

Slate watched his eyes and animated hands, a side of him she had not seen.

"And you think you can do something about this?" Slate asked.

"Yes. A solar-powered water pump, polyethylene tubing, and a storage tank could supply water to a hundred families and save hundreds of hours of toil each week. The cost is under a thousand dollars per package."

"Wow, you've done your homework."

Miller leaned back in his chair, eating a pastry he had added to his order.

"This is where you come in, Sarah. I could hang on as dean, grow moss, and become more antiquated. It's not a bad gig, and I know enough university secrets that most wouldn't mess with me."

He laughed to himself. "At sixty-four, I have a window to start something new before I get too fat or my health goes south. This water idea may be bullshit, but it might be worth the smiles of very grateful people."

Slate's eyes got big, and with a smile, she said, "I like the vision you've created."

"Enough about me, what are you up to these days, besides becoming famous for saving the Everglades and all that good stuff?"

Slate finished the last of her Bangkok bistro wrap, wondering why the dean had drifted so far off his usual track.

"Wow, busy. Snakes, snakes, and more snakes." She laughed and made a wiggle motion with her finger.

"I'm sure. I meant, what will you do after the project? Have you given that any thought?"

"Oh. Tell you what. I'm getting a Bavarian cream to help me think. Want anything?"

Standing in line, she thought about his question, wondering the reason for his impromptu social invitation. It wasn't to show me his new car.

Maybe he's lonely. Or excited about the water idea. Perhaps just feeling chatty. Or maybe, being single, his libido spiked. No, I don't think that's it.

Back at the table. "This should do it," she said, holding up the treat, the whipped cream dripping from the fill hole. She bent her mouth sideways and took a bite. Miller tossed a napkin across the table.

"That's a good question, my plans after the project. Until a few weeks ago, I wasn't sure we could do it. There is still a lot that could go wrong. If luck holds, pythons will no longer pose a threat to the Everglades parks in a few weeks. That's 3,500 square miles. Another thousand square miles of Everglades habitat lies north of the parks. My company owns the technology, so we'll likely get that contract. I'm also working on a way to find python nests and destroy them. In a few years, pythons will be a bad memory in Florida."

Miller listened intently, his fingers together on the table, his thumbs circling each other.

"Then, I suppose you can license your technology or adapt it for other invasive species like feral pigs?" he asked.

"Yes, the algorithm isn't picky on what it learns to recognize if we have the right sensors. No doubt, you're aware I've been talking with the Defense Department."

Miller nodded.

"Do you like building start-ups and becoming filthy rich?" he asked.

Slate hadn't really thought about it, given that the horse was already on the track.

Am I having fun? Is this what I want to do? Is it the money? Is it for Jamie? Yes, I did it for him. Or at least it began like that. What am I giving up?

Miller watched her and waited.

"That's a good question, Dean. One I'll have to think about."

"If I can use your pastry as a cliché, it's food for thought." He smiled, pleased at his cleverness. "You applied research and knowledge from your studies to solve the python problem. Consider what you are leaving behind in the wonderful world of academia. Your accomplishments and notoriety would pull in enormous outside support and funding for new science projects and solutions."

Slate listened and thought about his words, weighing options, both personal and professional.

"I've given this a lot of thought, Sarah. There's no hurry, but I think you would be an outstanding dean as my replacement."

Slate slid against the back of her seat, stunned.

"I don't know what to say."

"It may not be for you. It's a pain in the ass most of the time. The whining drives me crazy, and I can't stand the pompous bastards, of which there are many. Still, I think we put out a good product of capable engineers."

Slate watched his face display the emotions behind his thoughts.

"If you structured your company correctly, you wouldn't need to divest. That would keep your options open in the private sector."

Slate nodded in agreement, sipping the last of her coffee.

"So, you think about it, Snake Lady. You're my first choice. Plenty of time to finish your project."

Miller extended his hand, and Slate shook it gently.

"Thank you, Dean. You have no idea how much your confidence and offer mean to me."

They gathered up their items for the trash. Both slid their chairs in. Slate turned to leave, her back to him.

Miller leaned forward near her ear. "Nick told me T-Zee is home with his parents. I'm happy about that."

Without turning, Slate reached her hand back and found his. She held it until they reached the restaurant door.

42

End of the World

Slate parked her new Lexus SUV near the front door of Barney's. Not expecting her, most team members in the private room were already halfway through their first plastic cup of draft beer. Slate walked up behind Jeremy, the captain of Team Bobcat and the unofficial group leader, as he wrote results for week six on the whiteboard.

"How's it going?" Slate asked, startling him.

He recognized her voice and twirled around, almost swiping the red marker across her white blouse.

"Oh, hi, Doctor Warner," he said, looking behind her for other management types who would dampen the party.

"It's good. Week six was our longest week yet." Reading from the whiteboard, "Six days, three hundred total flight hours, fifteen grids cleared, and 29,243 dead pythons."

"You look tired, Jeremy." Slate scanned the room and said, "You all look tired."

Groups of different sizes clustered around the keg and sat at tables. Some sat alone with their phones or iPads.

"Let's put it this way. One more week is a good thing. Not that we don't love saving the Everglades," Jeremy laughed.

Slate patted him on the shoulder.

"It would be an easy job, if it weren't for the people," she said with a wink and a smile.

"Tell me about it. At times, I think we're on a reality show."

"Which one?" she asked, laughing out loud.

"You're funny, Doctor Warner. How about a combination of Survivor, Fear Factor, and Love Island?"

"You should write a book," Slate laughed. "Oh, I forgot, you signed an NDA. Forget about the book."

Jeremy finished writing the team standings for the week and cumulative results. Team Dragon won week six, but Team Iguana, where Sandy remained the co-pilot, had the most total kills by a wide margin.

Personality conflicts and disputes developed over the weeks, both inside and outside the RVs. At the end of week three, Shannon suggested Slate reshuffle the teams. Console captains remained on their original RVs. Co-pilots and the three drone crew chiefs of each team submitted confidential wish lists to Slate on Saturday, December 15th. Each person ranked teams and members. Four teams requested to stay put, with no change. Slate tried to accommodate their requests.

Shannon published the new team lineups on Sunday, and people moved their stuff. Unable to satisfy everyone, some were trapped with bottom-ranked captains, like Jerry Jones, of Team Hyena. Flounder became an all-girls team.

Slate included a reminder in the reassignment memo. "I appreciate your commitment and endurance. Living and working in close quarters is challenging. I hope you're having some fun or at least making the best of your off-duty time.

"I compare your job as drone operators to pilots. The great majority of a pilot's time is spent precisely following set procedures while being ready for the thousand unexpected events that might occur. Self-discipline and professionalism are imperative in our work. In other words, leave any personal issues in the RVs when you are on duty.

"If you have personal conflicts, notify Shannon, so we can accommodate everyone as best we can."

Although not officially authorized, if the physical proximity of RVs allowed, and members agreed, people switched RVs for sleepovers. Shannon shared juicy tidbits about hook-ups and break-ups with Slate.

Slate thought about the complexity that humans added to the project. The more humans involved, the more problems. She imagined the problems managing thousands of human hunters, if not for her drones. Then she envisioned technology that only required one or two humans to command a swarm of hunter-killer platforms firing beam weapons.

Slate made her way around groups of team members. Having only one short week remaining, they appeared upbeat and in high spirits. The most common complaint, which Slate heard often, was the stench of dead pythons and swarms of turkey vultures—some vultures even learned to follow drones like pelicans followed fishing trawlers and hung out at their RV sites.

A crew chief from Team Cheetah told Slate, "It's something you never get used to. The odor permeates the RVs. I smell it on my sheets."

"I'm sorry about the odor. We hadn't considered that as a factor. Dispatch is adjusting grid assignments to favor upwind locations when possible. Anyway, we've knocked weeks off the original schedule with our adjustments. It could have been worse, I guess."

"At least the vultures and alligators are happy, and we've seen raccoons and even coyotes eating dead pythons," the crew chief said.

Slate asked for the group's attention and was about to speak when Carter and Taylor walked in. Taylor gave Slate a warm hug, with a look of complete happiness on her face.

"We can't stay," Carter said. "Taylor has started her last semester and has homework."

"Honors organic chemistry. It's brutal," Taylor said.

Slate told the group, "Get some pizza. Then, I have an announcement before I skedaddle."

Carter grabbed a box of pizza and left. The others loaded their plates and sat down.

Slate continued. "Listen up, gang. Raven tells me we can complete the final ten grids by flying four hours a day, Monday through Friday, next week.

"A couple of notes. I apologize for the gun jams last week. It was bad ammunition. We have a new supplier.

"We're seeing more gawkers, YouTubers, small drones, and reporters out there, so be careful. FWC is assigning another officer to each Zcolt team, and additional sheriff's deputies are patrolling roads.

"One last thing. Because we will finish clearing 3,500 square miles of Everglades parks earlier than projected, we qualify for contract incentives. What does that mean to you? If next week goes smoothly, I'll see you here on Friday with an envelope for each of you, a thousand dollars in cash."

Everyone jumped to their feet, cheering and toasting each other.

***

Leaving Barney's, Slate drove west to the coast. Her overnight bag contained a long-sleeve, sea foam-colored shirt, lightweight, form-fitting capris, water shoes, a wide-brimmed Panama hat, and a silky lace nightgown. Crossing the bridge to Chokoloskee Island down Calusa Drive, the path ended at a vacant lot on the water's edge.

Jake stood watching the sun settle behind puffy clouds. His back to her, she thought he looked rugged and delicious. Hearing her car on the sand and shells, he turned to see her waving above the steering wheel of her new Lexus SUV.

He held her hand while the sun edged toward the sea.

She smelled the salt air and took in the solitude. "I so needed this," she said.

"Where's your Highlander?"

"Gone. How do you like it? It has all-wheel drive. We can drive on the beach."

"Good for you. I like to see you happy, but you can't drive on this beach.

"The house is right over there."

She showed him her car, and he carried her bag to the two-story beach house, which belonged to a client friend.

They caught the sunset from the rooftop deck, having wine she had bought.

"My boat is over there." He pointed to a twenty-one-foot fishing boat sitting on a lift above the water. The aluminum T-top gleamed gold in light from the sunset.

"You have your choice. We can go out for seafood, or I'll make shrimp scampi with capers and sliced avocado over angel hair. Drinks are on the house."

She pointed to the kitchen. The owner of the beach house left a bottle of champagne as a gift. They had a second glass on the deck off the living room, her bare feet on the wood railing. She leaned back in the chair with her eyes closed, letting the spirits fill her mind.

Jake came up behind, bent over, and kissed her upside down. She reached up, ran her fingers through his hair, and pulled him into her mouth. She stopped his hand as he reached under her blouse.

"We'd better slow down if we want to eat," she laughed.

Dinner was delightful at the small table overlooking the estuary. Slate asked about the three kids down on a wooden dock.

"They're fishing for mangrove snapper under the dock light. They fight like fish ten times their size. And they're excellent eating."

"Sounds fun."

"Want to try it, Cowgirl?"

"Ah, well, I'm thinking of an indoor sport." Slate held up her glass for the last splash of champagne.

"I like how you think. First, let's make a plan for the morning." Jake turned the handheld marine radio to the automated weather station. For Slate, much of the transmission sounded like gibberish.

Jake interpreted for her. "Early morning fog, sea state one-foot, light winds, forecast calls for more of the same. Looks good. We'll cast a net for bait on the way out, have fishing lines in the water by eight, and be back by noon. We can't keep snook, but we'll catch red drum and sea trout for lunch. That's the plan, what do you think, Hot Stuff?"

"Yes, I like it. This is all new to me, and I'm excited. I so want to see what your life is like. You really do love it here, don't you?"

"There's no place quite like my world. It's remote and provides everything nature has to offer. "Hey, did you watch your Survivor show this week?"

"Not yet."

"Well, I recorded it," Jake said proudly. "Want to watch it in the bedroom? I bought gourmet caramel corn from Granny's general store."

When together in the RV, there was always the pressure of time. Tonight was different. They relaxed, watched TV, and let the night develop. Moonshine reflected off the sea into the room.

Her mind drifted to places only he'd taken her. Delicious royal blues, pinks, and purples swirled and lifted her. Jake was her captain on a ship sailing high in a night sky of galaxies and shooting stars. Spent and fulfilled, they lay wrapped around each other.

"You're phenomenal," he said.

She smiled. "Only with you, Cowboy."

Jake was in the bathroom when she noticed a message from the governor on her phone.

He thinks I'm at my condo.

Jake returned and snuggled behind her in a spoon. His breathing settled as he relaxed and drifted off to sleep. Slate watched shadows flicker across the wall as light filtered through a palm tree swaying in the breeze.

She liked everything about the man cradling her. She ran down the list in her mind.

He's grounded, predictable, dependable, trustworthy, honest, respectful, clean, organized, unpretentious, and intelligent. And he's amazing in bed.

She laughed to herself.

That sounds like a scout oath, minus the sex part.

The wind must have increased or changed direction. A shutter rattled. She remembered the drive from Miami. With each mile, she felt further removed from her world. Slate searched for the word to describe the feeling of this place—precarious.

She recalled as a teenager being on the thin ridge trail on a rocky outcrop at the Grand Canyon. Four feet wide, a thousand-foot drop on each side, the trail ended on a gravel-covered rock platform the size of a camper. A few people waited there for sunset pictures. They jostled for position, some with tripods. Someone bumped her. Her foot slipped on loose stones. Her balance tipped. "Excuse me," someone said. She froze and sat down in panic. Two people helped her off the precipice. She remained on a park bench until long after the sun had set. Back at the lodge, she called her mother, her safety net, from a payphone.

Jake is perfectly at home here. For me, Chokoloskee Island feels like that rocky outcrop.

The morning ride in the fog on Jake's boat excited Slate. They caught two fish called red drum on an oyster bar, one large enough to keep. Slate caught the biggest of three sea trout on sea-grass beds. Back at the beach house, Jake filleted the fish, then pan-fried them in an iron skillet with butter and herbs. They split a beer.

He noticed Slate glance at her watch and, with a gleam in his eye, said, "One hour. You up for it?"

Slate jumped up. "I'll race you to the bed. Go!"

***

On the way home, Slate thought about the complications of life, the crazy mix of puzzle pieces. At her condo on Sunday afternoon, first she called Jake, who wanted to know if she got back alright.

Next, she called the governor, crossed her fingers, and told him she'd been out with girlfriends the night before, and one, who visited from out of town, had stayed over.

They discussed being on track to wrap up the Everglades project by Friday. He gave her an update on enhancements at Pa-Hay-Okee and a rough schedule for the commemorative events.

Slate brought up the next phase.

"I know this came up at the last meeting and we should have decided earlier, but while we have drone assets and teams in the field, it makes sense to clear the adjacent conservation areas north of the parks. They total about 1,000 square miles and would take about four weeks if we employ ten teams. I've talked with Brent and Newman."

"What did they say?"

"They need a week to coordinate, and we need a week to lay out a grid plan. So, we could hunt the last week of this month, and the following week, then take off the week before the Pa-Hay-Okee commemorative. We hunt the last two to three weeks of February, and we're done."

"What about money?"

"I'm fine with amending our contract using the same conditions. The State will save millions on mobilization costs," Slate said.

"Perfect. We can announce this at Pa-Hay-Okee on February 16th."

Before calling, Slate touched up her makeup and considered offering to video chat, knowing John would not bring it up again after their last call and her underwear flub. He seemed a bit perfunctory, efficient, and reserved. *Is he wary of me? Afraid of being rejected? Decided I'm too complicated or a tease? Has someone else captured his attention? Whatever it is, I don't like it.*

"I thought about doing a video chat, John, but figured you might only be wearing a tie," she laughed while pushing the video chat invite button.

He didn't reply. She wondered if he had heard her, and she thought about turning her video off. *What's wrong with me?*

He popped into view.

"You're funny," he said. "I'm disappointed to see that you're also dressed. That's a joke. I'm not a perv."

"I know you're not, John. I'm the one sticking my foot in my mouth. But in our last video chat, I really was trying to cool down from a scorching day in the Everglades."

"No worries. We're laughing, and that's the important part."

"You're sweet and respectful and a gentleman."

"You don't make it easy, Cowgirl. There's so much about you that I find irresistible," he said.

"I'm blushing. By the way, you look great in boots and a cowboy hat," she said.

Sitting at his desk at home, he reached over, picked up the hat, and put it on.

"Quite handsome, Mr. Governor."

With a big smile, looking directly into her eyes, he said, "So, what happens after Pay-Hay-Okee?"

Slate cocked her head to one side and gave him a sly smile. "Oh, you mean after the project?"

He nodded, his eyes locked onto hers.

"Well, there's a lot to think about, but I'd say that all options are on the table."

He tipped his hat with his fingers. She winked at him.

43

We're Good

February 16th, 2030, the first anniversary of the massacre at Pa-Hay-Okee.

Preparations for the commemorative event concluded late Friday evening, February 15th.

The next morning, shuttle buses operated from the main parking area, located two miles away at the turnoff from State Highway 9336, where, one year earlier, Sheriff Palmer's command center had coordinated search and recovery operations. A bronze statue depicting scouts hiking toward a sunset replaced a tent where the scouts' families had gathered.

Pa-Hay-Okee Lookout was completely refurbished. A sixty-foot-tall observation tower, constructed of cypress and oak, featured three viewing platforms and a cedar shake roof. A circular area near the tower represented a scouting campsite. In place of a campfire, the center held a reflecting pool. Eleven cypress benches surrounded the pool. A brass plaque on the back of each bench had the name, age, and rank of each scout, including the only survivors: Taylor, Owen, and Cindy.

The new Everglades Heritage Lodge housed a wildlife museum, a large meeting room, and a park ranger's office. Made of limestone, rough-hewn timber, and cypress logs, the lodge, like the tower and memorial site, complemented the natural surroundings.

The original boardwalk was extended. Ignoring rules, park staff had thrown baitfish from the viewing alcoves along the wooden walkway. This attracted Snowy Egrets, Great Blue Herons, smaller Tricolored Herons, Wood Storks, Anhinga, and the Roseate Spoonbills.

Extensive efforts had created a manicured trail over the three-mile route the scouts had taken to the forested hammock. On the

286

western end, a quarter mile from the site of the massacre, the National Park Service built a permanent camping area. It included tent platforms for fifty scouts, cabins for adult leaders, and facilities for teaching wilderness skills.

The audience waited for the ceremony to begin. VIPs had wooden folding chairs on the stage, and the audience sat in semicircular rows. The US Secretary of the Interior, members of Congress, state legislators, chaplains, and other officials chatted among themselves on stage. The Florida Attorney General sat off to the side, talking on her phone and taking notes.

To the relief of organizers, puffy white clouds and a light breeze combined with a perfect temperature of seventy-two. The light fragrance of sweet magnolia blossoms, the rustling of leaves high in the canopy, and sunlight trading places with shadows had a calming effect. Still, many were anxious. The anniversary of the event unleashed a kaleidoscope of emotions. This, the place where the bodies were brought, where Cindy almost died, and where Taylor escaped with Owen, dredged up painful memories.

Commemorating the anniversary in an area still infested with Burmese pythons would have been unbearable. Organizers had reasons to celebrate incredible successes that seemed impossible, let alone achieved, in only twelve months. The catalyst for those achievements was, sadly, the loss of eight bright young lives.

* * *

A deep, pulsating throb, a whomp-whomp unlike any other, advanced on Pa-Hay-Okee from the east. The V-22 Osprey had departed Homestead Air Base twenty minutes earlier. It banked sharply, circled the assembly, then slowed as the propellers transitioned from airplane to helicopter mode. Escorted by Blackhawk helicopters of the Florida National Guard, it landed nearby on the entrance road. The governor, with Slate beside him, stood with other dignitaries, bracing against the prop wash. The Osprey engines shut down, and the Vice President of the United States descended the steps.

The governor escorted the vice president to the front row of the audience, where family members sat. He greeted each person, giving special attention to the three survivors. As the vice president shook Taylor's hand, he noticed a bird land on the lookout tower.

He pointed to a Bald Eagle. "Is that your eagle, Taylor?"

She, wearing her uniform with an Eagle Scout medal suspended from a red, white, and blue ribbon, looked up, then pointed to her medal, and replied, "It is now, Mr. Vice President." They laughed.

The reporter from Channel 12, Ashley Fox, now with a copper-colored bob hairstyle and frameless cat-eyeglasses, wore a butter yellow linen sundress. She captured Taylor's witty reply to the vice president on her iPhone, and the segment opened the six o'clock newscast.

Taylor had invited Wendy Cooper, the sheriff's deputy who interviewed her in the hospital, to sit next to her and her mother. Slate took the seat between Mathew and Rick, her brother and Jamie's father. Rick's former wife, Fran, sat next to Mathew. Lottie Lohman, the owner of Banana the dog, and her grandson, Andrew, also sat in the section for victims' families.

Sheriff Palmer and first responders, plus Jake Calhoun and his two dozen python hunters who had recovered the scouts, sat in a designated section of bleacher seats. Other sections housed members of the Red Riders, Never Again, and Bring Them Back, formerly known as Mothers Against the FWC, who now focused on restoring native animals to South Florida.

ZKuul Solutions had a separate bleacher for ninety representatives, including fifty members of the ten Zcolt teams. Each wore a flight suit, the same color as the Blue Angels, with name tags and epaulettes indicating their position on the team. A badge over the left breast had the team mascot, and a shoulder patch displaying a coiled Burmese python, that was embroidered with the number of recorded team kills. At Slate's suggestion, the owner of Barney's Bar, and their staff, plus the Gator Park staff, and the airboat captains were invited, and sat with the Zcolt teams.

In the bleachers next to ZKuul, sat Florida State FWC staff and officers who provided security and logistical support.

Scoutmaster Flanagan and the two adult leaders who had dropped off the eleven scouts on February 17th, 2029, sat with their troop and sixty uniformed scouts from ten troops across South Florida.

Flags in Florida had flown at half-mast all week.

A scout approached the podium, lifted a bugle, and waited.

Four F-35 Lightning fighter jets from the Jacksonville Air National Guard flew over the assembly at one thousand feet and three hundred miles per hour. One jet pulled up vertically, lit its afterburner, and disappeared into high cirrus clouds, a traditional salute to the fallen. A pressure wave swept over the audience with a thundering roar.

The scout played taps with deep emotion, bringing out tissues and eliciting hugs.

Sheriff Palmer's color guard marched in front of the stage, stopping before the families of each lost scout to present them with a tri-cornered American flag. Rick held the flag in front of Slate and the four embraced.

"Thank you for what you've done, Sister. Jamie would be so proud of you."

A Christian pastor and a Jewish rabbi gave invocations.

Governor Prescott sat next to the vice president on the stage. The governor walked to the podium as Slate's staff rolled a Zcolt drone on a platform to the middle of the stage. Having flown 120 missions, it looked like the battle-scarred space shuttle at the Kennedy Space Center. Carter had placed a new blue and white ZKuul Solutions decal on the body of the Zcolt above the Humboldt.

The governor gave opening remarks, acknowledged the families and the large contingent of scouts. He explained the vice president had two additional events and would be leaving shortly, then welcomed him to the podium.

"Thank you, Governor Prescott. What a beautiful job you've done on upgrades to Pa-Hay-Okee, a place I visited as a young scout. There's no place like the Everglades. I've been concerned about the python invasion and the loss of native animals for many years.

"Here we are in 2030. Due to the tragic loss of young lives represented by families here today, newly elected Governor Prescott committed to finding a solution. Because of his leadership, the Burmese python is no longer a threat. I'm truly amazed at what Florida has accomplished on their own, thanks to Governor Prescott and his team."

The vice president walked a few steps to the weathered Zcolt, turned one of the six rotors, and bent over to see the gun. "Pardon my language, but that's one bad-ass machine. I've never seen anything quite like this."

He leaned to read a number on the decal of a coiled python below the ZKuul logo. "Amazing. 14, 879 kills."

Returning to the microphone, he said, "Governor Prescott told me of meeting a research scientist after his first press conference in Miami following the tragedy. He read a note from the scientist which said, 'I can kill your snakes, every damn one of them.' As it turned out, she was the chair of the University of Miami's computer science and robotics departments. The governor did not know at the time that her nephew, Jamie, was one of the scout leaders taken at Pa-Hay-Okee. Call it a coincidence or destiny, but this led to a novel solution, the first of its kind anywhere in the world.

"Professor Sarah Warner, can you come to the stage?"

Surprised, Slate looked toward the governor for an explanation. She walked onto the stage, shook hands with the vice president, and stood beside the podium.

"I'm told Dr. Warner's parents nicknamed her Slate as a baby who cried like chalk screeching on a chalkboard."

The audience laughed, and Slate blushed.

The vice president picked up a leather binder as his female chief of staff approached with a small box.

"Doctor Sarah Slate Warner, on behalf of the President of the United States, I award you the National Medal of Technology and Innovation."

The VP read the citation while his chief of staff pinned the medal on Slate's lapel.

"Doctor Warner has pushed the boundaries of computer science and robotics in designing custom algorithms and aerial platforms that will save lives and restore biodiversity to South Florida. Her discoveries will benefit our country in many additional ways."

The chief of staff led Slate from the stage, pausing for dignitaries to congratulate her.

The VP gave closing remarks and departed the stage in an SUV for the short ride to the waiting Osprey.

Governor Prescott continued his presentation, stopping for the gritty growl of giant propellers. Lifting off, the Osprey banked to pass over the assembly. The VP, against protocol, stood in the open door, waving to the crowd. Ashley elbowed her cameraman just in time to capture the VP practically hanging out the door as if he was leaving a battleground for home.

"The loss of young lives happened one year ago today. On the following Friday, I held a press conference on the lawn of Sheriff Palmer's headquarters in Miami.

"That was when I outlined a plan. Having failed to prevent or issue a warning about the potential for pythons to attack humans, I fired five high-ranking public officials.

"I cancelled three worthless and costly state python programs and the ridiculous annual python challenge that accomplished little and left tons of garbage in the Everglades.

"I tasked the Florida Department of Law Enforcement to investigate actions and motivations of public officials since the year 2000, who might have realized special private gains from the commercialization and perpetuation of the python menace. Our attorney general, Pam Barnett, will say more about that in a minute.

"Lastly, I created a task force led by Brent Howard, Dr. Leslie Paton, and FWC Director Anthony Newman to explore all possible methods for removing pythons and restoring native birds and animals. Will the task force members please stand? Brent, please tell us your findings and what happened."

Brent unfolded his notes. "Hi, I'm the governor's director of science and technology. We worked closely with our academic community and industry partners to seek cost-effective methods for removing pythons. Long story short, the University of Miami, under Dean Miller's leadership, submitted Dr. Warner's idea, which was judged as the only plausible solution. Dean Miller, could you please stand and be recognized?"

The dean stood, waved, and quickly sat.

"Governor Prescott worked with the legislature on both sides of the aisle. They funded a proof-of-concept contract, a pilot project, and the final ten-week removal phase, which was completed four weeks ago. Florida State agencies provided logistics and security.

"Next, I'll let Dr. Warner tell you how they did it."

Slate made her way back to the stage, sunlight reflecting brightly off her medal.

"Thank you, Brent. First, it has been such an incredible experience working alongside talented people from the FWC, DOT, DEP, the University of Florida, and Save Native Wildlife of Florida.

"Like many, Dean Miller and I were caught off guard by the python threat in our own backyard. We discovered that most of our native animals had been wiped out. Dean Miller made university resources available across various disciplines.

"I assembled a small team to assist me. Jake, Brad, Carter, and Shannon, please stand."

Slate pointed to the Zcolt. "This is what we created. It has sensors and a computer program that I adapted to find pythons. A weapons computer aims the gun, which shoots a single bullet into the python's brain. The computer is fast and precise. Does anyone want to see it fly?"

Cheers rose, and hands shot into the air. A sound like an army of machines marching on air, drew the audience's attention toward the entrance road. The lead Zcolt had two drones on the left and right. Fifty feet behind the first three-ship formation was a second set. Then a third, a fourth, and a fifth, for a total of fifteen Zcolts. At thirty feet above ground, flying at eight miles per hour, they resembled an alien invasion. Slate saw reactions span a range of human emotions—shock, amazement, awe, and fear. Many stepped back or put a hand to their mouth. Others stared with mouths open. She saw members of the Red Riders pointing at the Zcolt gun barrels. The members of Zcolt teams not operating the drones from nearby control trailers called out the team names as they passed—Albatross, Cheetah, Eagle, Gator, and Iguana.

After passing between the audience and the stage, the line of Zcolts climbed up and over cypress trees, turned right behind the new lookout tower, and descended out of sight. It took a moment, but the applause caught, and cheers went up.

"It's amazing none of this existed one year ago," Slate said. "There was no blueprint. Only ideas, trials, and errors. Five teams, each consisting of five members, flew the drones you saw. More precisely, they operated the computers that fly the drones. Members of the other five teams are over there in the bleachers. Please give them a round of applause."

Slate signaled to Dr. Paton, who stood and approached the podium.

"As Governor Prescott said, removing pythons was the first step. Now the hard work begins of repopulating the Everglades with native animals and birds. The person in charge of that is Dr. Leslie Paton, Director of Wildlife Ecology and Conservation at the University of Florida. Please welcome Dr. Paton as she comes to the podium."

Dr. Paton smiled. "Hello, everyone. Such a beautiful day in so many ways. If you think we are excited, you should see the animals. They can't wait to come home."

To the left of the assembly area, near the edge where the park ended in marsh grass and bushes, the FWC had lined up twelve covered trailers in a V shape, with the wide end facing the audience and the narrow end facing the marsh, like a funnel.

"Through a combination of captive breeding and the help of rescue centers, our staff and hundreds of volunteers are collecting animals that will bring the Everglades back to life. Are you ready for a homecoming?"

Cheers and clapping filled the air.

One by one, FWC officers opened a trailer door, then the door of each interior cage. A family of raccoons, ten in all, sniffed the air and jumped to the ground, then ran for the marsh. The crowd applauded and cheered. The audience let out oohs and aahs at the sight of the two panthers, young brothers, in separate cages. They leaped to the ground, and one rebounded in a vertical jump to the top of a trailer. The other took off for the marsh. A wildlife officer shooed with his arms, and the young male jumped from the trailer and chased after his brother.

Dr. Paton followed a script that announced the names of animals and interesting facts about each species. There were foxes, opossums, white tailed deer, bobcats, marsh rabbits, fox squirrels, and box turtles.

"I can only imagine what they must be thinking. A whole new world reclaimed for them. The actual program is more methodical and structured. It will take years for the population to recover and for the Everglades to become a thriving ecosystem once again—thanks to the incredible work of Slate Warner, the governor, and all who found a way to beat the pythons."

Governor Prescott came to the podium. "Thank you for your contributions, Dr. Paton.

"Now I'd like our attorney general, Pam Barnett, to speak."

She thanked the governor and opened a folder.

"The investigation opened by Governor Prescott progressed, and like many, developed new leads and trails to find the truth. At a certain point, it became necessary to convene a grand jury, which I ordered. For the past three months, the grand jury has called witnesses and developed additional lines of inquiry. They considered wildlife policy decisions, programs, business relationships, grant award processes, contract bidding and evaluation, contract deliverables and compliance, hiring practices, expense substantiation, and auditing."

The attorney general paused to survey the audience. Silence and tension replaced the euphoria of Dr. Paton's animal releases.

"The grand jury found probable cause to bring charges of fraud, misappropriation of funds, bid-rigging, shell companies, willful ignorance by public officials, unsubstantiated income windfalls, criminal hiring practices, quid-pro-quo relationships, and conspiracy."

Public officials looked at each other with raised eyebrows. Shannon made eye contact with Slate, and they nodded with satisfaction. Slate glanced at Nick. He stood off to the side under a tree, wearing a baseball cap and sunglasses, next to someone she didn't recognize.

"As such, yesterday, the grand jury filed indictments against two business owners, a non-profit organization, and three public officials. As I speak, law enforcement is issuing summonses and arrest warrants.

"As your attorney general, I value public trust and justice—the cornerstones of this administration. Governor Prescott pledged to find the how and why behind the proliferation and cover-up of the python crisis. The upcoming trials promise jaw-dropping revelations."

Whispers and murmurs wafted through the audience.

The governor thanked the attorney general and asked Scoutmaster Flanagan to form-up the scouts.

"So, what have we accomplished and what comes next? Here are the numbers. In three months of operations, ZKuul Solutions eliminated 289,451 pythons from 3,500 square miles in the Florida Everglades and

Big Cypress. Over the next several weeks, they will finish clearing the roughly 1,000 square miles of FWC wildlife conservation areas, which hold approximately 65,000 pythons.

"Smaller pythons, under three feet in length, remain. We have four years before they reach breeding age. Meanwhile, ZKuul Solutions is close to finalizing a technology that locates python nests in May and June. Females remain on their eggs for two months, plenty of time for drones and human hunters to destroy the females and their nests. Burmese pythons could be eliminated in Florida in three years. As for costs, the State has invested less than sixty million in this project, far less than the one hundred million in fraud, waste, and abuse with minimal results over the past three decades."

Prescott noticed the Bald Eagle had returned to the top of the tower. Flanagan and the scouts were assembled behind the bleachers. He looked at Slate and winked. She raised two fingers in a small wave.

"It's been a good day. Thanks for coming, for honoring the young lives lost, and for celebrating our achievements."

A screech sounded. The eagle peeled off its perch and dove, sweeping down in a curve to level flight between the stage and audience. Talons came out like grappling hooks. A rabbit, one of a dozen Dr. Paton released, nibbled grass under an oak. The collision crushed the rabbit into the ground. The raptor flapped its wings, lifting the bunny into the sky. The governor took the interruption in stride.

"And there we see nature as it's meant to be. I was about to say, the last event before a reception in the new Heritage Lodge, is the departure of campers who are hiking to the new Three Mile Hammock."

Owen, the scout rescued from a python by Taylor, was six inches taller than last year. He held a staff with the troop flag displaying the number 44 and the words "Tamiami, Florida." Owen, a tall pack on his back, led the column. Taylor followed, the survival knife sheathed to her belt. Carter followed her. Cindy, the scout who scrambled barefoot in the dark for half a mile to escape, brought her younger brother. Shannon and Brad looked out of place with their shiny new camping gear. Eight additional Troop 44 scouts, new to wilderness camping, completed the section. Each one stood in silence, respectful of the departure of eleven scouts from this spot one year earlier.

Families watched and cried, many uncontrollably.

Scouts from four other troops formed behind Troop 44. A bugler sounded the assembly and the call to march. The scout band played "The Scout Salute" and "Scouting We Shall Go."

From the podium, Scoutmaster Flanagan wiped away tears, called the formation to attention, gave the order to march, and returned a salute initiated by Scout Owen.

As the campers departed, FWC officers uncovered bird cages and opened the wire tops. Hundreds of Northern Bobwhite Quail erupted in a covey. They flew low and disappeared down the trail ahead of the scouts.

* * *

Slate said goodbye to her brother as they boarded the shuttle bus. Dean Miller waited for her in the control trailer.

"You were right, Dean. I'm a scientist and researcher. I would be honored to fill your position when you retire. In any event, I've decided to remain with the University, and I've set aside my official involvement with ZKuul. I'm consulting as a third-party advisor until the completion of the contract extension."

Dean Miller shook her hand.

"You made the right choice. I can retire with satisfaction, knowing that our college's future prominence is in good hands. Anticipating your decision, I've already submitted you as my first choice. No worries."

She agreed to meet him in four weeks and walked him to his car.

Slate enjoyed the quiet of the short walk to the new lodge. When she opened the massive oak door, she saw Zcolt teams in the banquet hall on the right. In the corner to her left, by a wall of bookcases, Jake sat at a table by the window. He drank coffee from a metal cup and was reading the commemoration brochure. He looked up as she walked over.

"Hi, Jake."

"Hi, yourself. Are you glad it's over, Professor?"

She nodded and sat down, her back to the room.

"It went well. I'm happy and sad. My head is swimming."

"Can I get you something?"

She pointed to his coffee. "One of those, please."

He fixed it the way she liked and set it down.

She sipped from the cup in thought, then looked up.

"You can have any job you want at ZKuul, Jake. This is only the beginning. The applications for what we've created are endless. You can be rich and famous."

He looked at her, his expression unchanged.

"Any job you want. I'm serious."

He reached across and touched her nose.

"I like your shiny new ribbon and medal. Don't worry about me. I'm fine."

"You didn't get enough recognition for what you have done, Jake."

Jake looked at the woman he'd come to know and love. "We're a good combination. I have no complaints or regrets."

Jeremy, from Team Bobcat, walked over.

"Hey, Boss, I think the governor is looking for you."

"Oh, thanks, Jeremy." She turned to see Prescott through a side window by the entrance, talking to Senator Grant.

"I'll be right back, Jake."

Slate made her way through groups of people, shaking hands and accepting compliments. On the porch outside the entrance, she walked up to the governor and shook hands with the senator. The senator said his goodbyes and left. Prescott turned to her.

"Wow, quite a day. Your Zcolt fly-by blew me away."

She laughed. "I thought you might like that. Your attorney general's announcement blew me away."

He laughed. "Yeah, there are at least a dozen looking over their shoulders."

The governor leaned closer to say, "You just shook hands with one of them."

She looked at her hand and back at the governor, wrinkling her nose.

"Thank you for your part in my receiving the national technology medal," she said.

"You completely deserve it. Did you see your 'Welcome Home' mural in the museum, like the picture I gave you?"

"No way, there's one inside?"

"Yep." He smiled with satisfaction.

"Thanks. That means a lot to me. That's how I want to be remembered."

"I know. Okay, I'm heading out to wrap up a couple of things. I'll see you when I see you."

"Gotcha."

Inside the lodge, Slate excused herself to Jake again.

"Please stay. I'll be right back."

Filling an entire wall, the hand-painted mural had an airborne Zcolt in the background guarding the Everglades. A favorable caricature of Slate in the lower right corner joined lines of animals. A panther sat next to Slate, leaning against her leg, her hand on its head.

Back at Jake's table with a big smile, Slate said, "Wow, there's a mural in the museum welcoming the animals home."

"I saw it. It's very nice. And it's you. You did it."

They talked about the events of the day, laughing at the animals running away from each other and into the swamp. They reflected on the emotions their friends would face on the campout.

"I need to make an appearance with the teams before I leave," she said.

Jake tipped his cup up, emptying the last of his coffee, and looked at her for a long moment.

She interrupted the silence. "So, we're good, right, Cowboy?"

With the smile she had grown to love, he said, "We're good, Cowgirl."

* * *

The cloud-burst gray-colored Lexus still smelled new. Slate inhaled deeply and listened to the silence inside her car. Happy to be alone behind dark-tinted windows, a shuttle bus passed, taking people to their vehicles. She opened the weather app on her phone: partly cloudy skies, seventy degrees, light winds, and no rain at Pa-Hay-Okee tonight.

That's good. A good night for camping and loving nature. New beginnings. Sleep well, my friends.

She started the engine, quiet and alien, unlike the killing machines she created. She thought about the eagle and the rabbit—Jamie and Taylor that awful night. She pushed back images of exploding snake heads and the sound of Lucy announcing, "python, python."

You're almost home. It's almost over.

The Lexus glided over crunchy gravel. In the rear-view mirror, she saw the place in the parking lot, and her mind shifted to that night, the demonstration flight. She imagined Carter's face in the Zcolt camera with the python wrapped around him. She recalled Brad holding the fat, ugly head, trying to shoot it.

Slate shuddered and twisted the mirror away.

It's almost over.

On the access road, the Lexus rolled past her memories.

Right there! Remember the eerie snakeskin? That creeped me out good—those crazy boys and their chainsaw. No one got hurt. What was I thinking, choosing this place for the demonstration?

Slate laughed. Up ahead, she saw the stop sign at the turnoff and smiled. A left turn went to Everglades City, a right to Miami. Stopped, she adjusted the mirror and removed the cap from her new lipstick, Addiction Pink. She took her time to get it right, smacked her lips, and said, "You're looking good, girl."

Epilogue

She walked in silence on plush carpet down a long hallway lined with wall sconces. At door 7111, she faced the camera. A speaker announced softly, "Welcome, Miss Warner." The door unlocked with a hushed click.

Larger than she had expected, the room featured a cream-colored leather loveseat and two navy blue armchairs arranged beside a glass coffee table. In the center, a hand-embossed welcome note leaned against a single white orchid in a crystal vase. A bottle of Veuve Clicquot occupied a silver ice bucket, and a bowl of chocolate-dipped strawberries, figs, and sugared almonds was centered on a marble credenza beneath a television. She plucked a strawberry and took a bite.

A six-inch-high, polished mahogany platform supported an oversized king bed with a diamond-tufted, champagne-colored silk headboard. Centered on the bed in front of layers of pillows, hundreds of red rose petals lay in the shape of a heart. Slate stepped onto the platform, picked up a petal, and inhaled.

The French door opened to a veranda and a balcony wall of tempered glass below a teak railing. A slight breeze carried a salty scent and the sound of machinery. Slate looked across the bay, past the downtown skyline, to the condominiums. Down below, forklifts gunned engines and maneuvered heavy pallets.

At the bar, she opened the refrigerator, happy to see Rose's lime juice, and made herself a vodka gimlet. She sat at the vanity, sipped her drink, applied mascara and eyeliner, and dabbed Coco by Chanel behind her ears. Hearing the text tone from her phone on the credenza, Slate finished her drink and touched up her lipstick.

"Hi, I'm here," the text said.

Slate took a deep breath and texted back. "Do you mean here? As in, here, here?"

"Yes."

"I'm here too."

Slate slid the deadbolt and opened her door as the door to the adjoining room opened. They stood, taking each other in.

"Your place or mine?" she asked, giggling.

They sat on the loveseat in her room, made small talk about their cruise to Chile, and sipped champagne. She offered him a strawberry. He opened his mouth, and she popped it in. A long blast from the ship's horn sounded.

"Want anything else?" she asked.

"We do have unfinished business."

"Like what?"

"You offered me one kiss. One that was interrupted by a fire truck."

"When do you want to finish?"

"How about now?"

About the Author

Henry Kuhlman has lived in Florida for twenty-five years, first in Miami and currently near Orlando. A retired Air Force fighter pilot and international airline captain, he has traveled to over ninety countries.

Raised on a farm in Nebraska, he holds a master's degree from the University of Utah, worked as an executive at a Fortune 100 company, and has owned small businesses.

His current hobbies are drone flying, photography, creative writing, and Tai Chi.

Previous interests include offshore fishing, scuba diving, skydiving, ultralight flying, wild boar hunting, cattle ranching, and adventure travel.

He has been published in aviation and travel magazines and was a finalist in a Florida Writers Association competition.

Henry draws on far-reaching experiences to illuminate an environmental catastrophe that has, until now, remained largely invisible.